Katie Mettner wears the title of '~~t~~ her leg after falling down th~~~~ decorating her prosthetic le~~~~ Northern Wisconsin wi~~~~ ~~~~d wishes for a dog now ~~~~ Katie has an addiction to coff~~~~ ~~~~g aversion to Pinterest—now that she ~~~~ ~~~~ke the things she pins.

Jennifer D. Bokal is the author of several books, including the Heroes series Rocky Mountain Justice, Wyoming Nights, Texas Law and several books that are part of the Colton continuity. Happily married to her own alpha male for more than twenty-five years, she enjoys writing stories that explore the wonders of love. Jen and her manly husband have three beautiful grown daughters, two very spoiled dogs and a cat who runs the house.

THE MASQUERADING TWIN

KATIE METTNER

COLTON UNDERCOVER

JENNIFER D. BOKAL

MILLS & BOON

First Published in Great Britain 2024
by Mills & Boon, an imprint of HarperCollins*Publishers* Ltd
1 London Bridge Street, London, SE1 9GF

www.harpercollins.co.uk

HarperCollins*Publishers*
Macken House, 39/40 Mayor Street Upper,
Dublin 1, D01 C9W8, Ireland

The Masquerading Twin © 2024 Katie Mettner
Colton Undercover © 2024 by Harlequin Enterprises ULC

Special thanks and acknowledgment are given to Jennifer D. Bokal for her contribution to *The Coltons of Owl Creek* series.

ISBN: 978-0-263-32255-2

1124

THE MASQUERADING TWIN

KATIE METTNER

Chapter One

"Getting shot sucks," Selina grumped, shifting to find a more comfortable position. "What's worse is this damn hospital bed. It's like a board with sheets."

Efren glanced up from his crossword puzzle and raised a brow. "Next time, don't walk in front of a bullet."

Her eye roll was epically dramatic. She noticed her reflection in the mirror across from her bed and gave herself a score of twelve out of ten. The airtime before those drugged-up eyes returned to center had earned her the two extra points.

"If I recall correctly, I didn't, but I'll keep that in mind. What were you and Eric whispering about while everyone else tried to save my life?"

His sigh was notably a six out of ten on the exasperation scale. "Has anyone ever told you that you're incredibly dramatic?"

"Not before today. It must be a new skill. You didn't answer my question."

"Nothing," he said pointedly. This time, he didn't even look up from the crossword puzzle.

"Seemed like a lot of nothing considering the time it took. I was surprised you parted ways without a hug or a secret handshake."

When he lifted his head, agitation was written all over his face. Good, she was getting to him. Maybe he'd finally leave her hospital room for more than ten seconds. "Is this contrary banter supposed to convince me to leave?" She raised a brow as an answer. "You'll have to try harder. I've protected kids with more game than you've got."

He was so irritating! Selina forced herself to take a deep breath, or at least as deep as she could without pain.

Don't let him see you sweat. It's bad enough he sees you in pain. He doesn't need to know all your weaknesses.

Efren Brenna had been a burr in her side since the day he started working for Secure One. He'd moved down a spot now that she had a bullet wound in her side, but at least that would heal and the pain would disappear. Not the case with Brenna, it appeared. His reputation was that of a hero, and his ego matched. Okay, that wasn't fair. He was a hero. He'd saved countless lives while bleeding out from a traumatic leg amputation. On the other hand, his ego was too big for her liking. It filled up the room and left no space for anyone else. At least that was her story, and she was sticking to it.

She studied the man who sat engrossed in the newspaper crossword puzzle. Selina knew he was also paying full attention to everything around him in the hospital room and the hallway. She could see his profile from her bed, and she had to admit that some might consider him handsome. His brown hair was cut short in the back with a swoop of hair over his forehead. His skin was the perfect shade of desert tan, and his brown eyes were giant with lashes that any woman would kill for. He was tall to her five and a half feet, but thin and wiry. Under his left pant leg, he wore a high-tech above-knee skin-fit prosthesis with a running blade attached. He always wore his blade when they went on missions, and since he hadn't returned to Secure One, he hadn't changed into his everyday leg. She suspected Eric would return with it soon but wouldn't ask. She didn't want him to think she cared one way or the other about his comfort when she was the one in the hospital bed.

"If you must know," he said, setting the paper aside and leaning forward in his chair, "we were talking about the case—"

Motion caught her eye and she peered through the narrow window in the door. What she saw had her heart rate climbing fast. She put her finger to her lips, her gaze glued to the nurses' station outside her door. Efren swung his head around slowly. Selina wondered if he saw her, too. If she was real. A woman with long blond hair that fell in waves against her back where it blended into her white fur coat stood tapping her bloodred nails on the counter. The door was open a crack so they could hear the discussion between the nurse and the woman.

"I'm looking for Eva Shannon. I was told she was brought to this hospital."

"I'm sorry," the nurse said. "I can only give out information to family. Are you a direct family member?"

"Yes, I'm her sister," the woman answered in a rather bored tone.

Efren raised a brow at Selina in question, and she swallowed hard. There was no way that woman was her sister. She'd put her sister in a body bag eight years ago.

"Let me check," the nurse said, typing into the computer. "I'm sorry, but I don't have an Eva Shannon on this floor.

You could try two floors up. That's Med-Surg. She might be there since that's overflow when our floor gets full."

"I'll do that," the woman said.

Selina recognized the signature sass, and sweat broke out on her brow as the woman turned and sashayed toward the elevator. That woman was her sister. The one who was supposed to be dead.

Efren stood by the door until he heard the elevator's ding, then closed the door the rest of the way, jammed a chair under it and spun on her. "Get ready. I'm going to let Eric know we're moving."

"Get ready? Moving? I just had surgery to remove a bullet from my gut. I'm not going anywhere!"

Efren stalked to her bed in a way she'd never seen him move before. A lion patiently hunting prey came to mind. When he stood over her, his entire demeanor had changed. "Did you hear who that woman asked for?"

Selina swallowed before she answered, afraid nothing but a scream of terror would leave her lips if she didn't. "Eva Shannon. I don't know who that is, so I don't know what you're so worried about, Efren."

He braced his hands on the bed and leaned in until he was inches from her face. "You wanted to know what Eric and I were whispering about earlier?" He raised a brow, and she nodded. Having him this close to her was unnerving, and she blinked, afraid to breathe. "It was about the moment before you were shot. Randall Jr. said Ava Shannon right before he put a bullet in you. It was a question, not a statement. Vic also kept mumbling about you being dead, which tells me two things. That woman out there is Ava Shannon, and the woman I'm staring at is Eva Shannon. Cute play on the names. I give your mom props for that. I don't need to know the rest right now, but I need you to stop playing games. Let that fear you keep trying to swallow down motivate you to get up and get out of here before they finish the job!" The growl of exclamation was intense before he turned and picked up his bag, pulling out an encoded phone all Secure One operatives used.

With the phone to his ear, he stared her down, and she closed her eyes because if looks could kill, he'd do a better job than Randall's bullet had. The woman from a few moments ago filled her mind as terror shot through her soul. It was like looking in a mirror in a house of horrors. Ava was supposed to be dead. Selina had been the one to shoot her in the chest. The ME had assured her the bullet had done the trick and ended her reign of terror—all evidence to the contrary. Ava was alive and well, wearing her signature fur. That meant one thing. She was out for blood. Ava did not take well to being wronged, especially by her family.

Her mind warred with what she had just seen and what it already knew. How? Where had she been all these years? That night, the night they raided Randall Loraine's home, things hadn't gone as planned, but Selina wasn't sad to put her twin in a body bag at the end of the night, even if it put a target on her back.

"Listen, Eva, we have to talk about your sister," her police chief said as they strapped on their vests and readied their weapons.

"What's to talk about?" she asked, tightening the straps.

"You can't be a risk to the lives of the team. If she's going to distract you, you need to stand down."

"You should know me better than that by now," she answered, and then lined up with the rest of the team.

Eva could only hope her sister was inside those four ostentatious walls. The task force could prove she knew about the counterfeiting ring, but not that she had her hands in it. She did. They'd find that proof tonight. There was no way Ava Shannon-Loraine would let her husband run the ring alone. She was too controlling—too diabolical—to let an opportunity to manipulate and dominate Randall Sr. pass her by. They should both be behind bars, but first, they had to find the proof. Once they did, Eva had no problem being the one to put Ava in handcuffs.

The team spread out around the perimeter of the Loraine mansion. It had so many doors to cover that they'd had to pull in the SWAT teams from two separate counties. The last thing they wanted was for Randall or Ava to escape and disappear when they'd been building a case against them for over a year. If they went underground, they'd be in the wind forever.

Intel told them the couple spent their evenings in the library. Eva snickered to herself. She was the intel. She's spent enough time inside the mansion to know Ava and Randall's routine. Their sniper on the hill had confirmed they were there. That meant entering the front door, turning right down a hallway, and right into the first door. The room was small, which left them little room to hide, but Eva suspected they had a way out that even she didn't know existed.

With a nod from the chief, they rammed their way into the house from both ends. Eva tried to tune out the shouting and shrill alarm as she swung into the room where her sister and *brother-in-law sat enjoying a glass of bourbon they'd bought with blood money.*

"Freeze! You're under arrest!" her chief yelled at Randall as he crawled through a hatch in the floor.

Two SWAT guys hauled him out before he could shut it and handcuffed him before he got a word out. Eva swung her gun around the room. "Where is she?" It wasn't a question as much as a rebel yell at the man who had somehow helped her twin escape.

"Tag, you're it. Run, run as fast as you can, big sister, but little sister can't be caught." Randall's words were spat at her with so much distaste it made Eva laugh.

"You don't know me very well then, Randall." She swept her gun and flashlight down the hatch, but her twin was nowhere in sight. She didn't let that stop her. Eva's feet barely touched the ladder's rungs before she jumped onto the concrete floor below. The tunnel only went one way, so on instinct, she ran, knowing it was leading her toward the property line to the south. Ava couldn't have that much of a jump on her. Maybe thirty seconds. How far could she get in that time? With her gun tight to her chest, Eva noticed movement ahead of her. The swish of long blond hair as she climbed a ladder before popping out into the night.

"Ava, stop! You're surrounded!" she yelled to her twin, but Ava didn't stop.

The adrenaline had Eva's legs and heart pumping as she ran full out toward her twin, knowing that if she escaped, Eva would never be safe. She'd always have to look over her shoulder for a bullet that one day would come. Ava believed in an eye for an eye, but if her family betrayed her, she would burn down the world.

Eva reached out, her fingers grasping Ava's long hair. She pulled her backward and to the ground, where she landed with an oof. "Stay down!" Eva yelled, pointing her gun at Ava's center mass.

"What are you going to do, sis? Shoot an unarmed woman?"

"If she doesn't stay down, I won't hesitate," Eva growled. Her body shook with anger, but her gun remained steady.

"What happened to you?" Ava asked, shaking her head in disdain.

"What happened to me? I'm not the one on the wrong side of the law, Ava."

"You think you're holier than thou because you're a cop. You have no idea what real life is like for me. You're about to find out."

Ava launched herself at her twin but didn't get far before Eva squeezed the trigger. The bullet knocked her back, and shock filled her eyes as she glanced down at her chest, where blood turned her white cashmere sweater bright red.

"You shot me," she hissed, that shock turning to fury. "I can't believe you shot me!"

"I warned you," Eva said, her gun still pointed at her twin. With one hand, she pushed the button on her walkie. "I need EMS on the south side of the property. I have Ava Loraine. She has a bullet wound to the chest."

"Selina!"

She started at the name, opening her eyes to stare right into Efren's brown ones.

"Sorry, what did you say?"

"I said it's time to get you up and dressed. We have to go."

There was a knock on the door, and Efren had his gun

out and was next to the door before she saw him move. He opened the door a hair, but Selina couldn't see who it was.

"Quickly," he whispered, and opened the door wide enough for a nurse to slide through. He had the door shut and the chair under the handle before the nurse made it to the side of her bed.

"I have your discharge papers," she said cheerily, as though there wasn't a man with a gun in her room.

"Discharge papers?" Selina asked, her heart pounding in her chest as she pushed herself up in the bed.

The nurse shook the papers in her hand. "Everything you need to finish your recovery elsewhere. Eric told us to be alert for anyone asking about you who looked suspicious," she explained as she busied herself with the machines by Selina's bed. "When that woman looked exactly like my patient, I decided chances were good that was who he was referring to. I know you're an APP, so I'm confident you can take care of your wound, correct?"

Selina nodded, and the nurse smiled. "Good, let's get your IV out and find you something to put on that's a little less memorable." The nurse turned to Efren. "I have enough medication for the day, but she will need more than this."

Efren dug in his bag and pulled out a slip of paper. "Call it into that pharmacy, under that name. We'll pick it up."

The nurse stuck it in her pocket and set about removing Selina's IV and checking her wound. The drugs had made her head hazy, but she forced herself to concentrate. Her twin had returned from the dead, and now Selina and Efren were in her crosshairs. Her gaze drifted to Efren, his backpack on and ready to go while he glared at her in confusion and anger. She was going to have to trust him to keep her safe, but she suspected she was anything but when it came to Efren Brenna.

Chapter Two

Efren's gaze bounced between his mirrors, the road and the woman beside him. Getting her out of the hospital had been a dangerous endeavor that wasn't over yet. This old Jeep bought them time but not safety. It was registered in a way that would take someone more than a few minutes to figure out that Secure One owned it. It would get them where they needed to go, but then it would have to go.

They hit a bump, and he noticed Selina grimace. She was white as a sheet but holding on, and he couldn't ask for more than that. Efren didn't know if it was the pain or seeing her twin again that stole all color from her cheeks, but he would guess it was a little of both. She'd have to tell him exactly what they were dealing with, but it could wait until they weren't running for their lives.

"What's an APP?" he asked, hoping to distract her. She glanced at him in confusion, and he motioned behind him. "At the hospital. The nurse said you were an APP."

"Oh, I already forgot. I'm a little stressed."

"Understandable," he said with a nod.

"It means advanced practice paramedic. I can provide extensive and advanced patient care on critical patients in the field or in an emergent disaster situation."

"I see. I guess I thought you were a nurse."

"That's what they call me at Secure One to put the guys at ease."

His laughter filled the cab of the small Jeep. "I don't think the guys need to be put at ease when it comes to you taking care of them. Not after the way you cared for Marlise, Charlotte and Bethany. It's easy to see you only want what's best for your patients."

He noticed the shrug from the corner of his eye, but she didn't say anything, so he thought it best to change the subject. "We've been on the road for ninety minutes and haven't picked up a tail, which is reassuring. We're about ten minutes from where we'll pick up your prescriptions, and then it's another thirty to the safe house."

"It's going to be tough to move," she said, her breath tight when she spoke. "Wheelchair or no wheelchair."

He nodded and squeezed her shoulder briefly before putting his hand back on the wheel. "The pharmacy has a drive-through and no monitoring cameras, which is why I picked it. Is there anything else you need? The safe house is stocked with food and supplies."

"First aid supplies?" she asked, shifting in her seat. "I'm going to need gauze and tape."

He was silent as he turned off the highway into a small town. "I'm sure there are first aid supplies, but I don't know how many. Write down what you need, and I'll have them send it out with the prescriptions." He pointed at the pad of paper in the cup holder.

It took effort, but by the time they got to the pharmacy, she had a list that he passed the pharmacist through the window. While they waited, he noticed Selina eyeing him.

"Do you always have fake IDs on you?"

"Yes," he answered, his gaze grabbing hers for a moment. "We work in the kind of business that can leave us injured and on the run. If you aren't prepared, you're dead. As soon as we get the scripts, Michael Fenstad will cease to exist, but we'll have what we need until we can get back to Secure One."

The pharmacist returned to the window and handed everything out to them. Efren gave the pain medication to Selina and money to the pharmacist. As he pulled away, he motioned at the water bottle in the cup holder.

"Take one of the pain pills."

"It's too early," she said, checking the clock.

"Listen. You'll have to walk in when we get to the safe house. The wheelchair won't go over the terrain."

"Where is this place? Canada?"

"Middle of nowhere Minnesota, so just about as bad," he answered, motioning at the water again with his chin. "Take the pill now, so it's on board by the time we get there."

She hesitated only a moment longer before she followed his order. "I'm not immobile," she said defiantly. "I'm just slow-moving."

"And when you're being hunted, slow-moving is a risk factor for death. I do not want you taking another bullet under my guard. I'll never be employed again."

"We can't have that," she muttered with an eye roll that he noticed as he checked the rearview mirror.

He'd kept an eye out since they left the town behind and noticed a pair of headlights follow them out of town. That didn't mean it was necessarily suspicious, but he couldn't risk driving to the safe house if someone followed them.

"Tag on the rudder," she said, her gaze pinned on her side mirror. "They've been there since we left town."

"Yep, I was just thinking it was time to get rid of them." Efren slowed the Jeep and waited to see if the car went around them. It didn't.

"Next idea?" she asked, glancing at him.

"I hate to do this with you in the car, but they've left me no choice. Hang on and don't scream. It throws off my concentration."

He noted the start of her eye roll right before he yanked the wheel to the right and accelerated into the turn. He had no idea where the road went, but when the car kept going, he pressed the accelerator to the floor to put some distance between them.

"Slow down. They're not following us."

"Yet," he said, concentrating on the road ahead as he drove twice the posted speed limit. "They could be turning around as we speak."

She watched her mirror and let out a rather unladylike curse when headlights turned down the road. "We can't outrun them, and we can't bail," Selina said, her words tight.

"Well, hell, you just ruined all my plans." His words were tongue in cheek, but he heard the frustration in them, too. "Can you shoot?"

"Am I dead?"

"Not yet."

"Then I can shoot. Where's your gun?"

"Take the wheel," he ordered, waiting for her to grip it before he reached behind him and lifted a semiautomatic from under a blanket.

Selina's whistle was long and happy. "Well, look at you! You came loaded for bear. Keep this up and I might start to like you, Brenna."

She took the gun, and he took the wheel. Rather than give orders, he decided to let her make the plan. Maybe she would start to like him a little if he didn't take all the control away from her the way everyone else at Secure One did. He had to admit that he wanted her to like him, and not because of his ego. Since he returned from the war, he vowed to himself that he'd live his life without caring whether someone liked or disliked him. He was his true self all the time, except when it came to Selina. At the very least, he didn't want her to hate him. "What's the plan, Colvert?" he asked, hoping she had one and that it would stop him from thinking about how much he wished she liked him.

"They're gaining on us fast," she observed. She carefully got herself onto the Jeep floor on her knees and aimed the gun out the window. "When I say now, stomp the brakes. When I say go, hammer it. In between those two words, duck, cover and pray."

Efren couldn't help it. He smiled. Then the first bullet smacked into the back of the Jeep.

"Guess there's no time like the present. Now!"

Efren stomped the brake as she let the first rounds go. He couldn't see if she gained any purchase while he tried to keep the Jeep from careening off the road. Another round of bullets slammed into them, taking out the back window and leaving a sucking wind on his back. The enemy was outgunned, but Selina had little time to prove it.

"Don't mind if I do," she yelled, resting the gun on the back of the seat and pulling the trigger, releasing a barrage of bullets that definitely hit home. He checked the rearview mirror again and saw the car headed for the ditch and a large tree. "Go!"

He threw his arm out to brace her as he slammed the accelerator, then held her in place until their speed evened out and she could sit up again. "Great shooting, partner," he said with a shake of his head. "Once we're off this road and at the safe house, you've got some 'splaining to do."

THE BRUSH WAS thick and wanted to pull them down with every step. Selina was tired, in pain and trying to protect a surgical wound. All of that said, she would never admit to Efren that she was glad he'd made her take that pain pill. After they found their way to the safe house using back roads, they had to bury the Jeep in a grove of trees and walk in. If the people following them had a team waiting, driving into a trap out here was certain death, even with a semiautomatic. She knew who was following them, though she wasn't quite ready to share that information with her bodyguard yet. If Ava was alive, then she had the henchmen for Chicago Mafia kingpin Medardo Vaccaro at her disposal. That meant one thing—they would never stop coming for her until she, or Ava, was dead.

Known in the crime world as the Snake, but known to her and Ava as Uncle Medardo, he was less than happy when Selina's team broke up his payday by arresting Randall Loraine and killing Ava. Why did they call him Uncle Medardo? Her father had been part of his lower management for longer than she and Ava had been alive. When her father went into debt to Vaccaro, his boss so kindly suggested that the best way to pay off his debts was to offer one of his daughter's hands in marriage to Randall Loraine.

When her father turned up dead with a cause of death as "indeterminate," that was probably also Vaccaro getting payment for his debts. Selina had been a cop long enough to know a bribe had been accepted by the ME to make Charles Shannon's death an accident. Then again, it was equally possible Ava killed their father for marrying her off. Either way, Vaccaro was once again Selina's problem.

"Please tell me we're almost there," she whispered, trying to slide through the hole in the branches he'd made for her.

"We're here." Efren pointed ahead into the dark.

She squinted but couldn't make out a structure. "All I see is rubble."

"Exactly. That rubble is the safe house. Or rather, underneath that rubble." He flipped his night-vision goggles down and scanned the area. She leaned over, bracing her hands on her thighs to keep her side from spasming.

Getting shot in the side sucked, but Selina knew she was lucky. The bullet had missed all vital organs other than her left ovary. She already knew she couldn't have children, so this would be nothing more than a scar and a memory of another successful Secure One case in a few short weeks. It would be grand if her entire body would stop hurting, though. She'd only been out of surgery twenty-four hours when her twin showed up, and since then, she'd pushed her body to its limit. If she weren't on pain pills, she'd take a stiff drink and a bed. Right about now, she'd settle for the bed.

Efren lifted his goggles and turned to her. "I don't see anyone lying in wait. Let's get you someplace a bit more comfortable. It involves a rung ladder. I'll go down first so I can help you."

"I won't even argue." She followed him through the door of the old cabin with three walls that you could consider up-right compared to the back wall, which was in shambles. The roof was gone, and the wooden floor was strewn with bricks, leaves and pine needles. Old mattresses littered the floor, along with cooking pans and metal buckets.

"There's nothing here, Efren."

"At first glance," he said. He slid one of the mattresses across the floor and revealed a hatch.

"A hidden hatch. Okay, but how do we re-cover it?"

"We don't," he answered, motioning her to follow him through the hole in the back of the cabin wall. "The ground cover will hide our footprints," he whispered, helping her around behind a row of trees. "That hatch is there to throw people off."

"What's in the hatch?"

"Pipes that look real but do nothing."

He knelt, swept his hand along the ground between two trees, and lifted a heavy metal door. "This is our hatch. I'll go down first, help you, and then come back up and close it."

Selina nodded and waited for him to climb down the rung ladder. She averted her eyes, because the memory of fol-lowing Ava down a ladder just like this one eight years ago assailed her. Logically, she knew it wouldn't end the same, but the fear of Ava finding her was intense enough to wipe logic off the table.

An emergency light lit the ladder, and she saw Efren set-ting the bags on the bunker's floor. Selina prayed she'd make it down without needing his assistance. It would be a mistake to have his hands wrapped around any part of her, and keeping her distance would be the only way to survive any type of forced proximity. She chuckled to herself. Talk about an oxymoron.

"Selina!" he hissed, and she started, forgetting where she was and what she was supposed to be doing. It must be the pain pills. It couldn't be the man waiting for her below.

"Sorry," she whispered. "I was planning out my descent."

Her eyes rolled at herself that time, but she managed to make it down the rung with minimal pain and without falling into his arms. He climbed the ladder again to shut the hatch, and she walked to a bunk bed in the room, sat down and promptly passed out.

Chapter Three

"I need your help, Kai."

Eva could see that the man in front of her was terrified, but he finally nodded. "And you're sure I won't get in trouble for this?"

"Positive," Eva promised. "You have to know I don't have any other options. I wouldn't do this if I did."

"I know, but Eva, he's going to be heartbroken. I don't know if he'll ever recover."

"Selina?" a voice asked. "Selina, wake up. You're moaning. It's time for medication."

She blinked several times as the man beside her morphed from Kai into someone else. Someone she didn't know. Had they found her that quickly? "Kai! Kai! Help!"

"Selina, relax!" the man said, his voice frantic. "I'm Efren. You work for Cal Newfellow at Secure One. Your friends are Mina, Marlise and Charlotte."

Efren. Secure One. She blinked again and swallowed down the fear before she sat up gingerly. "Sorry. I got confused."

"I understand," he said, handing her a water bottle. "I remember what that's like when you're tired, sore, taking medication and dredging up the past."

"What time is it?" she asked to change the subject. The last thing she wanted to talk about with Efren Brenna was the past, though she knew it was inevitable.

"It's two a.m. I've been in touch with Cal and taken a nap. I didn't want to wake you until you had a chance to sleep off the pain from walking in. You must be hurting."

"I've felt better, but I'm alive. I can thank you for that both times."

"We're a team, which means no thanks is needed. I wish I could have spared you the pain of getting here, though."

"We're a team, so no apology is needed," she said with a wink. "Besides, you managed to get me the medication I needed and to a safe place before daylight."

"Only because of your scary accurate marksman skills. Does Cal know you're a crack shot?"

"Yep," she answered, taking the pills he held out. After she tossed them back with a swig of water, she took a moment to take in the room. "Where are we?"

"Nice pivot, Colvert," he said with a shake of his head. She smirked and accepted the hand he held out to help her up. "This is the safe house Cal built when he realized if we continued with these kinds of cases, one day we would need it."

"I can't believe he built a replica of the bunker at Secure One."

"If it ain't broke, don't fix it," Efren said with a chuckle. "But you're correct other than the kitchen, compostable toilet and small wash basin. Everything runs on battery power, so you could stay here for a few weeks if you conserve water and power. At least we have the communication equipment available."

"With the amount of equipment here, you could run a small

country," she said jokingly. "I need to use that compostable toilet, and then I suppose I need to touch base with my boss."

"Probably would be a good idea," Efren agreed with a wink. He opened the bathroom door for her. "Water, soap, towels and clean clothes are in the cabinet," he said, pointing at the metal locker next to the toilet. "When you're done, you'll tell me everything from start to finish. If I'm going to keep you safe, I have to know what's coming at us."

Fear shot through her at the idea of breaking her silence after all these years. Rather than speak, all she did was close the bathroom door.

WHO'S KAI? That was the only question running through Efren's head. He was obviously someone from Selina's past and someone she relied on when she was in trouble. Was he an ex-boyfriend or an ex-partner? It wasn't a giant leap to assume that Selina, aka Eva, was a cop in her past life. She knew too much to be anything but a cop or a criminal, and he knew Cal didn't hire criminals. He would still make her spell everything out, from her prior career choices to what happened with her sister. Until he understood what they were dealing with, there was no way for him to make a plan to keep her safe. After they talked, they'd contact Secure One as a united front.

The bathroom door cracked open, and Selina walked out. Her steps were ginger, but she'd washed up and found clean joggers in the cabinet. "I have to say, a sponge bath and clean clothes do make me feel like a new woman."

"Maybe some food would, too?" Efren turned from the small camp stove with a pan of hot soup he set at the little two-person table, along with a bag of crackers and her water.

"I hate to admit that you're right, but you're right. Thanks for fixing it for me."

"Remember what I said about thank you?" Efren asked. "Chances are there will come a time when you'll do the same for me. In the meantime, why don't you tell me what we're dealing with here?"

Rather than speak, she focused on the soup and crackers, so he patiently waited for her to finish. Finally, she lowered the spoon and motioned toward the two accent chairs in the corner by the beds.

"If I'm going to give you my life story, we may as well be comfortable. It would be smart to call Cal so I only have to do this once. He knows some, but not all, of my past."

He helped her stand and walked with her to the two chairs in the corner. Once they were comfortable, he addressed her prior statement.

"I have it on good authority that they're sleeping right now, so they can be prepared to help us come daylight. Before sunup, I need a timeline of what happened since the night your sister 'died.'" He put air quotes around that word since they both knew she was alive and well. "Give it to me as you would if you were a witness giving a statement at the station. I'll write it down so we can pull out the pertinent and important information to give the team when we talk to them in the morning."

"You're assuming I was a cop?" she asked with a brow raised.

"Am I wrong?" he asked, raising the opposite brow.

"Unfortunately, no. That said, it's been eight years since I took any witness statements, so you'll have to forgive me if I'm a little rusty." She was going for levity, so he chuckled softly.

"I've got the pad and the time," he said with a wink, motioning at the paper on his lap. "I should ask if we're breaking any contracts with the United States Marshals Service by talking about this?"

"WITSEC?" she asked, and he nodded once. "No. I'm not part of WITSEC."

"Okay, then start whenever you're ready." Efren respected that it would be hard for her to trust him with the truth when she'd kept it a closely guarded secret for so long.

She shifted in the seat, and he got up, grabbed a pillow from the bed and handed it to her. After she slid it along her side, she cleared her throat. "I'd been a Chicago cop for four years when I joined a task force tracking a counterfeiting operation. I was aiming to make detective and knew shutting down the operation would be the feather in my cap to get the promotion."

"How long ago did you join the task force?" he asked, writing on the pad rather than making eye contact. He hoped that would make it easier for her to focus.

"That would be ten years ago now," she answered. "The task force suspected that the counterfeiting originated with Chicago Mafia kingpin Medardo the Snake Vaccaro. I was already intimate with him and his business, so when they asked me to join the task force, I readily agreed."

"Had you worked a case where Vaccaro was involved before the counterfeiting?"

"Nope," she said, popping the *P* harder than necessary. "My father worked for him my entire life. Lower management, if you catch my drift."

His brows went up. "That's wild. A cop's father was a Mafia henchman."

"It wasn't easy being that cop in the beginning. When they found out about my father, my superiors tried to fire me for being a Vaccaro plant. I fought back with the union and won since there was no evidence that I was tied to Vaccaro. I had worked hard to keep myself separated from anything my father did since I was in high school. Then my father got behind on some debts to his boss. The Snake offered him an opportunity to pay them off by giving the hand of one of his daughters to be married to a man within his organization."

"And that daughter sure as hell wasn't you?"

"Nope," she said again, staring at her lap. "My father knew I was working my way to detective, and I wouldn't hesitate to arrest anyone who got in my way of accomplishing that goal, including him."

"Did your sister have her own life by then as well?"

"Nope," she said a third time, much to his amusement.

"I'm sorry for laughing, but I can't help but wonder if this entire conversation will be punctuated with the word nope."

"Nope." This time she gave him a quirky smile. "To answer your other question, Ava did not have her own life. She was a spoiled, entitled debutante wannabe who thought Daddy would bankroll her for life. She never wanted to lift a finger or work for anything. She was fifteen minutes younger than me, and we were identical twins in everything but our work ethic and morals."

"Neither of which is genetically embedded in us," Efren said, and she pointed at him.

"Well said. As a result, my father racked up debts and favors while trying to pay for Ava's every whim. Things like her multiple college degrees that she started and stopped, her spa business that never took off because she was never there, and other random nonsense that my father bankrolled. When the Snake asked for a daughter's hand, it was a no-brainer. If my father could unload Ava, he'd stay out of debt and on the right side of favor with his boss."

"I'm going to go out on a limb and guess that her betrothed was Randall Loraine Sr."

"That's him," Selina answered, practically spitting the words from her lips. "He was twenty-three years older, had three sons and was already a widower. That didn't stop her. As soon as she realized he had money, she readily agreed to warm his bed."

"So, your sister marries Loraine and ends up helping him run a counterfeiting racket?"

"That's a short jump of a long story, but it's the nuts and bolts. Ava married him twelve years ago, and I suspect, though I can't prove it, he was already running the counterfeit operation out of his mansion in Bemidji. The Snake wanted Ava there to paint Randall as the consummate family man who found love again as well as a mother for his boys. Hilarious, since those boys were already teenagers or young adults."

"What happened to your father?"

"He was found floating facedown in the Chicago River. His death was ruled indeterminate, so I know money changed hands with that death certificate. They also didn't find any water in his lungs, which means he was dead when he landed in the river."

"Nothing fishy about that," Efren muttered, and Selina laughed.

"I can't say for certain that Ava didn't kill him and convince Randall to help her cover it up. She believes in an eye for an eye, and if family wrongs her, she will burn down the world."

"Why would she kill your father? Did he wrong her somehow?"

"I would have no way of knowing that for certain, but if Randall told her Daddy had to die, then she wouldn't hesitate to do it."

"Which explains why she came looking for you as soon as she knew where you were."

"Likely," she agreed, shifting again. She was getting tired, and he had to wrap this up before she was in too much pain to talk. "That or she always knew where I was and was biding her time. If that's the case, then she's smarter than I gave her credit for all these years."

"I doubt she was the brains behind any fake death operation." Efren felt terrible that Selina saw herself as less than her sister when she was the one standing on the right side of the law. "She would have needed help and that help had to come from somewhere."

"More like someone," Selina agreed with a nod. "Vaccaro. I was told that my twin went straight to hell. Obviously, someone got the message wrong."

"Or someone wanted you to think she went straight to hell," Efren pointed out.

"That could be if the EMTs were bought in that town. No way to know now, but I wouldn't put it past Vaccaro to reel Ava back in if Randall had been snagged. The fact that she showed her face now terrifies me."

"Tell me why," he encouraged, leaning forward to show her he was listening and interested in what she had to say.

He'd been listening and interested in what Selina Colvert had to say since the day he met her. While she treated him like a second-class citizen and with as much malice as is tolerable in the workplace, he'd always known it was an act. She was scared and hurting, but kept a tight lid on her emotions so as not to rock the boat. Now he understood why. She couldn't rock the boat. If she left Secure One, her life would be in jeopardy again.

"Well, her husband is still in prison, one of her stepsons is dead, another is going to prison, and she could still face charges for the counterfeiting operation. Showing her face again puts her at risk for arrest, if they found evidence she was involved, which I have no way of knowing. My main worry is that she started warming Vaccaro's bed after her 'death' and has become another head of the snake."

"Was there evidence that she was involved in the counterfeiting operation?"

"Before we raided the mansion, we only had circumstantial evidence. You and I both know she was involved, though. She was Randall's wife and secretary. Here's the thing, Ava is lazy, but she's incredibly smart and quick on the draw."

"Just like you are."

"I suppose genetics come into play there."

"You think she knew more than she let on."

"I think she was the brains behind the operation. Randall Sr. is polished, but he isn't smart or talented when it comes to the art of manipulation, if that makes sense."

"Of course it does. He was a puppet of the Snake. A smart man wouldn't allow himself to be controlled that way."

"That sums it up. I spent a lot of time with them as a couple, and Ava ruled the roost. Not just in a spoiled wife kind of way, either. She ruled that house with an iron fist, both with Randall and the two boys still at home. All of that said, we knew the information inside the house held the answers the task force needed to put together a case against them both. I don't know if evidence was ever found to prove she was involved," Selina said with a shake of her head.

"You were on the task force, so wouldn't you know that information?"

"If I had been part of the task force after that night, yes."

"Let me guess. You were put on administrative leave for shooting your sister?"

"Bingo. I was on mandatory administrative leave until the shooting was investigated. I never heard if they found evidence of her involvement, but I know Ava, so I suspect they didn't. If she was the one running the operation, she'd make sure her hands stayed squeaky clean while Randall's were all red."

"Do you think they pulled you because they thought you were a Vaccaro plant?"

"No." Her gaze dropped to her lap before she finished. "I knew being part of that task force would put me in grave danger. I'd be lucky to survive a few days outside of police protection before they'd find me floating facedown just like my father. So I turned in my badge and gun, drove to Wisconsin, and fell off a bluff with the raging Wisconsin River below. That was the last time anyone saw Eva Shannon."

Chapter Four

Selina noted the surprise on Efren's face, but to his credit, he simply glanced up and waited to see if she would continue. When she didn't, he set the pen down on his paper.

"How about we take a break? You can hardly keep your eyes open."

She shook her head. "No. I'm fine. If we're going to call Secure One in the morning, we have to work this out. Then I can sleep."

He picked up his pen again. "You decided falling off a cliff was easier than going into WITSEC?"

"Easier? Not in the beginning. Faster? Yes, and at the time, I needed to disappear quickly. Since I didn't have any family left, it didn't matter if I was in WITSEC or on my own. Besides, I couldn't be sure that the Snake didn't have a plant somewhere in the marshals' office. If I took protection, then I had to trust them and probably would end up with a bullet between my eyes sooner rather than later. I trusted myself and knew I wasn't going to double-cross me."

"Valid. Still had to have been hard."

"It was. I had my search-and-rescue dog to think about. I convinced my friend Kai Tanner to take him for me and to tell the authorities I fell. Since the Wisconsin River opens up into the Mississippi, if they didn't find a body, they wouldn't be surprised."

"He was willing to lie to authorities for you?"

"He may have had a bit of a crush on me," she said. "Maybe if our lives had been different, I could have seen us together, but there was no way I was dragging someone as honest and kind as Kai into something that could get him killed."

"You could have taken the dog and run."

"I could have," she agreed with a head nod, "but then the Snake would know I'd run. Taking Zeus would have been a dead giveaway, no pun intended. It was the hardest thing I've ever had to do to hand his leash over to Kai, but Zeus deserved better than what I could give him."

"Then what happened?"

"I don't know," she answered with a shrug. "I checked the *Tribune* but since I went missing in Wisconsin, it didn't even make the papers. At least not that I could find. The Wisconsin papers reported it as the death of a search-and-rescue agent that was a tragic accident. That told me Kai didn't get in trouble for falsely reporting my death."

"Man, sucked to be him," Efren muttered, making notes.

"Why do you say that?" She snapped her head up, immediately on the defense. "You don't think it sucked to be me?"

"I know it did. It had to be a difficult decision to know your choice was to trust the institution you worked for or go it on your own. It had to be a brutal decision to hand over your dog and walk away. I was simply saying from a guy's perspective, that it sucked for Kai, too. Not only did he have to give up the woman he cared about, but he had to pretend that she was dead for the rest of his life, when he knew you were still out there. It's hard to move on with life when your heart and mind are in a different place."

"Thanks for doing a better job of gutting me than the bullet did." She wrapped her arm around her belly. "I felt like hell asking him, but I had no one, and he knew that. He wanted to be my someone any way he could, and this was the only way he could, so he stepped up."

"What happened after you 'fell off the cliff'?" He put that whole phrase in air quotes, too.

Her sigh was loaded. What followed that day was hard. Harder than anything she'd ever done, and that said a lot when she grew up with a father who worked for the Mafia.

"I was lucky to have money, several new identities and the ability to change my appearance rather easily, but it was still hard to navigate a world where you couldn't trust a soul. You couldn't stay in one place more than a day, visit the same store or restaurant more than once, or even use public transportation. I was lucky the raid happened during the summer or I would have been in much deeper trouble."

"How did you move around?"

"I stole old cars from people's yards, rode ATVs or walked."

Selina stood and paced to her left, stretching her side out carefully. She was relieved it was feeling better after the food and medication. The longer she was down and weak, the easier it was for the Snake to find a way in. "She was dead, Efren. By the time EMS got to her, she had practically bled out."

"Did you see her code and them call her time of death?"

Selina turned back to him. "No. They ran with her to the ambulance, worked on her, and then I watched them go hands-off," she explained, holding her hands in the air near her chest. "The EMS guys waited a few moments and then one shook his head. They covered her with a sheet and told me she was gone, so they'd take her to the ME. When they pulled away, it was without lights and sirens."

Efren tapped his pen on the pad. "You didn't go to the morgue?"

"No. There was no reason to. I didn't need to identify the body since everyone knew who she was. I was busy dealing with the fallout of shooting her."

"Did they hold a service for her?"

Selina gave him the palms-out. "No way for me to know since I was gone less than twenty-four hours after it happened. I resisted the urge to google anything to do with her."

"Not even from the secure servers at Secure One?"

"Not even then." She shook her head. "You don't understand the ruthlessness that is Vaccaro, Efren. People romanticize the Mafia like they're some kind of antihero who can be redeemed with good morals and making the right choices. If only they knew these guys." She shook her head again in frustration. "They're more likely to be old fleshy men than young, sexy tatted guys in suits. They wouldn't think twice about putting a bullet in you because you're between them and their whiskey bottle. There is nothing romantic about the Mafia, and it's a dangerous ideation to lead women to believe they'd be loved or respected by one. Women are a pawn to these men, and that's why I know Vaccaro had to be involved in Ava's death and rebirth."

"I have to heed to your knowledge on the Mafia as mine is limited to movies and books, but I still agree that a kingpin only does what's best for him, regardless of who is in his way." She lowered herself to the chair and nodded. "I'll have Mina search and see what she can find in the archives."

"You're asking the wrong questions." She sat and leaned over her knees to rub her forehead.

There was no question that the surgery and medication were the reason she couldn't pull all of this information together logically as she usually would. It was frustrating. They were on a timeline that was a matter of life or death. She needed to get it together.

"I wish I knew the right questions, Selina. I'm afraid I'm a bit out of my depth here. I'm a bodyguard, not a cop," he reminded her. "You're telling the story."

Selina slumped over in the chair. "I shot her, Efren. She was dead."

"They wanted you to think she was dead. That doesn't mean she was. If you could have, I know you would have gone to the morgue and checked her cold dead body yourself, right?"

"I would have watched the autopsy." Her words held a bit more fire again, and he smiled.

"Money had to have changed hands."

"If Vaccaro was involved, then there's no question," she agreed. "What I want to know is, was there an autopsy report?"

Efren scribbled it down on his pad. "Because if there was, he paid off more than an EMT?"

"Bingo. Then it becomes a plan rather than a reaction."

"A plan instead of a reaction?"

"Think about it." She grimaced, but it wasn't physical pain. It was the kind of pain a person was in when their world was crumbling around them and they didn't know what to do.

The terror inside her had filled her head to toe. There was no room left, but the terror kept coming in waves. As much as she trusted Secure One, her experience with Vaccaro told her she was a dead woman walking. "They knew the task force was closing in, or at the very least, they knew we were looking for that final connection so we could arrest them. Randall and Ava had a plan in case they were arrested or killed."

"Or gravely wounded." Selina tipped her head in agreement to his statement. "Did you keep the task force a secret?"

"From the Snake?" Efren nodded. "We didn't broadcast it, but he was used to being under investigation. It wasn't a stretch for him to know we were looking for the head of the counterfeiting ring. Are you implying there was a mole somewhere? It wasn't me."

"It never crossed my mind that you were," he assured her. "That said, I'm not implying it. I'm assuming it. The Chicago PD is vast in its size and scope. It could have been a beat cop, lieutenant, detective, secretary or janitor. Whomever it was, they were reporting your progress to Vaccaro."

"Could be. It also could be they had a plan in place for every operation he had going on, which was also vast in its size and scope. That's less important now eight years later. What is important is why did she appear now, and how did they know I was working at Secure One?"

"The timing is suspicious. I'll give you that. We already know the Winged Templar killed Howie Loraine, but he had to have Vaccaro's approval to put out the hit. Then, unbeknownst to them, Secure One got involved. Suddenly, there you were, served up on a silver platter."

"I was never visible until the night we tried to rescue Kadie and Vic at the Loraine mansion," Selina reminded him. She hung her head and sat quietly, letting the information roll through her tired, drugged mind. When Victor Loraine's girlfriend Kadie had been kidnapped by his older brother in hopes of getting his hands on Vic's infant son, Secure One had sent Vic in to talk to his brother in hopes of finding Kadie. Instead, Randall Jr. kidnapped Vic too and it was up to Secure One to rescue them. She snapped her head up with her lips in a thin line. "Randall Jr. knew Ava was alive."

"Did he look like he knew she was alive right before he shot you?"

Selina chewed on her lip for a few seconds while she ran the interaction through her mind, forcing herself not to focus on the gunshot, but the seconds before. "No, but all he said was 'you're dead.' He didn't call me Ava Shannon."

"Vic did. Vic specifically said Ava Shannon and that he saw her die."

"Think about it, Brenna." She heard the frustration in her voice, but it wasn't with him. It was with this situation that she couldn't control. "We're twins and I 'died,'" she said, using air quotes, "the day after Ava. Randall said you're dead because he knew I was supposed to be dead, too. Wait." She held up a finger as though she was replaying something in her mind. "Vic said he saw Ava dead?" Efren nodded. "Then he really was knocked silly. He hadn't been to the mansion since he left for college until the day he went there looking for Kadie. I know for a fact he wasn't there the night of the raid."

Efren immediately scratched a sentence on the page and underlined it. "That's a breakthrough."

"That Vic was knocked silly?"

"No. He may have seen her dead. There could have been a service. I'll have Mina contact him and ask about it. It would answer the question of how hard they worked to prove she was dead. Mina is great at digging until she finds those answers, so let's leave it to her. No sense in beating our heads against the wall when we have no way to find out."

Selina pointed at the computers off to her side. "But we do. A little search would give us a lot of these answers."

"It could also open us up for an attack that I can't predict. Until I know how far we can go with those machines, I can't risk it." He set his pad aside and stood, holding out his hand to her. "You've been up long enough. You need to rest. You had a hysterectomy less than twenty-four hours ago."

Selina slipped her hand in his, and the sensation was like silk. He'd touched her before, but this time was different. There was trust there that he was going to help her, even if it were as simple as getting her out of the chair without pain. He ran his thumb over the back of her hand, and the simple motion gave her silent comfort and security that just a few seconds ago she didn't feel. She would never admit it, but whenever she spoke of Vaccaro, the terror was overpowering. Efren was the only reason she wasn't rocking in a ball in the corner. She was a cop, but when you have intimate knowledge about someone as dangerous as the Snake, it was hard not to be terrified.

"Wait," she said, freezing with her hand still in his. "A hysterectomy?"

"The doctor told us he had to take an ovary and without your uterus, you can't have children. I assumed that meant they did a hysterectomy. I'm sorry, Selina. I wish you'd had more time to deal with that before we had to run."

"Time to deal with it?" She pulled her hand from his and lifted her shirt, showing him a healed starburst wound on her abdomen just outside of the bandage from her latest incision. "I'd been a cop about three weeks when I caught a bullet the first time," she explained. "That one ripped through my uterus and tore it to shreds. I was twenty-two. You don't have to worry about me coming to terms with anything. The kid card sailed for me thirteen years ago."

He was silent for a moment as he took in the scars across her belly. "The first time?" She tipped her head in confusion and he traced his finger over the scar. "You said the first time you caught a bullet. How many?"

"The other night made four and the second gut shot. I also took one in my right arm that still has shrapnel left and one in my left thigh. Barely missed the femoral artery. I don't know why I keep cheating death, but there will come a day when I don't."

He took her hand again and tightened his around it. "Not if I have anything to say about it. It's my job to keep you alive, and I take that responsibility seriously. With that responsibility comes the right to order you to bed, and that's what I'm doing. You need more sleep."

When he turned to the bunk, her hand still in his, her eyes were barely open. "I'm relieved to know they didn't remove major organs yesterday. That means you're at less risk of massive bleeding if we have to run again. You need to get as much rest as possible over the next couple of days. I don't know when we'll have to move next."

After straightening the blankets, he helped her down and waited for her to get comfortable before he pulled the blanket over her. "You'll wake me as soon as the team is ready to talk?"

"You know I will," he promised, resting his hand on her

shoulder for comfort. "I'm going to doze a bit while keeping an eye on the cameras."

"That's kind of an oxymoron, Brenna," she said, her eyes almost closed and her tongue thick when she spoke. "You need to sleep, too."

"Shh," he whispered, powering down the lantern over the bed area. "Rest now and let your body heal."

"It may not matter," she murmured, and she heard the terror again. "If they find me, all the healing in the world won't help me."

"Not if I have anything to say about it," he whispered, and her tired mind grasped on to that and vowed never to let it go.

Chapter Five

As soon as Selina dropped off to sleep, Efren lowered himself to the chair next to the bunks and leaned over on his elbows to gaze at her. Since the day he'd met her, Selina had intrigued him. The push and pull between them was both frustrating and something to look forward to in his workday. What bothered him the most, though, was knowing she didn't like him. It wasn't his ego that was bothered, either. It was knowing that he *cared* that she didn't like him. A long time ago he'd promised himself he'd never care about anyone enough for their opinion of him to matter. The war taught him that caring about people ends in heartache and pain when they're taken from you in the blink of an eye. The Snake could certainly take Selina in the blink of an eye; he didn't even question that. He was an excellent bodyguard with a stellar record, but he could only do so much as one man.

Still, he had to admit he cared. He wanted to know why she hated him, and wondered if he'd done something to make her so standoffish from the get-go. Everyone at Secure One assured him that it had nothing to do with him, but he wasn't so sure about that. If nothing else, their forced togetherness might afford him the opportunity to discover why she hated him so he could set her straight and put them back on even ground. Whether it was something he could fix or not was another issue. For now, though, Selina needed sleep above all else.

His gut twisted as he stared at her gorgeous face finally relaxed in sleep. She had stolen his breath from their first meeting. Her long blond hair had been pulled back in a no-nonsense ponytail, but the waves still flowed down her back. Her blue eyes were sharp and assessing, but he could easily picture what those eyes would look like when the lights were low and she was relaxed. He wondered if she knew how much terror reflected back at him from those eyes when she spoke of Vaccaro. The answer was no because if she did, she'd use her iron will to shut that down, too. To say Selina Colvert intrigued him was an understatement.

He stood and walked to the computer screen that served as his eyes outside the bunker. The screen had four quadrants, each showing a camera view angled around the old cabin structure. All was quiet, so he clicked the mouse to check the four cameras that blanketed the woods in every direction. Those were quiet, too, other than a family of deer foraging through the underbrush.

Returning to the real reason he was here, he pondered their next move. The Snake had wrapped himself around Selina a long time ago. His goal was to snuff the life out of her to keep his secrets hidden. Efren had every intention of cutting off the head of the snake before he had the chance to do that, though. This was a case of hunting the hunter, but he was prepared to do anything to keep his body count at zero. There wasn't a chance in hell the body to break his winning streak would be hers. He'd make sure it was his body before hers. The idea of losing Selina ran a shiver of fear down his spine as a huff left his lips.

Sure, you want to protect Selina because it's your job, he told himself. *No, you want to protect her because she represents everything you'll never have. As long as she's alive, you can focus on the reasons why she doesn't like you rather than on the reasons why you like her.* Above all, he knew the main reason he wanted to focus on protecting her was to avoid thinking about why the idea of losing her made him instantly lonely. That, above all else, was an emotion he could not afford to entertain.

SELINA STAYED IN bed and watched the man across the room. He had pulled his socket off and was massaging his limb. If she knew one thing about Efren Brenna, it was that he'd never show weakness, and that meant never taking his prosthesis off. In fact, this was the first time she'd seen him take it off longer than to shower or sleep since she met him. The paramedic in her wished he was closer so she could check the skin, but since he wasn't, she'd have to trust that he'd tell her if there was a problem.

She laughed internally. As if he'd tell her anything about himself. Hard-core aloofness was a requirement to be in the boys' club at Secure One. Selina understood it, though. Everyone at Secure One, including herself, dealt with one type of PTSD or the other. You didn't go to war or work in law enforcement and not see things that changed you and stayed with you forever. You learned to compartmentalize it; once you did, you never spoke of it again. It had been heavily debated whether that was a smart way to approach it, but in the end, it didn't matter what anyone else thought was the correct answer. What mattered was getting through every single day trying to live in a society you no longer trusted.

Efren finished his towel massage and then used his pull sock to seat his limb back into the prosthesis. Her practiced eye watched and waited for his facial expression to change when he added the valve to the socket, but he appeared comfortable through the entire process. Since he wore a skin-fit prosthesis, meaning there was nothing between his limb and the socket, she made a mental note to keep an eye on his gait over the next few days. The running blade made him fast when in the field, but walking on it all day was going to be more difficult than on his leg with a computerized knee. Wearing the blade required him to use his limb differently to make the "knee" bend, and that would wear the skin in different places. She hated to admit that there was a weak link in their chain, but there was, and his leg was it. Not because he wasn't competent in his job, but because the situation they were in called for rough terrain that could damage his limb or his blade at any point and leave them vulnerable to Vaccaro.

The name bounced around her brain like a bullet, and she closed her eyes again. Vaccaro had done enough damage to her family and her friends at Secure One. She was happy that the person to take a bullet the other night was her. No one else deserved what Vaccaro doled out to get to her family. Well, namely her, since it appeared her twin was still in good favor with that monster. She and Ava were the last of the Shannon family tree, and she was never more grateful for that.

Selina didn't care what Uncle Medardo had planned for her. She'd beat him at every turn her entire life, and she had no intention of breaking that streak now. Besides, she had all of Secure One behind her, fighting for the answers she'd need before she faced him again. She hoped, anyway. Part of her knew that Secure One would have her back, but the other part worried that her fear the last few months had spread like a virus through the team. If Vaccaro sensed dissension among the ranks, he might be tempted to break them and force people to pick sides.

Since the Red River Slayer had been captured, Selina had been struggling to keep her demons hidden from everyone all the time. Caring for Marlise and Charlotte had been difficult when they first came to Secure One. They were abused and broken, and trusted no one but her. The things they told her and the scars they showed her would never leave her mind or her heart. Then Bethany arrived as they chased the Red River Slayer, and she nearly broke Selina. How did you care for someone who had been held hostage, assaulted repeatedly and groomed to be the sex slave of a madman? Cal and the team knew Bethany needed more help than Selina could give her, but they insisted she try. If only they had spent a few hours in her shoes. She might be an APP, and once a cop, but she was also a woman. She had spent the last three years caring for these women who needed her in the moment, but no one was there for her when she needed someone. That, above all else, was what hurt her the most.

When the Loraines popped back up in her life in a way that she couldn't escape, her illusions of safety shattered. All bets were off. Her demons came out to play all day, every day, and fighting them back had become a losing battle. She should have run the moment someone said the name Randall Loraine, but she had nowhere to go. Running meant certain death. Sticking with Secure One gave her a fighting chance.

"I'm not going to let him get to you," Efren said once he stood in his socket again.

His voice startled her, and she jumped. "I never thought you would."

As he walked toward her in the bed, she'd never felt more vulnerable, so she sat up and swung her feet to the floor. "Nice try, Colvert, but your fear filled the room and stole all the oxygen. How do you think I knew you were awake?"

"Eyes in the back of your head?" The question was sarcastic, just the way she wanted it. She had to keep Efren at arm's length if she was going to get through this with any kind of dignity.

"You don't know how often I wish that were the case. How are you feeling?"

After stretching side to side and gingerly probing her abdomen, she looked up at him. "It's better this morning. It still feels bruised, but the burning pain in my gut from the incision is mostly gone."

"Good, I'm happy to hear that. It won't stay that way if you overdo it, though. While in this bunker, I need you to be down more than you're up. If we have to move quickly, you'll need your reserves to get through it. The terrain out there is tough to traverse when you're in top form, much less recovering from surgery."

"Speaking of terrain. How's the leg?" she asked, nicer this time, as she rubbed her eyes. "I noticed you had your socket off."

If he thought she didn't notice the way his eyes widened when she said that, he didn't know her very well. His "it's fine" was also not an acceptable answer.

"Run it down," she ordered. "Skin, pinch points, pain, function."

Efren threw his hand onto his hip with a huff. "I've been an amputee a long time. I don't need help with managing my situation. My leg, or lack thereof, will not be a factor in keeping you safe."

"That might be true, but I need help managing my situation, and the only help I have is standing in front of me," she said, her voice full of fire. "So run it down and be honest. I have the skills to keep small problems from becoming big problems."

"The skin is fine, there are no pinch points, I'm managing my phantom pain by keeping the limb compressed and with towel massage, and the function is superb. I could run this leg at half function and it would still be more than we'd need to get your surly backside out of trouble."

"Ego much?" She stood and straightened completely, finally able to take a deep breath.

"Honesty isn't ego."

She lifted a brow and pinned him with an assessing gaze. "I'm surprised they didn't bring your other leg to you at the hospital before they left town."

He shook his head as though he was thoroughly fed up with her questions. "Eric intended to, but Mack took mobile command back to Secure One before he got there to get it. They were headed back with it when we had to bail. It's not a problem, Selina. Walking through that terrain last night on the computerized knee would have been much more difficult. The blade is thinner and easier to maneuver in those situations. They both have their pros and cons. Well, look at you. Standing up straight is an improvement."

Selina accepted that he wanted to change the subject, so she didn't push. "The faster, the better, if you ask me."

"In this situation, yes, but don't overdo it. This is a marathon, not a sprint."

"Speaking of, have you heard from anyone?"

"Cal contacted me. They're ready to meet when we are. Mina has been working for a few hours already."

"Good. Hopefully, she'll know something to help unravel this situation. I'll be right out." Selina closed the door to the small bathroom and stripped off her shirt. She had little time, but the most important thing was to check her incision and ensure there was no sign of infection. As she peeled back the bandage, the incision slowly revealed itself, and she couldn't help but grimace. She had seen it yesterday but hadn't been with it enough to consider the scope of the repair to her fascia. No wonder her entire abdomen was black and blue. The incision was jagged, leaving a zigzag down her skin with a puckered center where the entry wound was. She also had an exit wound when the bullet had left her body and slammed into the back of her vest. It took her a minute to realize she would have to rely on Efren to check that incision. The mirror didn't go low enough, and she couldn't twist around without pain to see it herself.

Her sigh was heavy, and he could probably hear it out there, but there was little she could do other than re-dress the front incision and run a washcloth around her face and belly. After quickly brushing her teeth, she pulled her sweatshirt back on. "You've got this," she told the woman in the mirror. "It's just a Band-Aid. You can handle having his hands on you for that long."

The truth was, she couldn't handle having Efren's hands on her at all. Last night, when he held her hand and rubbed his thumb over it, she nearly fell apart on the spot. If she hadn't been so exhausted, she probably would have. It had been eight years since she'd encountered the intimate touch of a man who cared. That day, those few minutes of her life, had haunted her every day since then. Whenever she thought about Kai Tanner, her heart broke again. Vaccaro's venom poisoned more than just his victim. It traveled insidiously through their loved ones until they, too, suffered the wrath of the Snake.

Chapter Six

Eva watched and waited while the man she had known, and probably loved, finished the short climb up the bluff in the middle of nowhere, Wisconsin, and then bent over to catch his breath.

"I need your help, Kai."

His head snapped up when she stepped into the open, her dog Zeus standing steadfastly by her side. She saw the flare of love in his eyes. The same flare she'd seen for the last several years whenever they met up on a rescue. "I'll do anything I can, Eva."

"I have to run, Kai, and I'm going to need your help to get out of this alive." She spent the next few minutes outlining her plan.

"You want me to make a false report of your death?" Kai asked, taking a step back. "I doubt the authorities would appreciate that, Eva. If the ruse was uncovered, I could be charged."

"You won't be," she promised. "That's why I picked the bluffs. Falling into the river from up here is certain death, and a body would be washed away before a witness could even get to civilization for help. You're a search-and-rescue

guy. *If you tell them I never resurfaced, they'll believe you.
They won't try hard to find me and assume my body will wash
ashore or end up in the Mississippi. Eventually, they'll forget
about me and move on with life."*

"I'll never forget about you, Eva," Kai said, his head shaking. "You've been the best partner a guy could have in this
business. I'll never work with someone like you again. You
lead with your moral compass, which is rare these days. I
don't want to do this." His lip trembled when he put his hand
on his hip in some form of defiance she didn't understand.

"Never say never, Kai. You're the kind of guy who attracts
like-minded people. In my opinion, you're the best of the best.
I hope you understand now why I always stayed hands-off
with you. I will always love you even though I can never love
you." She pressed Zeus's leash into his palm. "Take him for
me. Give him the life I can't now."

"No," he said before she even finished. "No. You aren't
leaving, Eva. Stay. We can work this out."

"There are only two ways of working this out, Kai. They
both require me to die, fake or real. If I stay, the Snake will
be certain my death is real." Eva wished she was wrong, but
she wasn't. She'd crossed the wrong man, and now, if she
wanted to stay alive, she would have to die.

"I'm not ready to say goodbye, Eva. There is so much
left unsaid."

"There's nothing you can do for me now, Kai," she insisted. "Except to promise me you'll take care of Zeus and
give him a good life."

She could see the terror that filled him, but he finally nodded. "And you're sure I won't get in trouble for this?"

"Positive," Eva promised. "You have to know I don't have any other option. I wouldn't do this if I did."

"I know, but Eva, he's going to be heartbroken. I don't know if he'll ever recover."

"Zeus will be fine." She hoped someday Kai would be, too. "As long as he's got you and Apollo and can search, he'll find his purpose."

He choked back a sob and nodded. "We'll take care of him."

"I left his papers and money for his care in my truck at the entrance to the park. It should get you through quite a few years. I'm sorry I can't do more."

"No," he said, trailing a finger down her cheek. "Don't apologize for doing the right thing despite knowing the right thing meant a bounty on your head. I'll do my best to give him the kind of life and love you would have."

She knelt and wrapped her arms around the German shepherd's neck, whispering into his ear and stroking his fur. The pain in her chest was almost overwhelming. She'd lost her family to the Snake, and now he was taking the final things she loved.

Eva stood, and Kai grasped her elbow. "When it's safe, check my blog. I'll post updates about Zeus and Apollo as they work together. There will be pictures. It's the best I can do."

"Thank you," she said, raising up on her toes to kiss his cheek. "You are a genuinely good human, Kai. Find someone to love who's deserving of yours."

He grasped her hand. "You are deserving of love, Eva." He held tight to her hand as she tried to turn away. "I'll go with you. Let me grab Apollo."

"No." The one word was firm and heartbreaking. "For this to work, I need you to play your part. The Snake will know I took off if you aren't here to run interference."

Kai nodded, and she noticed him blink back the tears that filled his eyes. "Okay, I've got your back."

She threw her arms around his neck and held him momentarily before doing the same to Zeus. "You know what to do?" she asked, standing again and holding his gaze.

"I'll set the scene. You get out of dodge. I love ya, partner. Be safe."

Eva blew him a kiss, turned and ran like the hounds of hell were after her.

"Selina?" Efren's voice snapped her from the daydream, and she gasped, the sound loud in the concrete room. "I'm coming in."

When he opened the door, their eyes locked, and before she had truly returned to the world, he pulled her from the bathroom and into his arms. Efren held her lightly, one arm wrapped around her back and one holding her head to his shoulder. She couldn't help but catalog everything about him in quick succession. His muscular chest was warm and tight. His cheek smelled like cedar soap and shaving cream as it rested against hers. His arm wrapped around her waist was soft and warm against her skin. It took her a moment to realize she hadn't pulled her shirt down all the way, and it was trapped above his arm, allowing his heat to pour into her. What settled in somewhere deep inside was the way he held her against him gently, and while careful of her wounds, he still made her feel safe in a world she knew wasn't.

"You look like you've seen a ghost," he murmured. "Are you in pain?"

"Not physically," she answered, her words rough to her own ears. "I was thinking about the last time I had to run from the Snake." Rather than go any further, she snapped her lips shut.

"I can't pretend to know what you're going through, Selina," Efren whispered, squeezing her a bit tighter. "Just know that we all have your back and we'll stop at nothing to protect you from Vaccaro."

"I know." The two words were whispered, but they held so many emotions. Fear. Gratefulness. Regret.

"We don't hold a grudge at Secure One." He'd turned his head so his lips brushed her ear when he spoke. The sensations rocketing through her made her want to collapse to the ground, and she would have, had he not been holding her. "Have you ever held it against any of them when their demons attacked you unexpectedly?"

"No."

"The same is true for you, Selina. We'll get through this, and the team will be stronger for it."

She lifted her head, prepared to pull away, but instead, she laid her lips on his. They were warm, moist and open, as though they'd been waiting for this moment their entire life. She couldn't help but notice how perfectly matched they were as his settled against hers for a hairbreadth before he leaned into the kiss. He caressed her lips, keeping it tender but barely contained until she forced herself to step back out of the hug and stand on her own.

She didn't want to. Lord, how she didn't want to, and that scared her, too. Efren was the enemy. You didn't kiss the enemy. Because of him, she had been overlooked and cast aside as an operative by Cal and the rest of the team. She was supposed to hate him, not find refuge in his arms and lips. Even if the game had changed and he was no longer her biggest enemy, she had to stay hands—and now lips—off. She couldn't help but notice the way his gaze raked her from head to toe and back up again to rest at her midsection, where her shirt still hung haphazardly, allowing her pink and puckered flesh to peek out. His gaze warmed her skin and insides, sending heat spiraling through her at an alarming speed. She had to put the brakes on whatever this was before things got out of control and she started to like the man in front of her. She already liked that kiss way too much.

"I—I need some help with the wound on my back." She had no idea how to address what happened, so her game plan was to pretend it didn't. "Will you check it and rebandage it? I can't reach it from any angle."

"Sure." The word was growled, and she couldn't help but notice that his hands were in fists as he walked to the bathroom for the first aid kit. "I'm glad you mentioned it, because I'd forgotten about the exit wound."

"I haven't," she said, tongue in cheek. "It's annoying to sleep on that bandage. I'm hoping we can cover it with a regular Band-Aid at this point."

He swung a chair around and had her sit on the edge so he had a clear view of her back. After the supplies were readied on the table, he started working the bandage off her skin a little at a time. "The team is ready as soon as we are," he said, giving her something else to focus on as he worked. "They're anxious to put eyes on you so they can see that you're okay."

"I'm worried they're angry," she admitted. The truth was easier to speak when not staring directly into his eyes.

"That's one thing you don't have to worry about." He

dabbed liquid around the wound. It stung for just a moment, but then cool air stole it away, telling her he was fanning her skin to avoid hurting her. "From what I can gather, Cal knew the truth?"

"Some of it, but not the full scope. He was going to run a background check on me, and there was no way that was going to work. He had a...reputation, so I leaned into that in hopes he'd understand."

"As the kind of guy you could trust with your secrets because he had a mountain of his own?"

"Bingo." She hissed as he probed the edges of the wound. "What are you doing?"

"Sorry," he said, popping his head around her shoulder. "It's a little pink, but your reaction said it's pink from healing and not infection."

"Take a picture of it," she said, waiting for him to grab the Secure One phone. He handed it around to her, and she inspected it closely, trying not to visibly grimace at how ugly it was. "Well, I've taken better pictures. Let's put some antibiotic ointment around the edges just to be on the safe side, but avoid the stitches."

He squeezed her shoulder. "You're alive. Remember that and use it to fight through this. Someone else tried to take you down, but you stood tall. That mark on your skin is a badge of honor."

"Change the narrative and change the world, right?"

"Not the world," he disagreed, as he swiped ointment around the wound and grabbed a large bandage from the pack. "Just your mindset. I already know you're a fighter, Selina, so keep fighting. Don't let a Loraine bullet be the bullet that takes you down, physically or emotionally. They don't deserve to hold that kind of power over you. That much you know for sure." He pulled her shirt down over the wound and patted her back. "You're good to go."

Selina stood and stretched her back before giving a nod. "Thanks. It feels better to get that big bandage off there."

"Happy to do it." He threw away the old bandages and cleaned up the first aid kit before he washed his hands.

"Brenna," she said, and he turned, drying his hands on a towel. "I appreciate the pep talk. I got caught up in the past and you helped me refocus."

"Understandable," he said, tipping his head to the side. "It happens to all of us, which is what I like about working at Secure One. There's always someone there who understands and can pull you back before that rabbit hole goes too deep."

"Speaking of Secure One, I suppose we should make that call."

"Deep breath," he said, walking toward her until he was standing chest to chest with her again. She followed his order, and they took a deep breath together and let it out. "Good. You didn't even grimace with that breath. You must be feeling better," he said with a wink.

"I'm glad for it, too. The less medication I have to take, the sharper my mind will be."

"That's true, but you also have to be able to move quickly with little or no notice."

Selina tipped her head back and forth. "I'll take over-the-counter painkillers, but keep the other ones on me. I can always pop one fast if we have to go. That said, I'd give anyone major props who can find the entrance to this place. Cal didn't even tell the team where it was or how to find it."

"He wanted it need-to-know, so I didn't find out until last night when he sent the location to my GPS."

"That's Cal for you. The fewer people who know, the better. Time to make that call," she finally said, settling herself down at the computer terminal. He sat next to her and leaned into her ear.

"You can pretend that kiss never happened, but it did, and I'm not going to pretend that I didn't feel the connection between us. Fair warning."

His piece said, he clicked a button on a device next to him without another word.

Chapter Seven

Efren's words replayed on repeat in her mind. "Fair warning." Was he implying that he planned to kiss her again? The
very idea made her nervous. Not because she didn't want him
to, but because she did. Getting involved with anyone could
mean instant death for them. If necessary, she'd remind herself of that every second of the day. She couldn't be the reason an innocent person died at Vaccaro's hands.

Before she could speak, a familiar voice filled their concrete prison. "Secure one, Charlie."

"Secure two, Tango," Efren responded, and the screen
flickered to life.

"Secure three, Sierra," she finished, and Cal's face filled
the screen.

"You're a sight for sore eyes," he said without preamble.
"How are you feeling?"

"Better. I've had worse injuries."

"Maybe, but our goal now is to get you through this without more." Cal set his jaw for a moment and then shook his
head. "I'm going to flip the camera."

Selina nodded, and they waited until the conference room
came into view. Mina, Roman, Mack, Eric, Lucas, Cal, Char-

lotte and Marlise sat around the table. That was their core team, and Cal couldn't make it clearer he was sticking with them to get this job done. Awkward wasn't Selina's style, but staring into the faces of the people she'd lied to for years was exactly that. So much so that she didn't know what to say.

"We're a team," Eric said, standing and leaning on the table with his hands to peer into the camera. "We've been a team for years, and that doesn't change now. Is that understood, Sierra?"

Her nod was instant and quick. "Heard and understood, Echo."

Eric sat with a nod.

Mina spoke next. "Good to see you, Selina. We've been getting updates from Efren, but it's not the same as talking to you. Before we go any further, we all want to know the answer to one question." She motioned around the circle of people, so Selina nodded for her to ask it. "Going forward, do you want to go by Eva or Selina?"

"Selina." There was no hesitation in her answer. "Eva Shannon is dead. Do you all understand? She must remain dead and buried for more reasons than I have time to go into right now."

"He already knows you're alive," Marlise said. "No matter what name you go by, the bounty is on your head."

"I understand that, but if I'm going to get through this and figure out how Ava Shannon came back from the dead and why, I need distance. The only way to separate myself from my twin is to pretend I am someone else entirely."

"You are," Efren said, slipping his arm around her back where no one else could see. "You may be twins genetically, but not in morals or anything else that matters."

"He's right," Cal said with a nod. "That's the reason I hired you eight years ago with the weak story that you were a domestic violence victim on the run. That's also the reason we've got your back today even knowing that story you sold was fiction." All the heads around the table nodded as he spoke, and it lifted her tired lips into a smile.

"Thanks, team. My greatest fear was my attitude over the last few months damaged our relationship and you wouldn't want to work with me."

"Never," Mack said before anyone else could speak. "We all have our own brand of attitude depending on the day and situation. That's accepted within this circle, as you well know. You've been on the receiving end of my attitude more often than not."

"I still feel bad about it," she said, biting her lip.

"That's because you're a good person in your heart, and you don't want to hurt people," Charlotte said. "You got me through those first few days after I turned myself in and I was too scared to speak. It was you who kept me calm and made me feel safe even when I wasn't. Let us do that for you now."

A breath escaped her chest as though she'd been punched. "Thank you, Charlotte. I needed to hear you say that. It shifted my guilt and brought the reason we're here into focus. Getting out of this alive."

"It was the least I could do," Charlotte assured her.

Cal drummed his fingers on the table, and all heads turned to him. It was magical how he made those metal and plastic fingers behave just like real ones. "It's time for full disclosure, Colvert. The moment someone said the Loraine name a few weeks ago you should have been in my office, but we can't go backward, so let's go forward. Tell us why you're in their crosshairs."

She took a deep breath, knowing she had to bare her soul if they were going to save it. Efren rubbed her hip, his warm hand what she needed to ground her in order to tell the sordid tale again. She did it with as little emotion as possible as she filled them in on her family's involvement with the Mafia and her crossing of them during her law enforcement career.

"You're saying your sister didn't die that night?" Roman asked when she finished telling them about the raid.

"That appears to be the case, since she showed up at the hospital asking for me."

Eric shook his head and chuckled. "When I told the charge nurse to watch for someone suspicious asking about you, I never dreamed that person would look exactly like you. I was expecting a hit man."

"Trust me, Eric, she was the hit man. If Efren hadn't gotten me out of there, you'd be attending my real funeral right now. My twin believes in the whole Mafia mentality of an eye for an eye, and when that eye is family, she will stop at nothing to make you pay. What I don't know is why she's not dead and how she knew I wasn't either."

"I've got some feelers out in regard to the Loraine family. Unfortunately, I don't have any answers," Mina interjected.

"Yet," Roman added with a wink.

"I've concentrated my efforts on Randall Loraine Sr.," she explained, clicking a slide up onto the screen for them to see. "As you know, he's resided at Federal Correctional Institution Pekin for the last eight years serving a fifty-year sentence for the counterfeiting scheme. Since he was convicted of a nonviolent crime, he is in a low-security institution."

Selina rolled her eyes. "The crime may have been non-violent, but trust me, Randall Sr. knows how to be violent."

"I have no doubt of that, considering who he worked for," Mina agreed. "From what I can see of his records, he hasn't had any visitors since Howie Loraine was last there to see him shortly before his death almost a month ago. However, prior to that, Howie visited him once every two weeks for the entire time he's been there. Randall Jr. visited him once a month without fail."

"So maybe Howie and Randall were continuing Daddy's business on the outside?"

"More than likely," Eric agreed. "But we already suspected that was the case."

"None of that explains how my twin came back to life." Selina heard the frustration in her voice and tried to curb it. This wasn't her friends' fault, and she needed their help if she was going to come out of this bunker alive.

"I'm working on that as well," Mina promised. "I've pulled the information from that night, and I'm following the chain of people who were in contact with your sister from the time you shot her until she was pronounced 'dead.'" She used air quotes around the word, considering the circumstances. "My hope is to follow the money. If any of them got a large influx of cash, I'll find it."

Selina leaned forward, partly to free herself of Efren's warm hand on her side and partly to be seen better, so no one misunderstood what she was saying. "If Ava didn't die eight years ago, there's a connection somewhere between her and Vaccaro. We need to find that connection and follow where it leads."

"That's easier said than done," Mina answered. "The Vaccaro organization is one organization I can't hack. I can use back channels to find out what the organization is doing, but anything personal is off-limits to me."

"The Snake doesn't allow anyone into his den who he doesn't invite in as a warm body or a meal." Selina shivered involuntarily. "Is there a way to find out who Randall Jr. talked to the night he was arrested?"

"Like, did he make any phone calls?" Mina asked, her hands poised over the keyboard.

"Or have any visitors," Selina said. "I wonder if Randall Jr. knew she wasn't dead since he hung out so much with his father in prison. If he did, he may have been the one to report to her or Vaccaro that I was alive."

"He knew it was you since he already knew that Ava was alive and where she was," Efren finished, nodding immediately.

Eric spoke up. "Honestly, Eva and Ava are impossible to tell the difference when lip reading. It was dark and we were all moving. Randall Jr. could have said Eva and I wouldn't know. That would explain why he shot you."

"There was a lot of law enforcement there that night. If one of them was a plant by Vaccaro, they could have reported back that they saw Selina," Roman suggested.

"Since Randall Jr. already knew Ava was alive, he knew it was me." Selina clenched her jaw in frustration.

"We're assuming that Randall, and thus Vaccaro, knew Ava was still alive," Cal said, holding up a finger. "Until we know that for sure, we can't assume anything."

"Easiest way to find out is to start with Randall Jr. I can hopefully have an answer in a few hours," Mina said without taking her hands off the keyboard.

Selina smiled at her friend and nodded. "I know it won't be easy, but until we know why she's back, our hands are tied. That said, I assure you that Vaccaro is aware that Ava is still alive. I would go so far as to say he's the *reason* she's still alive."

"You think she's been working in his organization all these years?" Mack asked.

Selina's nod was exaggerated. "Without a doubt."

Cal waved his hand in the air. "What I don't get is, why Vaccaro was building an organization outside of his family. Our basic understanding of him says he's over the age of sixty. Shouldn't his children be the ones layered up into his organization? Isn't that how the Mafia works?"

"You're correct." Selina pointed at the screen with a smile. "Here's where things get interesting. Vaccaro is the last of his line. His swimmers didn't swim if you catch my drift?" Heads nodded around the table. "Since he never had children, he made his wife his second-in-command. A queenpin if you will. She was ten years younger than him, but she died of cancer about ten years ago. I have no idea what's transpired since, whether he's remarried or not, but that's beside the point. There are no children, so his only choice was to find other families he could corrupt and pull in to build his organization."

"It seems that his choices were a bit off?" Roman asked.

"In hindsight," Selina agreed. "My father and Randall Sr. were his buddies from college, so it made sense for him to pull them in. He trusted them to have children and raise them to be part of the business. He forgot that children live what they learn, and corruption doesn't always swing in your favor when the chips are down."

"He also forgot that some are simply not corruptible," Efren said, giving her a gentle shoulder bump. "All of that said, it's time for us to get back to Secure One."

"No." Selina's objection was loud and precise when she stood on the two letters.

"Selina, we're safer behind the layers of security at home than we'll ever be anywhere else."

"Maybe," she said, spinning to stick her finger in his chest. He stood, which made her smile inside. He was not going to be the beta male in this game if he could help it. "But I won't risk opening Secure One to the Vaccaro organization. That would be certain death for every single person sitting around that table. Is that what you want?"

"You're overreacting." She noticed him grit his teeth and make a fist before he spoke again. "We can't stay here. We have to move, and the most logical place is back to Secure One."

"I disagree with you, Tango," Cal said from the head of the table. "We already put Secure One at risk by going into the Loraine mansion to get Kadie and Vic. It was the right thing to do, but it opened us up to an attack that even our security measures may not be able to withstand. All I can do is hope they're too busy scrambling to get Randall Jr. out of jail and find Selina to worry about what we are doing. The last thing I want is for them to get wind that Selina is here."

"To that end," Marlise said, "I've made you disappear. Your credit card was used to buy a ticket to Hawaii and you were seen getting on the plane with a male resembling Efren."

"I doubt that will buy us much time," Selina said. "Thanks for trying, though."

"That one may not," Cal said, wearing a smirk. "The other five will probably slow them down, though."

"You bought six different plane tickets?" Efren asked, laughter bubbling out of him. "That's diabolical level stuff."

"This is life-or-death level stuff," Cal said. "I know Vaccaro won't believe you're on one flight, but if he's suddenly faced with six, he has no choice but to check them out, just in case. My goal is to keep the heat off you long enough to get some healing time in and to buy me time to find you somewhere else to go. When I built that bunker, I didn't have hiding an operative from the Mafia on my bingo card."

"That's my fault, I know," Selina agreed. "I can tell you until I'm blue in the face how bad I feel about that, but I'd rather get through this alive so I can make it up to you on the next case."

"There's the spirit!" Mina exclaimed, giving her an air high five. "Hang tight there and get some rest. Let us work on things on our end and before you know it, you'll be back in your lab doing your thing."

Efren looked like he was about to object when Cal spoke. "I'll contact you on the secure line if I need you to call in. While you wait, rest, and if you think of anything more to help us find your sist—" He held his hand up. "I'm sorry, find Ava Shannon, let me know immediately. We'll be in touch again at 2100 hours for an update. If you have to move before that, you know the drill."

Efren gave him a salute right before the screen went dark. Selina paced to the other end of the bunker in silence. "The Snake will know it's a ruse." The words were muttered rather than spoken. "He won't take the bait. He'll know I'm still here. We have to move."

"No." Efren grasped her arms and held her in place. "We have nowhere to go."

"We can't stay here." She looked up into his eyes and wondered if hers told a louder story than her words. "He will find us and he will kill us!" Before she could say another word, his lips were on hers.

Chapter Eight

Stop kissing her. Efren's inner voice demanded he listen, but he wasn't. He dug in deeper, drawing her into him with a hand at her waist and his other hand buried deep in her long, silky hair. She was butter under his lips and sagged against him as they stood in the silent room. She poured her pain, anger, fear and guilt into him, and he willingly swallowed it all. He'd been with plenty of women over the years, but none of them could bring him to his knees with a kiss the way Selina did. And she would always be Selina to him. He would fight for her and with her until his dying breath, if need be, but he'd rather make love, not war. That was all he was thinking about as his lips stroked hers. Selina slid her arms around his waist and moaned softly, telling him she was as into it as he was, despite the danger they faced from Vaccaro and what getting personally involved might bring down on them.

Too damn bad.

"We have to stop," she murmured against his lips before pulling away. "We can't let this distract us and leave ourselves open to an attack."

"You're right." The words were as heavy as the breath in

his chest. "I just can't deny this spark between us any longer. We've fought against it for months, but this was inevitable."

"Was it though?" she asked as she walked to the bed and sat. "I'm still mad at you. Don't think for a minute that I've forgotten how you became part of the team at Secure One."

"What does that mean, Selina?"

"I can't do this right now, Brenna. I need to rest." She'd scooted under the blankets and closed her eyes by the time he approached the bunks.

"It's interesting how you call me by my last name as soon as I get a little too close or you feel a little too vulnerable. Sleep now, but know there will come a day where we'll work out this grudge you've got against me. The way you kiss me tells me it will be worth it."

He waited, but she never responded, just kept on with her fake sleep. He'd allow it, for now, but he'd spoken the truth. One day, they'd have it out and once the air was cleared, he had every intention of exploring this heat between them. For now, he had to do what he could to get them out of this bind. To do that, he'd have to understand the enemy.

Efren waited for Selina's breathing to even out so he knew she was actually sleeping and then grabbed the Secure One phone. He typed out a message to Mina, whose response came within minutes. Sure thing. While Selina slept, he intended to learn everything he could about Vaccaro and the Shannons. Not so much about Eva as much as Ava. He would have to have a handle on what her sister was capable of if he was going to stay one step ahead of them. If that was even possible. If Vaccaro was half as powerful as they said he was—and he had no reason to doubt them—then his only choice might be to go stealth mode and literally stay one step ahead of them until the team could figure out how to bring them in.

He grabbed a bottle of water and a package of trail mix, then fired up the direct link computer. He'd have to wait until the satellite passed over to get the transmission, but with any luck, the info Mina was sending would be what he needed to get to not only know the enemy but better understand the woman he one day wanted in his bed. That truth hit him in the gut. If they somehow managed to cut off the head of this snake, he'd stop at nothing to prove to Selina that letting go of her anger and making room for him in her life was worth the risk.

He glanced at her and couldn't help but smile. That may be easier said than done, but he was up for the challenge.

SELINA WOKE SLOWLY, her head pounding and her belly sore when she sat up. "Oh Lord, end me." The words were grunted in pain. Efren was beside her almost instantly, helping her stand.

"I'll do no such thing, but I think you may have hit the seventy-two-hour hell."

"I couldn't agree more." She couldn't stand up straight, so she just sat back down. The seventy-two-hour hell was a place no one wanted to be after surgery. It was always the third day that everything hit you like a ton of bricks. The pain, fatigue the healing, and for her the fear, combined to make the next few hours miserable until she got everything under control again.

"Take this," Efren said, handing her a pill, but she pushed it away. "Take it. This is not up for argument." He held out a bottle of water and she grudgingly took the pill and forced herself to drink most of the water.

"I can't keep taking the heavy stuff," she said, leaning over on her thighs. "I have to shake this pain off and get ready for battle."

"Not treating your pain is going to make that impossible," he said, pulling the chair over to sit across from her. "You had a bullet in your belly, and it did some funky stuff to your body. Acknowledge that and accept it, so we can stop having this same argument every time you wake up."

"Why did I get trapped in a bunker with a smart-ass?" Her words were tongue-in-cheek, but she also meant them.

"More like a badass," he answered with a wink. "A badass who made you more soup and crackers and wants you to feel better because he knows how miserable you are right now. Speaking in generalities of course, since my last surgery wasn't gut surgery."

"What was your last surgery?" He helped her up and walked with her to the table where she sat again and waited for him to bring her the soup that he'd been heating up for her. He knew when she woke up, she was going to need food.

"Limb revision." He set a bowl in front of her with rice and chicken in broth. "That was about six years ago."

"How long ago was the original amputation?"

"Ten. They originally left my knee, but that limited my options for prosthetics, so I opted to go above the knee when the original amputation had to be revised anyway."

"They should have gone above the knee to start, right?"

"It would have saved me a lot of headaches, but traumatic amputations, as you know, are tricky. They did the best they could, and I was functional with a through the knee, but I'm outstanding above the knee." He winked to tell her he was joking, but she shook her head.

"You actually are outstanding above the knee. Considering what you've been through, you've come back from it well. I just wish you gave your limb more time to rest. I never see you without the prosthesis. Do you sleep with it?"

"No." He lowered himself to the chair across from her. "After the revision, I developed strong phantom pain. With the original injury, it was there, but it was more a minor annoyance in the background. This is not that. It's mind numbing and distracting, and the only way I found to deal with it is to keep compression on the limb at all times. It feels good in the socket, so at night, I have a soft one I wear to help with the pain while I sleep. The medication I take helps as well."

"Do you have your meds with you?" She asked the question with the spoon halfway to her mouth and a brow raised. Once the question was out, she finished spooning in the soup while keeping a close eye on him. She would know if he was lying.

"Some."

"Not enough, right?"

"Not for an extended period, no. I'm rationing them for now."

"And if you run out?"

"Not an option, so if we can't get back to Secure One, Cal may have to make an unexpected airdrop. We'll cross that bridge when we come to it."

"I want to say it won't come to it, but I am all too familiar with this game. We aren't going back to Secure One anytime soon."

"After what I read, I have to agree." He tapped his fingers

on the table. "I knew from the moment I met you that you were someone special, but all of this leaves me speechless."

"All of what? My hot mess express?"

"No, that you willingly took on a kingpin knowing you were signing your own death warrant. There aren't many people in the world who would do that."

"They would if they'd seen what I had in life." Her shrug at the end probably told him more than her words, but she couldn't worry about that now. Her secrets were no longer secrets, but she still wasn't comfortable with him knowing even the little bit she'd told him.

"I spent the night reading through the articles Mina sent me, and I stand by my statement. Not many people would do what you did."

"Articles?" Selina laid her spoon down, the soup threatening to come back up at the idea that he had information outside of what she'd given him. If she couldn't control the narrative, then she had no control left whatsoever. For someone like her, that was more terrifying than facing off with a kingpin.

"Mina dug through the archives and found some old articles about the Snake. His moniker is fitting."

She exhaled a bit at his words. Old articles on the Snake were okay. Old articles about her would leave her open to more questions than she wanted to answer. She was no longer the woman who fell off that cliff eight years ago. He couldn't get that idea in his head or it would be too hard for him to consider her an equal going forward.

"I thought I had a lot of medals. Then I read your bio."

Selina's heart sank. "I don't know what you mean. I don't have any medals."

"Not what I read. Sounds like you were not only a decorated Chicago PD cop, but you were an up-and-comer in the search-and-rescue world as well. Did you know they awarded you the valor award posthumously?"

Selina stood, no longer caring about the pain in her belly. The pain in her chest overpowered it. She wanted out of this bunker and away from Efren Brenna. She'd gotten used to hiding out in the lab at Secure One to avoid him and his damn tempting eyes, but here, there was nowhere to go, and she suspected he was taking full advantage of the situation. He liked making her uncomfortable. It was probably something they taught them in the military, like, live on the edge of your comfort zone, and soon you'll be comfortable in all the zones. She snorted at herself and offered herself a mental high five for that gem.

What was she supposed to say? No, she had no idea they bestowed upon her the most respected award in law enforcement after she faked her death.

"It's okay, you know," he said from directly behind her. "They didn't award it to you because you died. They awarded it to you because you lived."

Her shoulders sank, and he wrapped his arms around them, holding her against his chest. Every time they touched, his settled her somewhere deep inside that even she couldn't pinpoint. Or maybe she didn't want to pinpoint it and admit that his touch had power over her.

"Maybe I lived honestly, but I died dishonestly. I bet they wouldn't have considered that so medal-worthy."

"It's no different than going into WITSEC and falling off the face of the earth. The difference is, when you go into WITSEC, you don't get to shape the narrative. At least you did it your way. You did it in a way that reminded people, sometimes the heroes that go out to save them don't always come back."

Selina grabbed his forearms and held on tight, letting his heat warm and relax her. "I suppose that's true, but some might call what I did taking the coward's way out."

"Anyone who thinks that hasn't read the articles I have on Medardo Vaccaro. You took the only out you had at the time. Never consider your contributions to taking that man down as less than because of the choices you had to make after the attempt. You had no good ones, so you took the one that hurt the fewest number of people."

"How do you figure?" She was curious to know why he thought that was the best choice she could have made.

"Listen, you're talking to someone who ran a lot of missions in a lot of hostile places. Our first instruction if we were caught was to take any opportunity to end our lives before they could get information from us. The movies make it look like you can escape any situation when captured in a war or hostile territory, but the truth is, no one escapes. The enemy gets the information from you in the most painful way possible, and then you die. Make no mistake. You were in a war with no team and no one willing to protect you from the enemy. You already knew the police department suspected you of being involved with the Snake. They weren't likely to bend over backward to protect you from him, right?"

"If I'd thought it was likely, I wouldn't have run."

"Then you did what soldiers do. Sure, you didn't die, but you've spent the years since you disappeared doing good for other people. You've continued to rescue those in need, even if the way you do it looks a little bit different."

Selina said nothing, she just leaned her head back and let the words he said settle deep inside her where she could call them up whenever she doubted the decisions she'd made over the years. There was one important thing she had to do before they spent any more time togeth—

"Secure one, Whiskey."

Efren dropped his arms and hurried to the console with Selina on his heels. "Secure two, Tango."

Mina's face popped up on the screen, and she eyed them both. "I have an update, and you may want to sit down for this."

Chapter Nine

Efren's gaze darted to Selina for a moment, and then he pulled out a chair, motioning for her to sit, which she did without argument. Whether it was fatigue from the surgery or opening up to him over the last few days that made her feel weak, he didn't know, but whatever Mina had to say was sure to change the game again.

"How bad is it?" Selina asked, her shoulders stiff as though she was preparing for battle.

"You'll have to answer that question. I learned through some back channels that Randall Sr. could be released on a technicality."

Silence. Efren counted to ten before he slid into the chair next to Selina and hooked his arm around her waist. He didn't care if Mina saw him do it, either. He could see in Selina's eyes that her world was spinning and she needed someone to ground her. While he couldn't be everything for her, as the only one here, he could support her.

"Do you know why he's being released?" Efren asked since Selina had opened her mouth, but only a puff of air escaped.

"I'm working on learning that and what his release date will be."

"That explains why Ava is back now." Selina said her sister's name as though it were venom on her tongue she had to spit out. "Still doesn't explain where she's been all these years."

"Working on that, too," Mina answered. "But if she's within the Vaccaro organization, I won't find much."

"I have no doubt she is," Selina said with conviction. "Did you get anywhere with Randall Jr.'s arrest?"

"I have a few feelers out. The information is fresh, so it will take a bit longer to get."

"Understood," Efren said. "Thanks for the update. At least we know why Ava has shown her face again."

"Ever the loving wife. Give me a break," Selina muttered. "Are you sure there were no unnamed visitors visiting Daddy Dearest in prison?"

Mina smiled the smile she wore when she was a dog with a bone. "Great minds think alike. I broke down his visitor list, and I'm looking into the names individually. If she was there, I'll find out."

"Thanks, Mina—"

Before he could say more, Cal loomed over Mina's shoulder. "My surveillance indicates our attempts to throw off anyone looking for Selina has failed. Someone has been sniffing around the Jeep, and I haven't been able to get it out of there. Stay on your toes."

"I've always got an eye on the trail cameras," he assured his boss. Did he feel guilty for lying since he spent half his time staring at Selina? Not even a little bit.

"Good. We'll be in touch as soon as we know Randall's court date and the technicality."

"Selina," Mina said before Cal could end the transmission.

"Would Vaccaro put out a hit on you, or do you think this is purely Ava's axe to grind?"

Selina was silent longer than necessary to think about the question, which told Efren she was hiding something. "If the Snake knows I'm alive, he would want me as dead as Ava does, so a hit would be pointless. He'd send my twin after me."

Mina turned and smiled at Cal. "Told ya."

When she turned back, she winked at Selina.

"You're saying the real person we need to track is Ava?" Cal asked, and this time, Selina nodded immediately.

"I have no question. Ava has her own agenda, but this time, it lines up with the Snake's, so he's probably given her his blessing to take me out by any means necessary."

"All because you were a cop?" Efren asked.

"If you cross Vaccaro, no matter how small, you will pay. I knew that going in, but I held on to hope that if we could bust Randall and Ava for counterfeiting, that trail would lead us to Vaccaro and we could finally arrest him."

"You don't know if that happened, right?" Mina asked.

"If they found evidence leading to Vaccaro?" she asked, and Mina nodded. "If we know he's not in prison, then they didn't find anything. I assume since Randall was tried and sent to prison, the police were able to prove he was running the ring."

"There's nothing you can think of offhand that would be a reason they'd be releasing Randall now?"

"No," Selina said. "This is so frustrating!" Her fist hit the table and bounced until Efren grabbed it and held it between his hands.

"Take a deep breath." His whisper calmed her immediately, and she inhaled and then exhaled.

"Sorry." She glanced up at Mina and Cal, still on the screen. "It's hard to be here and not there. It's like watching someone save your life, but you aren't a participant in it."

"You very much are, though," Cal said to reassure her. "Your job is to keep your wits about you there and to answer our questions as information comes in. I know it feels like you aren't doing anything, but hang in there. We've all got your back, and the one who has your physical back is the best in the business. If he says jump, you don't ask questions, got it?"

Selina gave him a salute, and Mina promised to be in touch soon before they signed off.

"I can't believe they're releasing that lying sack of human flesh," she said in a sudden gush of fury and vitriol. "I gave up my life for this, and now he's going to walk free again!"

Efren was still holding her hand, and he massaged it until she relaxed the fist and let him caress her palm. "We don't know that yet. Don't jump to conclusions."

"What other conclusion can there be?" she demanded.

"It could be a retrial situation or house arrest. Let's give Mina a bit more time."

"Time, time." She muttered the words as she stood and paced the room. "We have so much time and never enough time. We're trapped here with nothing but time that we're wasting doing nothing to help them."

"We can't help them." Efren grasped her waist and held her in place. "But we aren't wasting time. We're biding our time. There is a difference. You need to heal and once I think you're ready, we'll leave this place and spend our time clearing your name."

Selina stared him down for the longest time before she spoke. "First off, I'm the medical professional here, not you. Second, there is no clearing my name. I'm either alive, and Ava is dead, or I'm dead and Ava is alive. Those are the only two outcomes."

"As a forever optimist, I believe there's a third option and that is you're alive and Ava is in prison next to her husband and the monster who is pulling her strings. We can do that at Secure One if we work together."

She reached up and patted his face, letting her fingers linger as they trailed away from his skin. His cheek heated from her touch, and he forced himself to stay focused on calming her enough to sleep. There would be time to explore this connection between them when her life wasn't on the line. He feared if he didn't convince her to rest, he'd use the time in this bunker unwisely, and that would cloud his decision-making process going forward.

"You're so innocent in the ways of the Mafia. I wish you could stay that way, but by the time this is over, you'll see the only proper place for these people is ten feet under. There is evil in this world that can't be reformed, and Vaccaro is the captain of that bus."

"You're saying the movies got it all wrong?" His words were light as he walked her backward toward the bed.

"There have been a handful of movies I could relate to as someone who grew up on the fringes of that lifestyle. Understanding the Mafia is impossible unless you live it, which I don't recommend. Unfortunately for you, you're about to live it."

"Don't feel bad for me, Selina Colvert." His words were an order, and her eyes widened a touch as he lowered her to the bed. "I've taken out a lot of that evil you speak of. Mafia of a different kind, you could say. If I had guilt about it, that ended when I found scores of villagers dead with their tongues cut out. Those are the images I'll never unsee, but I don't lose any sleep at night over the men who I made sure never walked this earth again. I'm not afraid of doing the same thing to Vaccaro if it comes down to you or him. Understand?"

He waited for her to get comfortable, but she didn't—she pulled him down onto the bed next to her. "You're going to war for me?"

"Yes. Only because I want to, Selina." Efren turned and cradled her face in his hands. "Not because I have to."

"I'm sorry," she whispered, her hands grasping his wrists.

"For what, darling?"

"Asking you to wade into another war you didn't ask to fight."

His smile was gentle when he ran his thumbs across her lips. "You didn't ask. I offered. Those other wars I fought, they were faces I didn't see or know. This war... Well, this war has a name and a face of someone I care about, so I'm standing in front of you now asking for a gun and a chance to march beside you. Together we can end this war swiftly. First, you need some rest." His thumbs stroked her temples as her eyes drooped, despite how she fought to keep them open.

He leaned in and placed a gentle kiss on her lips. "Sleep now, my beauty. That is time not wasted while you heal your body."

"Lie with me," she murmured as he lowered her head to the pillow. "I don't want to be alone."

Before she finished the sentence he'd scooted her to the back of the bed, kicked off his shoe and lain next to her. After arranging his prosthesis so it didn't hurt her, he pulled her against him tightly and gently splayed his hand across her belly.

"Sleep now. Clear your mind and let it rest, too. I've got your back."

Selina may have drifted off to sleep, but that was the very last thing on Efren's mind. The thought of losing the woman in his arms to an animal like Loraine or Vaccaro filled his mind. He was trained to hunt animals hiding in a hole, smoke them out and then end their lives. He vowed he'd do the same thing with Vaccaro so Selina could have her life back, even if he had to sacrifice himself to do it.

An hour later, as he peeled himself away from her and walked to the cabinet where the go bags waited, he refused to look too deeply at why he was willing to sacrifice himself for a woman who had treated him with nothing but animosity since the day they'd met. Maybe it had something to do with the look in her eye when she did it, or maybe it had something to do with the way she touched him when her guard was down, but whatever the reason, when this job was over, he'd have to leave Secure One if he wanted solidarity again. A team was great, until someone got too close and opened you up to emotions you didn't know how to deal with after what you'd been through.

Death and destruction were the emotions he understood now. The soft caress of a woman desperate for a connection as her world spun out of control was something else entirely.

The first one he could prepare and plan for. The second could only lead to one thing, and he'd already had enough heartbreak in his life to add more.

The touch of a woman was okay when it was no strings attached and no expectations, but it could never be that with Selina, and he knew it. The cost of being a hero was one he'd paid dearly for over the years. He may have saved six men that day, but only three of them remained all these years later. The scars of war went deep, and he was not immune to them just because he'd been the one doing the saving. What he learned was, you could rescue someone, but it was up to them to save themselves. Some could and some couldn't, but that wasn't his job. His job was to rescue or protect and then walk away, and that was exactly what he'd do again, even if it broke him to say goodbye to the brotherhood he'd found at Secure One.

He glanced behind him at the woman he considered part of that brotherhood, even if no one else on the team acknowledged the contributions she'd made to the business at a significant cost to her soul. That was the part that scared him the most. He understood that she suffered in silence out of some misplaced idea that stoicism was required to be part of the club. To be part of the inner circle that allowed you to do more than fix battle wounds and babysit. What surprised him the most was how angry it made him that she had to. He wasn't supposed to care. He wasn't supposed to get angry. He was supposed to do his job and move on to the next one. For the life of him, he couldn't figure out when that had changed. That was a lie. He knew the exact moment it changed, but he couldn't, and didn't want to, give it space in his head.

Efren turned away from Selina with determination. Once

they made it through this battle, he was done pretending that protecting people would bring back those he'd already lost. It was time for a new path, and no matter how much he wished it were different, that path would not include Selina Colvert.

Chapter Ten

Selina woke with a start, immediately registering that all the lights were low. On guard, she sat up and searched the room until her gaze landed on Efren's back. He stood at the consoles in deep concentration.

"There are tactical clothes at the end of the bed. Get dressed in place. I'm not looking."

"Do we have a problem?"

"Potentially." His words were clipped and quiet. "Someone is sniffing around topside."

Selina stripped off her sweats and pulled on the black rip-stop pants. They were a little big, but they'd have to do for now. She strapped on a belt that came complete with a holster and 9mm. After she adjusted them to protect the incisions on her front and back, she stripped off her sweatshirt, pulled on the black T-shirt and covered it with the sweatshirt, and then a lightweight black coat. She eyed the boots and before she could decide on a way to put them on, Efren was kneeling in front of her, tying on the boots for her.

"I can put on my own boots."

"I'd rather you save the energy for what's ahead of us. Grab your pills and take one. Just in case."

"I'm fine." She stood and stretched side to side to prove it. "We've been here for a week now and it's nothing more than a slight twinge." His disapproving glance made her sigh, so she took two over-the-counter painkillers to satisfy him. "What are we dealing with here, Efren?"

They hadn't gotten an update from Mina since yesterday afternoon, which meant she wasn't breaking through any of Vaccaro's firewalls put up to keep her out, and keeping Mina Jacobs out was no easy feat.

"My eyes in the sky are showing me that the guys who found the Jeep didn't give up there. They've been poking around in the woods, too."

"Damn it. Have you let Secure One know?"

"Not yet. I'm not sure that they'll hang around if they don't find anything." He pointed at the camera where two groups of two guys moved through the woods, silent as ninjas. They wore night-vision goggles and carried big guns.

"How far out are they? Are we safe in here?"

"For now," he answered, his gaze still on the console. "They won't find our hatch in the dark if they don't know where it is. The daytime is a different story."

"You're saying we won't be here if they make it that far."

"Not if I have anything to say about it. Our go bags are packed. I made a small one for you to carry. It has the first aid kit and the little bit of tech we can take with us. I don't want you carrying anything heavier than that until we see how you do."

"Do you have a destination in mind?"

He turned and took her in, his gaze dark, intense and focused. "Somewhere that isn't here."

"Secure one, Whiskey."

Efren put his finger to his lips and then turned and answered the console quietly. "Secure two, Tango. Hush mode."

Selina waited until Mina's face popped up on the screen. She spoke, but it was impossible to hear what she was saying; all she could do was read the captions on the screen. Her first questions were, "Are you in danger? Should I get Cal?"

Efren sat and put the foldable keyboard on his lap, dulling the sound even more. She thought he was being paranoid. There was no way Cal didn't make this place soundproof, but she supposed, considering his job, safer was better than sorry. She waited while he typed out what he'd seen and then asked her if she had an update.

What was written had her seeing red. "His lawyers filed a writ of habeas corpus?"

Efren turned to her. "What is that? I'm not a law enforcement person."

"Unlawful imprisonment," she answered. "Ask her if she knows the content of the writ."

After typing, they waited for Mina to answer. It wasn't one Selina liked, and Efren must have sensed it. "She may not know yet, but give her time, and she will find out what it is."

"It won't do us any good if we aren't in contact with her by the time she knows." The words were hissed through her teeth. She wasn't mad at him, it wasn't his fault, but she was mad that Randall's lawyers were playing games. The man deserved to rot in prison for his crimes—both the ones they knew about and the ones they didn't. Letting him out of prison was a surefire way of having him disappear, leaving her on the run forever.

Selina grabbed the keyboard from him and typed her own question. "When does he go before the judge?"

"Monday."

Selina did the math in her head and realized they were coming up on early Thursday morning. "That doesn't give us much time," she whispered, her lips in a thin line as she typed back to Mina. "As soon as you know, I have to know." Mina gave her a thumbs-up and then stood, moving aside so Cal could sit down.

Selina paced the room. She wanted to pay attention, but her mind was still focused on Randall. If his lawyers had proof that he was being unlawfully detained, he could go free as soon as Monday. Since she hadn't been present for the trial, she had no idea if that was a possibility. Then again, she knew the Snake, and chances were good that money was changing hands as they spoke.

"Colvert," Efren whispered, and she snapped to attention. He was motioning her over and she leaned in next to him. "You and Cal need to talk strategy."

"Strategy? Isn't that your call?"

"This is your life, you should have a say in it, yes?"

She took his seat and pulled the keyboard onto her lap. Cal was speaking, and she waited for the captions to come up.

Avoid going west. Once you leave the state, it will be harder for me to help. You're much closer to the western border, so go east or southeast.

Do you have another safe house in any direction of this location?

Negative. You have experience with avoiding Vaccaro in the past. Fall back on that. Once you're clear, call in and we'll have a plan in place.

Selina frowned as she stared at the man who had given her a home, sharpened her skills and treated her like family the last eight years. *Is leaving the bunker the right decision, or should we stay put?*

What does your gut say? Cal asked.

Run. Three letters. One word. The story of her life.

Now you're in your element. Good luck, Sierra. Charlie, out.

Before she could wrap her head around the fact that might be the last time she ever spoke to her friend, a low, guttural curse came from Efren's side of the console. He pointed at the top left camera where one of the four guys was spinning the hatch open inside the old cabin. He held his finger to his lips, and she nodded, watching in silence as one of the men climbed down the ladder and inspected the small space. There was barely room for him to turn around, which meant he wouldn't see the camera hidden inside one of the pipes. They didn't miss the shot of his face, though. They captured it and Efren sent it to Mina for identification. The night-vision goggles might make that more difficult, but if Mina could get his name, she would.

The guy climbed the ladder and shook his head at his buddies. After whispered conversation they weren't privy to, the men broke off into teams of two again and spread out through the woods, headed back in the direction of the Jeep. Once they disappeared, Efren let out a breath.

"Chances are they're going to regroup at the Jeep and fan out in the next direction," he whispered.

"Which will make it hard to know which way to go, right?"

He waited another few minutes until the teams were past the second set of cameras in the woods, then he waited a few more minutes after that, she assumed to make sure they didn't come back again. Once an adequate amount of time had passed, he started unplugging and unhooking several devices.

"These are going with us. They're our only tie to Secure One."

Selina held her bag out for him to stow away the folding keyboard and receiver. Once safely tucked away in protective pockets, she closed the bag and lowered it to the ground. "What's the plan, Brenna?"

"You tell me. I'm following your lead."

Her nod was almost imperceptible, but it gave her the push she needed to make the decision. "I don't know how you feel about it, but I don't want to be here if they come back during the day and find our hatch."

"Same. Walk me through the plan."

"We know they're out there, but this is our only window. We'll give them a thirty-minute head start. It took us an hour to get here from the Jeep, but I was moving much slower than they were tonight. We know they're headed north. We can't be sure where they'll go from there, but my bet is north or west, thinking we'll head for the closest border. If we head southeast, we'll be clear of them before daybreak. What say you, Brenna?"

"I say, I'll follow you anywhere, Colvert."

Before she could react, he dragged her toward him by the back of her head until their lips collided in a kiss that heated to boiling instantly. If they were going to survive this, she would have to keep her lips off his. When he tipped his head to take the kiss deeper, she knew that was going to be easier said than done.

THE SUN WAS breaking on the horizon, and they'd been walking for nearly five hours. Efren could see Selina needed to rest sooner rather than later. She'd been a trouper keeping pace with him all night, but as 6:00 a.m. approached, she needed food, a place to sit down, and a few more Advil before they could continue their journey.

He followed her down along a shallow creek and started edging her closer to the road. They needed to find a restaurant where they could sit for a bit and give her side time to rest. First, they had to get close enough to the road to watch for civilization. He hoped she was tired enough that she wouldn't notice what he was doing. It was easy to let her lead. She was an excellent leader who thought of even the smallest things that could trip them up, but she wasn't good at admitting when she needed rest. She would push herself until she crossed the line, and then he'd be finding a hospital instead of a diner.

Their walk had been in silence, and he'd spent the majority of it replaying that last kiss they'd shared in the bunker before risking their lives to save them. He hadn't held back that time and moved it past closed-lipped and into territory he wasn't sure she wanted to go, until she'd willingly joined him in the hot tangle of tongues. When the kiss ended and they made their plans for leaving the bunker, he'd vowed to keep his hands and his lips to himself going forward, but nothing turned him on more than a strong, independent woman who could take care of herself. Selina Colvert was that and so much more.

Maybe that was how he should look at his time with Selina. Whatever happened between them happened because the feelings were mutual, but that didn't mean there were strings attached when the case ended. His hard and fast rule had always been never to get involved with anyone he was guarding, but Selina wasn't just anyone. She was a teammate, an equal, dare he say a friend now that they'd put their trust, and lives, in each other's hands.

"Brenna," Selina hissed from his left. "You're too close to the road. Fall back."

Well, he should have known she wouldn't miss his migration east. "We need to find someplace to rest. I'm watching for signs to a diner or a gas station."

"Negative," she whispered, grabbing his backpack to pull him to a stop. "What part of 'we can't be seen' do you not understand? We may have left those guys behind, but they aren't the only guys. Vaccaro has scouts all over this state, I can assure you."

"That may well be true, but you aren't going to make it much farther without resting. We need food and to check your incision."

"Fine," she said, pointing ahead. "We'll cross the creek up there and stop as soon as the sun is up. That will allow us to rebandage the wounds without using a flashlight and we can grab a protein bar and some water."

"Or," he said, taking her hand and keeping her level with him as he continued to walk closer to the road. "We can find someplace big enough that we can blend in and grab something hot to eat. It would be good to have hot water and soap so we don't get your wound infected."

She held up until he had to stop or risk pulling her over. "What happened to 'you're in charge, Colvert. You know this guy best'?"

Efren spun on his heel and tipped her chin up. "I stand by that until I see you pushing yourself too far. Then you start making bad decisions that can make your situation worse.

I've watched you go from a five to a six to a seven on the pain scale in the last two hours. It's time to rest your body."

"Now you're an expert on my pain scale?"

The sarcasm dripped from the sentence when she crossed her arms over her chest and waited for him to respond.

"Yes, because I saw you at ten when I forced you to walk through the woods for an hour after a perilous ride less than a day after surgery. I've cataloged in my mind what level of pain you're at when you take medication and when you don't. I may not be an expert on you, but I'm observant, and that's what keeps people alive when I protect them. While I stand behind you running the show with how Vaccaro will behave, and knowing the best way to avoid him, keeping you safe is still my job. I will override you with a snap of my fingers if I think you're putting yourself at risk." He snapped his fingers in front of her face and she jumped, but not before he noticed the smoke in her eyes catch a flame.

Good. Let her get fired up. That would keep her going until they got somewhere to rest.

Selina stepped up to him and put her finger on his chest. "If you think I can't deal with a little bit of pain, you're dead wrong. I'm going to hurt much worse if Vaccaro gets hold of me—"

A stick snapped to the left of them, announcing in no uncertain terms that they weren't alone.

Chapter Eleven

Selina slowly removed her finger from Efren's chest and reached for her gun as he did the same. The woods had fallen silent again and they waited, their only communication their eyes. "Could be an animal," he mouthed, and she nodded. It could be an animal. It could be a snake.

She motioned with her eyes to a tree less than five feet behind them. They just had to make it there without alerting anyone that they were so close. The detritus on the forest floor was going to make that difficult, but they needed cover in case whatever was in the woods was an animal that walked on two legs and carried a big gun.

His nod was slow and deliberate as he brought his hand up to point from his eyes to the woods, telling her he'd watch while she went first. There was no way to argue with him, and he was supposed to be her bodyguard, so she looked down at her feet and slowly inched her way toward the tree. It was a giant oak that would easily hide them from anyone walking past, as long as they didn't get too close. It felt like forever before she had her back plastered to the tree. She inhaled a breath, then slowly turned and stuck her gun around the side of the tree, a sign to Efren to move.

He had taken his first step when the first shot rang out. Efren used it for cover and tore at her, rolling behind the tree as the second shot hit the dirt not too far from where they were standing.

"Not an animal," he hissed as they each braced their gun around opposite sides of the tree.

"What's the plan, bodyguard?"

"As much as I hate to say it, we wait." He eyed his bag. "You're going to need a bigger gun."

He'd been carrying an assault rifle through the woods, while she'd kept her sidearm on her only. Carrying an extra eight pounds around her shoulder would wear her out too quickly, so he'd kept it on his pack. Selina slowly holstered her sidearm and reached for the gun as another shot peppered the ground to the left of the tree.

Haste had her grabbing the gun off his pack and bringing it up to her shoulder in one smooth motion. "Where are they shooting from?"

"I can't tell. The vegetation is too thick this time of year. Until they show their face, we can't shoot back in case it's an innocent."

"They're shooting at us!"

"They could think we're an animal."

Selina couldn't stop the eye roll. "It's not even hunting season. We need to move."

"Not until we know where they are," he hissed, his words barely audible in the silence of the forest. "We could be surrounded."

She hated that he was right, but he was. Just because the bullets were coming from in front of them didn't mean there wasn't a team on every side. They didn't have enough ammo for a gunfight of that size, so she had to hope that wasn't the case. There were four last night, and she had to pray there were only four this morning. She glanced at Efren, who had his gun up without a waver as he waited, sweeping the dark vegetation in front of them.

"Slowly bend down and find something to throw to your right," he whispered.

Drawing fire was an excellent way to determine their location. She searched around the tree for something to throw until she encountered a hefty rock. With a nod to him, she tossed it to the right, and it landed and rolled a few feet before someone lit it up. She wasn't expecting the pop-pop from next to her but was happy he had a shot. Then she heard a grunt, and a heavy object dropped to the forest floor.

Her eyes wide, she glanced at Efren, who used the suppressor on his rifle to point at the ground, and then he mouthed, "throw another."

The man was going to pick them off one after the other to protect her. She felt around and came up with a piece of bark. It wasn't big, but at least it wouldn't sound the same as the rock. Efren gave her a head nod and she tossed it to their left. The morning was immediately lit up by gunfire, and he used the illumination to send a few bullets their way until they heard another body hit the ground.

"They aren't the smartest blokes in the forest," he muttered.

"That's Vaccaro men for ya," she whispered with a grin. The situation wasn't funny, but leave it to Efren to ease her fear a little bit.

"Throw something else. I doubt they'll take the bait again, but we have to try."

She grabbed a rock and tossed it far to the right. They waited, but this time, nothing happened. They stood in silence another five minutes, but they couldn't wait all day. They had to make a decision.

"We need to move, Brenna," she said, gun in hand. "Last night, there were two teams of two. Maybe they split up."

"That's what I'm thinking, too. Back-to-back until we know for sure."

"What direction?" she asked, lining their backpacks up and sweeping her gun across the trees in front of her.

"To find the hunters who became the hunted."

Efren moved forward, and Selina followed, struggling to walk backward without falling on the uneven terrain. Her trained ear listened for footfalls or any sound to indicate another human in the woods. They were barely across the creek and into the deeper vegetation again when moaning reached their ears. He tipped his head twice to the right, and they sidestepped toward the sound, watching for an ambush. It wasn't likely, or the bullets would have rained down on them already.

She nearly tripped and fell on the first body until Efren tossed his arm back to grab her. Once she was solid again, he stuck his left leg out while he crouched on his right to check the guy's pulse.

"Dead." He put his finger to his lips and tipped his ear to the side to indicate they should listen.

Selina heard a soft gurgling and motioned forward and to the right frantically. The guy was still alive, but he wouldn't be for long. Efren held her back and followed the sound at the same pace, sweeping his gun across the brightening forest as the sun rose above them. The light revealed the man they were looking for as he lay against a tree trunk, blood running from his neck and mouth with every labored breath.

Efren motioned to the left, and she turned and brought her gun up as he knelt by the man. "Who are you and what do you want with us?"

"Her," he said, his hand slowly raising to point at Selina. "He wants her."

"Who's he?" Efren asked, but Selina didn't wait with bated breath. She already knew the answer.

The man hissed, then laughed, blood bubbling out of his mouth with the action. "He's coming for you, little Eva Shannon. You once were lost, but now you're found."

"How many more are there?" Efren asked the question but the man just smiled, as though his secret was her death sentence. Efren pressed the butt of his gun to the guy's neck wound. "I'm going to ask you one more time. How many are there?"

"None today," he croaked as Efren eased off on the gun. "Tomorrow, more than you can count and the next day, even more. You can't escape the Snake, sweet Eva. Tag, you're it. Run, run, as fast as you ca…"

The sentence hung in the air as the guy's head lolled to the side and a final breath left his body. Efren cursed and grabbed his flashlight, shining it across the body frantically.

"GPS," she whispered and ran to the other guy, searching his body for the tracker he likely wore. If they had activated it before they went down, Vaccaro would send reinforcements. It took a moment but then she spotted it. "Left side of the vest!"

Selina pulled his off and ran back to Efren, who was struggling. She helped him and then motioned for him to follow her. He did without question, this time taking the back position while she walked forward at a fast clip. She held up her fist in a stop motion and slung her gun around her chest. A fast dig through his pack, and she came up with a condom. They used them at Secure One for all types of things from water containers to boot liners. She had something else in mind as she rolled the condom over the beacons, blew air into it, and tied it off. Once she was satisfied with the vessel, she lowered it to the creek and let it go.

"Brilliant," Efren said with a chuckle as the beacons floated downstream at a leisurely walking pace.

"All that does is buy us time." Selina stood and shook her head as the sun came up. "The guy was right. This place will be crawling with snakes faster than we can kill them. We have to find a faster way to move."

"Agreed. For now, let's move as quick as we can the opposite direction of those beacons."

He took off at a pace that was going to be tough for her to match, but she dug deep and reminded herself if she didn't find a way, she would find herself in the snake's den, and the pain would be greater than anything she had dealt with thus far.

HER BODY WAS screaming at her, but she wouldn't stop. Couldn't stop until they had a place to hole up long enough to take a shower and contact Secure One. A little food wouldn't hurt, either. Efren was trailing her, not demanding answers, which surprised her if she were honest. He had been incredibly supportive of her plans, only pushing back when he wanted her to stop long enough to think about things from all angles. They hadn't had time for her to do that when they hopped a ride in an old potato truck about four hours ago. They didn't know where he was going, but it was better than where they were at the time. It afforded them time off their feet to rest their bodies while getting as far away from the two dead guys as quickly as possible. When the truck stopped to refuel, they opted to jump out and find a place to contact Secure One. Mina was their eyes in the sky, and they needed more information. Hopefully, she had it.

"Where are we going?" Efren asked, his voice nearly drowned out by the rushing of the Mississippi River. The Mighty Miss was raging today, and that told Selina a storm was coming. Actually, more than one storm was coming for them, which was why they needed to regroup and get better prepared.

"I'll know it when I see it." That was the only answer she could give since she hadn't found what she was looking for yet.

They'd taken a few more steps when her arm shot out in front of them. "There."

"A cabin?" He pulled her to a stop and forced her to make eye contact. "Why?"

"It's November, so the cabins are closed for the winter. At least that one is. With any luck, inside is a shower, food and a place to call home."

"Fine, but let me scout it. Better I'm caught on camera than you."

Selina wanted to argue, but she couldn't. He was right. She had to be a ghost if she wanted to survive long enough to clear this area and get back to Secure One alive. He tugged his gaiter up around his face to hide it the best he could before he leaned in to whisper, "If it's safe, I'll owl call."

With a nod from her, he took off, approaching the cabin from behind where cameras would be less likely. Selina watched the way he moved across the yard. Considering he'd been on his leg for almost a full day and still moved like a dancer, it was impressive. He disappeared around the end of the cabin, and she waited for him to pop back up at the front of the place. When he did, he was low and angled away from any cameras that might be pointing right at him. He moved in slowly, knowing that any doorbell with a camera would be easy to spot on a cabin this old.

She moved closer, her trained eye already knowing the cabin was as low-tech as they come. Her validation came in the form of an owl hoot from the porch of the small structure. By the time she joined him, he was holding up a key.

"Guess they aren't afraid of theft." He had the door open and held up his finger, doing a quick sweep of the three-room cabin before he motioned her in. "Shades."

In quick succession they pulled the shades and then dropped their packs. "I'm glad we found this place. A storm is blowing in." Selina unzipped her coat and pulled her gaiter off as she took a look around. "Doesn't look like anyone has been here for quite a few seasons."

"That was the vibe I got, too, by looking in the windows. Let's just hope no one decides now is the time to take a trip to Grandpa's cabin."

"Not likely this late in the season with a storm brewing. We need to get a call into Secure One now before we can't." To make her point, a gust of wind rattled the windowpanes and made her jump.

"Hey, it's okay." Efren walked over and rubbed her arms before he pulled her into a quick hug. "You did good, Colvert. I'm proud of you for not only hanging on but finding the opportunities we needed to get clear of that mess. Let's use this time to regroup and make our next plan."

"I'm glad we got the best of those two in the woods, but there will be more."

"I know." He kissed her cheek before he stepped back and held her out at arm's length. "We're a team, and we'll face whatever comes at us the same way we did with those guys. Together."

"I'd be screwed without you, Brenna."

"Did it hurt to admit that?" he asked, his lips quirking in humor.

"Surprisingly, no. I've taken many of my frustrations out on you for too long. You didn't deserve it, but you were convenient. When you went to bat for me with Cal in the bunker, I realized you didn't deserve attitude from me."

"Apology accepted." He winked while he set out the equipment to call Secure One. "I'm a big boy and always knew there was more to your dislike of me than met the eye."

He fell silent as though he were waiting for her to tell him what that was, but she had no intention of doing that, now or ever. Admitting that she didn't hate him was hard, but admitting that she cared about him in ways she shouldn't could be dangerous to her heart and her life.

Chapter Twelve

She had bigger fish to fry than Efren Brenna's ego, and his name was Vaccaro. Selina made a vow to remind herself of that every minute of every hour if need be. The console linked up, and Efren spoke.

"Secure one, Tango."

"Secure two, Whiskey," came the voice of an angel.

Selina dropped to the small couch in relief. "Secure three, Sierra."

The small screen came to life, and Mina's face reflected at them, grainy and barely visible, but smiling. She panned the camera out, and four other faces stared back at them. Cal, Mack, Roman and Eric also sat around the table. "So good to see you guys!" Mina said. "We've been cautiously optimistic you'd call soon."

"Is that your way of saying you've been worried?" Efren's question was in good fun, but Mina nodded immediately.

"More than worried, especially when you missed your check-in," Cal said.

"Sorry about that. We were in the back of a potato truck moving too fast for the phone."

"A potato truck? Never mind, I don't want to know. Fill us in."

Efren was about to speak when Selina did. "We ran into two of Vaccaro's guys about four hours south of the bunker. Mr. Sharpshooter over here took them both out with a shot."

"Before they died, one confirmed they were working for the Snake and that more were on their way."

"That's when we jumped on the potato truck," Selina said to clarify. "We had to get out of the area quickly and without being seen."

"I'm relieved you found a way out," Roman said. "What's your location?"

"The Mississippi is right outside the window. That's all I know, other than the name of the gas station the truck stopped at. We borrowed a cabin until the storm passes."

"Borrowed," Mina said with a snort. "I'm glad you found shelter. We have much to discuss and little time to do it. First, tell me the name of the gas station."

"Go for It Gas," Selina said as Efren laughed. "What?" She punched his arm playfully. "It was easy to remember."

Mina clicked the keyboard a few times and then smiled. "You're on the outskirts of Winona to the north. That's a good place to be. Now, let's fill you in on Daddy Dearest."

Selina leaned in toward the console. "Do we know why he's being released?"

"We do, or at least why he's going before the judge. I'm glad you're sitting down. The writ of habeas corpus they filed pertains to you."

"Me?" she asked, and Mina nodded with a grimace.

"Randall's original trial lawyer allowed your written testimony to be included in the trial paperwork despite it not being signed. He also didn't ask the prosecuting team to do the due diligence of finding your body."

"Is that a thing?" Efren asked, glancing at her.

Mina nodded. "It is, but I don't buy it. I suspect money has changed hands here and this is just a way to get Daddy Dearest out of prison."

"Why now, though?" Efren asked in confusion. "It's been years."

"Because Randall Jr. was arrested." Selina's answer was resigned. "Vaccaro probably planned this all along, and we walked right into the trap he set."

"I don't understand," everyone said at once.

"Explain it if you can," Efren encouraged her, and she stood, pacing back and forth behind him as the winds intensified.

"The Snake was setting Randall Jr. up to take a fall by killing Howie. There's no way to know for sure, but if Junior wasn't running the counterfeiting business the way Vaccaro wanted, or heaven forbid, was skimming off the top, he would make an example out of him. Since Howie was already cheating on the Winged Templar's daughter, it was easy to kill him. They drop his body in the storage unit since Sadie works there and set up Sadie to take the fall, already knowing that Randall had Kadie."

"He had no way to know we would be there that night, though," Eric said.

"As I said, we fell into his trap. We played his game perfectly. In the end, Randall was arrested on kidnapping charges, which will put him away for life. With Randall Jr. and Howie both out of the picture, Vaccaro needs someone to run the business. Now it's time to get Daddy out after having served just enough years to make it look like an injustice was corrected rather than a criminal walked. The original trial attorney left that unsigned statement of mine in there on purpose. It was planted for this very occasion. I'm honestly surprised Vaccaro didn't just kill Randall Jr. and be done with it."

Cal's gaze darted to Mina's, and Selina cleared her throat. "What?"

"They found Junior unresponsive in his jail cell this morning. He's not dead, but he's also not expected to live."

Selina threw her arms up. "More reason for Daddy to get out of prison. Now he's lost two sons since he was so unjustly incarcerated. I should have signed that statement before I started writing it!"

"Was there a reason you hadn't signed it?" Efren asked, taking her hand and leading her to the couch to sit. "Rest. You're still healing."

"I didn't sign it because I wasn't finished with it. I had it on my desk and was working on it when I got called in and suspended for the shooting. Once that happens, I'm not allowed back into the area for anything. They must have found it on my desk, but I don't know anyone who would have put a half-finished, unsigned statement in a trial packet, cop or lawyer alike."

"Remember when we talked about someone being a mole for Vaccaro?" Efren said, and she nodded. "This smells like a mole."

"It smells like a rat." Cal's voice was angry. "And snakes love nothing more than a rat for a snack."

"I'll look into it," Mina said, writing it down on her pad.

"Did you find anything about Randall Jr.'s arrest before his unfortunate accident?" Efren asked.

"He used his one phone call for his lawyer. That was it."

"Vaccaro likely pays his lawyer, so any mention of the missing twin being in his basement that night would easily flow back to the snake's den," Cal said. "For now, that's our working theory. We assume he knows Selina is alive from the lawyer and sent Ava to clean that mess up. Since she couldn't, he's hunting you while trying to free his head capo."

"Just another day in the life," Selina said with an eye roll.

"We have the information. What's our next move?" Efren asked, sitting beside Selina and putting his arm around her waist. She glanced at him questioningly, but he didn't seem bothered by his PDA in front of the team. Thankfully, only Mina seemed to have noticed the interaction when she looked back to the console.

"There's more," Mina said, holding up her finger and pointing at Roman, who held up a map of Minnesota. "It turns out, the house in Bemidji isn't the only property titled in Randall Sr.'s name."

"What?" Selina asked, leaning in to see the grainy video.

"I did some digging and discovered a house in Caledonia that Randall owns." Roman held the map up to the screen so they could see the house marked near Highway 44.

"Wait," Efren said, his eyes roving in his head for a minute. "If we're near Winona, that puts Caledonia somewhere around fifty klicks from here."

"It's close, for sure," Cal said, leaning forward, ready to take over. "We can't be certain, since we can't do much recon on the place, but our guess is that's where Randall Jr. moved the operation after the trial. He couldn't keep anything in the Bemidji place, but as long as he lived there, he could make authorities believe he was clean."

"Did Randall Jr. travel to Caledonia frequently?" Eric asked, suddenly interested in the conversation again.

"Not as often as Howie Loraine did prior to his untimely beheading."

"Interesting," Selina said. "Maybe Howie was the gopher to keep Junior's nose clean."

"Possible," Cal agreed. "What are you thinking? I can see your instincts are locked and loaded on this. You know the family and how the Snake runs. We're counting on you to tell us our next move."

Selina was silent for a moment. She hoped they thought she was thinking of a plan instead of trying not to cry. She'd longed to hear Cal say those words. To treat her as an equal. To acknowledge her skills as a cop and law enforcement professional. Now that he was, she was afraid to screw it up. All she ever wanted was for them to see her as an equal. Suddenly, she was at a loss for words.

"Follow your gut," Efren whispered in her ear. "It's telling you the right answer."

His words broke her internal freeze-up, and she nodded. "If he's released by the judge on Monday, and you think he will be?" She was addressing Mina, who nodded. "They'll do one of two things. Go to one of Vaccaro's places and regroup, or go to Caledonia."

"Which do you think is more likely?"

"Hard to know if I can't see the place in Caledonia."

Mina held up her finger and dug around in a pile by her computer, coming up with a paper she handed to Roman. He held it up to the camera. "I could only get a view from above, but as you can see it's—"

"Sprawling," Efren said.

"There," Selina said without conscious thought. "They'll go there. Ava's a spoiled brat. When she showed up at the hospital in a fur coat, it was obvious to me she hadn't changed her spots. She wants the cushy lifestyle, and that place affords them her every whim. Of that, I'm certain."

"Now that's your gut talking," Efren whispered, squeezing her hip.

"I'm inclined to agree with you," Cal said. "Not regarding Ava, but that Randall will want to check his operation immediately."

"Vaccaro will demand it," Selina said, standing to pace again. "It's been unattended or left in the care of an underling for too long. What time on Monday?"

"The docket says 11:00 a.m."

She paced a few more times, and an idea came to her that was dangerous but diabolical. "What if I was also there at 11:00 a.m. to give my sworn statement to the court? Signed, sealed and delivered."

"Not going to happen!" Efren said, jumping up and grasping her arms as though he forgot they weren't alone in the room. "Are you trying to get yourself killed?"

"The court would protect me. Is it dangerous, yes, but it would keep Randall Sr. in prison."

"Which doesn't solve our problem." It was Cal's voice, this time from behind them. She couldn't break eye contact with Efren. What she saw in his eyes said maybe he cared about her as more than just a job. "Randall is still in jail, but

Ava and the Snake won't be. Doing that signs your death warrant, too."

"He's right," Efren said between clenched teeth. "You know he's right. We've fought too hard to keep you alive. We think this out. We make the plan and then we follow it. If we don't, you won't make it out of that courtroom alive. We both know it. You always want to do the right thing, and I'm proud as hell of you for even suggesting it, even knowing you'd be giving up your life for it, but you'd be giving up your life for the low-hanging fruit. We need the apple at the top of the tree, and the only way to get that is to let the rotten apple out of prison."

"As long as Ava is free, she will hunt me, Efren. We can't live that kind of life. I've been hiding for years from Vaccaro. I can't hide forever."

"If that's the case," Cal said from behind them, "Brenna is right. Let Randall out of prison, get him back to Caledonia. If they're both there, then we have evidence that Ava knows about the operation."

"What did you just say?" Selina asked, spinning on her heel.

"That we'd have proof Ava knows about the operation."

Selina smacked herself in the forehead. "Of course she does! That's where she's been all this time."

"You think Vaccaro was letting her run the operation all these years?"

"Hell no." Her laughter was enough to make Efren smile, she noticed. "There's no way he'd trust a Shannon to run any of his operations. Even one who had proven herself to his organization. That doesn't mean she wasn't living there all this time and helping. It's the only thing that makes sense."

"You think there's proof there that she knew the operation had continued all these years?" Roman asked, and Selina nodded. "If that's the case, and we can find it, it would take one assassin off your heels."

"Just not the most dangerous one," Selina said, gnawing on her lip. "There's no 'we' here, either." She dropped her hands and leaned into the console. "I won't put any of you at risk again. This is not your war to fight, and God knows you've all lost enough fighting other people's wars. This is my problem and my problem alone. From the moment I saw Ava standing at the nurses' station, I knew my days were numbered. There is no escaping the reach the Snake has when your time comes. My time has come to face off with this cobra, and I accept that. I can't accept anyone else getting hurt because of me."

"He's a man," Cal said, standing to his full height and leaning into the camera. "Not a god. He is not untouchable, Selina Colvert, and this team is damn good at its job. We protect and we serve, we just do it a bit differently than you're used to. That doesn't mean we don't get results. The storm is ramping up and we're about to lose connection. Stay put. Rest. Prepare. As soon as the storm is over, call in. We'll have an actionable plan. Do you understand me, Sierra?"

Selina wanted to argue, but knew it would do no good. "Understood."

"Good. Charlie, out."

The screen went blank, and she looked up into the eyes of the man who had gotten her this far, but could end up a casualty of her past. She wasn't okay with that.

"I'm okay with it," he said, as though he were reading her

mind. "I've fought less just wars than the one we're about to wade into, Colvert."

"Vaccaro has an army of soldiers, Efren." She was desperate to make him understand. "This is another war you can't win, but this time you'll pay with your life. If you send me alone, then no innocents have to die."

His finger came down on her lips to hush her. "He may have an army of soldiers, but they protect him for money. We protect you for love. That's why he will fail and you won't. Never forget that."

Chapter Thirteen

He shouldn't have used the L-word. He saw it in her eyes the moment he'd said it. She was dealing with enough, and that put pressure on her that she didn't need. Not that he meant it in a romantic sense, not using "we" before it, but she was an intelligent woman who was good at reading between the lines after working with men all her life. There was nothing he could do about it now other than continue to reassure her that the team was behind her and not going to let her face Vaccaro alone.

When Selina disappeared into the small bathroom to clean up, Efren had rummaged around the kitchen in hopes of finding some kind of canned good that was still edible. He wasn't expecting to pull open the fridge and encounter someone's canning stash. Why it was in the fridge, he had no idea, but he wasn't going to look a gift horse in the mouth. Admittedly, he held his breath when he tried to light the stove, fearing the propane tank in the backyard had long been empty. He was pleasantly surprised when it lit up and he was able to warm their dinner. The temperature was dropping outside, so rather than freeze the entire night, he'd also started the small propane cabin heater on low. He didn't know how long the propane would last, but it was better to warm up the cabin for as long as possible. If the propane ran out, they'd stay warm the rest of the night with the blankets from the bedroom. Always a gentleman, he'd give her the bed to sleep while he kept watch. He wasn't worried, though. The storm raging outside wasn't fit for man nor beast, but most especially not Vaccaro's men. The wind whipped against the cabin walls, and the river roared her way past them. Anyone out there tonight had a death wish.

"What smells so good?" Selina asked as she walked into the room. She was wearing a sweatshirt and pants that were too big for her, but she had the shirt tied in a knot to show her midriff and the pants cuffed at the ankles.

The sight of her bare midriff had him staring rather than speaking. "Uh, dinner," he was finally able to stutter. "What's with the outfit?"

"I found clothes in the dresser in there that were warm and clean. Saved a pair for you, too. I was surprised that there was warm water."

"Propane tank," he said, his throat still dry as he stared at the incision on her belly. "I thought it would be empty, but it's not. Shouldn't you have a bandage on that?"

Efren motioned her to the table where he had two sets of silverware waiting. She sat and he carried the hot pot of stew over, with veggies and brown bread for their feast.

"Dang," Selina whispered low when he set out the food. "Did you make a run to Winn-Dixie?"

He snorted as he slid into his seat. "I'd have to go pretty far to find a Winn-Dixie around here. I found all of this in the fridge. They were storing it in there. I thought that was a bit odd."

"Mmm," she said, taking a bite of the bread and chewing. "Not odd. An unplugged fridge will keep the canned goods from freezing in the winter if there's no heat. Then you just move them back to the shelf in the spring."

"I thought if there was no heat then there was no water? Why is there running water?"

"Insulated pipes," she answered around a bite of beef stew. "These cabins are mainly for summer, but a lot of trappers and snow lovers use them throughout the seasons. I feel like whoever owns this place isn't one of them. They come early spring through late fall."

"We can hope." He glanced at the door again, and she laughed.

"No one is coming out tonight. Was the barricade necessary?"

He glanced at the door again, where he'd shoved a heavy chest full of raincoats and other fishing equipment against it. "Yes. It won't stop anyone, but it will slow them down enough for us to bail out the bedroom window. We still need to avoid light hitting any of the windows. I'm sure the neighbors are also long gone, but we can't risk it."

"Penlights only, aimed at the floor. Oh, this is so good," she moaned as she took another bite of the bread. "I haven't had canned brown bread in years."

"I'll admit when I saw that I thought it was one of those fake cans where you hide your valuables or something. Never saw anything like it when that bread came out onto the plate."

"Are you from Mars?"

"California," he answered, and her lips tipped up on one side.

"That explains it."

"California explains why I've never seen bread in a can?"

"It's a Boston thing that's moved west, but probably not quite that far west. We keep it handy for power outages and snowstorms. The carbs keep you going, and you can eat it straight out of the can."

"I've eaten much worse meals ready to eat." He pointed at her belly. "Why isn't that bandaged?"

"I'm letting it get some air," she explained between bites. "The skin is red around the stitches, so after dinner, we're going to have to remove them."

"Remove them?" He propped his spoon in his bowl. "It's only been seven days since the surgery."

"Plenty long for my skin. I heal fast. If I let them go too long, they'll fester until they're infected. Trust me. I've had enough stitches in my life to know."

"I'm going to need more than a penlight to get them out."

"The bathroom doesn't have a window," she said. "We can close the door and get it done. I can do the front ones. You'll have to do the back ones."

He shuddered, drawing a laugh from her as she finished her stew. "The big bad bodyguard can't handle a few stitches?"

"Reminds me of my military days. Getting stitches in the field, or watching them desperately try to stitch a friend's body part closed long enough to get them to safety before they bled out." He cleared his throat and stood. "I found some cinnamon applesauce for dessert. Let me grab it."

As he walked away from her, he shoved the memories bubbling up inside him back behind the black curtain. Every so often, they liked to peek their head around the corner to remind him why he didn't *care*. Caring led to pain. He'd had more than enough of that for a lifetime.

EFREN PACED THE front porch, holding the sat phone in his hand. He'd left Selina inside to stay warm with the excuse that he needed to check the phone for messages. The storm had slowed for a bit, but there was still no way to get coverage inside the cabin. Would there be any messages? No, but he wasn't looking for them. He wanted to call Secure One when she wasn't within earshot so he could suggest a plan he knew she would never agree to.

The cold sleet pellets pounded on his back as he dialed Cal's secure phone. The phone didn't even ring before he heard, "Secure one, Charlie."

"Secure two, Tango," he answered. It sounded like a greeting, but it wasn't. It was a go-ahead between team members that it was safe to speak. If they answered any other way, they knew the team member was being tracked or held by the enemy. Considering what Cal used to do before he started Secure One, it was a legitimate way to ensure everyone's safety.

"Everything okay?" Cal asked. "I'm surprised to hear from you again, but I'm glad you called. I need your opinion on how Selina is doing after the surgery."

"Storm is raging here, as I'm sure you can hear. We just finished removing her stitches."

"Already? It's been seven days."

"Exactly what I said, but she's completely healed. Most bizarre thing I've ever seen. Do you know how many times she's been shot?"

"I suspected this wasn't the first," Cal said with a chuckle. "She was way too calm when she climbed out of that hole."

"To answer your question, she's in decent shape considering a bullet to the gut. She has a good appetite and has semi-okay stamina. The less walking we have to do, the better, though, for me and her."

"Noted. I know you don't have your other leg. How are you holding up?"

Efren bit his tongue to keep from telling the truth about his limb. They had bigger problems to solve, and his whining wasn't going to help. "Good. I can wear both legs interchangeably, though the blade can tire me out faster if I wear it too long. I'll be fine until this is resolved. Before we lose our connection, I need to talk to you about something when Selina isn't around."

"Of course you have my permission to date her. Not that you need it."

"I'm sorry?" He couldn't hold in his laughter.

"You aren't calling to ask me for her hand in marriage?"

"Smart-ass," Efren grumped as the cold wind whipped hard against his neck. "No, I'm calling to suggest we keep the cops out of the situation in Caledonia."

"What's your reason?"

"If the chance is given, we need to take out Vaccaro and Ava. Cops make that messy."

"Not untrue, but also, we aren't cops, and that's breaking the law."

"Oh, come on," Efren huffed, burrowing deeper into his coat to block the rain. "How many times in your life have you had to do bad things to benefit the greater good?"

"Too many, but does killing the Snake and Ava benefit the greater good or does it benefit Selina?"

Efren bit his lip and stepped closer to the cabin to keep

from getting drenched. He was glad he'd saved his shower until after he made the call. He was going to need it. "It can't benefit both?"

"That depends on who comes out better off. Selina or the greater good."

Efren took a deep breath to keep from losing his temper with his boss. "It's like you want this guy to kill Selina, and he will, if we don't get to him first."

"Listen here, Brenna. The very last thing I want is to lose Selina from the team. She's paramount to everything we do here and while she may not see that, the rest of us do. I would take Vaccaro out with my bare hands if given the chance, but I can't risk the reputation of Secure One and what I've built here. What's the saying, cut off the head of a snake and a new one will take its place?"

Efren wasn't giving up. If they brought the cops in on this mission, Selina was going to die. "If the head of the snake is removed, you can bet the rest of the heads will be too busy scrambling to wonder where Selina Colvert has gone. All I'm asking is to wait and loop the cops in on this operation after the fact rather than before."

"Does Selina know you're asking this of the team?"

"Not yet."

Cal was silent, and Efren had to wonder what he was thinking. It was a big ask, but Selina would never be safe if they didn't stop Ava and Vaccaro. She deserved more out of life than constantly looking over her shoulder for the next bullet.

"I'll keep the cops out of our plans for now," Cal finally said. "For now. That could change depending on what we find when we get to Caledonia. Understood?"

"Loud and clear," Efren said, letting out a breath.

"Selina has always been the one to demand we bring the cops in. I'm not sure how she's going to feel about you going behind her back like this."

"Let me handle Selina. Do you have an actionable plan?"

"Working on it," Cal answered. "As soon as this storm clears, we're headed your way for backup."

"Is that safe? What if he's watching Secure One?"

"Let me worry about us here while you do your job there. Keep Selina safe tonight. Eat. Get rest. Try to remember we're a team and we do better working with each other instead of against each other. We'll be in contact in the morning. Charlie, out."

Efren dropped the phone to his side and turned to stare out at the storm. The wind whipped and howled, and the sleet pelted down, changing direction with each turn of the wind. If his soul were an image, that would be it. This had become more than an assignment the moment he'd put his lips on hers. If they were going to get out of this alive, he was going to have to keep his head in the game. It was his job to convince Selina that this was one time the cops didn't need to be involved until after Secure One had gone in and doled out a bit of karma to the two people who deserved it most. After spending the last few days with her, he suspected it wouldn't be a hard sell. This was one time Selina Colvert might agree that manipulating fate was the right thing to do.

Chapter Fourteen

The stitches were out and Selina was feeling much better about life, even as a storm rolled around outside their tiny wooden structure, a madman and her twin were after her, and the man she was trapped with had flipped a switch and turned into king jerk of the universe. There was nothing she could do about the storm, the madman or Ava, but she could talk to the man who had switched into defense mode to protect himself. He'd helped her with the stitches begrudgingly, more than a little surprised when her skin was perfectly healed as she'd predicted.

What he didn't know was that her trained eye picked up the bounce he did every three or four steps on his blade as he paced the small room. That was something he didn't normally do. They'd decided to stay in the main room for as long as the heater stayed running. Eventually, they'd take turns sleeping and keeping watch until the storm passed and they could connect with the team again. In the meantime, she was going to have to convince him to let her look at his limb and treat any problems with it before they became major ones. Considering his attitude over the last few hours, she suspected that would be easier said than done.

Efren was dealing with some internal battle Selina wasn't privy to. She could see it in his body language and the way he set his jaw. What he couldn't control was the look in his coffee-brown eyes every time he glanced at her. Every so often, he'd run his hand through his short, curly hair and sigh. An hour ago, he'd moved the wardrobe away from the front door and gone outside. She could see he was talking on the sat phone, but he refused to answer any of her questions about why he had to call Secure One. He paced, huffed and sighed like the entire world was on his shoulders. Considering the circumstances, it was a real possibility that was how he felt as he sat trapped in a cabin with her. They both knew what was coming, and their war would likely include fatalities. They just had to hope those fatalities were on the enemy's side.

She'd call him out about his phone call later. For now, she had a bigger problem to solve. "Stop." She stood in front of him so he had no choice but to. "You have a situation with your leg. Sit down so I can look at it."

"My leg is fine." He growled the words more than he spoke them, and she lifted a brow.

She wasn't new to dealing with surly guys who didn't want to take the time to deal with an injury. "It's not fine. Every four steps you're doing an unusual bounce to take pressure off the anterior side of the socket. Now, would you like to sit down so I can check the skin or would you like to stand here and argue about whether or not you have a problem when you know you're going to lose the argument anyway? I'm good either way. I have nothing else to do."

Efren glared at her with his lips pursed and his eyes flaming. "You need to understand that I'm not comfortable with that idea. Let it go."

"Not happening. I don't care if you're uncomfortable. You're going to be more uncomfortable when you can't walk and we need to run. Pretend I'm a nurse at the VA if you have to, but sit down and take your socket off."

"I can't pretend you're a nurse at the VA," he said between clenched teeth as she dragged him to the couch near the heater. It put off a bit of light, and she'd need it to find the problem and repair it.

"Why not? You don't think I have the chops to be a nurse at the VA?"

"Oh, you have the chops, but I'm far more interested in you as a woman than any nurse I've dealt with at the VA."

He sat and she knelt in front of him, zipping off his pant leg to turn them into shorts. It was Mack who had found creative ways to dress the crew, who all had different braces and prostheses to wear. These pants worked great for getting their clothes changed quickly without taking their devices off. No one realized what a pain that was until they no longer had to do it. She removed the valve in the prosthesis to release the suction and glanced up at him. "I can be both and separate myself as each. Take it off."

His sigh was heavy, but he finally grasped the socket and pulled, carefully working it back and forth until it was off and he could set it aside. Selina took in the limb as a whole. His skin bore the typical changes that came with wearing a skin-fit prosthesis for years. The scar at the distal end of the femur was well done and shaped the limb nicely, but there was an area where a sore had developed.

Selina glanced up at him. "There's a hell of a blister on the scar."

"Kind of figured," he said, grasping his thigh and rubbing it. "The longer I wear the blade, the worse the phantom pain gets, and that changes my gait."

"Yet you refuse to let me take care of it when I have the skills to do it. Someone told me you were smart." Rather than wait for a response, she grabbed the first aid kit from his bag, and a clean towel from the bathroom cabinet. They'd both showered, which wasn't easy for him, but he'd managed by using a kitchen chair to sit on. The fact that he showered, saw the problem and refused to do anything about it really jacked her pickles. "You could have a little respect for what I do at Secure One." She tossed him the towel in anger, and he caught it midair. "Do your massage while I work on the blister."

"What are you so peeved about? I'm out here trying to help you, and you're giving me attitude."

"I'm giving you attitude because you showered, saw the problem and still didn't ask for help!"

He slung the towel under his thigh and moved it back and forth in a pattern he'd mastered, while she readied the first aid supplies she'd need to treat the blister and keep it from getting bigger. "I don't like coming to you for help."

"Well, thanks for the vote of confidence." Her eye roll punctuated the sarcasm in the sentence.

"Not because you're incompetent, Selina." He grabbed her hand, and she glanced up at him. "I'm supposed to be the one protecting you. How do you have confidence in that when I show you my weakest link?"

"It's not your weakest link, Efren. This doesn't stop you."

She motioned at his leg. "What stops you is this." She tapped her temple. "You overthink things instead of following your gut. You're the one whispering in my ear to follow mine. Why aren't you doing the same?"

"Following my gut would be a dangerous thing for you, Selina Colvert. If you were wise, you'd rethink telling me to do so."

"I can hold my own with you, Efren Brenna." Without waiting for his response, she inspected the scar while he held the limb up with the towel. The blister had already popped, which made the cleaning and bandaging easier, but they'd have to watch for infection until they could get back to Secure One.

"Mina said you were injured by an IED but saved six men that day?" It was time to change the subject before she told him how much she wanted him to follow his gut when it came to her.

"For what it was worth, yes," he agreed.

"Purple Heart?" She swiped antiseptic over the wound.

His next words were hissed. "Yep, and Bronze Star."

"What does it feel like to be a hero? Like a real hero?"

"Don't be condescending, Selina." His words were cold, and she glanced up to meet his clouded gaze. Whether it was pain or anger clouding it, she couldn't be sure.

"I'm not, Efren. It's a sincere question."

"I could ask you the same thing. You did an awful lot of saving when you were Eva Shannon."

"Not like you. Not missing a limb and bleeding out on the field. That's next-level stuff right there. Besides, I wasn't a hero. I was a cop doing my job, and in the case of search-

and-rescue, that was something I enjoyed doing that benefited others. That's it."

"I'm sorry for being short, but you made my point. I don't like the word *hero*. It sets my teeth on edge."

"Because?" She wanted to keep him talking so he wouldn't notice what she was doing with his limb. Keeping his mind focused on something other than her messing with the sore would hopefully keep him from having worse phantom pain when she finished. The nervous system and mind were so closely connected that it was difficult for amputees to train their brains not to focus on the pain, which was understandable. Unfortunately, messing with his limb was going to make it worse for a few days.

"I don't believe in heroes. Heroes are people we inflate in our minds as being more than human, and that's not right. Did I save six men that day in the field? Yes. Are they all still here on this earth? No. Since returning that day, we've lost three—one to his injuries and two to the scars the event left on their mind."

"I'm sorry. That's a tough reality, considering you went through the same experiences."

"It is, which is why I agreed to be a bodyguard when the opportunity came my way. I could protect people in danger for any number of reasons and deliver them safely to the other side. Score another soul for Efren that he managed to keep on this earth, at least for a little while longer. I know it isn't a healthy way to deal with the aftermath of the war, but I haven't figured out any other way."

"I wouldn't say it's unhealthy." Her fingers deftly applied a special transparent skin to the limb, and she held it gently while it settled in. "There are much worse ways of dealing with it."

"I've seen those ways, too, and didn't want to go down that road. I thought going back over there as a contractor would be better. It would give me more power to help those people, but it didn't. If anything, it gave me less power. I didn't like it, so I came back stateside and started protecting witnesses and domestic abuse survivors. That's where I found satisfaction in using my skills to help others."

"Why Secure One, then?"

"I came running because Mina called. That was the only reason. Mina, Roman and I worked together quite frequently when they were FBI. As one of the main bodyguards for WITSEC witnesses, we did a lot of coordinating."

"Ah, that explains why you were so concerned I was part of the program." Selina lowered his limb to the couch for support and pulled off her gloves to clean up the mess.

"That explains why I was so surprised to find out you did this on your own. Most people struggle to do it with the government behind them. I could only imagine how hard it was without them."

"It was a struggle, but I always knew that one day I might have to run, so I had planned for the contingency in the way I lived my life."

"What was it like growing up with a dad who was part of the Mafia? What did your mom think about it?"

"My mother died in childbirth. I was born first, but Ava was breech. They saved Ava, but my mother was gone. Dad named me Eva because it means life and her Ava because it means to live. My mother was Italian and her name was Bibiana, which meant full of life. Dad always said we carried her life. All of that said, he had no idea how to raise two baby girls, so he hired a nanny who cared for us until we were old enough to go to school."

"Your dad never remarried?"

"Thankfully, no. We found out shortly after he died that my parents had only been married eight months before we were born."

"A shotgun wedding?"

"Apparently, and not one based on love. Uncle Medardo had insisted he make an honest woman out of her. He wanted my father to play the part of the family man to bolster Medardo's attempt to change the face of the organization."

"Uncle?"

"That's what we called him growing up," Selina said with a shrug. "Looking back on it, it was weird, but we didn't know that he was a cold-blooded killer who used people like napkins and threw them away when he was done. Hell, we lived with a man who would kill on command."

"Did you know what your dad's job was? Seems like an odd thing to tell your kids."

"He didn't tell us. According to him, he was Uncle Medardo's business partner. I was twelve when I learned what he did for a living." She pointed at his socket. "Do you have pads you can put in there to protect that spot?"

"The small black bag in the front zipper. What happened when you were twelve?"

Selina walked to his go bag and knelt, pulling out the smaller supply bag and carrying it over to him. "I was supposed to wait in the car that night." She sat next to him and took his limb onto her lap, starting the towel massage so he could fix the socket. "He was taking forever and I was hungry. Since he'd gone into a pizzeria, I figured I'd run in, grab a snack and be back before he missed me."

"Instead?"

"Instead, I walked into the restaurant to see my father aiming a gun at a man who was on the ground groveling for his life. The man next to him already had a bullet between his eyes. My father said, this is done by order of the Snake, and then put a bullet between that guy's eyes. Thankfully, they were in a side room and my father never knew I was there. I got back in the car and waited for him like I hadn't just witnessed him kill someone. Intrinsically, I knew it would be dangerous to my life if I let on about what I saw, so instead, I spent six years plotting out a way to take him down when I got old enough. I saw police work as the only way, so as soon as I graduated from high school, I went to the academy. I had dreamed of one day being in the FBI, but I knew a dream was all it would ever be. What about you? Are your parents alive?"

"Yep, alive and well," he said as he added a pad to the socket. "My dad is from Italy, and my mom is from Bolivia. My dad worked for the UN, so I was born here in the States. They eventually became citizens when they retired."

"That explains the exotic skin tone," she said, running her hand up his forearm. "Mina always says you're the epitome of tall, dark and handsome."

"Do you agree?"

"It would be hard to disagree with that statement. Do you talk to your parents often?"

"Nice pivot, Colvert," he said, chuckling. "I talk to them every Sunday and keep them updated about where I am. I got a message to them while you were at the hospital that I was on a new case and didn't know when I'd call next. They've always been supportive of what I do, but they've enjoyed me working at Secure One. They like that I've found a way to do what I love and have a brotherhood again. They've seen how the loner lifestyle changed me, I suppose, and as parents do, they worry."

"Is that why you've stayed at Secure One? For the brotherhood?" Selina was trying to concentrate on doing the massage the way he did while they talked. It was her fault he was in this bind, so she would do what she could to give him some relief.

"That's one of the reasons I've stayed. It's refreshing to work with a team of people I trust where we're doing good things to help people. Even if we have to operate under the law a bit to do it."

"I try to avoid that," she said with a bit of a lip tilt. "Sometimes we can, sometimes we can't. When it came to Randall Jr., we couldn't. When it comes to the Snake, we will, and I fully support that."

His brows went up. "Seriously? You're okay with not bringing the cops in on this?"

"There's a certain finesse that will be needed on this case. No one knows that better than me. Is that what your little tête-à-tête was about out there? You could have talked to me about it before you went to Cal."

"I was going to, but I wanted his approval before I presented it as an option to you. It doesn't matter what our plans are if Cal's are different. He runs the show."

"True. We'll have to bring the cops in, but it can be after the fact."

"After what fact? After Ava and Vaccaro are dead?"

"If that's what has to happen," she answered. "Are you going to leave Secure One after this and go back to body-guarding?"

His laughter was quiet as he shook his head. "We'll have to discuss the plan in further detail, but I'll let it go until morning when we meet with the team. As for what happens after this case, no, I'm not leaving Secure One." He finished with the socket and set the leg down. "Cal has hired me on full-time. He's starting the cybersecurity division now with Mina, and he needs a strong team for the rest of the security work. I'll be bodyguarding, but for Secure One instead of the government. It will be a tighter team when this op is over."

"What does that mean?" She paused with the towel, confused by his statement.

"It means that it's time for you to set your stethoscope aside and pick up your gun again. You proved yourself last week as an invaluable operative. If Cal wants me to stay, we're a package deal."

"You're going to quit if he doesn't move me to operations from medical?"

"Without a moment's hesitation. My goal in life is to right wrongs, and you're a wrong that Cal needs to make right. You have the training and the chops to do what all those other guys do, the only difference is, you're a woman. I would hope by now, Cal has seen the difference all the women who have joined Secure One have made to his business. If he doesn't, then I don't want to work for him."

"Despite how I've treated you?"

"Partly because of the way you treated me. It intrigued me. I wanted to know why you were so upset that I was there when the team so obviously needed help. I understand now."

His finger traced her cheek, and the sensation sent a skitter of desire through her. "You didn't hate me. You hated what I represent."

"It wasn't fair to you." Her whispered admittance released a tightness in her chest she'd been carrying for too long. "I hated you for coming in and stealing my chance to take down the Red River Slayer."

"That's nonsense. I had nothing to do with that capture. I was there to guard the senator's daughter."

"But had they needed another person, they weren't going to pull the nurse off the injured woman, were they? No, they were going to go to the tall, dark and handsome stranger who had proven himself in the same war they'd fought."

"That's fair, and logical. Coupled with what you were dealing with as the caretaker of these women, I can understand the hostility you felt toward the newcomer. The Red River Slayer case has been over for almost a year. Why the continued animosity?"

"I'm always nervous when Cal brings someone new in. The Snake's reach is far and wide."

"I'm not a Vaccaro plant. I've only been to Chicago once."

"I know. And that's not why I've kept you at arm's length. There's this draw between us that's too hard to fight if I don't put up a wall." He gently pushed her hands aside and rolled on an elastic sock.

"That will control the nerves for now. As much as I love having your hands on me, I can't handle having your hands on me." He tugged her up onto the couch next to him and grasped her hands. "I feel the draw, too. Why do you want to fight it?"

Why did she want to fight it? That was a complicated answer to a simple question. "For starters, I'm a woman in a man's world."

"That's not the reason," he said, grasping her chin and forcing eye contact. "Mina is a woman in a man's world. So are Charlotte and Marlise."

"I'm not them." Her words were defensive. "I've had different life experiences. I don't know how to connect the way they do. Even if we wanted to explore this draw, I wouldn't know how."

"Wrong. You're scared. Just admit it, and then we can move on. We have to stop being afraid to be afraid. We have to stop letting the fear control us and use the fear to motivate us. Do you want me to admit it first? Okay. I'm scared of what this draw between us could mean. Every look, every interaction, every time I kiss you, it's a reminder that I can still feel. After I lost my leg and the men I cared about, I swore that I would never fall in love or have a long-term relationship. Life can change in an instant and someone you love can be taken just as quickly. Then I met you, and your attitude toward me hurt. Suddenly, I cared that you didn't like me even though you didn't know me. Those were dangerous feelings. I'm not supposed to care, but when it comes to you, I do. I care what you think about me, and I worry that this—" he motioned at his leg "—makes you think that I can't protect you as well as Roman or Cal could."

"No." The word was said quickly and with conviction. "I would trust you to protect me as much or more than I'd trust Cal or Roman."

"Why?"

"You've proved your mettle, Efren. You've kept me alive longer than I ever thought possible when Vaccaro entered our lives again. You haven't just kept me alive, but you've included me in the decisions that affect my life. That's more than anyone else at Secure One has done. You demand respect for yourself and the same respect for me. The only time the amputation is a factor is when you're limping and not taking care of yourself. That doesn't mean you can't protect me. You would lay down your life for me, which, while misguided, is the true definition of protection."

"Misguided? Why would dying for you be misguided?"

"Because no matter how much you give, you can't save me, Efren. You'd lay down your life and he'd slither right over you to get to me."

"Maybe you're right. Maybe I can't save you, but I can support you while you save yourself. You don't need a hero, Selina. You can fight Vaccaro and win as long as you have the right team behind you. Secure One is the right team. Every single one of your friends back home is busy making a plan to defend you. Find that woman inside you who stood on the top of a bluff and asked a man who loved her to support her one last time. Find the woman who survived and thrived on her own despite having the deck stacked against her. Let her guide you again, and the rest of us become soldiers in *your* army."

She was straddling him now to get closer. To be closer to the man who saw things in her that she didn't see in herself. "What if I want you to be more than a soldier?" Her question was soft as she lowered her head toward his, their noses touching as she waited for him to answer.

"I thought you were scared to be more with me."

"You told me to stop being afraid of being afraid. It sent me back to the woman who stood on a bluff and broke a man's heart in order to do the right thing. She used fear as motivation. Right now, that fear is motivating her to kiss you, Efren Brenna."

"Then she should quit talking about it—"

He didn't have a chance to finish the sentence before her lips were on his and the storm inside was stronger than the one knocking on their door.

Chapter Fifteen

"Selina, we have to stop," Efren said against her warm lips. Lord knew he didn't want to, but he also knew if he had this woman once, he'd want her every day for the rest of his life, and that was not in the cards for him.

Stop being afraid of being afraid.

He inhaled a breath, hating that voice for being right and being wrong at the same time. This wasn't being afraid of being afraid. This was protection. This was the way he protected himself from having to live in a world where his failures as a man and a soldier were always with him.

"We don't." Selina leaned back and took his face in her hands. "This connection between us has already been made. Trying to fight it will only be a lesson in frustration."

"Oh, trust me, I'm frustrated," he assured her, shifting under the sweet warmth of her draped across his lap. "That doesn't mean it's a good idea. Emotions complicate everything."

"You're right," she said, kissing the right side of his lips. "The biggest thing they complicate is our internal fight to protect our hearts from the pain of losing someone. It's an unfortunate side effect of the jobs we've done in the past. Those memories stay with us and shape every decision we make in the future. If we let them." She whispered the final sentence in his ear, and it sent a shiver of anticipation, expectation and desire down his spine. "How long are we going to give it that power before we pull it back and control our future again?"

"Up until a year ago, I'd planned to give it the power for the rest of my life. Tonight, here with you on my lap, I'm re-thinking that plan."

"I bet I can make you rethink it quicker," She lifted a brow, and it transformed her from the beautiful woman she was to a sexy vixen whom he wanted to make love to for the rest of his life. Selina slipped her hand between them and caressed his undeniable source of frustration.

He grasped her face and attacked her lips, thrusting against her hand while he searched for relief from the sweet torture she doled out. "Let me put my leg on," he said against her lips. "We'll go to the bedroom."

She leaned out of the kiss and lifted herself on her knees. Her shirt came off in a slow striptease, offering a full frontal that turned him on and hurt him at the same time. He traced the scars that marred her skin while he held her eye. It wasn't until his hands moved toward the clasp on her bra that she spoke. "We're not going to the bedroom. I want to make love to you right here, being open and honest with each other with all of our scars visible. These scars are part of us and will remain that way forever. I accept yours, Efren. Do you accept mine?"

He didn't answer with words. He deftly twisted her until she was on her back on the small sofa and he was kissing every scar across her belly, his featherlight touch raising goose bumps across her bare skin as he moved farther north.

It wasn't until those kisses landed on her nipples that she inhaled deeply. "Efren, make me yours. Now."

Her words shot fire through him, and he finished relieving them of their clothes until every painful scar and emotion was laid bare. "I have to grab some protection," he whispered as he kissed his way up the inside of her thigh.

"We don't need any."

The way she said it made him lift his head to meet her gaze. Her eyes were open and honest, and he chastised himself for forgetting something so important in the moment. He slid alongside her until he was able to kiss her lips. "I'm sorry. I forgot. Can we even do this? It hasn't been that long since your surgery."

"I'm fine," she assured him, running her hand through his hair. "I just want to feel something other than scared tonight. I'm not afraid of being with you anymore. I have no control over the storm outside, but I have control of the one inside me. That storm says only you can calm it, but first, you're going to have to fight through the waves threatening to take you under."

"I'm not afraid of those waves," he promised, scooting back on the couch and lifting her gently by her waist to sit across him. "Let's dive in and let them take us under together."

Selina leaned forward and took his lips with hers, kissing him senseless while her warmth settled around him. It was a moment before the sensation broke through the high he was on from holding her sweet body. When it did, he thrust upward with a moan nearly as loud as the ones from the storm outside.

"Selina," he hissed, thrusting his hips against hers until they were locked together in harmony and ecstasy.

She leaned back and braced herself on his thigh, taking him under the waves for a moment before she brought him back up, setting him on top to savor the pleasure. She paused, their heightened senses meshing as they entangled their hands and rode out the storm. With a satisfied sigh, they rested together in the calmness of their connection.

SELINA PACED THE small cabin as she tried to put together in her mind a way to make Vaccaro and Ava disappear from her life. She paused near the couch where the man she'd made love to three times in the same number of hours now rested. She'd insisted he catch a nap since she knew she wouldn't sleep. She was energized by the great sex but riddled with anxiety about what was to come—both with Vaccaro and her life now that she'd admitted she cared for Efren.

Stop being afraid of being afraid.

Those six words echoed through her head as she kept an eye on the perimeter of the cabin. The lesson she took from those words was to live life afraid. Playing it safe means the only winner is fear. In this case, playing it safe with Vaccaro meant he would be the winner in this decades-long game of cat and mouse. Playing it safe with Efren meant they'd both lose. They were good together, both as work partners and as life partners.

"Life partners?" she muttered. Back up the wagon. They shared some secrets and made love—no, they had sex three times. Not the definition of life partners. The question she kept trying to block from her mind—the one where the answer made her afraid—was, could they be life partners given a little more time and trust?

She was afraid because the answer, at least for her, was yes. She had always had feelings for Efren that went beyond basic colleagues. This night made their lives so much more complicated, especially considering she was still being hunted by a madwoman with an axe to grind. And she had no doubt they were still being hunted. This little interlude had been too good to be true, and as soon as the sun came up in a few hours, a memory was all it would be. A memory was all it would ever be if she didn't figure out a way to get Vaccaro and Ava off her back and keep Randall Sr. in prison.

Selina's heart pounded hard in her chest at the thoughts running through her head. If she could get that witness statement signed before Randall went before the judge, she might be able to keep him in prison. Efren's words came back to her then, and her shoulders slumped. He was right. Even if she did get the statement signed, if Vaccaro had already paid off the judge, she was risking her life for nothing. There had to be a better way.

Fear was keeping her from thinking through the better way. The fear she'd carried for so long wanted her to run back to Secure One and hide behind the fortress while someone else fought her battles. The other side of the fear told her she'd done that long enough. It was time she stepped up and took control of her own destiny again. When she was Eva Shannon, she was the kind of person who didn't hesitate when a decision had to be made, fear or no fear. She faced the fear head-on in her job so many times that it had simply become how she lived her life until her entire life became a calculated risk.

Selina had spent too long not taking any risks, calculated or otherwise. That, she realized, was why she hadn't pushed Cal to make her part of the core team as something other than medical. While she was mad about it, she was also afraid to rock the boat. If Cal did make her part of the team, then the safety she'd found in the med bay would be gone. She'd have to expose herself to the outside world again. Her life had become a yin-yang that she couldn't break. She wanted something she couldn't have but didn't want what she already had.

Selina recalled the woman who stood on that bluff eight years ago. That woman had an actionable plan that put her in complete control. That woman wasn't afraid to ask for everything from someone when she couldn't repay him. That woman was not afraid of the fear that engulfed her because the fear kept her alive.

She paused and gazed at Efren, his hair tousled in sleep and a deep five-o'clock shadow covering his chin. She wanted him more than any man she'd wanted in her lifetime. Fear rocketed through her at the idea of asking someone to be part of her life when her life was always a calculated risk. She'd let fear stop her from asking Kai. She couldn't make the same mistake with Efren, right? They had survived bombs, bullets and pain to get here. Those bombs and bullets didn't take their lives, which meant they shouldn't let them take their future.

Determined to get her life back, she grabbed a notebook and pen, then stood to the side of the window to use the light of the moon to write. The storm had blown out of town about an hour ago, and as happened in Minnesota, the sky cleared off immediately, dropping the temps to a teeth-chattering cold. The rain and sleet that had fallen was surely going to freeze, turning everything into an ice-skating rink until the sun came out to melt it. They'd have to be extra careful when they left the cabin so Efren didn't slip. His limb was already in rough shape, and falling could mean life or death for them. Thankfully, he had his spiked sole and his all-terrain sole with him.

What was that sound? Her brain registered it and dropped her to the floor under the window. She crab-walked to the other side of the cabin to peer out the window on that side from under the curtain. Her fear had been confirmed. A drone hovered around the yard, obviously trying to get a look inside the cabin. They had turned the propane heater off and with no lights on, as long as they stayed low, the drone would show its pilot nothing but an empty cabin.

Still in a crouch, Selina moved to the couch and put her hand on Efren's chest from where she sat on the ground. His eyes opened immediately and met hers. "Drone," she mouthed, and he slid off the couch onto the floor, curling himself around her as they listened for the faint sound of the flying spy to disappear—if it disappeared.

"How did they find us?" he whispered into her ear.

"Vaccaro has eyes everywhere, but this is a stretch even for me. We've left no digital trail and made no purchases."

"That's not entirely true," Efren whispered. "The sat phone leaves a digital trail when it goes to the service provider for billing, but Cal assured me it was safe to use."

"Nothing and no one is safe from Vaccaro. You used the phone what, five hours ago? They already found us. I'm surprised all we have is a drone in the air and not ten guys knocking down the door."

"Only because a satellite phone can't pinpoint where the call is coming from. It will give them a quadrant to search, so they know we are in the area, but they don't know our precise location. Using a drone makes sense. As soon as it's gone, so are we."

"To where?" Selina asked, rolling over to make eye contact.

"Anywhere but here. We need to get free of this place and then get connected with the team. I'm done letting this idiot control our lives."

"Me, too," she whispered with a nod. "I have a plan, but it's going to require backup from Secure One and a dance with a devil who's the spitting image of me."

"Wrong," he hissed, slamming his lips into hers to quiet them. "You may be identical twins, but that woman wears her evil like a fine linen cloak. You're like night and day. Remember, your fear feeds the devil, but if you stay strong, you'll starve her for good."

"That's where you're wrong," she whispered. "The devil gets her power from a snake, but once we've shredded his scaly body and buried him ten feet deep, the devil will become mortal once again. I no longer fear Ava or Vaccaro. I fear giving up another second of my life to them. Eva Shannon may be dead, but before she went over that cliff, she transferred her power to Selina Colvert. The time to bide is over. The time to do is upon us." She paused and they listened, but the night was silent again. "Are you ready to act rather than react?"

He pushed himself up and then held out his hand for her. "Secure one, Tango."

Selina slid her palm into his and let him pull her up. "Secure two, Sierra."

Quickly, they dressed for the weather and readied their bags. Selina held up a fist at the door of the cabin and they listened for several moments, but heard nothing but silence. "When we get out there, follow me and don't ask questions."

"Ten-four."

Efren pressed against her back, but she paused. "Ten-four? No arguments?"

"I knew from the moment I met you that I'd follow you anywhere, Sierra."

A ghost of a smile played on her lips as she opened the door. Today was the day she took her life back.

Chapter Sixteen

The night was as cold as Efren was expecting it to be, but he'd stayed close on Selina's heels, his gun out and his head on a swivel as they worked their way downstream, following the river. She had a plan, so he was going to let her lead until she asked for help. Selina didn't need anyone to save her. She could save herself as soon as she channeled the woman she'd hidden away so many years ago. That must have happened during the hour he'd been asleep, because the woman leading him now was completely different than the one he'd known over the last year.

Then again, as he thought about it, he'd been watching it happen over the course of the last week. Slowly, she was coming to realize that waiting around for someone else to help her out of this jam wasn't the answer. If she wanted to be free of Ava and Vaccaro, she was going to have to do the saving herself, even if it scared her.

And it scared her.

He could see it in her eyes when the drone was flying over their heads, but she hadn't buckled to the fear. She'd used it to spur her forward, and something told him she was just getting started. Their lovemaking came back to him, and he couldn't help but smile, even as they trudged along the cold, wet banks of the Mississippi. He loved nothing more than when a woman was willing to dominate him in the bedroom. Did he always allow it? No, but last night, he sensed that it was a first step for Selina to be in control again, and he was all too happy to give her that power. She deserved it. She harnessed it, and now she would use it to find her twin and put an end to this game of hide and seek.

For him, the most challenging part would be to put the image of her sweet, hot body on top of his out of his mind long enough to help her get the job done. Especially since the things his body told him about his time with her confused his mind and heart. Selina deserved a better life than she'd lived the last decade, but that didn't mean he could be the one to give her that life. Damn if he didn't want to, though. He couldn't remember the last time someone turned him on with a lifted brow and a snide remark, but Selina did every time.

His body contracted at the memories of the way she turned him on. His mind was blown at the number of times he'd made love to her last night and still couldn't get enough of her. He wanted her now. Cold, tired, hungry and sore, he'd still lay her down on the beach and frolic in the sand with her.

"Almost there," she whispered through a huffed breath as they hurried through the woods.

"Almost where?" He hoped she knew where she was going, because he was utterly lost. They'd been running parallel to the river, but other than that, it looked like trees and not much else.

"We need to get somewhere safe to call into Secure One before daybreak. We can't risk turning on the emergency tracking beacon, even if Cal says it's hidden from everyone but him. Vaccaro has bested us at every turn."

Selina was right, and Efren ran the crew at Secure One through his mind, looking for a mole. Their newest hire, Sadie Cook, had suffered at the hands of the Loraines, which was what prompted all of this just a few weeks ago, so there was no way it was her. He made a mental note to suggest to Cal that he check his people again. Efren hadn't been at Secure One long enough to know everyone well, but if there was a Vaccaro mole in play, Cal would find them.

"That drone could still be out here," he whispered as they pulled up to a tree and stopped. Selina leaned over to give her side a break and take a breather. He rubbed her back, hoping to relieve some tension there from the injury she was still dealing with despite her rapid improvement. "I haven't heard it again, though, so Vaccaro doesn't have a lock on us yet. My gut says that could still change."

"That's why we moved as fast as we did," she agreed. "We couldn't get picked up by their drone, but I also didn't want to miss our ride out of here."

"Our ride out of here?"

After straightening again and doing a bit of a side stretch, she pointed at the area in front of them that was still pitch black. "What time is it?"

He flipped his wrist to check his watch. "It's 4:37. Daybreak will be coming soon."

"So will our ride."

"Did you hire a rescue chariot? Because all I see is darkness."

"What you don't see are the train tracks in front of us," she whispered with a satisfied glint in her eye. "There will be a train coming along in the next few minutes. It's our ticket out of town."

Efren slid his hand into hers and turned her to face him. "We can't jump a train, Selina. That's crazy dangerous. I've already lost a leg. I can't afford to lose an arm, too."

"Why do you think I picked this spot? We could have picked up the tracks not too far from the cabin, but the train would be going too fast. By the time the train gets to this part of the track, it's slowing for a junction ahead. Your grandma could get on it at that point, so jumping the train will be safe and easy. Finding an open boxcar will be harder. Worst case, we take the stairs on the caboose, but that will leave us open to sight once the sun comes up."

"How do you know all this? We don't even know exactly where we are."

"Last night, while you were sleeping, I heard a whistle off in the distance. Mina said we were north of Winona, so that meant there was a cargo train moving through the area. All I had to do was be here when one went by. Luckily, we won't have to wait long. I'll have to thank Vaccaro when I see him for sending that drone up and getting us out the door early."

"How do you know all of this?" he asked as she kept her head turned up the track.

When she turned back, she wore a sad smile. "This is my old stomping grounds for search-and-rescue, Efren. We did a lot of work on the Mississippi and the surrounding areas. The bluffs near La Crosse are just downriver from here a bit."

"Are those the bluffs you—"

"No," she said with a shake of her head, already knowing what he was thinking. "But it's the same type of topography. Being here, it makes me nostalgic for those days and the days I used to spend with Zeus and Kai tracking the lost and wounded. On the other side of the coin, it makes me angry that Vaccaro stole my passion and turned me into someone else entirely."

"That's not true," he said, stepping up and taking her face in his hands. "You're still the same caring person who wants to rescue others. You just do it in a different way now."

Her head tipped in his hands, and her beautiful navy blue eyes turned confused. "I put Band-Aids on scrapes and hydrate grown men who push themselves too far?"

"You also nursed hurt and scared women back to health to the point that they can now lead healthy, happy lives with a man, which is a testament to the care they got at Secure One. Just a few weeks ago you took on the role of caregiver again when you took care of a scared baby and his aunt, while terrified of the man after them, I may add. Then you set the fear aside and stepped up with the information the team needed to prepare for a mission. A mission you went on to rescue two people in danger where you paid heavily. If that weren't enough, over the last year, week and last night, you rescued me." He leaned in to kiss her softly without lingering, but did allow his thumb to keep caressing her temple.

"Rescued you from what?"

"The need to be everyone's savior. The self-hatred I carried about the men I've lost since returning to friendly soil. The fear that I would never be enough for anyone and the loneliness I've been drowning in for years."

"My catty attitude toward you did all of that?" She tipped her head up to make eye contact, and he saw the truth in her eyes. She needed to know that he didn't hold any of that against her.

He hoped what she saw there was more than his words could convey. "It did, sweetheart. That attitude set an ember burning in my chest again. It gave me a reason to fight when I no longer had the spirit. This past week, when you've put your trust in me to keep you safe, it reminded me that I can still do the job. Last night, when you put your trust in me as a woman, it reminded me that I still have something to offer the right person, even if we come from different experiences in life." She gazed at him, as though she was unsure what to say, so he dropped a soft kiss on her lips and then tipped his head upstream. "I think I hear the train."

That sentence snapped her out of her trance, and she whipped her head to the right, listening for a moment before she nodded. "It's coming. We need to get in position, which means still in the trees, but once the conductor is past, we get as close to the cars as we can. As soon as we see a workable situation, we go for it."

"The conductor won't see us?"

"Not in the dark and on his flank." She moved to the edge of the trees and flipped down her night-vision goggles. "You with me, Tango?"

After flipping his goggles down, he nodded with a smile. "Right behind you, Sierra."

Somewhere between the time the train passed and the time he followed her onto an empty train car, he knew he'd always be behind her, rooting for her, and probably, if he were honest, loving her, even if from afar.

THE TRAIN RIDE had been slow, but Selina was happy for a chance to sit down and give her side a break. It was healing, but her stamina was minimal, which meant pushing herself when all her body wanted to do was rest. Preferably rest in bed with the man who had held her during the train trip so she could lean against his chest and be comfortable.

Physically, she'd been comfortable, but emotionally, she'd been fighting against the things he'd said to her in the dark woods. His words made her rethink her place at Secure One again and what she wanted when this mission was over. Then again, wanting and getting were two entirely different words in the English language; no matter what she wanted, she would get what Vaccaro wanted her to have and nothing more. Unless they could take him and Ava down, she'd only get another ticket to run.

Selina shook off those thoughts and hung her legs over the edge of the doorway, motioning for Efren to do the same. "As soon as it starts to slow a bit more, push yourself off, drop and roll. Don't try to land on your feet."

"Got it, boss," he said, readying his hands to copy hers.

Jumping on and off trains was dangerous business that no one should be doing, but when it was a matter of living another day or falling into the Snake's hands, she'd take her chances with the train. At least she could walk away from the train with her life and limbs. The same couldn't be said of the Snake. She felt the slowing of the train under her and glanced at Efren. "See that opening in the trees?" Her finger swung out to the right, and he nodded. "Let's aim for that."

"You jump first. I'll follow once you land. That way, we won't land on each other."

Her nod was quick as she scooted to the edge, waiting for the right moment. Selina had no doubt that sticking this landing would hurt, but landing in the Snake's den would hurt worse. With a deep breath in, she pushed off the car, being sure to land on her right side, not that it mattered much when the hard earth smacked her ribs and sent a ricochet of pain through her entire body. Her momentum rolled her once before her backpack stopped her on the second roll. Selina scrambled to her feet, barely breathing, and ran for the opening in the woods as she watched Efren do the same from his southern position.

"You okay?" he asked as soon as he'd joined her, grasping her elbows to steady her. "I saw you land pretty hard on your side."

"There wasn't a choice, but I'm fine," she said between hissed breaths as she tried to make that statement true. "How's your leg?"

"Better than your side." He was eyeing her closely, probably trying to decide if he needed to carry her.

She forced herself to stand straight and then stretched side to side, trying to work out any last cramps from the fall and to keep new ones from starting. "We missed our check-in time with Secure One. It couldn't be helped, but we need to call in."

"Using the sat phone means another pin of our location for Vaccaro."

"Do we have a choice?" she asked, pulling the phone from her bag. "Last time it took him five hours to get the info. We'll be long gone in five hours."

When the screen came alive, Selina turned it so Efren could read the message. "Shady Lakes Campground. Number 117. ASAP. How are we supposed to know where that is? We don't even know where we are right now."

"You don't, but I do, and Cal knows it." Selina lowered the phone, but she couldn't keep her hand from shaking. Twisting to face south, she pointed to her left. "Ahead half a klick is the marina near Brownsville, which means we're about four klicks from the campground."

Without another word, Selina took off through the woods, knowing he would follow her without question. She had her compass out, following it south and then jogging west, praying her stamina held long enough to get to the campground. A mile and a half in, she slowed to a walk, bending over to catch her breath while Efren came up behind her, rubbing her side the way he did when she was hurting. Before she could speak, he relieved her of the backpack and carefully slipped his hand under her jacket to massage her side until the cramping eased.

"You gotta take it easy, sweetheart," he whispered in her ear. "This is a marathon, not a sprint."

"I know," she said, her breath still coming in spurts. "But the sooner we can link up with the team, the better. Wasting time because I'm weak could be a death sentence." She kicked the ground in front of her in frustration.

Efren wrapped his arms all the way around her and held her to him. "You're not weak. A weak person wouldn't have jumped a train, jumped off a train and then run for two miles without stopping. You're recovering. You're not weak. There's a difference. Now, before we go any farther, are you familiar with the campground?"

"I've been there a few times for search-and-rescue, and it's a mix of modern and remote. The number he gave us is remote. We can bypass the campground through the woods and come at the site from the back side."

"When you're ready and at your pace," he said, releasing her, but slinging her backpack over his shoulders.

He would lighten the burden for her any way he could. She offered him a smile and then took off again, at a slower pace, not wanting to go too far past the campground. She was running blind without the convenience of a map or GPS, so she had to use her memory of her past to guide her. Those were painful. Those memories conjured the face of the man she'd left behind and the companion who had loved her unconditionally and understood her completely. How she had missed them both.

Memories of last night played through her mind, and she couldn't help but smile. She couldn't live in the past. She could only learn from it. She made a vow to herself right there as she slowed, sidestepping toward the edge of the trees and motioning for Efren to follow, that she'd take her life back. She'd find a way to be Selina Colvert and Eva Shannon for the benefit of others again.

She waved her hand at her throat as Efren stepped up to her. "That's 117, but it's empty. Did they leave?"

"Not without sending another coordinate," Efren answered, his eyes firing all around them. "The hair on the back of my neck is standing up, though, so we need to make a decision."

With clarity comes wisdom. That was a line Kai always said when they couldn't find their target on searches. "With clarity comes wisdom," Selina whispered. "Watch my back."

Before he could stop her, she broke through the brush and jogged to the wooden sign that said 117. She felt the thin ledge under it near the stake it was attached to. Sure enough, there was a piece of paper waiting. She grabbed it and ran back to Efren, who had his gun out and was sweeping the woods intently. Something had him spooked. He held his finger to his lips and waved his hand at his throat as he pointed at the note, then motioned for her to go south again.

She read the note as she pulled her gun from her holster and started forward. One klick west. That was it. Something told her getting one klick west was going to be hard won.

Chapter Seventeen

There had to be a mole in Secure One. Nothing else made sense. Efren motioned for Selina to move behind a tree, where they paused, listening for footsteps. If there wasn't a mole, then Vaccaro had a beacon on their location without Cal's knowledge. Considering the lengths Cal went to in order to ensure their security, that was saying something. Then again, if you ran a large crime organization, it was doubtful anyone could keep you from getting what you needed in a timely manner.

"What did the note say?" The whisper into her ear was barely audible.

She didn't speak; she held up one finger and then three. He nodded. One klick west. That wasn't far, unless they were ambushed on the way, and the hair on the back of his neck said that was a real possibility.

He leaned in closer again, keeping his gun pointed forward. "They're breaking through Cal's security layers. We can't lead them to Cal's front door."

"We can't have a gunfight this close to the campground," she hissed. "Too many civilians."

"I'm afraid that choice may not be ours. Let's move south-west and see what develops. Stay close. We don't have the big guns." Selina glanced down at her handgun and grimaced, which was exactly how he felt. The bad guys had the big guns this time, and they were at a deadly disadvantage.

They hadn't made it ten steps when motion caught his eye. "Behind you!" They yelled in unison, both swinging around on instinct with their guns, right into a hulking body in black.

Efren threw a punch blindly, hoping to connect with the assailant who had knocked his gun away already. His fist glanced off the guy's shoulder but when he brought his knee up, it landed square in the nether regions. The guy grunted and doubled over, stunned long enough for Efren to finish him off with a hit to the trachea. The dude dropped and Efren recovered his gun and rolled, coming up in the shooter's stance, searching for Selina. A grunt whipped his head around and he saw Selina stumble backward as the guy pummeled her in the kidneys, rendering her motionless. She couldn't take much more, so he waited for her to drop to the ground and then fired off one perfectly placed round. The guy spun like a ballerina before he dropped like a rock, his carotid emptying his lifeblood onto the ground.

"Selina!" Efren whisper-yelled, scrambling to the woman who was now writhing on the ground. On his way, he scooped up her weapon and grabbed her by her jacket, pulling her behind a tree. "Talk to me, baby." He knelt over her, his lips near her ear as he waited for her to breathe normally again.

"I'm okay." The words were huffed, and he knew she wasn't okay, but she would be. "I'm real sick and tired of these guys popping up like Whac-A-Moles."

He smiled. Yeah, she was going to be fine. "Can you sit up? Lean against the tree for support." He helped her into a seated position, but his gaze darted around the woods, searching for more goons. "We will have to move as soon as you're able. There could be more out there."

"Two or four but never more," she recited as she rubbed at her side with a grimace. "Uncle Medardo used to say that to my father all the time. Dad told us it was a rule about nails and how many go in a board. How dumb was I?"

"You weren't dumb," he whispered with half a chuckle. "You were a kid. The theory being more than four leaves room for capture?"

"That's my assumption," Selina said, pushing herself up when they heard a pop.

They dropped, both waiting for a bullet to slam into one of them or a tree above their heads, but there was nothing. Efren glanced at Selina and motioned her to him, just as another pop reached their ears, followed by a growly moan.

"Secure one, Echo."

Efren let out the breath he was holding and stood. "Secure two, Tango."

"Secure three, Charlie," Cal said as he broke through the trees, dragging someone behind him. "Welcome back. Good to see you. We were getting a little worried." He tossed the guy in front of their feet and knelt. "This can go one of two ways," Cal told him. "I can finish you off and leave your corpse to rot in the woods, or you can tell me how many more of you undertrained, uneducated, technology-reliant infants are out here, and I'll give you a fighting chance with that gut wound."

Efren noted the guy was barely old enough to drink and the color of paste. Cal better get him to talk fast, because he had no fighting chance against that gut wound. Hopefully the kid didn't realize that yet.

"If I talk, I die," he murmured.

"The Snake has his ways, right?" Cal asked, turning chummy with the kid. "You just follow orders and keep your head down so you aren't the next target. How'd you get tied up with this jackass anyway? You seem like a nice kid."

Efren couldn't help but snicker, willingly playing along with Cal's technique. "Did you just call the kingpin of Chicago's Mafia a jackass?"

"If the shoe fits," Cal answered without looking at him.

"Vaccaro wants her," the kid said, lifting his arm to point at Selina. "The first guy to bring her to him gets promoted."

"Promoted?" Cal said, acting impressed. "To what? Head henchman?"

"Something like that," he said with a groan.

"That doesn't answer my question. How many more are coming?"

"If we don't come back, another team will follow, and another. It's impossible to escape the Snake once you're in his sights."

"That's true," Selina said, crouching beside the kid. "How about if I save you all the trouble and turn myself over to the Snake?"

"Only if you want to die, Eva," he said, spittle and blood starting to bubble up from his lips. "That's your real name, right? Your sister is good and tight with the Snake now, if you know what I mean." He turned his head and spit, more blood bubbling up as he did so. Efren saw the moment he realized he was dying. There was no fear, just resignation. "I don't know who you all are, but if I were you," he said, pointing at Selina, "I'd run as fast and as far as you can, and I would have left ten minutes ago." He coughed, blood flowing freely from his lips as it also flowed over his hands, holding his stomach. "The next round will reach this location in thirty minutes. Less once I hit this." His bloody hand reached for his vest, but Eric stepped down on his stomach wound, stopping the guy cold.

"But you're not going to hit that," Eric said, his tone cold, hard and angry.

Cal searched the guy and found a beacon that he carefully unhooked from the vest.

"How many were there?" Selina asked, motioning toward the woods with her head.

"Two. The other guy is taking a dirt nap for eternity."

"Same for us," Efren said, motioning at the guys on the ground.

"We need to move," Cal said. "But first." He handed the beacon to Eric. "Get the rest of them and set them off somewhere before you double back."

Selina pointed upstream and to the right. "About a quarter mile back, a creek runs east toward the river. Toss them in there. It will buy us some more time."

With a nod, Eric disappeared into the trees like a ghost. Laughter bubbled up from the kid on the ground, though weak. "Tag, you're it. Run, run as fast as you can, sweet Eva…"

His words trailed off as his head lolled to the side, his eyes staring blankly at the ground. Efren shuddered and looked away. "That's the second guy to say the exact same thing as he was dying."

"This is a game to Vaccaro," Selina said, holstering her

gun. "It's the same thing Randall said to me the night I shot Ava eight years ago. Vaccaro makes the game rules, and he expects everyone to play."

"Well," Cal said as he started forward. "I don't know about you, but I'm not in the mood to play games with this idiot. I'd rather end his reign of terror the good old-fashioned way."

"With a bullet or brawn?" Efren asked as they hurried along behind him.

"First with brains, then brawn, but a bullet if necessary."

"Trust me," Selina huffed. "A bullet will be necessary."

CAL PULLED THEM up short near a gravel driveway. He reached for his phone, but Selina noticed Efren stop him. "Somehow, he knows your every move. Either you have a Vaccaro mole in Secure One or he has a mole in your communications company."

Cal sighed and shook his head. "I reran specs on all my people, and no one has connections to him other than Sadie and Selina, which we already knew. The communications company? Really?"

"I made that call to you last night on the sat phone and five hours later a drone was hovering over our cabin. You sent us the coordinates for the campground and an hour later, guys are in the woods looking for us."

"Damn it. Someone is inside my carrier, and they're supposed to be the best."

"The Snake's tentacles are many and wide," Selina said. "If you owe him a debt, you repay it when he comes to you. If you don't, you're dead. Even if you do, you're dead. As soon as you're no longer useful to him, he'll make sure you find a way out of his life for good."

"Comms are out then," Cal said with a shake of his head. "We'll have to use burner phones. I hate to do it, but by the time he figures out what we're doing by not using the carrier, we'll be knocking on his front door."

As they crept up the driveway, Selina was glad he'd had the forethought to bring burners with him, but then again, if he had mobile command, they had everything they'd need at their fingertips.

She had never been happier to see her friends show up when they did. If they hadn't, it would have been a dangerous endeavor to take on four guys by themselves. Especially worrying about civilian injuries if bullets started flying. The moment Cal tossed the guy down in front of them, dread filled her. People were dying, and her friends were going to be next if she didn't do something.

Her spine stiffened as she went back over the plan that she'd prepared this morning. She would have to stand her ground and force them to listen to her if they were going to come out of this alive as a team.

"Roman and Mina are waiting for us at mobile command," Cal said as he grabbed his birdcall from his pocket. He brought it to his lips and blew until a clicking, almost drumlike, sound filled the air.

A shudder went through Efren, and she stepped up against his back. "You okay?"

"Yeah," he whispered, shaking his head a bit. "The call of the white stork sends me back to the sandbox every time. It's how we called to each other since there were so many storks there. That's the first time I've heard it since I left."

Cal pocketed the birdcall and held their position, waiting and watching until they heard, "Secure one, Romeo."

"Secure two, Charlie," Cal answered, and Roman stepped out of the brush.

"It's good to see you guys," he said, shaking Efren's hand before he hugged Selina to his side. "Where's Echo?"

"He's running some interference for us."

"Why the birdcall?" Roman asked as they walked up the driveway, keeping an eye on both sides.

"Vaccaro has compromised our comms. I'll explain once we're inside."

When the vehicle came into view, Selina started. "This is new." The RV was white and had a rental company logo all over it.

"It's less conspicuous than mobile command," Cal explained. "I couldn't roll into town in that and expect Vaccaro not to notice. That's why it's tucked back here on private property. It's rented, so let's avoid putting any bullet holes in it."

They climbed the stairs and instantly, Mina was running toward them, grabbing Selina in a bear hug. "I'm so glad you're here. I've been worried sick about you guys."

"We're fine, Mina," Selina promised before she released her from the hug.

Mina eyed her carefully. "You don't look fine. You've got a bruise on your jaw and a black eye. Oh, wait, don't forget the busted lip."

Selina touched her lip and grimaced. "Better than getting punched in the gut." That was her only response.

When Selina glanced at Efren, she noticed he'd received the same treatment from their friends in the woods. His beautifully sculpted face now sported a black eye and a bruise across his nose. She'd have to check that it wasn't broken.

"Those guys aren't going to bother us again," Cal said, stripping off a few layers of clothes. "We do have a problem, Mina. Our comms are compromised."

Mina lifted her brow. "By Vaccaro?"

Cal motioned to Efren, who filled Mina in on what they'd experienced the last few days.

"That's not good," Mina said, her hand in her hair. "No wonder they could find us so easily. Burner phones?"

"Yep," Cal answered. "We'll use a burner phone app."

"A burner phone app on a burner phone?" Roman asked, digging out a bucket from under the table.

"A double layer of protection by using numbers that go away each time we make a call or send a text," Cal explained. "Best we can do under the circumstances."

Roman jumped up and ran for the door. "Eric doesn't know not to use comms," he said halfway out the door. "I'll find him and be back."

He was out the door and Mina was already shutting off her phones and equipment in a mad hurry. "This is going to cramp my style," she muttered. "It's going to be hard to track you guys with burner phones."

"You won't have to," Selina said, stepping toward Cal. "I have a plan. If we follow it to a T, most of us come out of this alive and unhurt. I will lay it out, but first, I need to tend to our injuries and address his leg."

"Everyone will come out of this alive and unhurt," Efren ground out, his eyes flaming when he looked at her. "Most especially you."

Mina raised a brow, but Selina ignored it. She didn't have time to argue with them. She'd lay out her plan, convince them it was the best way and then divert at the last minute.

Sacrificing her life was worth it if it meant Secure One could continue to help people when this was finally over. They had their mission, and she had hers. As she walked to the back of the RV with Efren, his hand sitting naturally in hers, Selina knew the hardest part of the mission would be coming to terms with never feeling his touch again. It was just another item on her long list of things she hated Uncle Medardo for—a list she'd been keeping for twenty-three years. Now it was time to face the man, read him the list of sins and let him atone for them one bullet at a time.

Chapter Eighteen

Efren pulled Mina aside after Selina had set his broken nose and added a couple of butterfly bandages to his cheekbone. He probably needed stitches, but he wasn't interested in taking the time to do that right now. The rest of the team was preparing for battle, while he was preparing not to lose the woman he'd come to care about.

"Have you heard anything more about Daddy Dearest? Is the hearing still scheduled for tomorrow?"

"It is, but it won't be an in-person judgment."

"I don't understand."

"Randall will remain at the penitentiary and be connected via closed-circuit television. The prosecution is afraid that taking him out of prison for the judgment puts too many people at risk."

"They're naive enough to think that the judgment will go their way?"

Mina shrugged. "I can't tell you what they're thinking, only what they're doing."

"If the judgment goes his way, when will he be released?"

"The following day," Mina answered. "There's paperwork to be done and filed before he can be released."

"Which means they won't return to the Caledonia house for two more days. That's if they come at all."

"It appears so. At least the best that I can figure. Now, not being able to use my equipment, I'm limited with what I can do."

"Understood," Efren said with a nod. "We need to do recon and then be prepared to move on the place as soon as they show up, and they will. They have nowhere else to go, and there's not a chance in hell Daddy Dearest is returning to Vaccaro's den. He'll want to separate himself as though he's an upstanding citizen who was wrongly accused, tried and convicted."

"All orchestrated by a madman who wants one of our own dead. We cannot let that happen," Efren emphasized. "Are we on the same page with that?"

"You can be assured of it," Mina said firmly. "Selina has been part of Secure One for longer than either of us has, and the teams' loyalty to her runs deep. They respect her and what she does as much as what Cal does. She may not see that, but it's the truth. Besides, it's not like her interactions with Vaccaro in the past made her a bad person. Just the opposite is true. She tried to stop Vaccaro once and never got the chance. Now she's got the chance again. Let's do everything we can to make it happen."

Efren held up his finger. "While keeping her safe."

"As safe as we can without taking away her power," Mina said, lowering his finger.

"Power means nothing if you're dead, Mina." The sentence was rough and revealed all the emotions inside him. "We have to protect her."

"You love her, I understand that feeling, but she's not looking for a hero. She's looking for a partner."

"No one said anything about love." The words were tight and clipped, which made Mina smile. He didn't care. His only goal was to get across to her the importance of keeping Selina tight to them so she didn't get hurt.

"They didn't need to. I can see it all over that handsome, if slightly dented, face." Her grin was wide as she waved her finger around his nose. Then she turned and walked back to the front of the RV, where everyone was gathered.

Everyone but one.

Selina was cleaning up and changing in the bedroom of the RV. Efren walked to the back and slid the door aside just in time to see her shirt fall over a nasty bruise across her ribs.

"Selina," he said, slipping through the door and sliding it closed. "Did you see that bruise?"

Her laughter was soft. "Didn't need to see it. I can feel it."

Efren lifted her shirt again and inspected the damage to her side. "This is from the train. Did you land on a rock?"

"Probably the backpack," she answered, pulling the shirt from his hands. "You threw yours, but I kept mine, hoping to use it to break my fall. It is what it is."

"Is it broken?"

"No," she assured him, sliding her arms into a black windbreaker. "It's sore, but I can breathe just fine." Selina turned and put a hand to his chest. "I'll live to see another day, Brenna."

"Let's make it many more days, okay?" he asked, pulling her to him by her coat and planting his lips on hers in a kiss he hoped would remind her why she wanted to.

"Keep kissing me like that," she whispered when he pulled back, "and I won't want to leave this room for many more years."

"That's kind of the point." His wink was playful but was

underlined by nervousness. She patted his chest and then walked past him, slid open the door and went to the front where everyone was gathered.

"I want to say thank you for having my back," Selina said to the group assembled around her. Cal had brought Roman, Mina, Eric, Mack and Lucas, but Mack and Lucas were currently setting up closer to Caledonia so they had a command station ready when they arrived. It was less than fifteen minutes from their current location, but he felt like they'd fight for every mile. "Mina, do you have an update on the Randalls?"

"Yes." She shuffled some papers around and came up with one. "Randall Jr. is still in a coma. They can't pull the plug until a direct relative signs off on it."

"How convenient," Selina said, rolling her eyes.

"Exactly. I would guess that means Daddy Dearest has to sign the papers. Maybe from prison, or maybe he has to go there to do it. I wasn't able to find that information before we went dark."

"That may delay their arrival to Caledonia," Selina said, pacing in front of the small table.

"Or, he will leave his son in a coma and play the part for the cameras."

"While likely, that doesn't help us make a plan to take them down."

"But it does," Selina said, pacing the floor. "I tried to think of every way possible to sign that witness statement before Daddy Dearest has his hearing, but there's no way to do it without exposing me and the entire team. Instead, we'll just have to get him here and catch him in the act."

"You're thinking paperwork with his name on it, or...?" Mina asked, her head cocked in confusion.

"If it's there when the cops raid the house, then sure. In the meantime, our plan of action starts way before that."

"We're all in agreement that we keep the cops out of this," Cal said, his gaze darting to Efren, who nodded once.

Selina stopped pacing. "At least until I've gone in with the wire and gotten some confessions."

"Are you kidding me?" Efren exclaimed. "I didn't keep you alive for the last week to have you walk to your execution!"

"First of all, you didn't keep me alive," she said, stalking over to him. "We kept each other alive. That's what partners do. The other thing partners do is support each other. You're the one who told me to stop being afraid of being afraid and harness the woman who used to use fear as motivation. That's what I'm doing, so you can either respect that and participate in the planning of this mission, or you can disrespect it, stand here and keep your trap shut, but you can't have it both ways."

Mina was nearly biting her tongue off to keep from laughing by the time Selina stalked away from him, but he wasn't amused. What was she thinking? She was going to get herself killed, and none of their fancy guns or tactical skills could stop that from happening.

"She could shoot you on sight," Cal said, playing the devil's advocate. "Then we've got nothing to take them down with, their business stays open, and we all become Vaccaro's targets."

"You don't know my twin, Cal," Selina said, facing him. "She's dying to have it out with me. Ava wants to spew all her hatred for me before she kills me. She won't shoot me on sight. Will I get out of there alive? Depends on how good your snipers are." She glared at him, and he stepped back. Selina wanted him to take out her sister right in front of her?

"This time, I'll make sure she's dead, make no mistake." His words were firm, and even Cal lifted his brow. Efren didn't care what they thought about him and Selina at this point. Let their tongues wag; he had more important things to do, like protect Selina.

"What about Vaccaro?" Roman asked, putting his arm around Mina's waist. "It's bad enough that Secure One is on his radar. We don't want to be his targets."

Selina leaned against the table and crossed her ankles. Efren knew she wasn't nearly as relaxed as she looked, but she wanted the team to focus on what she was saying and not how she was feeling. He noticed she was always good at that, especially when an injury was in immediate need of care and the patient resisted. "Ava isn't the only target on the table. Anyone in the house is fair game as far as I'm concerned, including Vaccaro."

Cal's brows went up. "Now you're talking about a lot of death hanging over my head. I'm not sure I'm superbly comfortable with that."

"Let's be real here," Selina said, eyeing each one of them. "You've all been special ops at one point in your life. You all understand that sometimes we have to do bad things for the betterment of society. I can live with their deaths if the Snake stops hurting people for money. If it means the Snake stops destroying families and traumatizing children. If it means the Snake stops selling drugs that are killing people and making millions doing it. We are not above the law, but we do have a responsibility to the country, even if they walk around in their lives completely clueless about the things we're faced with in this job. That's how I want it. I've taken that burden on myself in the past and been okay with it because it meant good, honest, innocent people could continue to help others in the light, untouched by the darkness we see."

You could hear a pin drop in the small space when she finished speaking. Efren's chest had swelled the longer she spoke, and he stepped forward, finally joining the rest of the group. "She's right. It kills me to put her in danger, but she's right. Our entire mission at Secure One is to keep people safe. You've done that for a countless number of people already. We can do it again, safely, so we all go home at the end of the day. No one knows this man like Selina does, so I say we follow her lead." His gaze caught hers, and she smiled then mouthed "thank you." It was killing him inside to put her in danger, but he had told her to take her power back and let her fear motivate her. He couldn't turn around and tell her she was doing it wrong now. All he could do was make sure she was protected from harm, the one way he was best at.

Cal took a step forward. "Sierra is the mission commander. I expect you to have assignments ready when we get to Caledonia."

"Already done," she said, standing up and moving beside Efren. "Everyone has a specific role in making this a happy ending, but I've played to your strengths."

"Mina does not leave home base," Roman said without room for argument. "She's desk duty now for oh, at least the next six months." He put a protective hand on her belly and kissed her cheek.

Selina squealed and ran to hug her as everyone started talking at once. As Efren shook Roman's hand and hugged

Mina, then pulled Selina into him, he was sure of one thing. He had found his home, and now it was time to protect it from evil.

Chapter Nineteen

The trip to Caledonia had been surprisingly uneventful, even if they had to hide in the back of a food truck headed for a Caledonia bar and restaurant. Selina would have ridden a horse if it meant they could end this decades-long feud between the Shannons and Vaccaro—at least the only Shannon who mattered. Ava may have sold her soul to the devil, but Selina would take a bullet before she did. Hopefully, the man sitting beside her would ensure that didn't happen.

Once there, they met up with Lucas and Mack, who had set them up in a small cabin just outside the Loraine property. They had set up a communications system to rival no other, only to learn they couldn't use it. Instead, they'd have to rely on flip phones to communicate. If one took too long to send a message… Selina hated to think about the consequences of that, so she shook it off. She had to keep her head in the game or she risked losing it to the Snake.

"I'm still not sure about the wire," Cal said as he leaned against a table in front of them. "You're the cop, so you know more than I do, but I didn't think you could submit a hidden wire as evidence."

"Depends on the state," Selina answered. "Minnesota allows it as long as one person in the conversation is aware of the wire." She pointed at herself. "In Illinois, laws are a bit tighter, but we aren't in Illinois. We're in Minnesota, and I'm technically still an officer of the law. That's why I'm wearing the wire and no one else."

"Run it down then," Cal said, motioning that she had the floor.

"The mission objective is to take Ava Shannon and Randall Sr. into custody after getting their confessions on tape to implicate them both in the counterfeiting operation."

"What about Vaccaro?" Roman asked from where he stood by Mina.

"Vaccaro doesn't come into play here," Selina said, facing him. "He won't return to Caledonia with the happily reunited couple."

"I'm aware, but the question was more geared at how do we stop him from coming after us?"

"We don't." Selina turned and leaned on the table to look them all in the eye. "Once we have Randall and Ava in custody, Vaccaro will cut all ties with them and anyone around them."

"I don't buy it." Roman shook his head with his lips in a thin line. "He's had thugs out searching for you for over a week now, and if this counterfeiting operation is as important as you say it is, he'll be looking for revenge that we shut it down."

Selina held her finger up as she stood. "We aren't shutting it down. We took two people into custody. We didn't burn down the house. He'll have that place cleaned out and the operation moved faster than we can book Ava and Randall into jail. At that point, he slithers back to Chicago never to be seen again." She glanced at all of them one at a time and could see they didn't believe her. "You're going to have to take my word on this, team. I've known Medardo my entire life. I've seen how cold, calculating and evil he is. One day you're his favorite person in the world and the next you no longer exist to him. Are there thugs hunting me right now? Yes, but not at Vaccaro's direction. Ava is behind all of this. I'm surprised Vaccaro bought in, but then again, I'm not. Ava can be—" she motioned around in the air for a bit as she searched for the right word "—convincing? Relentless? If Ava Shannon wants something, she gets it. Right now, she wants me dead."

"Well, she's not going to get that," Efren growled from the corner.

Selina shook her head. "No, she's not, but we can let her think she is. Imagine her face when I waltz through the front door and into the study while they drink to Randall's release."

"She could have a gun," Lucas pointed out. "Then what?"

"Then I put my hands in the air and start talking. I know her. She will not shoot until she's had a chance to spew all her hatred at me. I'm the root cause for everything that's wrong with her life." She added an eye roll to assure them it was sarcasm. "Besides, if she gets trigger-happy, we'll have people in place who have a faster trigger finger than she does."

"That makes it complicated." Cal's grimace was felt by all of them, including Selina.

"That makes it attempted murder on her part and self-defense on mine. Case closed."

Eric looked up from his notebook. "What happens if you don't get anything incriminating on the wire?"

"We take them into custody anyway," Selina said with a

shrug. "Then we call in the cops and let them tear the place apart to find the evidence they need to send them to prison."

"Where Vaccaro will get them out again?" Mina asked, a brow raised.

A sigh escaped Selina's lips. "Not likely. Again, Vaccaro has a line, and if we capture Ava and Randall, he will be done with them. They will pay for his crimes, which is always the way he likes it."

"Even if the cops come in and take the evidence before he gets there to get it?"

"I assure you, there will be no information in that house proving Vaccaro is involved in the scheme, just like last time. Randall went to prison, but Vaccaro was never even mentioned, even though we all knew he was behind it. The same thing will happen this time. The only way we could get Vaccaro for the counterfeiting is if Ava or Randall confirm it on tape. Even then, his lawyers will get him off."

"And if they both end up dead?" Lucas asked.

"Then we turn their cameras back on after I walk out the door and we walk away. Someone will find them and assume Vaccaro took care of his problem. Case closed."

"Except that the evilest one of the three is still walking around sucking air and ruining people's lives," Eric hissed. "I don't like that idea."

"You were a cop, Eric. You know that we can't get all the bad guys. All we can do is our best and let the law take care of the rest."

"We aren't cops, though," Efren said. "If I think for one second that woman is going to get trigger-happy, she's going down. Messy or not, she's going down. I don't like any of this."

"Neither do I," Cal agreed. "Like it or not, we're between

a rock and a hard place. We can't call the cops in since we have no proof of the operation being moved here. They can't get a warrant on 'we think this is what they're doing.'"

Selina shook her head. "There is no rock or hard place here, Cal. There is only one choice and we've made it. I will reprise my role of Eva Shannon long enough to take my twin and Randall down, and then Eva dies again."

"As long as Selina lives," Efren said between clenched teeth as all the heads around the table nodded.

She gave the final nod. "I apologize for putting you all in this position. If I could do it over, I would, but all we can do now is play the hand we were given."

"Don't apologize to us," Roman said with a shake of his head. "We've all done much worse things for the betterment of the world than what we're facing here tonight. My conscience is clear. It will be clearer if we can get Vaccaro, but two are better than none."

"With that decided, it's time for assignments." Cal pushed off the wall where he was standing and walked to the center. "You must memorize what Sierra tells you. I want no written evidence." Cal pointed at Selina's notebook. "Once the assignments are given, Mina will burn that."

"Ten-four," Selina said, spreading the notebook open on the table. "Let's walk through it."

As she handed out assignments and went over the plan of attack, Selina couldn't keep her gaze from drifting to the man who sat with his lips in a thin line and his arms crossed over his chest. He wasn't happy. Neither was she, but she understood one thing he didn't. If they ever wanted a chance to be together. To really have the chance to make a life together, then Ava had to die. Selina would squeeze the trigger without hesitation if she had to, and all she could do was pray he would do the same.

AVA SHANNON IS on the property.

Those words had sent a chill down Selina's spine when the scout team had reported in. They were surprised to find her look-alike sitting in the den sipping sangria when they did a sweep of the property. Like it or not, she had to act now, even if they all said it was too dangerous. If she could apprehend Ava, and then do a video testimony to send to the judge before the trial tomorrow, she could keep Randall in prison and send Ava there, too. Maybe she was being too idealistic, but she was using those ideals as her motivating factor. It was time to bring all of them some peace. If the only way to do that was to clash with her twin, then so be it.

Selina lifted her shirt, threaded the black leather belt through her pant loops, and buckled it in the front. There was a small recorder inside the buckle with an antenna running through the belt. It was voice activated, so it should easily pick up any conversation she had with her twin face-to-face. Since they wanted to avoid a digital signal, she couldn't wear a transmitter that would send a signal back and allow Mina to listen in. It would be all on her to get the audio they needed to put Ava behind bars with her husband. This was one time she was lucky that they had to go low-tech. The team didn't see the bigger picture, but she did, and the picture was ugly. It would be up to her to erase the past and start over.

Selina grabbed a secondary voice-activated recorder to ensure she got the recordings she needed. It was the length of a paperclip and slid into her pocket without leaving an outline on the material. She positioned her concealed holster at the back of her pants and tucked a small 9mm into it. She wasn't going in unprepared, and wasn't afraid to use the gun if push came to shove, and it just might. Her only goal was not to put that decision or action on any of her friends, especially Efren. "I killed for you" didn't feel like a winning basis for a healthy relationship.

Were they in a relationship, though? That was a question she couldn't answer without consulting Efren. She suspected any theoretical relationship they may have had would be destroyed when she left this cabin. It couldn't be helped. Selina was the only one who understood how volatile her twin was and how any plan wholly depended on Ava's choices, not theirs.

Knowing Ava was here meant the plan disappeared, and instinct kicked in. The Shannon twins were finally in the same place again, and in an hour, this would all be over. If they waited until after the trial and planned the mission down to the very last detail, it would be too late. Selina would text them she was going in right before she approached the front door. She felt bad that the team would have to scramble to get into place, but she'd tried to reason with them. Once again, they all disregarded her knowledge—despite the lack of their own—when it came to her family. She planned to buy them time by talking to Ava to get all the dirt she could on Vaccaro and Randall.

More than likely, Ava was at the house to destroy anything tying them to the counterfeiting operation. Once that was done, she would return to Chicago to join her husband before they disappeared for good. Selina couldn't risk it. Her past was her past, not the team's, and she would do whatever she had to do to protect them even if that meant dying. That was a real possibility, and even though Efren refused to address it, Selina was honest with herself at all times. These could be her last few minutes on this earth. She'd fight like hell to make sure that didn't happen, but if it did, she was taking Ava down with her.

The only thing she regretted was not kissing Efren before he left to scout out his sniper position, and not whispering three words in his ear after the kiss ended. She'd hold on to the emotions and those words, using it all as motivation to walk out of that house alive tonight. Efren may not want to hear it, but if she made it out, she'd tell him anyway. For the first time in her life, she'd be honest with a man about her feelings, even if he rejected her. And he might. She wouldn't blame him if he did, either. She was breaking his trust by going rogue, but what none of them understood was, she had no other choice. It was now or never if they wanted to apprehend Ava Shannon and put this to rest.

She slid her arms inside the sleeves of her Secure One jacket and zipped it to cover the holster and the belt. After slipping past the closed bathroom door, where Mina was cleaning up, she slid out the door of the cabin silently. This would be the shortest and longest walk of her life, but one way or the other, the game would be over tonight.

Chapter Twenty

Efren swung through the cabin door and immediately switched out his all-terrain sole on his blade for his spiked sole. He'd found the perfect spot that would allow him to cover Selina when she was inside the house. He was more than surprised when he looked through his scope, and Selina's face stared back at him. He had to remind himself that the woman inside that house was nothing like her sister. Selina had a soul and she wasn't afraid to do the right thing, even when the right thing was the hardest thing to do.

Temptation had called to him when he had Ava Shannon dead to rights under his rifle scope. He could have ended the whole thing right then and there, and the desire to squeeze that trigger and make it look like an assassination so they could all go home was almost overwhelming. Instead, he did the right thing and took his finger off the trigger. The satisfaction he'd get in taking out Ava Shannon would be short-lived when he screwed up the rest of the mission by not hearing what she had to say.

"Selina?" he called, walking to the back of the cabin where several beds sat in a row. This was obviously someone's hunting cabin, as it was well cared for but utilitarian.

There was a figure on one of the beds, but it wasn't Selina. "Mina? Are you okay?"

"Hey, yeah," she said, sitting up and rubbing her eyes. "I was just catching some sleep. I was sick earlier, and the long hours are taking a toll on me. We couldn't have picked a worse time to get pregnant."

Efren chuckled as he leaned against the door. "I didn't know you guys were trying."

"We weren't," she said, sliding her leg into her prosthesis. "It was, what do you say, a happy surprise? Heavy on the surprise in the beginning. Our work doesn't lend itself to having a family, so I'm glad Cal is starting the new cybersecurity division *and* hired Sadie. She's going to be a godsend in more ways than one."

Efren held his hand out to help her up. "It's a great idea, honestly. We have more requests for cybersecurity than we do physical security now. Cal is lucky to have you at the helm. You're the reason it will be a successful endeavor for Secure One."

Mina playfully leaned into him. "You are good for my ego, Efren Brenna. As soon as this mission is over, I'll start looking for others to join the team. We'll have to recruit, and how we live at Secure One will be a tough sell, but if I can build a solid core team, we can always expand if needed."

"You mean like satellite offices?"

"More like the way Elliot works security around the upper portion of Minnesota. We'd have people who live off Secure One property who can go into businesses and fix systems that have been hacked, then build new security in. Remote, but still doing Secure One business."

"So needed, too," Efren said as they walked back into the

main room. "Do you want me to flip through my Rolodex to see if anyone is looking for a change?"

"Yes, thank you! You have connections everywhere, so I know Cal would appreciate it as much as I do."

"No problem, I'll do it as soon as we get back to base." He paused and glanced around the empty room. "I thought Selina was staying with you and out of sight."

"I did, too. After I horked my guts out for fifteen minutes, I passed out on the bed. I thought she was out here."

Efren got a bad feeling in the pit of his stomach. "Did anyone report back what we found at the house when we did our recon?"

"You mean about Ava Shannon being on the property? Yeah, Cal, Mack and Roman checked in to let us know. They wanted us to arm ourselves but stay in the cabin. Selina argued with them for a while before they left again."

"What did they argue about?" A bad feeling filled the pit of his gut to overflowing.

"Honestly, I was sick, but I think it had something to do with them not listening to her?"

Efren cursed and ran for the back where they'd set up a makeshift equipment area. It didn't take but a second for him to see that her jacket and boots were missing. He jogged back to the front of the cabin. "What kind of wire is Selina wearing into the house?"

"We decided on the belt recorder. It's voice activated, so she doesn't have to worry about it not coming on when she needs it to." Mina pointed at the table but then cocked her head. "The belt is gone."

Efren cursed again. "She's going in alone tonight."

"You're jumping to conclusions, Efren," Mina said. "She's

probably just out getting some air and you missed her on the way in."

"She's out getting air after Cal told you to stay hidden? No, she's going to have it out with her sister before we have anything in place to protect her—"

He was interrupted by a sharp report that had him jumping in front of Mina. When he realized it was too far away, he grabbed his jacket and ran for the door. "Text Cal! Tell him Selina's inside that house."

Efren pumped his legs as fast and as hard as he could as he ran to where his rifle was hidden. That shot could mean it was too late, but he had to try. He wanted to plow through the house's front door, grab Selina and then shake her silly for going off alone, but he couldn't risk it. For all he knew, Selina was the one to do the shooting, so it was better to get in place and assess the situation than go off half-cocked, the same way she had.

He scrambled up the ladder against the small shed, then army-crawled toward where he'd left his gun. The entire time he prayed to anyone listening that when he looked through that scope, the twin he loved was still standing. He'd planned to tell her how he felt before the mission, but now he was glad he hadn't. This little stunt was proof that trust was easily broken and that losing someone you love can happen in the blink of an eye. He couldn't, wouldn't, get involved with someone he couldn't trust, and Selina had proved that here tonight. She was the mission manager. If she'd wanted to change the plan, she could have easily called everyone in and prepped them for the change, but she hadn't done that. Instead, she decided she would handle this herself, without so much as the courtesy of a heads-up, and that told him all he needed to know about Selina Colvert.

SELINA SLIPPED THE phone in her pocket after texting the team. Get in position. I'm going in. Six words that would shape her future from here on out. She'd either walk out alive or be rolled out dead, but either way, this nightmare would be over for the rest of the team.

After a deep breath in and out, she walked to the front door, assured by the team that there were no cameras they could see on the house's perimeter. She found that odd at first until she remembered they had to fit into small-town Caledonia, and you don't do that by making your house a fortress. Selina had no doubt there were cameras somewhere, so rather than ring the doorbell, she tried the knob, not surprised when the door swung open. Her twin was expecting her. Good. That meant she wanted to talk. If she knew Selina was here and wanted her dead, she would have done that already. No, Ava wanted to have a chat with her, so she'd welcome her to her home.

Selina strolled through the house leisurely, giving the team time to get in place after getting her text. Before long, she found her twin, a replica of herself, sitting on the couch in a small den.

"Well, well, if it isn't big sister," Ava said without standing. "So glad you could stop in. I'm sure you've been dying to know how I'm still breathing. Considering, you know, you shot me."

"You don't give me enough credit, Ava," Selina said, inching her way into the room, but standing to the side of the window, just in case Efren needed a clear shot. "It's not hard to put your return from the dead squarely on Uncle Medardo's shoulders."

Ava smiled, and it chilled Selina to the bone. They may share the same features, but Ava's twisted into evilness with every expression. "Good old Uncle Medardo. We aren't blood related, but he's been better family than my own. He's taken care of me and made sure I had a roof over my head all these years. That's more than I can say for you."

"Considering I thought you were dead, I'm unsure what you expected me to do."

"Funny how that turned out. I thought you were dead, too. For over seven years, I lived in bliss, knowing I had not only done the heavy lifting to get rid of our father, but you had fallen to your untimely death just days after mine. Maybe I should say timely, at least as far as I was concerned."

"You killed our father?"

"Of course. He had to go. Uncle Medardo was too loyal to him. Daddy needed to be out of the picture so I could take his place. Funny how that works. He sold me for the price of a debt, but in the end, he was the one who paid."

"The debt he incurred trying to make you happy!" Selina exclaimed, anger filling her as she listened to her deranged twin. "You're the problem, Ava."

"No, you're the problem, Eva. You keep turning up like a bad penny, which has to end. That's why about a year ago, I happened to be in Seattle on business for Uncle Medardo. Did you know your old friend Kai Tanner lives there now? Well, not in Seattle, some little town around there, but he wasn't hard to find."

"You saw Kai?" Selina asked with her hands in fists at her

side. She wanted to pull her sidearm and end this right now, but shooting an unarmed woman was murder.

"Such a lovesick fool," Eva said, brushing at her skirt. "He sure had a lot to say when he thought I was you, though. A chance meeting, a couple of spiked drinks and a roll in the hay gave me all the information I needed to know that my intuition was right. Your fall off the cliff was nothing more than a swan dive."

"Did Randall Jr. know you were alive?" Selina asked, forcing her mind away from Kai and concentrating on asking the right questions to get the answers they needed to put her away.

"Of course he did. Howie and I were running the operation here at the Caledonia house while he kept his father's other businesses going."

Selina finally understood why Randall had shot her in the tunnel. He knew his stepmother was still alive, so when he came face-to-face with someone who looked like her, but was working with the law, he knew it had to be her.

"How did you manage to keep the counterfeiting operation going when Randall was in prison? He was the brains behind the operation."

"Wrong," Ava said haughtily. "My husband is nothing more than a puppet who makes Medardo look good. Medardo wanted to get rid of Randall before he even made it to trial, but I talked him out of it. I showed him the operation here and that I was the mastermind behind its success, not Randall. Keeping Randall in jail took the pressure off me and let me continue with the business here, while keeping him somewhere safe for use at a later date, if need be."

"And suddenly, because I'm alive, now is the time to use

him?" Selina knew she was getting it all on tape, and wanted to keep her talking for as long as she could before she had to face down the inevitable gun her twin had somewhere in this room.

"More like a lucky coincidence. You see, the business here has run its course, and Medardo has a different assignment for us."

Selina smiled with satisfaction. If they'd followed the original plan and waited until after Randall was released from prison, they would have missed their opportunity to take them down.

"That's why you sent all the goons after me?" Selina asked, refusing to splint her side despite the pain. There wasn't a chance in hell she would give Ava the satisfaction of knowing she'd hurt her. "So I didn't screw up your new assignment?"

"I sent the goons after you based on nothing more than revenge," Ava spat, standing to get in Selina's face. She dug her finger into her chest. "You tried to put me in the grave, so tit for a tat, big sister." Ava's eyes were wild as she shook with vengeance. "You always thought you were so important, so righteous. The truth is, you're just like me, but you hide behind a badge to make your revenge heroic."

"I didn't realize you were so close to Uncle Medardo," Selina said, the words sticking in her throat. "What's it like letting that snake make love to you at night? The idea makes me sick," she hissed, the sound loud in the room.

Ava hauled off and slapped Selina across the face, but Selina didn't flinch. "Don't you talk about him that way! He loves me!"

The report of gunfire was so close to Selina's left ear that it sent her spiraling backward for several steps. She righted herself and dialed in on the scene in front of her. Ava was on the ground, blood bubbling out of her mouth as Vaccaro stood over her with a gun.

"You talk too much." That same voice from childhood drove a shiver down her spine. It had been so many years since she'd had the displeasure to be in his company that seeing him again was doing weird things to her equilibrium. "For the record, I never loved you, but you sure were easy to manipulate with those three little words, you poor misguided woman. Your daddy issues were your downfall, but I happily manipulated them to my advantage. Did you hear the news? Randall Jr. didn't make it out of the coma. He passed just an hour ago. So sad." He shook his head as though he had a heart. "I suppose the news will come out in the morning that his father died by suicide in prison when he learned the news. What a sad, sad family you all were."

Medardo swung the gun in Selina's direction. "Speaking of sad families, how lucky am I to get a twofer? In my opinion, it's more than time to make sure no more Shannons walk this earth. All the bickering in this family is exhausting—first, your father, then your sister. You were refreshing, Eva. You never kowtowed to your father, and you always did your own thing. I could respect you as an adversary, but my respect has limits. This whole mess has to go away." He motioned around the room with his gun while Selina slid her gaze to her twin. Blood pooled around her on the couch where she'd fallen. Blood no longer bubbled from her mouth, and her eyes were fixed on the ceiling in the stare of death. There was no doubt that this time, Ava Shannon was dead.

"Eva Shannon is already dead," she said, and Medardo

snapped the gun and his attention back to her. "As far as I'm concerned, we can come to an agreement."

"An agreement?" The question was filled with curiosity, so Selina shrugged as though none of it really mattered to her.

"We both walk away from here tonight and forget the other exists. I have a new life now that I'd like to continue to live, so I'm happy to strike a deal with the devil in order to do that."

Medardo laughed the laugh she remembered from their Sunday dinners when she was a child. "You always could make me laugh, little girl. Unfortunately, I won't be able to forget you exist. You're far too noble to pretend that I don't exist, either. No, the only way to make sure my interests are served is to dispatch the Shannon twins and be on my way. Especially since this place is about to go up in flames. It's a shame there's no fire hydrant way out here. When the house becomes an inferno, they'll have no choice but to let it burn itself out."

Medardo smiled the smile that reminded her of the snake he was. His gun lowered to her center mass, and she had to make a split decision. Try to run or go for her gun. Before she could do either, Medardo jerked backward with a shriek.

They both looked down at his arm to see half of it had been blown off, and the gun was nowhere to be found. Medardo grabbed his elbow as he fell to the couch next to her sister, blood pouring from the destroyed tissue.

"You shot me," he said, shock setting in. "I can't believe you shot me."

"I didn't shoot you," Selina said, a smile tugging her lips up. "You see, I have friends who don't take kindly to bullies who threaten other people. They shot you. I'm surprised it took them as long as it did, to be honest."

Selina pulled her gun from the holster and glanced around the room. "An inferno, you say?" She sniffed the air, and the scent of accelerant reached her nostrils. It was hard to distinguish it over the coppery smell of her sister's blood, but it was there, and she had to get out sooner rather than later. He probably had the system on a timer to ignite on his way out the door. "You know, they say in life, you get back what you put in." Selina aimed at his kneecap and pulled the trigger. Medardo yowled in pain, unsure what to grab with his only free hand.

"That was for stealing my innocence," Selina said, backing toward the door. She couldn't risk being in the house when it went up. She didn't want any of her team seeing the flames and running in to save her.

"You can't leave me here!" he screamed. "My bodyguards are just outside the door."

"Are they, though?" Selina asked with a smile. "I suspect they're taking a nap just like all the other guys you sent out to find me. When they wake up and discover the house on fire, do you think they'll come running to save you? I'm going to guess no. I can't think of a better place for you to die, Uncle Medardo," she said with enough venom to poison the man in front of her. "You see, I right injustices regardless of the consequences, and that is something I will continue to do while you rot in hell right next to my sister."

Selina smiled, turned and gingerly walked to the front door. One spark and this place was going up. She didn't want to be in it when it did. With a final smile, she tucked her gun in her holster, pulled the door open and slammed it behind her. She'd seen the spark, and as she ran for the woods, she heard the telltale whoosh of the accelerant igniting. It was then that she knew it was over.

Chapter Twenty-One

The team was back at Secure One and gathered in the conference room. Last night had been a blur, and Efren hadn't had a second to breathe since they'd pulled in, all in separate vehicles. They didn't have time to talk, much less argue, about anything that had happened if they wanted to be out of the area before the fire engines arrived. They'd emptied the cabin and been on the road in under fifteen minutes, which was when they passed the fire engines heading to the inferno on the outskirts of Caledonia. All of them had watched that house go up and knew there would be nothing to save by the time they got there. Not the house and not the people inside it.

"Well, that was not our finest hour," Cal said to open the meeting. All heads turned to Selina, who sat at the end of the table in silence.

"I accept full responsibility for that." She stood and pulled off her belt and tossed a small device on the table.

"What's that?" Cal asked, pulling it toward him.

"Proof, should we ever need it."

"Unless his bodyguards wake up and decide to tell the police all about their involvement with a Mafia kingpin, I doubt that will be necessary, but I'll log it in."

"No, you're going to listen to it. Now." She pointed at the computer Mina had in front of her, and Mina hooked up the small device and did some fiddling. When she was done, she glanced at Cal, who nodded. Mina clicked the mouse and the room filled with Ava's voice. They listened in silence to the information unfolding.

Efren couldn't help but notice the expressions on their faces as they took in and processed the information. He also noticed how Selina subconsciously grimaced when the first shot rang out and then how she flinched when Medardo howled. Efren had hit his target dead-on. He could have killed the man, but that wasn't his goal. He wanted to get rid of the weapon and give Selina the upper hand to get out of the situation herself. In the end, it hadn't mattered, since Vaccaro was now dust.

When the recording ended, Cal glanced up at Selina. "What were you thinking?"

Efren noticed Selina's jaw tic once, and she blinked several times before she spoke. "We're supposed to be a team, but not one of you listened to me. You heard her," she said, pointing at the computer. "She was leaving Caledonia and never coming back. Had we waited until after the hearing, they would have disappeared. As soon as you said she was in the house, I knew. She was waiting for me. That entire game, her showing up at the hospital and pushing us farther and farther south, was on purpose. She wanted me to die tonight, and her ego was too big to consider it would be her who died."

"You both could have died!" Cal exclaimed. "I can't even wrap my mind around what happened. Not only did you break rank and go rogue, but you put yourself and this entire business at risk! If anyone figures out that we were there tonight,

I'm done. Do you understand me? This business is over. We have protocols and plans for a reason!"

"You're right," she said, standing and walking to the front of the room. "This is my fault, and I take responsibility for it. If I wasn't willing to, I wouldn't have done it. You will have no legal trouble from what happened tonight. There is nothing left, and if they figure out Medardo died in that fire, you won't see the FBI crying about it. As you heard, Randall and Randall are no more, so this case is closed." She lifted her lanyard from her neck and set it on the table in front of Cal. "I hereby resign my position as chief medical officer at Secure One. I committed too many inexcusable offenses tonight to be trusted as an operative again. I will clean out the lab of my personal belongings and head out in the morning. Thank you for everything. I mean that," she whispered as she wrapped her arms around the man in front of her.

Cal hugged her awkwardly, his gaze holding Efren's in a look of terror and desperation. Efren wondered if he wore the same look. Was he angry at Selina for what she had done? Yes. Did she put them in a tough position? Yes. Did he want her to leave Secure One? His head said yes, she was a liability they couldn't keep around, but his heart said he'd follow her wherever she went and that was his internal battle now.

Selina ended the hug and turned to the team. The tears on her face had clearly surprised everyone as they glanced at one another around the table. "I owe all of you my life, and that is something I can never repay. The only thing I can do is say thank you for everything and for understanding that all of this—" she motioned at the devices on the table as she wiped a tear away "—started long before I ever had a say in how any of it would end. For the record, it ended the best possible way, and that's because all of you took it on your shoulders to do the right thing by doing the wrong thing. I'll never again lose sleep knowing that Vaccaro is still hurting people and I could do nothing to stop it. We stopped it. We did the wrong thing for the right reasons. That's enough for me."

"That's enough for me, too," Lucas said, standing and saluting.

"It's enough for me, too," Roman said, following Lucas.

"It's enough for me, too," Eric and Mack said, standing and saluting.

"I won't lose any sleep tonight," Mina said, standing and giving Selina a smile.

Efren stood slowly, pushing the chair back with his knee and meeting Selina's gaze right before he walked out of the room.

SELINA BLEW OUT a breath as the man she'd fallen in love with walked out on her. She expected him to be upset, but she also expected him to act like an adult. She was right about only one, apparently.

"Give him time," Cal said, resting his hand on her shoulder. "He's stared fear in the face a lot over the last week, and came to the realization too many times that he might lose you. Quite a few of us in this room have gone through it. Right?" She glanced up to nodding heads. "Give him some time, and he'll come around. Now, about your job."

"I'll head to the med bay and clean out my things." Her heart was heavy now that she was faced with the realization that this team would no longer be her team. "If you don't mind, I'll need to take care of my wounds, too." She lifted her shirt to show him her abdomen, but it was Mina who gasped.

"How are you even upright?" she asked, coming around the table to look at her ribs. "You need a hospital."

"Nothing's broken." Selina lowered her shirt. "I'll tape up my ribs and fix my incision before I head out."

"You're not going anywhere." Cal handed her the Secure One badge back. "You may have pulled rank tonight, but in hindsight, you did what had to be done. We, as a team, failed to listen to you about a lot of things when it came to Vaccaro, and that's on us, not you. When the going got tough, you walked in and took care of business. Do I like having an operative on the team who does her own thing, whether it's right or wrong? No. We will have to talk about that, but I do like having an operative on my team who is quick on their feet, competent and perceptive. You're all of those things, which is what made you a good cop back in the day. I think it's time we move you onto the team as the valuable op that you are, as I know you've been unhappy in your position for some time now."

"You want me to stay?" She lowered herself to the table in surprise. "As an operative?"

"Yes, but we can talk about it later when we're all rested. Promise me you won't go anywhere until we've talked, and you've talked to Efren. He deserves that much if nothing else."

He deserved so much more, but suddenly, Selina wasn't so sure she was the woman to give it to him anymore. She understood how he felt, and couldn't pretend that she didn't. She'd betrayed him by going after her twin by herself. It was a chance she had to take for the betterment of the entire world, but whether he believed that or not was up to him.

Cal dismissed everyone with instructions to get some sleep

and meet up in the morning for a debriefing once the news reports about the Caledonia house, and the two Randalls, started to generate.

"Mina, could I ask a favor?" Selina asked before the woman could walk out of the room. She didn't know how to ask her this question without looking like she didn't care about the man who didn't think she'd done the right thing.

Mina smiled and pulled a piece of paper from her pocket. She handed it to Selina without a word and disappeared with a wink.

Selina looked down at the paper and all it said was, *Kai Tanner, Cliff, Washington. 425-555-4577.*

BEFORE SHE LOST her nerve, she knocked on Efren's door and waited. Selina had followed Cal's advice and given him an hour before she followed him, but she wondered if even that was enough. What happened in the next ten minutes would direct Selina's life going forward. If she and Efren couldn't come to an understanding, she would leave Secure One, despite Cal insisting otherwise. While she had screwed up the mission, she had also done the right thing, and that was something none of them could argue with.

The door cracked open, and Efren looked out. "Not into talking tonight, Selina."

She stuck her hand in the door before he could close it. "How about listening, then?"

Selina heard his heavy sigh, but he opened the door the rest of the way and let her into the room. "I'm sorry." Those were the first words out of her mouth, and he lowered his brow.

"Are you, though? It doesn't seem like you were too

sorry when you were defending your actions in the conference room."

"I'm sorry for breaking the planned mission," she clarified. "And I'm sorry you were put in the position to shoot Medardo. I'm not sorry that they're dead."

Efren tipped his head to the side in agreement. "I don't have a problem that they're dead either. I took out his hand to give you a chance to do the rest. I do have a problem with my trust being broken."

"I know." She stared at her shoes for a moment before she glanced up into his deeply troubled eyes. "When I made the decision to do it, there was no question in my mind you'd feel betrayed. The problem was, no matter what angle I argued from, no one was listening to me."

"Including me," he admitted with a sigh.

"I spent a long time with the team after you left, helping them understand that what I did put my life in danger, but I did that so that they'd remain safe. If Ava had disappeared, I shudder to think how long it would have been before she turned up again, but I do know we'd all be looking over our shoulder. I want you to understand that is the reason I chose to betray your trust and risk my life. Better my life than any of yours, considering this was my fight. Did I play into Ava's game? Yes. I bit hook, line and sinker into it, but there was no other choice. I just hope you all see there was no other choice." Her voice was barely above a whisper by the time she finished her impassioned plea. Her hands fell to her sides, and she lowered her head. "You risked your life to keep me safe this last week, and for that, I'm eternally grateful, Efren. I'm sure when you got that text that I was going in, you felt as though it had all been for naught, but it wasn't, I promise.

I will continue to do good things to help other people because that is who I am."

"Wait. Text? You sent a text?"

"Of course I did. I sent it right before I went in to tell you to get into position. How else would you know I was going in?"

Efren gripped her forearms gently and held her gaze. "I didn't get a text message. I was in the cabin with Mina and heard the first shot. I ran like a man possessed to where I'd left the rifle and looked through the scope to see Vaccaro holding the gun on you. You don't know how badly I wanted to end him."

"Why didn't you?"

"You needed to take your power back. You needed to be the one who made the decision you could live with. Doing anything else was being a hero you didn't need. That's why."

"I love you, Efren," Selina said the words in a rush of breath and tears. Her lips trembled as she tried to form words, but she hiccuped and had to start over. "You were the only thing on my mind the entire time I was in that house. How mad you were going to be at me and how I was going to lose you, but how I had to protect you. I had to protect you from those people so you could continue to help others. My decisions tonight meant I would lose you, but I couldn't leave Vaccaro on your doorstep for the rest of your life. That would have been wrong and the exact opposite of what it means to love someone."

Efren ran his hand through his hair as he stared at her. "You went into the house for me?" Her nod was shaky as she sucked up air, but she didn't speak, just lowered herself to the bed and tried not to sob.

He didn't say anything, just paced back and forth in front

of her with his hands in his hair until finally, he joined her on the bed and tipped her chin toward him. "Do you know how I know that I love you?" Her eyes widened, but she didn't answer. "I let you see my leg. I made love to you without my prosthesis. I let you see me. The other night in the cabin was the first time I let anyone see me in twelve years. That's when I knew that I loved you."

"You love me, too?" Her voice was shaky, but she noted a little hope in the words.

"Probably since the first day you made a snide remark about my ability to guard someone. Do I love what you did tonight? No. Can I respect it for what it was? Yes. Do I ever want you to do something that stupid ever again? No. No. Never. Do you understand me?"

He had grasped her upper arms and held her so close she could feel his warm breath on her cheek. "Never again," she whispered.

"Did you really quit?" he asked, his gaze holding hers as their noses touched.

"I tried, but Cal wouldn't let me. He said we're going to talk about it tomorrow, but as long as I don't go rogue again, I earned my spot as an operative. I may take it, I may not. I'll talk to him first and then decide. That is, if you are willing to continue to work with me despite what happened between us."

"Despite what happened between us? Do you mean making love to you? Kissing you? Loving you?" She nodded against his forehead, and he smiled. "I'll only continue to work with you as long as we can still do those things, Selina. Do you think we can still have a relationship with all the baggage we carry?"

She gazed into his clear, open, accepting eyes. "I'll carry yours if you'll carry mine."

"That sounds like a mission we can work together on."

"Are you okay with knowing I can't have your child?"

"You're all I'll ever need in this life. Our lifestyle doesn't lend itself to little ones, and I'm okay with that if you are. I love you, Selina." He lowered his lips to hers.

"Not as much as I love you, Efren Brenna," she said against his lips right before he captured them for the first kiss of the rest of their lives.

Epilogue

Selina flipped through the news stories about the death of "known Mafia kingpin Medardo Vaccaro." It had taken authorities almost a week to identify the bodies in the house. The fact that it took so long told her that Vaccaro's bodyguards had indeed dipped rather than try to rescue their boss. Conspiracy theories were already rampant less then twelve hours since it was determined that the body found in the charred home in Caledonia was Vaccaro. The second body found next to him had been identified as Ava Shannon, a woman the world thought was already dead. While Selina's bullet eight years ago hadn't killed her twin, it had done enough damage to her heart that she required a pacemaker and defibrillator to keep ticking. Those devices were registered to the patient, and that was how they determined which Shannon twin had been found dead...again. As far as Selina was concerned, Eva Shannon was dead and she was happy to let it remain that way.

True to his word, Vaccaro had taken out both Randalls as well. To think Randall Sr. was so overcome with grief about his son that he hung himself with his bedsheets in his cell just hours from being released. The first thing Secure One had done was make sure that the only living Loraine son, Victor, was still alive and well in Bemidji, where he was recovering from being kidnapped by his brother just a few weeks ago while trying to save his fiancée. They were fine and rejoicing that Vaccaro, his father and his brother were dead. Now he could live an everyday life with Kadie and his son without leaving Bemidji. Since the Loraine home was now empty, they'd sell it and use the money to start their life together. Selina had never been happier to hear that something good would come from this debacle. Sadie, Kadie's sister and aunt to Houston, was even more thrilled. She worked at Secure One now as the chef, but if her sister and nephew remained in Bemidji, she could maintain her relationship with them easily, which was important to her.

There had been multiple times over the last week when she had to stop and ask herself if she had done the right thing. Each time, she got another sign that she had, so she decided to bury it in the box where she kept all the memories of her life as Eva Shannon. All but one part, that is. There was a thread dangling that would have to be tied up, but she had yet to find the courage to dial the number Mina had given her.

Cal had come to her a few days ago to talk about her job. He began by apologizing for treating her as an afterthought when the business took an unexpected turn. He admitted he should have asked her if she was comfortable caring for the women who had found their way to Secure One for safety, and not assumed she was a robot who could continue to care for them without help or someone to talk to about what she was going through as their caregiver. Selina had taken some of that responsibility on her shoulders, as she could have spoken up and told Cal of the toll it was taking.

In the end, he offered her a full-time operative position, which, after much thought, she'd turned down. After the last case, she realized she was far more valuable to the team as a floater. She would remain the chief medical officer at the compound, ensuring the men were healthy and eating correctly by working with Sadie. When they went on cases, she would also go, using the mobile command as her home base where she would be their medic or jump in as an operative if the occasion called for it. She would also be the medical informant for the new cybersecurity division. She'd help out when something came up with a medical clinic or hospital that the team needed help translating. It was a lot of hats to wear, but that had been her life for as long as she could remember, and she wouldn't want it any other way.

"Selina?" She turned and made eye contact with the man who had been there to hold her up through each new revelation over the last few days. Efren had spent some time in the med bay with her. His limb had been damaged more than she was happy with, but he assured her he had hurt it worse in the past. He came in for treatment of the skin twice a day and was unfortunately using his fancy wheelchair rather than his prosthesis at the advice of his medical team. He took it unexpectedly well when she told him he had to stay off it if he expected the damaged skin to heal, which told her that it was bothering him far more than he was letting on.

"Hi," she said, walking to the door. She bent down and kissed his lips in a work-appropriate buss. "Did you need something? How's the limb?"

"My leg is fine, but Cal sent me down to get you. He needs you in the comms room. I'm here to give you a ride."

Her laughter filled the hallway after she locked the med bay door. "I can walk, but thanks."

Efren grabbed her hand and pulled her down onto his lap. "I know you can walk, but if you walk, I don't get the pleasure of having you on my lap." They wheeled down to the comms room where she kissed him and then hopped off his lap, walking into the room.

"Cal?" she asked, but the room was empty. She turned back to the hallway. "I thought Cal wanted me."

"He did, but he also wanted you to have some privacy, so he sent me to get you. Sit." He motioned at the chair in front of a bank of computer screens.

She took the chair and he rolled over, hitting a button and waiting until the screen illuminated. Selina's gasp was loud when the face staring back at her was the only happy part of her past.

"Kai!" she exclaimed, leaning in closer to the screen.

"Eva," the man said, his voice awed for a moment until he held up his hand. "Sorry, Selina. I'm just so stunned to see you again."

"Same," she said with a smile. "I never checked your blog, I'm ashamed to say. I was too afraid to want a life I couldn't have. I was afraid I'd do something not to the benefit of my health. Yesterday, I spent the day going through your posts from the first ones to the last. Thank you for being so good to Zeus."

"He was my buddy," Kai said with a smile. "From the day you handed him to me, he never left my side. It was like he knew I was his only connection to you and he was my final connection to you. Until the day he died he made me walk him with the leash you left him with that day."

Selina had her hand to her heart with a smile on her face and tears in her eyes. "I never doubted that you would care for him better than I could in my situation. You did such great things as a team. I'm so proud of your accomplishments. Look at you running your own team. I always knew you could and would do it one day. That's why I left. Had I stayed, I would have held you back and put you at risk."

"I can see that now," he agreed.

"Listen, about the elephant in the room," she said, glancing at Efren, who slipped his hand in hers.

"It wasn't you," he said before she could. "She approached me in a dark bar, and I'm embarrassed to say I fell for it in the beginning."

"Don't be embarrassed," she interrupted. "My twin was manipulative and calculating. You didn't stand a chance."

"Still, part of me knew. All of me knew when she barely touched my dog's head, much less loved him up the way you would have. By then it was too late. She'd drugged my last drink with ketamine."

"So she got her answers, but you don't remember a thing."

"Nothing other than bringing her home and then waking up naked and alone, with this feeling of being gutted all over again."

"Kai, I can't begin to tell you how sorry I am. When I left, I thought she was dead. I didn't know she was alive until a week ago."

"That much I figured. Part of me knew that you would have somehow let me know she was alive if you knew. It wouldn't be hard for her to find your old relationships and leverage them, especially since I took Zeus. I was more than a little surprised when someone named Cal reached out yesterday."

"I wasn't aware he had." Selina rubbed her hand on her leg nervously. "I was going to, I wanted to apologize for Ava. I just had to build up the courage I'd need to see you again."

"You always were my one who got away, but I hear you've found the one you're meant to be with."

"This is Efren Brenna. He's the only reason I'm sitting here talking to you. The last few weeks have been tumultuous."

"From what I heard, you did some search-and-rescue of your own kind. At least that's what I understood from reading between the lines. Let me offer my congratulations on that search. It was more than time. I'm proud of you for staying in the light and fighting the darkness with integrity."

"I don't know about all that, but I'm glad their reign has come to an end."

"He's right," Efren said, kissing the fingers of the hand he held. It felt to Selina a bit like a power play for Kai, but she'd allow it considering what they'd been through. "Your integrity in the face of bad odds is the reason the country is a much safer place."

Selina smiled at him for a moment before she focused on the screen again. "Gosh, it's just so good to see you. I want to hear about the Cliff Badgers and how you started the team!"

"Let's just say you weren't the only one looking for a fresh start. This was mine. I won't bore you with the details, but let me say this, friend. If you two are ever looking for a new line of work, you've always got a place on my team."

Selina lifted a brow at Efren, who lifted one right back.

* * * * *

COLTON UNDERCOVER

JENNIFER D. BOKAL

To my forever love, John.

Chapter One

Special Agent Liam Hill, FBI, sat at his desk in a cubicle. His workspace was located in the middle of a group of similar cubicles. The large, windowless room located in the FBI's headquarters was affectionately referred to as the Rat Maze. The Hoover Building itself was named for the organization's longest-serving director, J. Edgar Hoover. Squat, plain, yet imposing, it was reminiscent of its namesake.

His cubicle mate, Constance Hernandez, sat at a desk across from his own. For the past two weeks, Liam and Constance had been tracking down documents associated with a church outside Owl Creek, Idaho. So far, they hadn't found enough information to bring charges. They'd received a report that the pastor was coercing his followers into giving him their life savings.

"I don't like this as a federal violation," said Constance. "It's not against the law to give away cash. If people want to give all their money to this church, so be it."

"But what if they feel as if they don't have any choice?"

He paused. "Besides, he advertises online. Communicates with potential followers through the internet. That could be wire fraud."

"Weak sauce," said his colleague.

He knew her opinion already. Still, Liam was determined to conduct a full investigation. It was more than his job. It was his duty. "You know, they put Al Capone in jail for tax fraud."

Every FBI agent knew about the mob boss from the 1920s. The agency that put him in jail was a grandfather of what would become the modern-day Bureau. "In case you forgot," said Constance, "we don't investigate tax crimes. That's the IRS."

"All I'm saying is that Capone committed much worse crimes than tax evasion. But that's what got him locked up. And jail is jail."

Constance pursed her lips. He couldn't tell if she was considering what he said or thinking up a new argument.

"Hill. Hernandez." The two names were fired, like bullets. Liam looked up to find his supervisor leaning on the cubicle wall. Wayne Parsons, a Black man from Detroit, fit his name. He was the son and grandson of preachers. What's more, he'd inherited a clear and deep baritone voice that was perfect for the pulpit. "Tell me everything you know about the Ever After Church. Start with how you came across the information."

It was Liam who'd gotten the lead two weeks earlier. He said, "My mom's former receptionist, Helena, joined the church after a nasty divorce. She eventually moved to their compound in the mountains. Since she had secretarial skills, she was put to work in the church's administration building. Once she realized that the church's leader, a guy named Markus Acker, kept most of the money being raised for personal expenses, she became disillusioned and left. She reached out to me because she remembered I was with the FBI. According to Helena, Markus has his financial records on a separate computer that is never connected to the internet."

"That's odd," said Wayne.

Constance picked up the story. "I've been piecing together Acker's background. He's a shady dude, even if he's never been charged with anything. Been pastor at several failed churches over the years."

"Collect all your information," said Wayne. "Kate Dubois wants a briefing."

Assistant to the Director, or A-DIC, Kate Dubois oversaw all units that investigated financial crimes for the FBI. Constance lifted her brows. Giving a briefing to the A-DIC was a big deal. She asked, "When does Dubois want to hear from us?"

"She wants a presentation now," said Wayne. "But I convinced her to give you ten minutes."

"Are you kidding?" There was no way he could put together a coherent presentation in such a short amount of time.

"No joke. Get to work." Wayne took two steps, stopped, and turned around. "Just so you both know, I put in my retirement papers yesterday. On May first, I'll be a free man. The career board is meeting in the next few weeks to pick my replacement. The two of you are at the top of the list. Do a good job on this briefing and you might just end up with a promotion."

For years, Liam had worked with Constance. She was a smart agent, and the closest thing to a friend he had in Washington, DC. It was a shame that she was now his rival. For too long, he'd been stuck in the warren of cubicles. He wanted the promotion and intended to get it.

"Whoever the career board picks," he said, "no hard feelings."

Constance sighed. "Get to work, Liam. We only have nine minutes left."

LIAM STOOD IN front of a screen. A large conference table with room for eighteen took up most of the floor space. Chairs on casters surrounded the table. Only seven seats were filled. Aside from Liam, Constance and Wayne, the A-DIC sat at the foot of the table with her entourage of two special agents and a financial analyst.

Everyone in the room was an employee of the FBI. It was true that the Bureau didn't assign uniforms, like in the military. But there was an unspoken dress code for those who worked at the Hoover Building. Everyone wore a dark suit. All the men were also in a white button-down shirt and a necktie. The women had all donned blouses along with understated jewelry.

Liam held a tablet computer that controlled his part of the briefing. He pointed to the enlarged image of a tax document that filled the monitor. "This is the last return filed with the IRS by the Ever After Church. As you can see, they claim only modest income. According to our sources, the church has taken in well over a million dollars this year alone through member donations." In his opinion, the donations were coerced from those people.

"Upstairs, you mentioned something about the church's

leader having a computer that never goes online," said Wayne. "Tell us more."

"The CI thinks that Markus enters all his correct financial information into that device." It felt odd to refer to Helena, a lady who used to make him cookies, as a confidential informant. But this was work—nothing personal. "Acker is the only person with access to the device."

"So, the only way to see the information is to physically have the computer?" asked Wayne.

"That," said Liam, "or copy the hard drive."

"How would we do that?" asked Constance.

"Someone has to infiltrate the church," he said.

"But that will take months—maybe even years." Constance continued, "Does the Bureau have the resources to spare on such a small case?"

True, most financial crimes the FBI investigated were worth several million dollars or more. But other things were also true. "First, we don't know how much Markus Acker has taken from his followers." The amount could be astronomical—but he'd serve nobody by speculating. "Also, he's doing more than depleting bank accounts. He's ruining lives."

"This case merits our attention. Markus Acker is suspected of laundering money for some nefarious organizations. The church is also connected to several deaths," said Kate Dubois, the first words she'd spoken since the meeting began. She continued, "I'd like to hear how you plan to get an agent into the church."

In that moment, he knew what he needed to do to get out of the Rat Maze. And how he'd get the promotion. "I wouldn't just send any agent," he began. "I'll go undercover."

"You?" Constance's tone was filled with concern. "You

haven't been in the field, well, ever. How're you going to handle an undercover operation?"

The thing was, she wasn't wrong. Liam had passed his CPA exam after his first try—an unheard-of feat. He'd then applied to the Bureau and been hired at the age of twenty-four. In the last seven years, he'd been assigned to the financial crimes unit. While he'd worked a variety of cases, he spent most of his time in the Hoover Building. It left a gap in his résumé that would be filled by being the undercover agent on the case.

"But why are you the one to go undercover?" asked Wayne.

"For one," he said, "I'm from Idaho. I grew up in Boise. It's close to Owl Creek. So, I'll know how to talk to the locals."

The A-DIC said, "I don't like it. You might run into someone from your past. Or someone who still knows your family."

This was his moment. If he could convince the A-DIC to let him go to Owl Creek, the next move in his career would be assured. Inhaling, he began, "My parents moved to Arizona five years ago. I have one sister, Allison, who's stationed on an airbase in Okinawa. She left seven years back when she got into the Air Force Academy."

For a full minute, Dubois said nothing. Then, she slowly shook her head and his stomach dropped. "It's still too close. We can't give you an alias if it could be easily blown." Then, with the next breath, she looked at Constance. "You have information on Markus Acker?"

Constance sat up taller. "Yes, ma'am." Her presentation was already loaded into the smartboard and was controlled by her own laptop. She typed a few keystrokes and Markus's face filled the screen with a professional headshot.

One couldn't tell by the photo, but Liam knew that the other man was tall and still fit. He wore his dark blond hair short, and by the looks of it, cut by an expensive stylist. In the photo, he wore a black suit, white shirt and yellow tie.

"Markus is fifty-five years old," Constance began. "He has degrees in both communication and finance."

He knew all the information already and was hardly listening. How had he blown his chance to work undercover? Then again, he should be asking a different question. How could he get the A-DIC to change her mind?

The first photo was replaced by another. "I pulled this recent picture off the church's website. The woman in the picture has been identified as Markus's fiancée. Jessie Colton."

His gaze snapped to the screen. He recognized the woman at once. "Damn," he said without much thought. "She hasn't changed at all."

"You know Ms. Colton?" Constance asked.

How many years had it been since he'd spoken to anyone in the Colton family? The last time would've been the summer that Allison graduated from high school, and he entered the FBI Academy. "I used to know her, at least. She's the mom of my kid sister's best friend. My dad used to joke that if Sarah came over for one more sleepover, he'd be able to write her off on the taxes." Sure, it was lame dad humor but there'd also been a nugget of truth to the jest. Sarah was constantly at his house.

"To be honest, I'm surprised that you didn't know the subject was dating the mother of a former friend," said the A-DIC.

A sick feeling dropped into his stomach, like he'd just stepped into something unpleasant. "Like I said, after my parents left Boise, we really haven't kept in touch with anyone from Idaho."

"That's not what I meant, Special Agent Hill. You've been building a case on Markus Acker and the Ever After Church, have you not? You should know about his personal life," she snapped.

There was only one thing for him to say. "You're right, ma'am."

"If I may," said Constance. "Liam and I divided the work duties. Since he's been working so closely with the financials, I did a background investigation on Acker. To be honest, this is the first time we're sharing information."

"I expect my teams to work as a cohesive unit. But I understand that this investigation is moving quickly. From now one, consult with one another. We're the FBI, not the Keystone Cops for chrissake." Leaning forward, Dubois rested her elbows on the tabletop. "The fact that you know Jessie Colton is interesting."

"I wouldn't say that I know her," he said carefully. Correcting a superior was the same as swimming in dangerous waters. "But as a teenager, I knew her daughter well. Hell, she used to go on vacation with us."

"Why is that?" asked Wayne. "What was the Colton home like?"

To be honest, Liam hadn't thought about Sarah since he left Idaho. But now that she was top of mind, it was amazing how much he could remember. She'd been a sweet kid who liked to read. In fact, her taste in books was well beyond her years. He recalled a specific weekend that he'd come home from college. Sitting at the kitchen table, he read *War and Peace* while eating breakfast. Sarah wandered into the kitchen and pointed to the book in his hand. *Tolstoy, huh? I liked* Anna Karenina *better.* They'd spent the next hour talking about literature.

The squeaking of casters brought him back to the conference room. He'd been quiet for too long. He could feel Wayne's question hanging in the air. *What was the Colton home like?*

He let out a long breath. "Sarah's home life was crap. Her parents weren't abusive, or anything like that. But her mother and father split up when she was in elementary school. Dad was only around sometimes. Mom always had a flair for the dramatic. Her brother was a good guy—older than her, younger than me."

"Do you think she'd remember you?" A-DIC Dubois asked.

"I'd hope so," he said, offended that anyone suggest Sarah forgot about him. "I was the one who taught her how to drive."

Dubois leaned back in her seat. The image of Jessie Colton still filled the screen. "Special Agent Hill, you're certain that your family hasn't kept in touch with the crowd from Boise?"

He wasn't sure if it were a question or a comment. Still, there was only one thing he could say. "That's correct."

"What about your sister?" she asked.

When the family gathered for Christmas last year, Liam and Allison had sat outside in the balmy Tucson evening. Lamenting the heat, she'd complained, *"I miss Idaho. It's not Christmas without a little snow."*

"You're on leave," he'd said. *"You could take a week and visit old friends."*

Shaking her head, Allison had said, *"I lost touch with everyone when I graduated. The Air Force Academy doesn't leave much time for socialization—especially for people who live hundreds of miles away."*

"Even Sarah?" he'd asked, incredulous.

"Even Sarah," she'd echoed. *"I think we're social media friends. But I never use those apps so I'm not even sure."*

Liam's memory came and went in the span of a heartbeat. He didn't hesitate to answer the A-DIC's question this time. "Allison hasn't had any contact with the Coltons, either."

"So, neither Sarah Colton nor her mother know that you're in the FBI." Again, not quite a question, not quite a statement.

"Well, that's not entirely accurate," he said, measuring his words. "Sarah and my sister had just graduated from high school right before I headed off to Quantico for training. I assume she remembers that I was going to the academy." Liam becoming an FBI agent had been a big deal for the family. His parents had thrown a going-away party. Of course, Sarah had attended.

"But she doesn't know what you're doing now."

He knew what Dubois was thinking. His pulse began to race with excitement and apprehension both. "We haven't been in touch personally since that summer, so I doubt she knows any more about me than I know about her." Which was absolutely nothing.

"Do we have any intel on Jessie Colton's children?" Dubois directed her gaze at Constance.

"Um, no, ma'am." Her shoulders were shrugged in tight, probably preparing for another brutal comment.

Using his tablet computer, Liam accessed his sister's little-used social media accounts. From there, he found the friends list. Sarah Colton was among those with whom Allison had connected. He followed the link to Sarah's profile. The lanky kid with braces had been replaced by a statuesque woman. "Sarah still lives in Boise," he said, reading the details listed on her profile. "She graduated from Boise State with a master's degree in library sciences. She works at the downtown library. Never married. No kids. No current romantic partner. But she does have a cat named Tolstoy."

"Where'd you get all that information?" Wayne asked.

"My sister's social media profile," said Liam.

"I thought you said your sister and Sarah weren't friends anymore," said Wayne.

Liam exited Sarah's profile and opened his sister's. He checked for the latest post. "Allison hasn't accessed the account for three years but it's still online."

Dubois picked up a pen and tapped the end on the table. There was no other sound in the room and Liam's heart began to beat with the tempo. "You've got your wish, Special Agent Hill. I'm sending you to Idaho, but you won't be undercover per se. You'll go to Boise and contact Sarah Colton. From there, I want you to rekindle your friendship. If she trusts you, her mother might, too. These two women are the shortest path to Acker, I can feel it."

Liam was getting exactly what he wanted. Why was his gut twisted into knots of unease? "Sarah knows that I'm with the Bureau. Even if she's not suspicious, her mother and Acker will be."

"Leave that to us," said the A-DIC. "We'll change your life, online at least. You'll be given a new background." She paused, seeming to consider what to say next. "You'll be a banker who's in Boise looking for real estate for a client."

"It should work," he said. Still, the apprehension coiled in his gut.

"Of course it will work." Dubois stood. Everyone else in the room got to their feet, as well.

Liam rose slowly. "Thank you for this opportunity, ma'am."

"Don't thank me yet. I expect results, Special Agent Hill. And soon."

Dubois left. Her retinue followed.

Only Constance and Wayne remained.

"I'll be in touch with the particulars of your background and some training to get you up to speed on undercover work," said his supervisor. "But go home and make arrangements to leave. You'll be out of DC soon. A word of advice?" Wayne dropped his hand on Liam's shoulder. "You're a good agent but don't screw up. What happens over the next few weeks has the power to define your career for good or bad."

"Point taken."

With that, Wayne left the conference room.

Constance quietly packed up her laptop. For a moment, neither said anything. Finally, he cleared his throat. "I should probably thank you for covering for me with Dubois."

She gave a quiet laugh. "You probably should." She zipped up her bag before saying, "Looks like that promotion will be yours when you get back."

She was probably right. Still, he knew enough to say, "You never know. You're a hell of an agent."

"It's probably for the best. My wife doesn't like all the late hours I'm keeping now. Although the raise would've helped to pay for IVF." His work friend had shared the cost of each round of in vitro fertilization. The cost was astronomical. It almost made him feel guilty for wanting the promotion so damn bad.

Slipping the strap of her computer bag over her shoulder,

she continued, "I'll keep looking into Markus Acker's personal life. Anything I find that's germane will get passed on."

"I appreciate having you in my corner."

"Just remember me when you're assistant to the director and get to pick your own minions," she joked.

He laughed. "It's a deal. Although, you'll never be a minion."

With a small wave, she slipped through the door and was gone. It left him alone. He knew he should be happy about the case—elated, really. He'd gotten the chance to prove that he was a capable field agent and not just another bean counter with a badge and gun.

Yet, blood hummed through his veins and left him jittery.

Was it because this would be his first foray out of the confines of Washington, DC? Or was there more?

He picked up his tablet computer and pressed the home button. His sister's social media account was still open. Instead of exiting the app, he found Sarah Colton's profile for a second time. In the picture, she wore a light blue dress and held her striped tabby, Tolstoy. Her light brown hair brushed the tops of her shoulders, and the corners of her green eyes crinkled with her smile. The last time he saw her, she'd been a skinny kid, barely out of high school and only eighteen years old. The long lines of youth had been replaced with womanly curves.

Looking at her profile, he sighed. He knew what was bothering him and why.

It was no secret that Sarah had harbored a huge crush on Liam when they were growing up. For years, he didn't care. After all, she was just a kid. But all of that changed right before he went away to the FBI Academy. Sarah, who'd recently turned eighteen years old, mentioned that she was legally an adult but still hadn't gotten her driver's license.

He remembered the conversation like it happened last week and not over seven years ago.

"Why no license?" he'd asked.

Sarah sat at the breakfast bar in the kitchen. *"Nate tried to teach me,"* she said, mentioning her brother. *"But we fought. Mom tried, but she freaked out."* She sighed, her shoulders slumping. *"I make progress with Dad, but he's not around much."*

"I'm home for a few weeks. I can take you out," he offered, happy to fill his days somehow.

It had only taken a week's worth of lessons and she passed the test on the first try.

Outside the DMV, she proudly held up her temporary license. With a big smile on her face, she'd announced, *"I couldn't have gotten this without you."*

He'd been so proud that he'd opened his arms for a hug.

She stepped into his embrace, and an instant later her lips found his.

Even now, his face burned with shame. Over the years he'd seen the looks on Sarah's face each time she glanced in his direction. He'd been a fool to ignore her longing.

He stepped away. *"Sarah,"* he mumbled, the feeling of her kiss still on his lips. *"I can't. We can't. I'm so much older than you."*

Her eyes flooded with tears. *"I just thought. I hoped."* She wiped her cheeks with her sleeve and dropped her gaze. *"Ohmigod, I'm so embarrassed."*

"Don't be embarrassed," he said, trying to sound soothing. *"It happened once, but it can't happen again."*

She ran off crying. In the moment, he convinced himself that it was best to let her go. Even then, he knew that he should have done or said something.

He left for the FBI Academy a week later. Sarah attended his going-away party but the two didn't speak to the other.

He glanced once more at her profile picture. Soon, he was going to have to face the grown-up version of Sarah Colton. And to be honest, he wasn't sure what kind of reaction he was going to get.

Chapter Two

One week later
Boise, Idaho

Sarah Colton's office was on the third floor of the Boise Public Library's downtown branch. The building, built in 1908, was made of local stone and filled half a city block. The residents of Boise affectionately called it The Castle. The multitude of rooms was perfect for reading areas, separating fiction from non, children's books from YA, and YA from fiction for adults. But the downside of such a large structure was that it was hard to keep temperate. In the summer, the building was sweltering. In the winter, the rooms were like iceboxes. And on this gloomy Tuesday in March, the damp had settled into the cramped spaces.

Huddled behind her desk, she gripped a cup of tea for warmth with both hands and stared at the screen of her desktop computer. The latest gas and electric bill had just landed in her inbox and honestly, she wished it hadn't.

"Knock, knock." Her friend and coworker Margaret Rhodes stood on the threshold. A Black woman, she wore her long hair in braids. Today, she'd donned a bright pink sweater with a lipstick to match. "So? How'd it go?"

Of course, Margaret would want all the details of last night's date. Taking a sip of tea, Sarah made a face.

Margaret's smile faded. "That bad?"

"He was fine," Sarah sighed. "Just a little young."

"Young?" Margaret echoed. "He's twenty-four. You're twenty-five. There can only be twelve months between your birthdays."

"He's a grad student at Boise State but he acted like an undergrad."

"I'm not saying that you should marry the guy—or anyone at all, for that matter. But you keep saying that you want to find someone to care about. Was he really *that* bad?"

Sighing, she took the last swallow of her tea. "He called me bro all night."

It was Margaret's turn to make a face. "Okay, that's bad."

"Tell me about it." She gave her friend a quick wink. "Bro."

"What're you working on? Anything I can do to help?"

"We just got the heating bill. If you have a million dollars just lying around, I'll take it," she joked.

"Sorry, no extra cash," said Margaret.

She sighed and looked at the amount due again. The budget was already stretched thin. Sarah had no idea how she was going to find the extra money. And yet, she had other things to worry about beyond the tight budget and her lousy romantic life. Her father had passed away only months earlier, and his death had sent out shock waves that still reverberated. Sarah and her brother, Nate, had ten half siblings. Of course, her parents' illicit affair had caused heartache for all the other Coltons. She was still trying to navigate her newfound family relationships. Then, there was her mother's new boyfriend. *Ugh.*

Pushing all her problems aside, she tried to smile. "What're you up to this morning?"

"Last night's shift didn't put away any of the returns. I'm going to get all the books on the shelves before it gets too busy."

"I'll help you put the books away." Anything was better than looking at the bill she didn't have the funds to pay. After exiting her account, she slipped on the loose cardigan she kept in her office. Standing, she said, "You take nonfiction and I'll take fiction."

"Deal," said Margaret.

On the first floor, two trolleys filled with books sat behind the circulation desk. "This one is yours," said Margaret, wheeling a cart toward Sarah.

From the number of volumes, she figured that the task would take the better part of an hour. It was 10:03 a.m. The library had opened only minutes before. If history served, patrons wouldn't start arriving for another thirty minutes.

She scanned the titles. Not only had the late shift failed to reshelve any books, but they also hadn't organized them alphabetically, either. Sighing, she realized that this task might take her closer to two hours. She picked up the first book.

The Gospel According to the Son. Mailer, Norman.

Pushing the cart through the stacks, she found the correct shelf and replaced the book.

Riffling through the titles, she found five more that should be placed close by. She picked up the next book in the pile, a heavy tome. *War and Peace. Tolstoy, Leo.*

Honestly, she couldn't look at a work by the Russian writer

without thinking of Liam Hill. When she was in middle school, she'd talked to him about books. He was the first person she'd ever related to through literature. It had led directly to her current profession.

Then again, she couldn't look at another guy without thinking of Liam, either. Unquestionably, he was the yardstick she used to measure every other man. She'd yet to meet a guy who was his equal.

Maybe it was time to let go of her preoccupation with Liam.

The front door opened and closed. The sun caught on the glass and reflected on the back wall. She peered through a gap between the books and caught the glimpse of a man. He was tall with dark hair. She only saw his profile before he disappeared behind another shelf. Her heart skipped a beat.

Had it really been him?

She dropped her gaze to the book in her hand. Of course, it wasn't Liam. After all, he'd just been on her mind.

After setting the book back onto the cart, Sarah smoothed down the front of her button-up blouse. She needed to find the early-morning patron and offer help. She walked to the end of the stacks and turned the corner. The middle of the library's main room consisted of the checkout/help desk. A double shelf of fiction books ringed the perimeter. Periodicals were to the left and computer workstations were to the right.

The man she'd seen was gone.

Certainly, she wasn't imagining things—even if he had reminded her of Liam Hill.

Perhaps he'd gone to one of the other rooms. Well, if he needed anything, he'd find Sarah.

Retracing her steps, she rounded the corner at the end of

a tall shelf and stopped. The man stood next to her cart. He held the volume of *War and Peace*. Her heart thundered in her chest, a wild beast trying to break free of its cage.

He was still tall with the same dark hair and brown eyes. She hadn't seen him in years, yet it was unmistakably him. Her throat tightened. She squeaked his name. "Liam?"

Looking up slowly, his eyes widened in surprise. "Sarah Colton? Is that you?"

"It is. Wow. I haven't seen you in forever." Her pulse still raced—it was a combination of shock and the fact that Liam had actually gotten better-looking since she'd seen him last. "How have you been? How's Allison? I haven't spoken to her in ages, either."

He wore his winter coat unzipped. Underneath was a white oxford shirt and pair of gray trousers. A pair of black loafers completed his outfit. "Allison's good. Still in the air force. Stationed in Japan right now. Parents are good, too. Life in the desert suits them." He paused. "It's so weird to run into you. I just got into town for work and need to do a little research on some property. I figured I could pick up a book to read, and who knew we'd both be at the library as soon as it opened?"

"Actually." Sarah held the fabric of her loose cardigan taut. Her name tag was no longer hidden in the folds of fabric. "I work here."

He peered at the metal tag affixed near her chest. "Head Librarian. That's impressive. Congrats."

"What about you? The last that I remember, you were heading to the FBI's training academy in Virginia."

He sighed and gave a quick shake of his head. "It didn't

work out. Living on a civil servant's salary is hard. A bank offered me a job managing their investments and I took it."

"Oh." She choked on a kernel of grief. Yet, why did his job choices cause her any angst? She remembered Liam as being such a principled person, it was a shame to see him give up his ideals for cash. Then again, he was right. Even as head librarian, living on a civil servant's salary was hard. "Well, congrats on your new job."

"It's not really a new position, but thanks anyway. How 'bout you? How long have you been working for the library?"

"It'll be a year in May." She'd been hired right after finishing her master's degree. "So, you said you were here doing research. Can I help you with anything?"

"I'm looking for information on some buildings downtown. I have a client who wants to expand his business."

"Let me put you in touch with Margaret. She's our research librarian and can help you find all those things that aren't on the internet."

The nonfiction room was adjacent to the main room. Margaret was easy to find. The cart of books she was sorting was nearly empty. It reminded Sarah of all the tasks she'd yet to complete.

Her friend and coworker looked up as she approached. "Hi. Something I can help you with?"

"This is an old friend of mine. He's looking at some investment properties and wants to see what we have on file. Liam, this is Margaret. She can help with any of your questions."

Holding up one finger, Margaret said, "Let me put away the last of these books. I'll be right back." Wheeling her cart to the end of an aisle, she turned the corner and disappeared behind a set of shelves.

There was really no reason for Sarah to stay. But it brought up an interesting question. What did she do now? Shake his hand? Give him a hug? Since the last time they'd embraced had led to the most embarrassing moment of her life, she held out her hand. "It was really great seeing you."

He slipped his palm into hers. A tingling traveled up her arm, leaving her pulse racing once more. "Well." She was breathless. "Take care of yourself." She walked away. The feeling of his eyes on the back of her neck was like a lover's caress.

"Hey, Sarah."

She turned back quickly. "Yes?"

Damn. Why'd she have to look so eager?

He said, "I'm going to be in town for a few days. Any chance we can grab dinner one night? We can catch up more. You'd save me from a week of eating alone."

"Yeah, sure." The feeling of Liam's hand in hers still danced along her skin. Pressing her thumb into her palm, she rubbed a small circle into her flesh. She couldn't decide if she was trying to preserve the sensation or get rid of it. "That would be nice."

"Is tonight too soon?"

Honestly, she didn't have any plans after work. But did accepting a date last minute make her look desperate? No. This wasn't a date, despite the fact that her skin tingled from a single touch. Liam was simply an old acquaintance. "Tonight's fine. Meet me out front at six thirty. There are some nice restaurants nearby."

"Six thirty it is," he repeated.

Margaret approached. "Sorry to keep you waiting. What can I help you find?"

Sarah gave Liam a small wave and walked away. Her day started off lousy. But seeing Liam after all these years had definitely improved her morning. What's more, she hoped her love life was about to rally, as well.

BY 6:10 P.M., Liam had checked into a downtown hotel not far from the library. His orders were to brief A-DIC Dubois daily. He'd called three minutes and forty-seven seconds earlier only to be put on hold. Sitting at a small table, he propped his socked feet on the bed and watched the seconds ticking by.

Before leaving DC, Liam had attended a crash course in working as an undercover agent. The first rule was to always maintain his cover. It meant that he'd spent hours looking for a property that he would never purchase for a client who didn't exist. To him, it seemed like a waste of time. Especially since he only had one objective: to reconnect with Sarah Colton.

He'd achieved that goal. But there was more.

If he wanted Sarah to reintroduce him to her mother—and Markus, as well—she had to think they were more than friends. A make-believe romance felt slimy. He hated to fool Sarah, especially since she'd been a good friend to Allison.

"Special Agent Hill." Dubois came onto the line, pulling him from his thoughts. "What have you got for me?"

"To start with, I made contact with Sarah Colton." He spent the next several minutes filling in the A-DIC on the particulars of his run-in at the library. He also outlined how he'd worked with her colleague to find out information about several of the buildings in downtown Boise. "I'm meeting Sarah for dinner soon."

"Good job. I'll let you get back to work, unless there's anything else."

There was, but did he bother bringing it up to A-DIC Dubois? "When we were younger, Sarah had a crush on me. When I saw her today, I could tell that her feelings haven't changed much." It was more than the electric charge that shot up his arm the minute she placed her hand in his. He'd paid attention to her reaction. All the physical signs were there. Her pupils had dilated. Her pulse fluttered at the base of her neck. "It seems smarmy to use her crush against her."

After a moment, Dubois said, "I suppose using Sarah Colton's old feelings for you is grubby. But sometimes, you need to get a little dirty if you're going to clean up a mess. Trust me, the Ever After Church is one huge effing cluster. Let me know if you aren't up to the task. We can send in another agent. But like it or not, Sarah Colton will be used to access her mother and Markus Acker."

"I'm in," he said. "Forget I had any hesitation."

"You're a decent man, I won't forget that. But for now, stow away that decency."

"Will do." He glanced at the time. 6:27 p.m. "Crap," he cursed. "I'm sorry, ma'am, but I have to meet Sarah."

"Go," she ordered. "Keep me updated."

He ended the call while scooping up the keycard for his room. A hooded parka hung on the back of the chair. While wrestling his jacket free, he shoved his feet into his loafers. He was out the door in seconds. At one end of the hall was a bank of elevators; at the other were stairs. He didn't have time to wait for an elevator to make it to the tenth floor and back to the lobby. He jogged to the stairs and pushed the heavy fire door open. Descending, he took the steps two at a time. His footfalls clanged on each metal step.

The stairwell ended at a side entrance, and he stepped onto the street. Fat gray clouds hung low in the sky. Cold air bit into his skin. Zipping his jacket, he strode purposefully down the street. By the time he reached the corner, he was at a jog. On the next block, he started to run. A clock hung outside a bank. 6:38 p.m.

Damn it. He was more than a little late.

He sprinted down the empty sidewalk as fat snowflakes started swirling in the sky. The front doors to the library stood in the middle of the block. A long figure, clad in a puffy coat and voluminous scarf, stood in a pool of light cast by a lamppost.

"Sarah," he wheezed. She turned at the sound of his voice. He waved, slowing to a jog. "Sorry for being late. I had to call into my office and the time got away from me. I didn't have your number to let you know. Hope you haven't been standing here long."

"Not long," she said. Her words were clipped. "In fact, I just stepped outside and since you weren't here, I was worried that you'd come and gone." The strap to a small bag was draped across her torso. She unzipped the bag and pulled out her phone. Holding up the device, she said, "Enter your contact information. Then we can text each other if you need more help with your research."

He entered a number from the fake account set up by the FBI.

"Here you go." He handed Sarah her phone.

She tapped on her phone's screen.

His phone pinged with an incoming text a second later. He glanced at the screen.

Sarah had sent him a message with a book emoji.

"Now you have my contact information, too." Slipping her phone back into her bag, she asked, "Anywhere special you want to eat?"

For the first time in years, he was back in Boise. True, he'd never live in Idaho again. But still, this place would always be his home. "How 'bout some finger steaks?"

"I thought you might want some of those." Deep-fried strips of beef, finger steaks were a local delicacy. They were also something he'd never find in Washington, DC. Sarah smiled, and his pulse jumped. She really had gotten pretty. "Come with me. I know a place."

She started to walk, and he fell in step beside her.

During his undercover training, Liam had learned about more than just how to stay undercover. He'd become an expert in Sarah Colton, as well. Like, he knew that she spoke to her coworker Margaret Rhodes every evening for an hour. On Wednesday nights, Sarah attended a barre class and then had dinner with friends. She was a member of two different book clubs. The last guy she dated had been a match on an app. Sarah's father, Robert, had died several months ago. Jessie joined the Ever After Church not long after Sarah went to college. He also knew that each parent had abandoned a family of their own to be together. Combined, Jessie and Robert had ten other children. Most of them lived near Owl Creek.

Knowing so much about her was supposed to make it easier to connect. The thing was, he wanted to hear it all from her.

A cold wind sent snowflakes skittering across the sidewalk. Liam shoved his nose into the collar of his coat.

Well, the weather was always a safe topic. "In Washington, it's already spring. Sunny days and mild nights. The cherry blossoms will be blooming by the end of the month."

"Must be nice," said Sarah. "You remember how it is here. We might get snow in June."

"Spring is nice," he agreed. "But summer in DC is brutal. It's too hot and humid to go outside during the day."

She stopped in front of a restaurant. The front door was made from tempered glass. Light spilled onto the sidewalk. "This place is new, but they have the best finger steaks in the city." She pulled the door open. The scent of cooking meat wafted into the night air.

"Heaven," he said, crossing the threshold. "This must smell like heaven."

She laughed and followed him inside. "You have an interesting take on the afterlife."

The room was filled with two dozen round tables. Only half were filled. A wooden bar ran the length of one wall. A sign on a post read Seat Yourself.

"Let's grab a table by the window," Sarah suggested.

"After you."

She wound her way to an empty table set for four. After slipping out of her coat, she draped the jacket on one of the chairs. Dropping into the seat, she sighed.

"Long day?" he asked, taking a seat across from her.

"Let's just say it's been a long few months."

Was Markus Acker a part of the problem? "Anything you want to talk about?"

Sarah scrubbed her face with both hands, letting her palms

drop to the tabletop. "There's a lot going on in my life. Too much, really."

"I know we never really kept in touch after my family moved, but that doesn't mean I don't care. You were able to count on me when we were younger. I hope you know that you can count on me still."

She shook her head and sighed. "It's just that…"

"It's just what?" He reached for her hand. A current of electricity ran from his fingertips to his shoulder.

Sarah met his gaze, her eyes wide. She looked down at the table, letting her hands slip into her lap. "I don't want to bore you with all my problems."

Before he could press her for more, a female server approached. She set two menus on the table. "I wanted to drop these off. I'll be back in a second to get your drink order."

Sarah studied her menu. Liam picked up his own menu. True, he knew what he was going to order. But the conversation was over—at least for now.

Another rule from undercover agent training was to be patient.

Had he been too pushy?

Then again, she was still at the table. It meant he was still in the game.

Relaxing, he watched Sarah. Her light brown hair fell to her shoulders. She tucked a strand behind her ear and sighed. The sound landed in his belly, and he dropped his gaze once more to the menu.

His arm still buzzed with the current of energy that passed between them. It was an interesting physical response and one he didn't want to analyze. In fact, it was best if the reaction was just ignored.

Chapter Three

Sarah pressed her back into the chair to make more room at the table. The server set a large tray on a stand next to the table. There were two identical orders on the platter. Finger steaks, cooked carrots and fries. Steam wafted off the plates as the savory scent of meat mixed with the sweet smell of the carrots.

"Enjoy," said the server as she set plates in front of Liam and Sarah. Tucking the tray under one arm and holding the stand in the other hand, she walked across the restaurant.

"I never realized how much I missed these." Liam lifted a strip of beef from the plate and popped it in his mouth. "Tease me if you want about the afterlife, this *is* heaven."

"Maybe they just remind you of Boise," she said.

"Could be." He unrolled a set of silverware and placed the paper napkin on his lap. "For me, home and heaven are kinda the same thing."

"You've been in DC for so long, that must be home for you now."

Liam took a sip of his beer. "I live and work in DC. But it's not home."

"Well, at least you're here now." She lifted her glass of

soda from the table and held it up. Liam touched the edge of his bottle to the rim of her glass.

"Cheers," he said.

She took a sip of soda and tried to calm the excited butterflies that started fluttering in her middle. If DC didn't feel like home, she doubted that he was in a relationship. Picking up her own roll of silverware, she removed a fork and stabbed a piece of beef. She popped it into her mouth, chewed and swallowed. "How's Allison? She never posts anything on social media, so I don't know what's going on in her life."

Liam washed down a bite with a swig of beer before speaking. "She's good. Still in the air force. Still flying jets. I saw her at Christmas. She was complaining about the heat in Arizona. She wanted some snow for the holidays."

"Next time you talk to her, remind her that we get snow in June." Sarah picked up a French fry and bit off the end. "And tell her I said hi. How're your folks?"

"They're good, too. After my parents retired, they started traveling. With Allison being in Japan, they've been all over Asia. Mom's hoping that she gets stationed in Europe next."

She tried to swallow, but her throat was filled with regret. She washed her food down with a drink of soda. At one time, the Hill family had been a major part of her life. Now, she knew next to nothing about them. "Your parents always liked to travel. I'm sure they love getting to see the world."

"Remember when we all went to Disneyland?" he asked. "I still have that group picture of us in front of the castle."

She recalled the trip well. The Hills had packed up their minivan and taken a road trip to California. They booked a suite at a fancy resort on the park's property. She and Allison shared one of the beds. Mr. and Mrs. Hill had been in another. Liam had been relegated to a pullout sofa in the living room. The family had covered all the expenses for Sarah. At the time, she was just excited to go on a fun trip. Now, she knew how much they'd truly given to her. "Your folks were good to me. They were like a second set of parents."

"They thought of you as one of their own, so I guess the feeling was mutual."

"I hate that I lost touch with everyone." She'd finished half of her meal. The rest could be saved for leftovers. After wiping her lips with a napkin, she said. "But I guess that's life."

"It's hard once everyone moves and there's nothing tethering you to a place." Liam finished the last swallow of his beer. "But I do miss Boise. I didn't think I would…" With a shake of his head, he placed the empty bottle on the table. "Being back has brought up a lot of memories. Well, I guess living here wouldn't be the same without family around."

Family. The one word was a punch to the chest. Sarah always knew her family was imperfect. It was part of the reason she was so drawn to the Hills. But she hadn't realized how many secrets both her parents were hiding. "My dad died a few months back," she said, without much thought.

"Oh, Sarah. I'm so sorry. What happened?"

Since her father passed away, she'd heard enough sympathies to last her a lifetime. But with Liam they seemed more sincere. Or maybe she just wanted him to care. "It's more than losing my dad." Though that was bad enough. "But I found something out after he died."

"Really? What?"

In all these months, she hadn't shared the entire truth with many people. Nate, her brother, obviously knew. She'd told Margaret. Sarah's mom refused to discuss her own past. And yet, "My parents had families before they got together. The kicker is—Mom was married to Dad's brother and Dad was married to Mom's sister. Between the two of them, Nate and I have ten half siblings."

Liam stared for a moment. "Are you joking?"

She shook her head. Her eyes burned but she refused to cry—not anymore, at least. "The worst of it all is that things are so awkward with the other Coltons. I worry that they blame us for stealing their parents."

"That's crazy. You aren't responsible for anything your folks did."

"I wish you could talk to them," she said with a listless laugh.

Liam sat taller. "Here's what I want to do. Go to Owl Creek right now and clear everything up." He poked the table with his finger, emphasizing his final two words.

Her meal sat heavy in her stomach. "How'd you know they all live in Owl Creek?"

"What?"

"You just said that you wanted to go to Owl Creek and chat with all my siblings. I never told you where they live."

"Oh, that." He paused. "I remember that's where your parents had lived before Boise. I guess I just assumed."

Her cheeks warmed. Had he remembered that much over the years? "You have a stellar memory."

A bead of sweat rolled down the side of his cheek. He wiped it away with his thumb. "Thanks."

The server approached the table. "Can I get you two dessert or coffee?"

Liam looked at Sarah. "You up for anything else?"

Pulling back the cuff of her sweater, she checked her watch

for the time: 8:42 p.m. "I better get home. My cat was expecting his dinner more than an hour ago."

To the server, Liam said, "We'll take the check." Then, to Sarah, "Looks like the weather's gotten nasty." The percussion of sleet against the window had been a constant. He continued, "I'll order us a rideshare. I can drop you off at work before going back to the hotel."

"A ride back to work would be nice."

Liam pulled his cell from a pocket. After opening an app, he tapped on the screen. "The car will be here in three minutes." The waitress returned with the bill on a mobile payment device. Liam used his phone to pay. As he signed for the meal with a finger, his phone pinged. Glancing at his phone once more, he said, "Looks like our ride is here."

Sarah slipped on her coat as she walked through the restaurant. Outside, a black sedan sat at the curb. Icy rain fell in a sheet. Ducking down, she sprinted to the car. She settled in the back seat. Her hands were numb with the cold. Liam sat beside her. His strong thigh pressed into her knee.

A wave of desire washed over her. For a moment, she was lost in a fantasy of his mouth on hers.

Lifting her gaze, she looked in his direction. He was watching her.

The temptation to place her lips on his was strong. Then, she remembered the last time she tried to kiss Liam. Shifting, she pulled her leg away from his.

Within minutes, the rideshare driver pulled into the parking lot behind the library. Her small station wagon sat next to the building. An exterior light reflected on a thin layer of ice that coated her car.

"Thanks for everything," she said, reaching for the handle. "It was great to catch up."

Liam opened his own door. "Looks like you can use some help. Get in the car and start the engine. Do you have an ice scraper?"

Using a fob, she unlocked the door and started the engine. She kept an ice scraper tucked into a pouch on the back of the driver's seat. Back in the storm, she ran the blade over the windshield. Liam reached for her. His hand covered hers. "Let me."

The icy rain soaked her hair and dripped down the collar of her coat. But she didn't mind the wind and the cold. In the moment, there was nothing beyond Liam and his touch.

Then, another image filled her mind. This time, it was a memory and not fantasy. Liam's arms had been around her waist. Her hands were clasped behind his neck. She'd given in to the moment and placed her lips on his.

He'd broken away the instant the kiss began.

"I can't. We can't. You're a great girl—but I'm so much older than you."

"Six years, that's not much," she tried to reason, even as her eyes burned with unshed tears.

"Maybe one day, it won't be. Right now, it is."

Then, she was back in the parking lot and in the middle of the miserable weather. Her cheeks burned. "You should go. Your ride's waiting."

"I'm not leaving you by yourself."

"I'll be fine. You go on."

Liam spoke to the driver through an open window. The black car slipped into the dark. Soon, the only thing she could see were the taillights. Then, even those were gone.

"Get inside," Liam urged. "I'll clear the windshield. You can drive me back to the hotel."

This time, she slid behind the driver's seat. The inside of the car was already warm. She turned up the heat and held her fingers in the slipstream of hot air. Liam ran the scraper's blade across the glass. With the defrost turned up to its highest setting, the ice had already started to melt. It took only minutes to clear all the windows.

Liam opened the passenger door. "I forgot how the cold can slice into your bones," he said, getting settled into the seat.

"I'll drop you off before the weather gets worse."

She eased out of the parking lot and turned onto the road. Holding tight to the steering wheel, she stared into the headlights. The beams captured the sleet, making it look as though they flew through outer space. The hotel came into view, and she parked at the curb.

"Thanks for everything," she said, keenly aware that he watched her still.

"I'd like to see you again," he said.

Did he want another friendly dinner? Or was Liam interested in more?

"Reach out anytime while you're in town."

"What about tomorrow night?"

"Tomorrow night?" she echoed with a laugh. "You must really be bored. Don't you have friends to see while you're here?"

"I guess there are, but I want to see you."

She studied him. When she was a kid, she always thought that Liam was the best-looking guy in the world. Now, she was a grown woman. Still, he was the most handsome man she'd ever met. "I can see you again tomorrow."

He smiled. A breath caught in her chest. "Good. Great. Tomorrow, it is. I'll meet you outside the library."

Sarah remembered almost nothing of her drive home. As she opened the front door, Tolstoy launched himself off the sofa in the adjoining living room and ran toward her. Her apartment was modest but comfortable. Aside from the living room, there was a kitchen to the left and her bedroom suite to the right.

"Hey, buddy." The cat wrapped his body around her leg. She picked him up and he tucked his head under her chin. "Miss me?"

With a meow, he wiggled from her grasp. Then, he ran straight to his food dish.

"I know. I know." After slipping out of her coat, she draped it over the back of a chair. Continuing to chat with the cat, she walked toward the kitchen. "You must be starved."

Tolstoy's dish sat on the floor. A layer of kibble filled the bottom of his bowl, so the cat wasn't exactly famished. Still, he'd become used to eating a can of food promptly at 7:00 p.m. It was rare that she made him wait. She emptied his food into the dish. Purring loudly, he stuck his face into the bowl.

Sarah scratched the cat's back before wandering to her bedroom. She flipped on a bedside lamp. It filled her room with a warm glow. Outside, sleet continued to tap against the window. The storm outside made her small apartment feel cozy. But for the first time, Sarah was more than alone. She felt the shadow of loneliness creeping in from the corners.

She shrugged off the mood. After all, she'd always been fine with her own company.

After setting her phone on a charger, she stripped out of her work clothes and threw them into a hamper. A pair of flannel sleep pants and a sweatshirt—the same set she'd worn the night before—lay on her pillow. She put on her pajamas and completed her nighttime routine. With her face washed and her teeth brushed, she settled into bed. Books, stacked into a tower, teetered on her bedside table. From where she sat, Sarah scanned the titles. They were a combination of genres: mystery, literary fiction and a few romance novels. None of them piqued her interest.

She padded quietly into the living room. A floor-to-ceiling bookcase sat in the corner. She knew the shelf without looking. Sarah reached for her favorite book. Holding it to her chest, she returned to her bedroom and slipped under the covers. Sarah opened her copy of *Anna Karenina* and tried to read. The words meant nothing, and her thoughts kept slipping back to her evening with Liam.

True, he was just in town for one week. It was also true that they'd only gone out to dinner once and he hadn't even tried to kiss her. It could also be true that he still only saw her as his kid sister's friend. Tolstoy jumped onto the mattress. Purring, he shoved his nose under the book, making himself impossible to ignore.

Setting the book aside, she lifted the cat onto her lap. Since starting the job at the library, she'd spent many evenings at home with a good book and her cat. While she loved her fur-baby with everything inside her, she wanted more from life.

She wanted a house. Kids. A husband.

Liam's face flashed through her mind.

Lifting her phone from the charger, she found her mom's contact and placed a call. Without a single ring, voice mail answered.

"This is Jessie." Her mom's voice was bright and cheery. "You know what to do."

"Hey, Mom. It's me. You won't believe who I saw today. Liam Hill. He was Allison's big brother. Anyway, he left the FBI and is a banker now, and is looking for investment properties for a client who wants to relocate in Boise. We had dinner." She sighed. Leaving a message wasn't the same as chatting with her mother. "Call me back when you can. Love you."

She ended the call.

Liam's reappearing in her life seemed like news that should be shared. It was too late to call Margaret, but they'd certainly chat about it tomorrow. Her brother, Nate, was a good guy. Even with his new girlfriend, Vivian, he was too practical to be romantic.

She opened a social media app and scrolled through her list of friends. Allison Hill, Liam's sister, was easy to find. From there, she typed out a direct message:

You won't believe who I ran into today. Your brother!! He's in Boise on behalf of a client who wants to buy an investment property. Liam and I had dinner. It was good to catch up. I'd love to hear from you, too.

Take care of yourself.

She hit Send and pressed the phone to her chest.

Her favorite childhood daydream had been to become Mrs. Liam Hill. Now, she was an adult and couldn't help but wonder—*what if?*

JESSIE COLTON LEANED back into the sofa and sipped her wine. She loved a French rosé. Cold wind whipped down from the mountain peaks and rattled the windows in their frames. A fire danced in the hearth and warmed the chilly room. This house, with its floor-to-ceiling windows and beautiful views, was the first permanent property for what would be the Ever After Church's complex. It's too bad that not everyone who belonged to the church could live in such a large and well-appointed house.

In fact, many braved the bitter night in not much more than a tent.

But as Markus said, the Lord provides. Everyone was working so hard to create a utopia for all members. Soon, they'd all have lovely homes—although none would be quite as nice as hers.

A pang of guilt stabbed her in the chest. She took another sip of wine. It turned to vinegar in her mouth. Inhaling, she counted to ten, before exhaling. The feelings of remorse slipped away with her breath.

They were replaced with another thought. Really, it befits the church leader to have the nicest accommodations, right?

She took another sip of wine and sighed. The vintage was perfect.

Her phone pinged and she glanced at the screen.

She'd missed one call and had a single voice mail.

Both were from Sarah.

Spotty cellular coverage was one of the things she loathed about living in the woods.

Still, Markus felt that too much technology separated people from the divine. He was probably right. But it made getting calls difficult. She opened the message app and read the transcript.

Hey, Mom. It's me. You won't believe who I saw today. Liam Hill. He was Allison's big brother. Anyway, he left the FBI and is a banker now, and is looking for investment properties for a client in Boise. We had dinner. Call me back when you can. Love you.

Jessie closed the app and took a long swallow of wine. She remembered the Hill family well. Besides Allison being a permanent fixture in Sarah's life from kindergarten through graduation, the Hills had taken Sarah on several vacations over the years. The back of her throat pricked with envy.

Sarah had been fortunate to go on all those trips, especially since Jessie couldn't afford to go anywhere.

The large diamond solitaire on her engagement ring caught the lamplight, sending rainbow sparkles through the room. Now, it was her turn to be lucky. Markus really was a generous man.

Like her thoughts had made him manifest, Markus walked into the room. He moved like a predatory cat with loose limbs and a steady gait. "What are you doing?"

"Sarah just called but the phone never rang. She left a message, though. Seems like she re-met an old friend. He's a banker, in town for business." She paused, memories of the Hill family coming to her from over the years. "It's odd that he works for a bank."

"Why's that?" he asked. "Lots of people work for banks."

"Well, he used to be an FBI agent is all." She recalled his going-away party. The Hills had deemed to invite her, too.

She'd awkwardly stood on the patio and tried to make small talk with the other guests. Sarah moved through the crowd like the Hill's third child. And if Jessie wasn't her daughter's mother, then who was she? That night, she'd gotten on the internet and found the Ever After Church community.

"You're right," he said, a scowl creasing his brow. "That is odd. I don't like your daughter dating a fed."

"They aren't dating." Markus and his constant suspicions were enough to make her head throb. She rubbed her brow. "I'm sure there's a reasonable explanation about why he changed jobs."

"Then why did you say it's weird?"

"It was a big deal that he'd gotten into the Bureau so young. Could be that he just didn't know what he was getting into," she suggested.

"Maybe," he echoed.

She could tell that he wasn't convinced. "I can ask Sarah. I was just going to return her call."

Markus slid next to her on the sofa, his body fitting perfectly next to hers. "Oh, okay." The two words were filled to the brim with disappointment.

"What's the matter?" She felt the heat of anger rising in her cheeks. "You said that if I moved here with you, you'd never keep me from my kids."

"Of course, you're right. It's just that I was feeling a little lonely and wanted some time with my blushing, future bride."

Leaning into his side, she laughed. "Blushing bride. That makes me sound like an eighteen-year-old virgin."

"You know that every time that we're together is like the first time."

He stroked her breast through her shirt. Her nipple hardened. Honestly, Jessie had never known a man who wanted sex as much as Markus. It was just another way she had gotten lucky. Not every woman her age was with a man as virile as her fiancé.

He laid her back on the sofa and situated his hips between her thighs. He was already hard. She was already wet. They really were perfect for one another. In the moment, nothing else mattered.

Chapter Four

A-DIC Dubois had set up a daily briefing on the Ever After Church case. At 9:00 a.m. on his second day in Boise, Liam sat at the small table in his hotel room. His laptop was open, and a secure connection had been established with the Hoover Building. His screen was filled with the same image those in the conference room saw on the smartboard.

"We were able to get approval for aerial photographs of the compound," said Constance, narrating from off-camera. "After obtaining a warrant from a federal judge, we deployed a drone last night." A dark image filled with a jumble of darker shapes appeared on the screen. The same image appeared again. This time, there were three circles—red, yellow and green—around the largest shapes. "The red circle is around the home that belongs to Markus Acker and his fiancée, Jessie Colton. The yellow is the building that doubles as a cafeteria and sanctuary. The green is the church's administrative building."

"What else is in this image?" asked Dubois. "It looks like all the toys my kid leaves on the floor at night."

"Those are dwellings where the rest of the church members live. It's a combination of tents and shacks made of whatever's available." Constance continued, "I was able to access other images of the compound." She rotated through several photographs of the compound. Armed guards, dressed in black, were posted at the gate and wandered throughout the compound. People, lean and dirty, huddled over a small camp stove for warmth.

The images lit a fire in Liam's chest that burned with anger. He had a small printer in the room and would print off the pictures. They'd serve as a reminder as to why he'd returned to Idaho.

"For the privilege of giving Acker all your worldly possessions, you get to live in squalor." Dubois's tone was filled with snark. "It's our job to nail this bastard. Any updates from you, Special Agent Hill?"

"I arrived in Boise on Sunday night and made contact with Sarah Colton yesterday morning. We had dinner together. We also made plans to go out again tonight."

"That's decent progress," said Dubois. "But we need results. Did she buy your story about being in town for work?"

Constance stopped sharing her presentation. The image of the Ever After Church property was replaced by a view of the conference room at the Hoover Building. Liam's own image also appeared in a smaller square.

Dinner with Sarah had been one of the best dates he'd been on in months. She was easy to talk with—not like in DC where everyone was posturing. She'd been charming, funny and had taken him for finger steaks. Too bad it had all been a lie.

"I think she believed every word I said, ma'am. Of course, she remembered that I'd been with the FBI. When I told her that I left the Bureau for better pay, she seemed disappointed, not doubtful."

"What are you going to do tonight?" asked Constance. "I hope you're taking her somewhere special."

"Honestly, I haven't put much thought into where we're going. Last night, she picked the restaurant. The food was good."

"The FBI didn't send you to Boise on a gastro tour. Get tight with Sarah Colton again and quickly," said Dubois.

From her seat in the conference room, Constance held up her phone. "I found just the place for you. Chez Henri is the highest-rated restaurant in Boise."

He didn't remember any place called Chez Henri. It must be new. Or, newish. "I'll look it up and make a reservation."

"I've already taken care of it for you," said Constance. "I booked you a table for two at seven."

"You'll keep me informed of your progress," said Dubois, rising from her seat. The rest of those in the room stood, as well. They filed out of the conference room.

Constance remained in her seat. "How's it going?" she asked. "Honestly."

He wasn't going to tell his friend that he felt like a jerk for lying. He'd already tried that with Dubois and almost got pulled from the investigation. Instead, he said, "I didn't think I'd enjoy being back in Idaho, but I do. Plus, it's good to catch up with Sarah."

"Plus, plus," she added. "She's cute. That can't hurt."

"She's more than cute," he said.

"That's what I thought," said Constance. "Well, have fun. But not too much fun."

He ignored whatever she meant to imply. "I'll chat with you later," he said.

Then, his computer screen went blank.

With the briefing complete, he had hours until his dinner date but nothing to do with his time. Looking out the window, he surveyed people on the street. From ten stories up, their lives seemed uncomplicated.

As he watched, he understood the schism between his real life and his undercover persona. If the real Liam Hill had been in Idaho for work, he'd reach out to old friends. But undercover Liam knew enough to stay away from people who would ask questions he'd never answer.

Moving from the table to the bed, he placed a call. His mother answered after the second ring. "Liam, honey. It's great to hear from you. Everything okay?"

Damn. Had someone seen him in town and called his parents already? "Why would you think something's wrong?"

"You never call in the middle of the day, is all."

"I'm fine, but I have a favor to ask. If anyone from Boise asks about me, don't say anything."

"That seems rude."

"It's not rude. It's national security."

His mom sighed. "I guess you can't tell me what's going on, then."

"I can't," he said. "Sorry."

"Anything else I can do for you?"

Actually, there was. "I've been trying to get a hold of Allison." Since she was stationed overseas, the family used a messaging app to keep in touch. Once the investigation had been approved, he'd tried to reach his sister several times. He needed to alert her to ignore any messages from Idaho, as well. So far, she hadn't messaged him back. "Any idea why she's incommunicado?"

"Your sister's part of a joint military exercise in Asia. It's all very hush-hush. She told me not to expect to hear from her for a few weeks."

Liam exhaled and sank back in the chair. Allison's being off the grid for the Air Force explained everything. It also meant that Sarah wouldn't be able to get in touch with her, either. "Looks like both your kids have to worry about national security."

"You know that your father and I are very proud of you and your sister, even if we don't always get to know what you're doing."

"Thanks, Mom." He was tempted to give his mother an update on Sarah Colton. Before he got into real trouble, he said, "I need to get back to work. Give Dad my love."

"Take care of yourself, Liam."

The call ended and he rose from the seat. Sure, he wanted to avoid people whom he used to know. But he couldn't just sit in the hotel room all day and wait for his date. Slipping into his coat, he shoved his phone and room key into his pocket. Liam turned for the stairs and came down all ten flights. At the ground level, he pushed the door open and stepped onto the street.

Every building he passed held a memory. There was the building where his buddy's dad had a law practice. Over the years, they'd stopped by his work more than once. A nice assistant always made the boys a cup of hot chocolate. Across the street was the building where his mother practiced medicine until she retired. At the corner, where his favorite diner had been, a used bookstore.

As he walked, he realized something important. For seven years he'd devoted himself to his job. He believed in the Bureau's mission. *Fidelity. Bravery. Integrity.* But he'd spent so much time at work that he hadn't bothered to make a life. Even his mom, who'd been a doctor, had gotten married and had kids. When was it going to be his turn?

No, that wasn't a fair question.

He should be asking something else.

When was he going to make having a life his priority? At the end of the block, a striped awning hung over the sidewalk. Years ago, it had been one of his dad's favorite restaurants. Was it still the same, or had that changed, too?

A sign was taped to the door: Now Serving Breakfast.

Back in DC it was 11:27 a.m.—almost time for lunch. He'd already burned off the bagel he'd eaten at the hotel. A second breakfast wouldn't be the worst thing. Pushing the door open, he stepped inside. The room looked just like he remembered. Dark paneling covered the walls. Chairs, wrapped in green vinyl, surrounded twenty-plus tables draped with white cloths. A set of stairs led to a balcony that also served as a private party space. His mom had hosted a surprise fiftieth birthday party for his dad on the upper level.

A young man stepped up to the host's stand. "Can I help you?"

"Table for one," said Liam.

It was easy to find a seat. Aside from Liam, the restaurant was empty. The host led him to a table next to a line of windows overlooking the street. He handed Liam a menu. "What can I get you to drink?"

"Coffee and an orange juice," said Liam.

"Be right back."

Alone, it was time to get back to work. Pulling out his phone, he found Sarah's contact information. He sent her a text.

Hope your cat wasn't upset that I kept you out late last night.

She replied immediately.

Once Tolstoy got his dinner, all was forgiven.

He typed out another message.

I made us a reservation for tonight, so it might be late. Chez Henri. 7:00 p.m. I'll pick you up at your work.

Sarah replied:

Chez Henri? I'm impressed. If I'd known we were going someplace that fancy, I would've dressed nicer for work.

He chuckled as he read her text. She was funny and smart. Besides, he couldn't imagine her looking anything other than beautiful.

You looked fabulous to me last night.

STANDING BEHIND THE circulation desk, Sarah read LIAM'S TEXT. HE definitely knew how to flatter a girl, that's for sure. A dozen flirty responses came to mind, but with him, she wanted to play it cool. Slipping the phone into the slouchy pocket on her loose cardigan, she smiled.

"I saw that expression," said Margaret while scanning a

book into the system. "Let me guess. You just got a text from a handsome banker."

Margaret was a good friend and the only other full-time employee at the library. It meant the two shared a lot of their lives, but they had an unwritten rule to never gossip at work. Since the room was empty, Sarah decided it was okay to break their rule this once. "Liam made us reservations at Chez Henri."

"Très fancy," Margaret said with a fake French accent. "What're you going to wear?"

She shoved her hands into the pockets of her sweater and opened the front. "He's picking me up from work, so I'm wearing what I'm in."

"Read Banned Books?" Margaret read the front of her T-shirt out loud. "I love your sentiments, but you cannot wear that to Chez Henri. Quin took me there for our last anniversary. That place is swanky. You'll want to dress up." Her husband, Quin, was an engineer for the city, and one of the most considerate people Sarah had ever met.

"Of course your husband took you to Chez Henri because he's amazing." She wasn't ready to give up. "But Liam said I looked fabulous just the way I am."

"Well, isn't he a sweet talker? That just gives you another reason to look your best."

"It's not all about looks," she countered. Then again, she couldn't remember the last time she wanted to look good for another person. But she did want to wow Liam. "Besides, our reservation is at seven. I can't stay here until six thirty, go home and change, and be back to meet him."

"Go home early," Margaret suggested. "Take a shower. Put on that floral dress you wore to the last library trustees meeting. Then, have him pick you up at your place."

"I can't leave you alone."

Margaret said, "I am perfectly capable of running the library by myself until we close. Nobody's here now, and if we get a rush, I can handle it. I'll even have Quin stop by on his way home to keep me company."

Most people didn't consider it wild to leave work early to get ready for a date. But Sarah was conscientious and dependable and going home before closing time felt reckless. "Only if you're sure."

"Not only am I sure, but I insist."

Pulling her phone out of her pocket, she sent Liam another message.

Change of plans. I can get out of work early. Can you pick me up at my place?

She also gave him the address.

Her phone pinged with his reply.

Sounds perfect. See you at 6:30

A swarm of butterflies flitted in her stomach. Seriously, she shouldn't be this giddy over a guy. But Liam wasn't *a guy*. In fact, he was *the guy*.

She didn't believe in fate or luck or a higher power—especially after her mother got involved with Markus Acker. But something good had brought Liam back to her life and she was eager to see what would happen next.

At 6:25 p.m., Sarah checked her reflection in the bathroom mirror. Her hair fell in loose waves to her shoulders. Her makeup brought out the green of her eyes and her lips were full and glossy. Margaret had been right to suggest that she wear her floral dress. The bodice hugged her breasts before the skirt fell in folds around her legs.

It was the most effort she'd put into her appearance in months—hell, maybe all year.

She couldn't help but wonder if Liam would appreciate her effort.

A knocking came from the front door. Tolstoy, who sat on the back of the toilet, jumped down from his perch and scampered to the living room. Sarah followed her cat to the front door and looked through the peephole. Liam stood on the stoop. He held a bouquet of pink roses wrapped in cellophane and a small paper bag.

Placing her hand on the doorknob, she tried to remember the last guy who brought her flowers. Then again, it didn't matter. None of the guys were Liam. She pulled the door open. Cold air rushed into her apartment.

Liam's gaze met hers. Time turned into molasses in the winter. A smile spread across his face. "You look fantastic."

She couldn't help but smile back. "Thanks."

He handed her the roses. "These are for you." The sweet scent of flowers filled the air. Then, he held up the small bag. From inside, he removed a bag of cat treats. "These are for your cat." He shook the bag. "It's the least I can do since I'm taking you out two nights in a row."

Tolstoy heard the treats and wound his body around Sarah's ankles.

"You know," she said, "most guys just send a text when they show up and expect me to meet them in the parking lot. Not only do you come to the door, but you bring gifts."

"I'd like to think that I'm not most guys."

Oh, he was far from average. Stepping back from the threshold, she said, "Come in for a second. It'll give me time to give Tolstoy some treats and put the flowers into a vase."

Sarah dumped a few treats into the cat's dish. The cat ran to his food bowl. Sticking his nose inside, he started to purr as he ate.

"I think he likes them."

"I hope so," said Liam. "I figure with a name like Tolstoy he'd only want the best."

"Some cats are picky," she said, pulling a vase from a cabinet. She placed the container in the sink and filled it with water. "Not him. He's like a dog and will eat most anything."

"Next time, I'll pick up dog treats."

So, he thought there'd be a next time. That was promising. She bit her lip to keep from smiling again. Sarah unwrapped the flowers. She placed them in the vase and set the arrangement on the middle of the kitchen table. "There," she said. "They look perfect."

Liam knelt next to the cat and ruffled the fur behind his ears. "I've always been a big fan of Tolstoy's work."

"Yeah, I remember," she said.

"You do?" He smiled. The expression lit up his whole face. Even the corners of his eyes turned up in their own version of a smile. Sarah's heart skipped a beat and he continued, "I'm surprised."

"You shouldn't be. We talked about Tolstoy a million years ago. You were in college. I was in middle school. That conversation made me realize that literature and reading and books could be more than a hobby but a career. It took me a bit to figure out that I wanted to be a librarian. But here I am."

The last words tumbled out of her mouth. Once she started

speaking, it had been impossible to stop. Why had she decided to be so honest?

"I'm humbled that anything I said made an impact."

"It's more than just the one talk or the fact that you taught me how to drive. You've always done so much for me. From the time I was a kid, your family was my shelter in the storm. If it weren't for all of you, I'd be a very different person."

Liam worked his jaw back and forth. "There's something I need to tell you."

Her interest was piqued. "That sounds ominous."

"Well, it's not horrible. But I need to clear the air." He paused.

In the silence, a million different disasters came to her at once. One of his parents was gravely ill. He was the one who was sick. He was involved with someone else. He was married. "What—" she began. The word came out as a croak. She cleared her throat. "What is it?"

He dropped his gaze to the floor. "We have a reservation, and the rideshare is waiting. We really need to get going."

Obviously, that wasn't what he was going to say to her at all. What was she supposed to do now? Argue with him until he confessed? Demand that he tell her the truth? Neither option was her style. "Let me get my coat and my purse." Both were tucked into a small closet. After slipping on her coat, she draped her purse over her shoulder. "You ready?" she asked, opening the door.

Liam nodded and walked out of the apartment. Sarah followed, pulling the door closed and twisting the handle to make sure the automatic lock engaged. It had. She walked across the outdoor landing toward the steps. All the while, she tried to ignore the nagging thought that there was more to Liam's story.

Her apartment was located on the second floor of an apartment building with sixteen units. There were four floors and an open stairwell that bisected the building. A frigid gust blew up the steps and the icy wind bit her flesh. Zipping her jacket to the chin, she asked, "When will winter end?"

"According to the calendar, spring is about three weeks away," he said. "But in DC, the weather's already warm enough for flowers to bloom."

"You keep saying that. Sounds to me like you're bragging."

"Maybe a little bit," he said.

Glancing over her shoulder, she gave him a fake scowl. She turned and took a step down. That's when it happened.

Her foot hit the edge of the stair. She slipped, pitching forward. Then, gravity took over and she started to fall. As she went over, Liam reached around her waist. He pulled her back, holding her to his chest. Her pulse thundered in her ears.

"Are you okay?" His words tickled her neck.

She was keenly aware of him. His arms were strong. His pecs were hard, and his legs were long. But it was more than his toned physique—although that was impressive enough. "Thanks for catching me," she said.

"I've always had your back. You know that."

She wanted to believe that was true. But there was something important that he wanted to tell her and at the last minute, he changed his mind. True, she hadn't seen Liam in years. Even before then, she was hardly entitled to know everything about him. She drew in a deep breath. Icy air froze in her nose. The cold was bracing and brought with it a so-bering thought.

She could not get lost in a fairy tale.

She and Liam were not going to have a happily-ever-after.

"We better go," she said, stepping carefully on the next stair.

Liam followed but said nothing.

A blue SUV sat in the parking lot. The driver flashed his lights as they approached. "That's our ride."

Liam opened the passenger door for Sarah. "My lady, your carriage," he kidded.

Yeah, the joke was cheesy. Still, she laughed. "Thank you, kind sir."

She climbed into the back seat. Liam closed her door and rounded to the other side of the car, sitting behind the driver.

The SUV pulled out of the parking lot. After a minute, she glanced in Liam's direction. Resting his chin on his hand, he stared out the window. The glass caught his reflection. Lines of worry ran along his forehead.

"Rough day?" she asked.

"What?" he started, obviously lost in his own thoughts.

"You look worried. I wondered if you'd had a rough day."

Liam sighed. "Jet lag is catching up with me." He gave a wan smile. "Besides, I'm not having much luck finding the right building for my client."

"Tell me about your job." She knew next to nothing about banking.

"There's not much to tell," he sighed. "It's boring and complicated."

To her it sounded awful—no matter how much money he

made. "Why'd you leave the FBI, then? You used to want to save the world. What changed?"

"I don't know how to answer that question. It's just that…"

In the darkened back seat, he pinned her with his gaze. She had the feeling that whatever he said next was going to be important—not just for him but for her, too. Holding her breath, she waited for him to keep speaking. He didn't. "It's just that, what?" she prodded.

The car slowed to a stop.

"It's just that I think we're here," he said.

She glanced out the window. Dual electric sconces, made to look like flames, stood on either side of a wooden door. Located in a renovated home, the white stone structure was built by a silver baron in the late 1800s and Chez Henri had kept much of the Victorian-era charm. From the sconces to the wrought iron railing to the room with the round turret and peaked roof on the third floor, everything was as it had been in Boise's heyday.

Liam opened his door and stepped from the car. Leaning into the auto, he held out his hand. She placed her palm in his. Her flesh warmed with his touch. Together, they walked up the stone steps to the front door.

Inside, a hostess stood behind a wooden stand. "Good evening," she said with a smile. "Do you have a reservation?"

"Hill," said Liam. "Party of two."

"Can I take your coats?" Sarah removed her jacket and handed it to the hostess. Liam did the same. The hostess disappeared through a door marked Coatroom. She returned a moment later and handed Liam two plastic tickets. "Follow me."

She led them down a short corridor. Smaller rooms

branched off the hallway and were set with two and three tables each. Most of the tables were filled with patrons. The crystal stemware at each place sparkled.

"Liam?" A male voice boomed from one of the dining rooms. "Is that you?" A man in a dark suit with thin, blond hair approached. He smiled wide, "Damn. It is you. How ya been?"

"Topher." The two men shook hands. "I didn't expect to see you here."

"Why wouldn't I be here? I still live in Boise. Still working for my old man at the law firm. What're you doing? Or can't you say because it's top-secret for the federal government."

Liam worked his jaw back and forth. "I left the Bureau a few years ago to go into the banking industry. I thought you knew that."

"Last I heard, you were still a G-man."

"Topher, do you remember Sarah Colton? She was one of Allison's friends."

The other man offered his palm. "Actually, I do remember you. Nate's little sister, right?"

"I am. Good to see you again." She recalled Liam's high school friend who played on the football team. Allison thought Topher was dreamy. Sarah was never interested in anyone other than Liam.

She shook Topher's hand. His skin was clammy, and the antiseptic scent of alcohol surrounded him. Turning his attention back to Liam, he asked, "So, what're you doing since you left the FBI?"

"Me?" Liam seemed surprised by the question. "I'm here for a client. They're looking for a building."

Topher's smile grew. "My law firm handles that kind of

transaction. Who's your client? What kind of property do you need?"

Liam said, "I can't really talk about that right now."

"We need to meet, then. There are lots of properties I can show you. Give me a call."

"Yeah. Sure." Liam shook hands with Topher again. "I'll reach out."

"Don't you want my number?"

"What? Of course." He removed his phone from his pocket before handing it over. "It'd be great to catch up."

"It'd be even better to do some business. Between me and you, my dad's always on my case about bringing in new clients," Topher confided as he entered his contact information. After handing back the phone, he extended his thumb and pinkie. Putting his hand to his ear, just like he was talking on a landline, he said, "Call me."

"Will do." Liam gave his friend a quick wave before walking away.

"That seems like a lucky break," she said as soon as Topher was out of earshot. "You two used to be tight, and now you can work together."

"Yeah," he said. "It'd be great."

Sarah might not know everything about Liam or his life. But she suspected that he wasn't in Boise to find property for a client. It brought up an interesting question. Why had he come home in the first place?

Chapter Five

Sarah and Liam sat at a table in the main dining room of Chez Henri. A marble fireplace, big enough to fit her car, dominated one wall. Flames danced in the grate. Several tables, covered in pristine white cloths, were scattered around the room. The walls were covered in golden wallpaper. A crystal chandelier hung from the ceiling.

"This place is beautiful," she said.

"It's almost as attractive as the company."

Picking up a pre-poured glass of water, she took a sip. "Now you're flattering me."

Liam lined up his silverware, although the table was perfectly set. "Can't a guy give a compliment?"

She held up her hands, surrendering. "You're right. I'll take the compliment."

"You're welcome."

Before he could say any more, the server approached the table. "My name is Douglas and I'll be taking care of you this evening." He handed them each a menu. "Can I get you started with something to drink?" The server continued, "We have a special on a French rosé."

French rosé. It was her mother's favorite wine. In fact,

this was the exact kind of place her mother always wanted to patronize. But money had been tight in the Colton household. She also knew that her mother felt the lack of cash like a physical pain. Suddenly, the cozy room was stifling. Her throat closed like a fist. "I think I'm okay with water for now," she croaked.

"Make that two. But leave the drink list."

Sarah tried to scan the food menu but saw nothing.

"Listen," Liam began. "My compliment made you uncomfortable. I was trying to be flirty but overshot the mark. You do look great, though. So, I'm not going to apologize for that."

"It's not your flirting. It's just…" She paused, not sure what to say. How was she supposed to explain her family? Then again, he knew a lot of the story—more even than most of her current close friends. "It's just that the wine recommendation reminded me of my mom."

"You think that's a bad thing."

"It's not bad, it just touches a nerve." She paused again. "My mom started dating a new guy. He's a minister, and his church is really successful. He has all sorts of money. My mom can buy all the things now that she couldn't afford before. French wines are one of those things—and rosé is her favorite."

"Sorry that it got brought up."

She waved away his apology. "You couldn't have known," she said. "How could you?"

He sat quietly for a moment. "So, what do you think of Markus?"

She lifted her shoulders. Ready to let them drop in a shrug, she stopped. "How'd you know his name is Markus?"

Liam looked up from the menu. "What's that?"

"My mom's fiancé *is* named Markus. But I never mentioned that."

Liam regarded her but said nothing.

"How'd you know his name?" she pressed.

Shaking his head, Liam smiled. She really did love his smile. "You caught me. After we ran into each other, I looked at your social media page. I found your mom and Nate, too. I'm not a creep. I was just curious about your lives." He paused. "I hope you aren't too mad."

Was she? "I guess everything we post online is meant to be seen. Did you send me a friend request?"

"I really don't get on social media much, so, no."

Funny, his sister was rarely online, either. Must be a Hill family thing.

The server approached and stood at the side of the table. "Are you ready to place your order?"

She'd barely glanced at the menu. Looking at the selections, she picked the first thing to catch her attention. "I'll take the chicken piccata."

"Soup or salad?"

It was too cold outside to eat a salad. "I'll have the soup."

Liam ordered a pork chop with apricot glaze. He also took the soup. Finishing the order, he said, "We'll take a bottle of local merlot."

After the server left, Liam said, "I hope you like red wine. I figured that it wasn't imported, and it wasn't a rosé."

"I'm sure everything will be delicious." As it turns out, Sarah was right.

The wine was earthy. The soup was a hearty tomato bisque. Her chicken was tender. The sauce was a perfect blend of creamy and tangy. For dessert, they shared a flour-less chocolate torte.

Scraping her fork across the dessert plate, she hummed with satisfaction. "If that meal had been any better, it'd be illegal."

"The only thing better than the food was the conversation." Liam opened his phone and tapped on the screen. "I just ordered a car to pick us up. But excuse me for a minute. I'm going to the men's room."

Sarah watched him walk away before pulling the phone from her purse. During the evening, she'd missed several texts and a call from her mother. Calling her mom back would have to wait, but she opened the texts. They were all from Margaret.

How's the date?

What outfit did you wear?

What do you think of the restaurant?

When are you going to text me back?

She sent Margaret a message: He brought flowers and cat treats. Wore the floral dress. Chez Henri is amazing.

Margaret replied instantly.

How's the date going? Do you still like him?

Sarah stared at the screen. Honestly, she wasn't sure how to answer the question. But she had to tell someone the truth.

Something seems off.

The text bubble was open for several seconds before Margaret's message appeared.

Maybe you're looking for a reason not to like him.

Sarah slumped back in the seat. Could Margaret be right? She sent another message.

I'll call you when I get home.

Her friend replied with a thumbs-up emoji.

She closed the conversation and that's when she noticed her social media. She had one new message. She opened the app and read. Her mouth went dry, and her pulse started to race. She read the message a second time and all the pieces of the puzzle clicked into place.

"Are you okay?" Liam stood next to the table.

How long had he been standing there? Then again, she was blind to everything other than her phone.

"Are you okay?" he asked again. "You look flushed. Do you have a fever?"

"I don't have a fever," she snapped. "But I'm not okay."

As if struck, he rocked back on his heels. "Okay," he said slowly. "What's going on?"

She read the note from Allison one more time.

Sarah!! It's so great to hear from you. I never get on social media, and I should. It's the best way to keep up with friends. It's weird that you ran into Liam. But are you sure it's him? When we talked about a month ago, he was still with the FBI. No mention of leaving the gov't to work for a bank. Let's keep in touch.

She handed Liam the phone. "Maybe you can explain all this."

LIAM READ HIS sister's message. Like falling off a cliff, his stomach dropped to his shoes. He hit the bottom, and it left him stunned and breathless. There was no way to salvage the investigation now.

Underneath his concern was a single thought. It was a patch of blue sky in the middle of a hurricane. At least Sarah knew the truth.

He hated lying to her from the beginning.

"Say something," she hissed.

"I'm sorry you had to find out." He held the phone out to her.

"That's the lamest thing I've ever heard." She rose from her seat and jerked the cell from his hand. Anger, like dancing flames, rolled off her. "I thought you were one of the good guys. What I don't get is why you lied."

Ouch. He was one of the good guys. It's just that he couldn't tell her what he was doing. Then again…

His phone pinged. He glanced at the screen. "Our ride's waiting. Can we talk about this at your place?"

"I'm not going anywhere with you. And you certainly aren't coming back to my apartment."

The more time he spent with his newest idea, the more he liked it. "I really think we need a few minutes alone."

She shook her head. "I'll get my own ride. Thank you very much." She turned and walked out of the dining room.

Liam followed her into the corridor. "Wait," he called out. "Just give me five minutes to explain."

Stopping at the hostess stand, she glared at Liam. "Do you have the ticket for my jacket?"

He fished the plastic tabs from his pocket before handing them over to the hostess. Once she disappeared into the coatroom, he lowered his voice. "Give me two minutes. If you don't like what I have to say, the rideshare is yours. I'll have this ride take you home and order my own car."

The hostess returned with their jackets. "Here you go."

Liam placed a tip on the stand before reaching for the coats. "Two minutes," he repeated.

"Talk quick." She held up the phone so he could see the screen. The timer had been set for 120 seconds.

He moved to a corner, far enough from the hostess that he wouldn't be overheard. He didn't have time to think about his decision or consider the consequences. He said, "Allison's right. Topher's right. I'm still with the FBI."

Sarah gaped. "Why didn't you say that from the beginning?"

"Because." He rubbed the back of his neck. His muscles were taut with tension. If this didn't work out, he'd lose more than this case. Certainly, Dubois would fire him. "I'm working undercover."

"That doesn't make sense. Why send in someone who used to live in Boise? Obviously, you were going to accidentally run into people you knew, like me and Topher."

He had to be honest with her. Playing games wouldn't work—not anymore, at least. "Meeting you wasn't an accident."

Her gaze hardened. "It wasn't?"

"I meant to find you. To get close to you."

She shook her head. He could feel her slipping away, like grains of sand through his fingers.

"Me?" She gazed at him. "Why am I important to the FBI?"

"I need Markus Aker."

"My mom's fiancé."

Liam wasn't sure how much time he had left, but he was determined to say his piece before the clock ran out. "He's not the pastor of a rich church. He's been extorting money from his followers for years."

"There's no way," she began. "That's not true…" Her words trailed off. "My mom would never…" And then, "How would you know?"

"I'm with the FBI, remember?"

"How can I forget?" For a moment, she stood without speaking. "What about my mom?"

"Right now," said Liam, "your mom isn't in any trouble with the FBI. The longer she stays, the more criminal exposure she'll have."

Her complexion paled. He imagined the reality of the situation was settling on her. "Do you think she's in physical danger?"

Liam had to tell her the truth. "To be honest, I'm not sure about your mom's safety. He is manipulative. It's possible that your mother doesn't know what's going on."

She raked her fingers through her hair. "I've always hated that bastard."

The question was, did she hate Markus enough to willingly betray her mother? There was only one way to find out. "I need your help."

"My help?" she echoed.

"There's a lot you don't know about Markus. He's not a good man. But I need more evidence before any charges can be filed." How much time did he have left? "I need to get onto the church compound. There's a computer with his financial records."

She shook her head. "My mom will be beyond pissed if she ever found out I helped you."

"She'll be upset if you let her stay involved with a criminal, too," he said.

Sarah's phone began to beep. His time was up. He'd told her everything. But was it enough?

SARAH HAD AGREED to hear everything Liam had to say. Together, they'd returned to his hotel room, and now she stood next to the bed. Funny that a few hours earlier, she shaved her legs in case her night ended at his place. Here she was, but this wasn't the evening she had hoped for at all.

The comforter was covered with papers and photographs. For the past hour, Liam had outlined the evidence.

The story was easy to follow. Members of the Ever After Church lived in desperate poverty as Markus extorted money from those same people and their families. He claimed the money was all for the good of humanity.

In every picture of Markus, her mother was at his side.

There were too many questions for her to think straight. Sure, she wanted to know how her mom got involved with a con man like Markus. Yet, there were other things she wanted to know, as well. Finally, she settled on a single question. "What was your plan before your original plan went to hell?"

Liam leaned against the wall. He folded his arms across his chest and stared at the pictures on the bed as he spoke. "I had hoped to rekindle our friendship. Once we were established, I'd talk you into connecting me to your mom. Then, your mom would introduce me to Markus."

"Friendship," she echoed. "That's a funny word choice for how aggressively flirty you've been. Flowers. Cat treats. Nice restaurants."

"Okay, fine. I was playing the romance card. And I am sorry for hurting your feelings."

Her feelings weren't just hurt. They'd been crushed to dust. "How could you do this to me?"

"I've got a confidential informant who used to be a member of the church. Markus coerces people into giving him money. There's no way to file charges because he didn't steal the cash. But he uses the internet to lure followers to him. That's wire fraud. Aside from that, there's speculation that he's laundering money for some seriously bad people. His real transactions are kept in the church's admin building. To find those documents, I need access. But…" He picked up another picture. In this one, a guard armed with a rifle stood next to a road leading to the Ever After Church. "Obviously, I can't sneak onto the property. What I need is an invitation."

In a way, she understood why he'd come to her. She was the most direct path to Jessie and, therefore, Markus. Knowing didn't help ease her hurt. In fact, the void inside her yawned wider.

The shambles of her love life aside, Sarah had to help her mom. She picked up a photograph. The image was black-

and-white. Taken from a distance, the subject was grainy, yet unmistakable. In it, her mother stood next to Markus. Jessie gestured to the large house where she lived. Sarah recognized the floor-to-ceiling windows from a video call when her mom gave her a virtual tour.

In the background of the picture was something her mother hadn't bothered to share. Shacks, constructed of boards and plastic tarps, were scattered around the beautiful home. People milled about in the picture. Everyone was thin, dirty and looked hungry—everyone, that is, other than Jessie and Markus.

Setting the photo back on the bed, she looked at Liam. "Tell me what you need."

Chapter Six

Sarah studied one of the photographs taken at the Ever After Church's compound. In it, her mother embraced Markus, the two of them laughing. The diamond in her engagement ring sparkled in the sun. In the background, a child with a dirty face cried.

How could Jessie happily ignore such suffering?

Then again, she knew the answer. Markus had money. Her mom had always wanted the security that came with a boatload of cash.

Maybe she should be asking another question—one that she didn't know how to answer. Was she willing to set up her mother with the FBI?

Sure, Jessie wasn't perfect. But what kind of daughter betrayed their mom?

Liam sat on the corner of the bed. "I know this a lot to take in."

"A lot to take in?" she snapped. Anger burned her from the inside out. She was furious at him for disrupting her boring life. She was furious at him for making her choose between helping to put a criminal in jail and deceiving her mom. But mostly, she was furious with herself. She'd trusted Liam completely. And even now, she couldn't walk away. "What can't I take in? The fact that my mom is dating a criminal or that you set me up?"

"Both, I guess." He was so damn calm, it made her want to scream.

She drew in a shaking breath. "If I were to help, what would you want me to do?"

"If?" He lifted an eyebrow.

"If," she repeated.

He exhaled. "You know I wouldn't ask you to do this if it wasn't important, right?"

"The thing is, I don't know anything about you." She didn't bother to keep the anger from her tone. "I used to know you. But now?" She shrugged.

"I've already shared a ton of confidential information about my case. If you aren't interested in helping, I really can't say anything else." He paused. "Just do me a favor and don't say anything to your mom about running into me."

"It's too late for that." Sarah shook her head. "I was so excited that you and I accidentally bumped into each other, I called her last night."

"Did you speak to her? What'd you say?"

"I had to leave her a message." Oh, yeah. Her mom had returned her call during dinner. "She called me back. We just haven't spoken yet."

"What can I say to get you to agree to help me?"

She didn't have much fight left in her. Still, she wasn't ready to give up or give in. Shaking her head, she said, "Give me some time to think things through."

"Fair enough. Can I call you in a few days?"

Oh, whom was she kidding? She couldn't let her mom stay

involved with someone like Markus. Even if Jessie wasn't personally charged with a crime, her life would be ruined. Suddenly exhausted, she slumped back in the chair. "I'll do it."

Liam slipped off the bed and knelt in front of her. He placed a hand on her knee. His touch sent energy buzzing through her veins. He asked, "Are you sure?"

"No, but I'm going to help my mom anyway. I want one thing from you," she said. "If my mom is implicated in any of this, you need to help her out."

"I'll do what I can to shield your mother." He pressed a hand to his chest. "I promise."

It wasn't the complete assurance she hoped for. Yet, it was the best she was going to get. "Now what?"

"You need to convince your mom that you and I are in love. More than in love. Tell her that we're talking about making the relationship permanent. With me as a future son-in-law, she'll have to introduce me to Markus."

Liam's plan was so simple, she knew it'd work.

Standing, she went to the chest of drawers. Her purse sat next to the TV. She dug through the bag until she found her phone. After pulling up her list of recent calls, she found her mom's number and placed the call. Turning on the speaker function, she counted each ring.

One. Two. Three. Four.

"They have really bad service," she said, not bothering to look at Liam. "It's why we have a hard time speaking to each other."

Before Liam could say anything, her mother's voice came out of the speaker. "Hi, hon. Are you still there?"

"Hi, Mom." Guilt twisted in her gut.

"Well, you know how big this house is. I heard the phone ringing but had to run to get it."

In that moment, she knew something to be both unpleasant and true. Her mother would ignore a lot to live in a large home and have lots of money. "I'm glad you answered. I've got news. I told you how I ran into Allison's older brother, right?"

"Well, I got your message," said Jessie. "What was his name? Ian?"

"It's Liam. We've been out twice, and Mom, I can't believe it. I'm in love."

"Love," her mom echoed. "Are you sure? You've only been on two dates, that's pretty quick."

"It is." She continued, trying her best to sound dreamy. "Kind of like you and Markus."

"That's great for you both," said her mom, sounding like she didn't mean a word.

She leaned against the dresser. The edge bit into her flesh. The pain seemed to be a recompense for what she was about to say next. "I was thinking since you don't work, you could come to Boise. I'd love for you to see him again."

"You know I can't get away from the church on short notice. Markus needs me. The congregation needs me, too."

Did her mother really believe she was helping? "Oh, that's too bad. Liam's going back to DC at the beginning of next week. He has meetings with his other clients," she added. Any mention of business—and therefore money—was sure to get her mom's attention.

"You never said why Liam is in Idaho."

"He works for a bank and is here trying to find a building for a client that's expanding their business," she said, repeating his well-worn lie. Then, she added one of her own. "He's even looking to donate money to local charities. You know, make a good impression for his client."

"Markus and I really can't get away from the church for long. We're going into Owl Creek on Thursday. He promised to take me to Hutch's Diner. We could meet for brunch at ten."

Just like Sarah had dangled a hook in front of her mom, Jessie saw the possibility of money and had taken the bite. "I'll have to check," she said, knowing full well that she was going to use a personal day. "Can I call you back in the morning?"

"Sure thing," said her mom. "Love you."

"Love you, too." The words caught in her throat. After ending the call, she slipped her phone into the pocket of her dress. "I'll take Thursday day off and we can go to Owl Creek together."

"I hate to ask this, but can you take off Friday, too? If we're lucky, I'll be able to get onto the compound. But getting an invitation will take more than one day."

The weight of the world dropped onto her shoulders, leaving her flattened. Then again, what was another day? "I'm sure I can take off two days."

Liam exhaled and smiled. Her heart skipped a beat. After everything, how could she still find him attractive? He said, "You did great on the phone, by the way. I really appreciate what you're doing for me."

"It's not for you," she snapped. "This is for my mom. She needs to get away from Markus before he causes her real trouble."

"I get that," said Liam, his tone conciliatory. "But you're the key."

She took out her phone and opened a rideshare app. "There's lots to do before Thursday. I have to get home."

Liam already had his phone out, too. "I'll get you a car. It's the least I can do." She started to argue. After all, she was an adult and could order her own ride. Then again, why should she incur expenses on the government's behalf? Saying nothing, she watched as he tapped on the phone's screen. "Looks like someone can pick you up in five minutes."

She had done the unthinkable by deceiving her mother. True, someone needed to save Jessie from her own bad decisions. But there was more. Deep down, Sarah knew that she hadn't made the call just for her mother's benefit. It was Liam. She'd had feelings for him her entire life. It was a habit. An addiction. And quitting Liam wasn't going to be easy. The room suddenly felt too hot. She started to sweat. "I'll wait in the lobby."

Liam rose from the bed. "I'll come with you. Make sure you get home safe."

Shaking her head, she said, "Everything you've told me is overwhelming. I need time to process. And besides…" She let her words trail off, knowing full well that it was better to keep some thoughts to herself.

"*And besides*, what?" he pressed.

She picked up her purse and coat, draping both over her arm. "Good night, Liam."

He stepped in front of her. "If we're going to work together, we need to be honest."

Honest? Until now, everything he'd said was a lie.

Before she could say anything, he added, "Besides, making sure you get home safely is the right thing to do."

"This isn't a real date. Stop acting like you care."

He stepped toward her. His scent, soap and sweat and pine of his cologne, washed over her. "Tell me what to say that will make this better between us."

"It's not my job to tell you how to fix things." She continued, "And there is no us."

His phone pinged. He glanced at the screen. "Your ride's here."

She shifted the coat from one arm to the other. "Well, then, I better go."

She maneuvered past him. Her shoulder brushed his chest. The side of her arm grazed his abs. Her pulse began to race.

He placed his fingers on the back of her hand. Electricity danced along her skin. "Look at me."

She couldn't lift her gaze. Her obsession had to end. "Good night, Liam."

Slipping away from his touch, she opened the door and stepped into the hallway. She walked down the corridor and drew in a deep breath. And then another. By the time she reached the elevator, Sarah's heart rate had slowed. She pushed the call button and the doors opened immediately. Stepping into the car, she rode the elevator to the ground floor. By the time the doors opened into the lobby, she was able to think.

The rideshare waited next to the front doors. She verified her driver before settling into the back seat. Looking out the window, she knew why Liam hadn't been honest with her from the beginning. Still, she hated that he'd lied to her. She also hated that she bought his lie. What she hated worst of all is that in being around Liam, she started to hope that all her adolescent dreams were about to become true.

Her phone pinged with an incoming text from Margaret.

Message me so I know you weren't kidnapped or something.

Instead of texting, Sarah opened her phone app and placed a call.

"Hey," said Margaret as she answered the phone. "I didn't mean to be a pest, just wanted to know that you were okay."

"I'm better than okay," said Sarah, forcing her tone to be bright. "I think I'm in love."

"Love?" her friend echoed. "That was fast."

"Not when you think about it. We've known each other our whole lives. Finding Liam was like coming home." Her chest tightened. Sarah was prepared to lie, but it was the truth that hurt. "I'm going to take a few personal days—Thursday and Friday—to take Liam to Owl Creek. That way he can meet my mom as my boyfriend, not just Allison's older brother."

"Well, you've got it bad."

Sarah tried to laugh. "You make it sound like I've come down with the flu."

"In a lot of ways, being in love *is* a sickness. I'm going to say one last thing, and then I'll stop. You know that he lives in DC and he's only here for work?"

It didn't matter. Once she helped Liam, the fake relationship would become a bogus breakup. "Yeah, I know. Can you stop by Friday and Saturday to check on Tolstoy?"

"Of course I can take care of your fur-baby, so long as you promise to be careful."

"You're the best." Would she ever tell her friend the entire truth? "I'll see you tomorrow," she said before ending the call.

Staring out the window, she watched her reflection in the glass. She tried to be an informed person. She watched the news. She read legal thrillers and nonfiction books on criminals and crimes. It was naive to think that she could slink away from the case like she was sneaking out the back door. If Markus was arrested, there'd be a trial. Sarah would be called as a witness. The minute she agreed to help, she became involved until the end.

Her phone pinged as another text landed on her phone. Sarah decided that if it was Margaret again, she'd tell the truth and ask for advice.

The text was from Liam.

I know there was a lot to absorb tonight. I wish things could be different.

Hoping for some kind of real relationship with Liam was like trying to grab fog. Sure, it seemed like something solid was there, but in the end, it was only mist.

She typed out a message, asking the only question that mattered.

Different, how?

He replied right away.

I wish your mom wasn't involved with Markus.

Well, that made two of them.

Agreed.

He sent another message.

I am sorry that I lied but there was no other way.

She typed out another text.

I'll be able to make the trip to Owl Creek on Thursday and Friday. I have the weekend off, too, if we need extra time.

Liam sent another message.

Thank you.

Another message followed the first.

I'll do what I can to help your mother. I swear.

He'd lied to her about...well, about everything. Was this another one of his fibs?

The car stopped in front of her building. Sarah unbuckled her seat belt. "Thanks for everything."

"You have a good night," said the driver as she opened the door.

"You, too," she said, stepping into the parking lot.

She jogged through the cold and up the stairs to her apartment. At the door, she unlatched the lock. The scent of roses filled her apartment. It seemed like it had been days since Liam showed up at her apartment, not hours.

Tolstoy ran across the room as she opened the door. She bent down and picked him up from the floor. Purring, he tucked his head under her chin. "Did you miss me, buddy?" she asked, scratching under his chin. She walked into her room and set him on the bed. "Then you're going to be unhappy with the next few days. I'm going on a trip."

Setting both her purse and coat on the end of her bed, she

sat down on the mattress. The cat nudged her side. She ran her hand over his silky fur. "You love me, right?"

He offered her the underside of his chin for a scratch.

"I'll take that as a *yes*."

Maybe Sarah was no good at love. Maybe it was her destiny to be alone—a librarian and her cat. Maybe she overlooked the good guys and was only interested in those who'd never love her back. She missed her father, truly she did. But he hadn't been around much when she was growing up. Of course, now she knew why. Maybe that was why she'd been so fixated on Liam. He'd showed her the attention she craved.

That was the biggest irony of them all. For years, she wanted Liam to need her. Now that she was crucial to his investigation, she wished that he'd forget that they knew each other at all.

Chapter Seven

Two days later
7:35 a.m.

Liam shifted his duffel bag from one shoulder to the other. Standing on the sidewalk in front of the hotel, he scanned the long line of early-morning commuters that clogged the downtown street with traffic. Sarah was supposed to have picked him up already. He glanced at his phone, checking for the time: 7:36 a.m.

A hard knot formed in his gut.

True, Sarah had agreed to help him. But he also knew she wasn't fully on board.

He didn't blame her.

He didn't like the lies or betrayal, either.

But like his boss said earlier, sometimes you have to get dirty to clean up a mess.

If truth were told, A-DIC Dubois was another reason for his roiling gut. By bringing Sarah Colton into the case, he'd opened a proverbial pandora's box. Instead of being filled with curses and evil, he'd found paperwork. Then again, paperwork was a curse all on its own. After several heated discussions, Dubois had given the okay to continue the investigation.

He exhaled, and his breath caught into a frozen cloud. The sky was already a brilliant shade of blue. Today was going to be one of those beautiful Idaho days that started the transition from winter into spring.

Being in the place where he grew up brought back all the reasons why he loved his home state. The weather was crisp and clear. The people were friendly and inviting. He had friends who shared his history, not just workmates who knew him professionally. Besides, Boise was the only place he could ever find good finger steaks.

Then, there was Sarah Colton.

He hadn't seen her since she left his hotel room on Tuesday night. They'd communicated, but only through texts. He had to brief her more about her undercover role but figured his instructions could wait. They would have time to go over things while stuck together on the drive to Owl Creek.

On Tuesday evening, he'd brought her flowers. When he stopped at the market to get the bouquet and the cat treats, he understood his motivations. Then, she opened the door, and he knew that he was in real trouble. It was more than her brown hair, her green eyes or the way her dress hugged her curves. It was her smile. It was her scent. It was the way she'd felt in his arms as he'd held her in the stairwell.

He rubbed his forearm, the memory of her body pressed against his still lingered on his flesh.

Oh sure, it could just be loneliness. After years of working in DC, Liam didn't have a single friend outside of work. Aside from Constance, those people were just friendly colleagues. Seeing Sarah, and being here, reminded him of all the things he'd missed.

The phone began to shimmy in his hand a moment before caller ID flashed on the screen.

Sarah Colton.

The knot in his middle hardened. Had she changed her mind? After fighting to bring her onto the case, what would happen if she backed out now?

Drawing in a lungful of icy air, he swiped the call open. "Hey."

"Sorry I'm late." She was breathless. "It took forever to decide what to pack. Now, I'm stuck in traffic. I'll be there in five minutes. Ten minutes, tops."

"Thanks for letting me know." A café sat across the street. He'd been so focused on getting out of town that he hadn't bothered with breakfast. Now he had a few minutes to spare. "How do you take your coffee?"

"Coffee?" she repeated, as if the word held no meaning for her. "I really don't drink coffee. I'm more of a tea person."

The café would have tea, too. "How do you take your tea, then?"

"Green tea with honey and lemon."

The cars on the road stopped for a traffic light. Liam stepped from the curb and wound his way past the bumpers. "I'll see you in a few."

On the opposite side of the street, the Winding River Café sat between an ophthalmologist's office and a shoe store. A sandwich board boasted fresh smoothies, açai bowls, organic coffees and teas, and a used bookstore. He opened the door and was greeted with the sweet scent of warm blueberry muffins. His stomach grumbled. Ten tables were scattered around the room. Most of them were filled. The server stood behind a long counter that was attached to a pastry case. She wore her hair pulled back in a blue bandanna and looked up as he entered. "Morning," she said. "What can I get started for you?"

"I'd like a medium green tea with honey and lemon, along with a black coffee."

"Anything else?"

The scent of the muffins was too much to ignore. "I'll take a muffin, as well." Sure, he didn't have to woo Sarah any longer. But really, she was doing him a solid favor. For that, he really was grateful. "You know," he said to the server. "Make that order for two muffins."

"I'll get those for you." As the server poured his coffee, Liam used his phone's app to pay.

"Here you go." At the end of the counter, the server set two cups in a drink container next to a paper bag. "The muffins are fresh from the oven."

Picking up his order, he hustled out the door. Traffic was stopped once again. Three vehicles back, a car beeped its horn. From the driver's seat, Sarah waved. Balancing the drink tray, the paper bag and his duffel over his shoulder, he hustled to where she idled.

After setting the drinks on the roof of her car, he opened the back door. Once his bag was set on the rear seat, he opened the front door and slid into the passenger seat. As he slammed the door shut, traffic started moving. "Your timing was perfect."

She inhaled deeply. "Are those blueberry muffins?"

"They are." He set the tea and coffee into the car's cupholders. Then, he opened the bag. "You want one?"

"Yes, please." He handed her a muffin. "Thanks for picking up a tea."

Traffic stopped again. She eased her foot onto the break while peeling away the paper wrapper. She took a bite of muffin and hummed with satisfaction. The sound reverberated in his chest. He cast a glance in her direction. A piece of muffin stuck to her lip. She licked it away. The gesture was unassuming and, still, undeniably sexy. The car's interior suddenly became sweltering. He closed the heating vents and blew onto his coffee.

In front of them, traffic rolled forward.

"Here." Sarah held out her muffin. "Hold this."

Liam placed his hand under hers. Their gazes held. For a split second, he swore that she saw into his soul. It was the first time he'd been seen in years. No longer was he a cog in the machinery that was the FBI.

From behind, a horn blared.

Pulling away his hands, he said, "I got it."

Eyes forward, Sarah clenched the steering wheel with both hands, and drove.

Easing back into the seat, Liam tried to relax. Yet the feeling of his hands on hers still vibrated from his fingers to his wrist. He placed the muffin back in the bag and picked up his coffee cup. He took a long swallow, hoping that the caffeine high would reset his system. Because Liam knew one thing—if he was going to spend the next few days with Sarah and be professional, he was going to have to get his libido in check.

SARAH HAD NEVER taken the trip from Boise to Owl Creek by herself. But when she learned about her numerous siblings, one thing was clear. They were part of the fabric that held Owl Creek together. If she wanted to see them, she'd be driving this way more often.

Leaning into the seatback, she sighed.

Liam looked at her from the passenger seat. "Everything okay?"

"There's a lot to deal with, you know? It's more than my mom being involved with Markus." Even his name tasted foul. "It's that Owl Creek is where they're from..."

"You mean all the other Colton kids?"

There was so much to say, but her throat was tight with emotions. "Yeah," she grumbled the single word. "I'm not sure what to do if I see one of them. Things still feel weird."

"What caused all the hurt feelings?"

"Honestly, I don't know why this is so difficult." Her shoulders slumped. "Since I don't know, anything I say will be a guess."

"You know, my middle name is Speculation."

"Your middle name is James," she said.

"Liam James Speculation Hill," he said. "I had it legally changed last year."

She didn't want to find him charming. But he was. With a quiet chuckle, she shook her head. "I forgot your corny sense of humor."

"You remembered that my middle name was James but forgot how I'm the King of Bad Jokes?"

Her shoulders relaxed, releasing some of the tension she'd been carrying for days.

"Honestly," he continued, "I'd like to hear what you think."

The highway ran between a forest on one side and a steep mountain peak on the other. Keeping her eyes on the road, she said, "I guess they were shocked to find out that Nate and I existed. Plus, who'd want a living and breathing reminder that your parents have been lying to you for years?" She lifted the tea from the cupholder and took a sip.

"I'm sure they don't blame you and Nate," said Liam. "How could they? You guys didn't ask to be born."

That was true. It was a thought that kept her awake on sleepless nights. "But we're a complication they can't ignore."

"I'm sure things will change," he said. "Once they get to know you, they'll come to love you."

She glanced at Liam and gave him a small smile. "I wish I had your optimism."

"We might not even run into any of your siblings."

"Now I know that you're optimistic. The Coltons are everywhere in Owl Creek." Like the fact that one of her Colton siblings, Ruby, was the local veterinarian. There was also Fletcher, an Owl Creek police detective. One sister owned a bookstore, and another owned a catering business. "It'll be me against them."

The tea in her stomach churned.

"I'll be with you." Liam smiled. The roiling changed to a quickening. "Besides, I am an FBI agent. They can't mess with you if I'm around."

She looked back at the road. "But they won't know that you're an agent. Besides, one of my brothers was with the FBI, too, I think."

He rubbed his forehead. "There are a lot of Colton kids. It's hard to wrap your head around all the siblings."

"Nate and I make a dozen."

She drove for several miles, neither one of them speaking. Finally, Liam cleared his throat. "We should probably discuss our cover story."

Cover story? "What do you mean? Are we supposed to have a made-up background? Because I'll be honest. I'm not going to be great with a lot of new details."

"For the most part, what we'll tell people is the truth. I'm Liam Hill—Allison's older brother. I came back to Boise for work and ran into you. We went out twice and realized that we have an amazing bond. Since we knew each other before, there's no awkward getting-to-know-you phase." He hooked air quotes around the words *getting to know you*. "So, sure, the relationship is moving fast, but who cares?"

"There are a lot of lies in our story. We aren't in a relationship." Picking up her tea, she took another sip. Working the cup back into the holder, she continued, "We don't care about each other."

"I get that you're mad at me still." Shifting in his seat, he turned to face her. "But if you carry your anger around like an accessory, nobody will believe that we're in love."

She inhaled and exhaled. "What will I have to do?"

"You and I will have to hold hands," said Liam. "Gaze into each other's eyes. Kiss in public."

Over the years, she'd wondered what it would be like to really kiss him. Was she about to find out? But there would be no real emotions in the act. In a lot of ways, it would be worse than never knowing. "What about the hotel situation?"

"I booked us one room but there are two beds." He paused. "Nothing will blow our cover quicker than someone not believing that we're a couple."

"Great. No pressure." Her hands ached. The ridges of the

steering wheel pressed into her palms. She loosened her grip. "So how does this whole investigation thing work?"

"Once I have the evidence, Markus will be arrested. Then, there'll be a trial to determine his guilt or innocence."

"I'll have to testify, right?"

"You will."

How would Jessie feel when Sarah took the stand? Actually, she didn't need to ask that question. She already knew the answer.

Her mom would be furious. She'd hate Sarah. It might destroy their relationship.

Might, hell.

Sarah couldn't worry about that right now. Instead, she asked another question. "Do you do this a lot? You know, work on undercover cases?"

She turned to glance in his direction. The sun caught him from behind and surrounded him with a golden halo. Then again, for much of her life, he'd seemed more like a deity than human.

"I barely get out of the Hoover Building," he said. "Most of my work has been analytics."

She asked, "Do you like it?"

"Define *like*," he joked. "Right now, it's all I do. It's all I know."

"You know the old saying about all work and no play."

Shaking his head, he gave a quick laugh. "Who knew a nursery rhyme was going to be the original slogan for a work/life balance?" He stretched his legs out. "I really don't have any kind of balance in my life. I only work. Right now, I'm hoping to get a promotion. Then again, the new job will mean longer hours and more responsibility. All the sacrifices will be worth it in the end."

"It's none of my business how much or little you work. It's no secret that I've always liked you. I just don't want you to have regrets." She waved a hand, as if erasing her words from the air. "Forget I said anything. You have a right to live the life you want. I'm not in any position to judge."

With an exhale, he looked out the window. Without turning to face her, he said, "Being back in Idaho made me realize all the things I've given up for my work." Liam leaned his chin on his fist and continued to stare out the window. "At the end of my life, I'll be able to look in the mirror and say, 'I worked hard.' Not a bad accomplishment. But think of the things I've missed already. Friends. Family. Love. The whole time, I've been so busy that I forgot that the whole point of life was to live."

She wanted to say something wise. Too bad she couldn't think of any advice. "Will this case help you get your promotion?"

"If I can bring down Markus Acker, my career is set."

"That's a good thing, right?"

"Yeah, it's a good thing."

She wasn't convinced.

A mileage sign stood on the side of the highway.

Owl Creek 20 Miles.

"Almost there," said Liam. "If you want to bail, now is the time. Call your mom and tell her we had a huge fight. Tell her that you're taking me back to Boise."

His plan was tempting. What's more, it would work.

Did she want to turn around now? Honestly, there was a part of her that just wanted to return to her uninteresting life. But could she live with herself if she ignored the people who lived at the compound? Also, what about Liam? Sure, she was hurt that he'd lied to her. But the wound was deep because she still cared.

She felt as if she stood on the edge of a cliff, wondering if she should jump. There was no turning back once she committed.

Rolling her shoulders back, conviction straightened her spine. "I'm in."

Chapter Eight

Liam sat in the passenger seat and gazed out the window. A mountain peak rose in the distance and tall pine trees stood on either side of the road. The view was breathtaking. Or it would've been, except for the fact that he'd been asking himself a single, important question.

Was he ready to work as an undercover agent?

True, he'd fought to open the case and to be assigned as the special agent in charge. It had been another fight to bring Sarah on board. But he'd spent his whole career in the Rat Maze at headquarters. He didn't even have experience working with a criminal unit and out in the field—let alone being a singleton.

A large wooden sign surrounded by a dormant flower bed stood at the side of the road.

Welcome to Owl Creek, Idaho.

A Great Place to Visit. A Better Place to Live.

Owl Creek was like many towns in the Mountain West. Their economy was based on tourism. Skiing in the winter. Boating and hiking in the summer. Early March would be their low season, and it explained why the streets were all but empty. The buildings that lined Main Street were an eclectic mix of Victorian-era brick and new constructions.

Sarah eased her car next to the curb and put the gearshift into Park. "We made it," she said. "Hutch's Diner is on the next block. It's the one with the blue-and-white-striped awning."

Liam opened the car door and stepped onto the sidewalk. The scent of pine hung in the air. "It's nice here." He slammed the door closed. "Not at all like DC."

Sarah had exited the car, as well. She stood next to the front bumper. "I thought you loved your city. What about spring coming early?"

He chuckled. "I guess I'm more of an Idaho boy than I thought."

Sarah stepped up onto the sidewalk and stood next to him. She was so close that he could touch her if he wanted. And honestly, he wanted to wrap his arms around her waist and pull her to him. But what did she want?

"I've never been to DC." Twisting from side to side, she stretched. "Obviously, I've read all about the monuments and museums. I'd love to see it one day."

For an instant, he wondered what it would be like to wander down the National Mall with Sarah. She'd want to read the entire quote wrapped around the inside of the Lincoln Monument. But what would she think of the words? Or if they visited the National Gallery, which exhibit would she like best?

The invitation clung to his lips.

He didn't know how to describe their relationship. Years ago, Sarah was his sister's best friend. Now, she was helping him catch a crook. She wasn't a coworker. She wasn't a friend. They weren't involved. Although he hoped they could fool everyone—including her mother—into thinking they were in love. Maybe their association was too complicated to define. "You should go one day."

"But only if it's in the spring, right?" She winked to show that she was teasing.

"We should probably cover some ground rules." The street was empty, but he lowered his voice to a whisper. After all, he couldn't be too careful. "Unless we're alone, we have to stay in character. You're you, Sarah Colton. I'm me, Liam Hill. We were childhood friends, and now we're in love. You don't have to say anything much about my job. But so long as you remember I work for a bank, we'll be okay."

"Got it," she said. And then, "Anything else?"

"We should probably hold hands."

"Yeah, sure." She slipped her palm into his.

An electric current ran up his arm and left his pulse racing. He wanted to think that his reaction was just natural tension. A lot was riding on this case. But he knew better. It was being close to Sarah.

They walked down the block. The restaurant's door opened. "There you are." Jessie Colton rushed toward the sidewalk with her arms opened wide. "I've missed you so much," she said, pulling Sarah into an embrace.

Stepping back, Sarah reached for his hand. "Mom, you remember Liam Hill. He's Allison's brother."

"It's been a while, but you haven't changed much," Jessie said, smiling.

"Well, you haven't changed at all."

Jessie squeezed his shoulder, and said, "It's good to see you, Liam." A large diamond ring flashed in the sunlight. "I saw you from our table and had to come out." She pointed to a window that overlooked the street.

"C'mon." Sarah's grip on his hand tightened. "Let's introduce you to Markus." Turning to her mother, she continued, "His client wants to invest in some nonprofits in Idaho. Since Markus is the pastor of a church, I thought that he might know some worthy charities."

Jessie's eyes went wide. "Of course Markus can help you. Tell me, would your client want to invest in a house of worship?"

Liam didn't need to worry about Sarah. She was a natural at working undercover. Turning to Jessie, he smiled. "That depends on the church."

Grasping his elbow, Jessie pulled him to the door. The snare had been set and it seemed like Jessie was interested in the bait. Only one question remained. Was the trap enough to fool someone as devious and dangerous as Markus Acker?

JESSIE STUDIED HER DAUGHTER, looking for signs that Sarah was really in love.

She was dressed nicer than usual—none of those T-shirts with sayings that she found so humorous. For the day, she had on turtleneck sweater in deep red. It matched her lipstick perfectly. She also wore a pair of black slacks and boots.

But more than Sarah's clothes were different.

Her cheeks were rosy. Her hair was shiny. She stood tall and proud—not slouched over like she spent too much time hunched over books. The changes were slight but unmistakable. Sarah had fallen for Liam—again.

Inside, questions practically bubbled up and out. How did Sarah's old crush happen to waltz back into her life? What kind of clients did he represent? And most important—how much money did he want to donate?

Unlike all her kids who lived in Owl Creek, Sarah and Nate were different. Maybe it's because those two kids had been Jessie's alone. She didn't have to share them with either of her exes, Buck or Robert—she'd left Buck and Robert hadn't been around all that much. She never had to raise those two in the shadow of her sister, Jenny—the saint.

Liam held open the door for Jessie and Sarah to pass. She glanced at his watch. The timepiece was expensive. She knew the brand. Markus wore one, as well.

As they squeezed across the threshold, she leaned in close to her daughter. "You and I need to find some time to talk. There are obviously some things you haven't told me."

"Oh?" Sarah's eye went wide with feigned innocence. It was the same look she'd used since she was a kid and trying to blame her brother for her own misdeeds. "What's that?"

"You didn't tell me how handsome Liam had gotten." She paused. "Or that he was so successful."

Sarah glanced over her shoulder. "You know I don't really care about money."

True, she didn't care about money. If she did, then she would have majored in prelaw or premed or even business. But no, Sarah insisted on library sciences. It didn't matter that she'd be poor her entire life. She loved books and wanted to be happy.

But Jessie knew different. Happiness without money was impossible.

"Well, he certainly is a catch," she said, her voice not much more than a whisper. She led them through Hutch's Diner.

It was the same place she'd come for years. The walls were

filled with memories, both good and bad. She was working as a waitress in this very restaurant the first time Buck asked her on a date. Years later, they'd brought Malcolm here to celebrate his first birthday. The original owner, Hutch, had still been alive and the celebration dinner had been on the house. The first time Robert suggested they leave Owl Creek was on the sidewalk in front of the diner. That last memory stabbed her in the side. Yet, she was intent on only being happy. And speaking of happiness, Markus waited at a table near the window.

"Darling," she said, placing both her hands in his. "I want you to meet Liam Hill. He's an old family friend and is in Idaho on business."

Markus didn't like new people, she knew. He had a hard time trusting others. Then again, who could blame him after all the lies that circulated on the internet? In fact, he hadn't wanted to come to brunch at all. But Jessie had insisted and now, she was happy that she had.

Smiling sweetly, she tossed her hair over her shoulder. "Liam's client is looking for a charity that might need a donation. Sarah thought of you and the church." That wasn't exactly what her daughter had suggested, but it was close enough to the truth. Besides, it was exactly what Markus would want to hear.

Her fiancé's face went slack for a moment. Then, he smiled. It was the same charm he exuded from the pulpit. "Sarah, honey," he said as he stood. "Good to see you." He pulled her in for a quick peck on the cheek. "And Liam." Markus held out his hand to shake. "Nice to meet you."

"Nice to meet you, as well," said Liam. "I hate to mix

business and family, but Jessie and Sarah think you can help me out."

Drawing his brows together, Markus nodded slowly. It was his grave-and-concerned look. She'd seen it more than once. One of the things she loved most about Markus was that he always knew what people wanted to see and hear. "I'll help if I can. Have a seat and tell me what you need."

Jessie waited until Liam sat next to Markus. Sarah sat to Liam's right. Finally, Jessie took her own chair. As she looked around the table, she felt light with contentment. This is what she'd always wanted—a loving relationship with her children, and a devoted man in her life. Sure, she'd made some mistakes. But she'd been treated poorly, too. Now, all the difficulties were in the past and she could finally live the life she wanted.

From here on, nothing could go wrong.

LIAM SAT BETWEEN Markus and Sarah. Just like he'd sprinted the last leg of a race, adrenaline surged through his system. Then again, sitting across from the target of his investigation was akin to crossing the finish line.

He picked up a pre-poured glass of water and took a sip. The gesture gave him a minute to get an initial read of Markus. He wore his dark blond hair short. Even for this lunch, he wore a well-tailored charcoal gray suit, white shirt and blue tie. Serious. Conventional. Trustworthy. In short, he dressed the part of a man who led a successful church.

But he'd seen the bank statements. According to the paperwork filed with the IRS, Markus and his church didn't take in much money. It was up to Liam to get the evidence proving all of that was a lie. So, he hadn't crossed the finish line at all. In fact, he'd just completed the first leg of a grueling multistage endurance event.

Markus watched Jessie as she chatted with her daughter. He smiled. The expression filled his eyes with genuine warmth. Did the pastor really love Sarah's mom? It seemed so.

Leaning toward Markus, he lowered his voice. "I remember Sarah's mom from when I was a kid. She was always anxious about one thing or another. Just seeing her for two minutes now, I can tell that she's more relaxed. Seems like she's a changed woman."

Markus sat straighter. "You think so?"

"I do." A twinge of guilt caught in his throat. He didn't like using Markus's feelings for Jessie against him. Then again, if he wasn't going to put Acker in jail, why was he in Owl Creek at all? "Seems like you showed up at the right time to save Jessie."

"Save Jessie," Markus repeated. "I'd like to think that I, along with the members of the Ever After Church, helped her through her grief."

"I'm sure it was more you than anyone else."

"Tell me." Markus turned to face Liam. "Are you a religious man?"

Liam sighed. "I don't go to church if that's what you're asking. But I do have a strict set of beliefs."

"Oh?" Markus picked up his own glass of water and took a drink. "What are those?"

"I do what's right for my clients—especially if we can both profit."

Throwing back his head, Markus laughed. "Who do you work for now?"

"My bank's headquarters is in Washington, DC." Liam gave Markus all the information from his undercover profile.

"What client has brought you to Owl Creek?"

"Well," he said, "it was Sarah who brought me to Owl Creek. I was working in Boise."

"Fair enough. But you still haven't told me much about your client."

Liam exhaled. "I'm sure you understand confidentiality— being the pastor of a large church and all. My clients expect discretion from me, much as your congregation expects it from you."

"I understand completely," said Markus. "What's more, I value a man who can keep his own counsel." He paused. "I understand that you used to work for the FBI."

Liam nodded. It'd be impossible to escape that truth. "I did."

"Can I ask why you left the Bureau? Don't most people stay with the federal government until they retire?"

"Have you seen how much FBI agents get paid?" he asked.

Markus shook his head. "Can't say that I have."

"Let's put it this way—it's not nearly enough money to live in a place like DC."

Markus chuckled. "Jessie mentioned something about investing in a charity."

The charity investment wasn't part of the original script, but something Sarah had added. Even though he'd never worked in the field, he knew that to be a successful undercover agent, he needed to improvise. He said, "It's one way to create a connection with a community."

"Does this charity have to be in Boise? I have some contacts in churches there, of course," Markus continued, wiping sweat from the side of his glass. "But if you could work with an organization closer to Owl Creek, I could personally help you out."

Liam recalled one time he and his father had gone fishing on the Payette River outside Boise. It had been boring just standing on the riverbank, waiting for a fish to bite. But one had.

Pull him in but slowly, his father had advised. *Otherwise, he won't swallow the hook all the way and might get loose. Make him think that he's coming for you. The fish has gotta think it was his idea all along.*

He had to follow his dad's advice from all those years ago. "I appreciate your offer to help locally, but this really isn't where my client plans to relocate." His mouth was dry. Picking up the water, he drained the glass in a single swallow. "But if you can make any introductions to organizations in Boise, that'd be great."

With a sigh, Markus smoothed down his tie. "Of course. There are plenty of worthy charities. How much do you plan to invest?"

A server, clad in a white shirt and black pants, walked past. Liam waved. "Do you have a slip of paper and a pen?"

"Of course." They removed both from the apron that was tied around their waist. Placing them on the table, the server said, "There you go."

Liam wrote a sum on the square of paper: $500,000. He slid it toward Markus. "This is confidential, of course."

"Of course," the pastor repeated. He removed a pair of reading glasses from the inside pocket of his suit jacket. After donning the glasses, he looked down at the sheet. His eyes widened for an instant. The change was gone as quick as it came. But Markus had swallowed the hook. "Let me make some calls on your behalf. Until then, maybe you'd like to see where we're building our next church."

"I'll have to talk to Sarah and see what she has planned..."

"I insist," said Markus. "Besides, I don't think that Sarah's been by our new home. I know that Jessie's proud of what we've built."

Yep, the hook was in very deep. "I'm sure we can figure something out. Sarah and I are in town until Sunday."

"Come by tomorrow morning. By then, I'll have a list of worthy charities for your client." He wiped his mouth with a napkin and stood. "Excuse me a minute. I need to make a call."

Jessie looked over as Markus rose. "Where are you going?"

"I just need to check on something."

"Now?" Jessie asked. "After Sarah and Liam came all this way to meet us? Can't it wait?"

Markus placed his lips on Jessie's cheek. Closing her eyes, she leaned into the kiss. He said, "I won't be gone for a minute. Order food. You know what I like. We're here to celebrate since Sarah's come to visit."

Sarah gave a tight-lipped smile.

Markus strode across the dining room. From a nearby table, two men with short haircuts and thick necks rose. They followed Markus from the dining room. He'd seen the photos from the church compound and the armed guards at the gate. It appeared that Markus had his own security detail, as well.

"What's up with the bodyguards?" he asked, as they left the restaurant.

Jessie sighed. "Markus has gotten some threats recently.

It's like that with important people. We felt it best to put extra protection in place."

"What kind of threats?" asked Sarah. "Are you safe?"

Jessie patted the back of her daughter's hand. "I didn't want to mention anything to you, hon. It's just trolling on the internet. Nothing to worry about."

Before Jessie could continue, Markus returned.

Smoothing down his tie, he smiled. "Crisis averted. Have we ordered yet? I'm starving."

"You look like you're in a good mood," said Jessie, leaning into Markus's side. "What's up?"

"I got some really great news, that's all."

Liam's phone pinged with a text. He checked his watch for the message. It was from Constance. "Someone searched you on the internet. The background we planted was all they found."

He wasn't surprised. Obviously, Markus had left the table and conducted a search for Liam. The fact that he'd only found what the FBI wanted him to see meant that everything was going as planned.

It also meant that Markus really had swallowed the bait completely. Now, it was up to Liam to reel him in.

Chapter Nine

Sarah hooked her arm through her mother's elbow as they left
the restaurant. A black SUV was parked at the curb. A man
jumped from the passenger seat and opened the back door.

"That's our ride." Jessie gave her arm a squeeze. "I'll see
you tomorrow."

"Looking forward to it." She pulled her mother in for a
quick hug. When had her mom gotten so thin? Thin, hell.
Jessie felt frail. "How are you, Mom?" she asked, whispering into her ear. "Honestly?"

Jessie held her at arm's length. "Right now, I'm thrilled.
I love having you here. Liam seems like a nice guy. Markus
likes him, too. I'm delighted for us all."

She studied her mother's face. "But are you always happy?"

"I always live in the now. And this moment is filled with
peace and bliss."

Her mother was with a man who needed armed guards.
How could that be peaceful? Liam and Markus stood up the
block. Heads bowed together, they talked.

Sarah felt the irrational need to tell her mom everything.
How Liam was actually with the FBI. That the feds had
Markus in their sights for stealing from his followers.

Then again, it wouldn't make a difference.

As soon as she got the chance, Jessie would tell Markus everything.

Her mom needed to see that he was a total creep for herself. Otherwise, she wouldn't believe what anyone—even Sarah—had to say.

"Earth to Sarah." Her mother waved her hand. "Come in, Sarah."

"Yeah, sorry," Had her mother been talking to her? "I zoned out for a minute."

"I'd say you did. I asked if you'd seen my new bag." Her mother held up a leather purse with red and green trim. "Markus bought it for me last week."

Sarah knew little about expensive brands, but she recognized the designer. "Wow, Mom. That's really nice. I bet it cost as much as my car's worth."

"Don't be silly." Jessie smoothed her hand over the glossy leather. "This cost twice what your car is worth."

Ouch.

Markus and Liam approached. Both men were laughing. Markus slid into the waiting SUV. "Let's go," he barked from inside the vehicle. "I have to stop at the post office before we go back."

Jessie reached for Sarah's hand. "Take care of yourself and I'll see you tomorrow."

Her mother's hand started slipping away. Sarah tightened her grip on Jessie's fingers. "Mom, you know I love you, right?"

"I know." She squeezed Sarah's hand once more before letting her fingers slip from her grasp. Her mother got into the SUV. The door closed and the vehicle drove away.

"As far as the Bureau is concerned, this brunch was a rousing success."

"Well, I'm super happy for your successes," she said, knowing that her tone was less than super happy.

"You don't sound pleased."

That was an understatement. "How am I supposed to feel? My mom is cozied up to the world's biggest scumbag. Why? Is it really for all the designer bags and flashy jewelry?"

"I'm sorry," said Liam. "I wish I could…"

She waved away his apology. "It's not your fault."

But that wasn't exactly true, either. As crazy as it sounded, even in her own mind, she wouldn't betray her mother for anyone other than Liam Hill.

"I know my mom," she said, her voice small. "She's never been a good person." Was she allowed to say that out loud? Sure, she'd thought it before. Even when she was a kid, her mom wasn't like most parents. She wasn't proud when Sarah or her brother did well. Instead, she was jealous of their accomplishments. And, of course, Jessie had been hiding a whole other family. "How could she keep me and Nate away from all our siblings?" But there was more. "How could she abandon all those kids?" The last word came out as a sob.

"Hey, hey, hey." Liam gripped her shoulders. His hands were warm and strong. She wanted to lean into his chest. Yet, she didn't dare. Because if she did, she'd never leave his side.

"I'm okay." She drew in a shaking breath. "I'll be okay." At least her second statement was closer to the truth. Whatever her mother did, Sarah always rallied.

"We've got a few hours before we can check in to the hotel. Owl Creek looks like a nice little town. Want to wander?" He pointed across the street. "There's a bookstore."

An hour of roving through stacks of books was the exact salve her soul needed. "You do know how to woo a lady— at least a librarian."

He reached for her hand.

For a moment, she ignored his outstretched palm. Then again, they were supposed to be a couple. Sarah slid her fingers between his. They fit together perfectly, like they'd been woven into a single being. She lifted her gaze to him. He was watching her with his big, brown eyes. She wanted to kiss him—just to see how his lips felt against hers. She moved closer and tilted her chin up. He moved closer still, erasing the distance between them.

A truck, its exhaust pipe rattling, roared past.

Sarah stepped back. "That was loud."

Liam ran a hand over his mouth. "Tell me about it." Another car passed. "Looks like it's all clear. Let's go."

Hand in hand, Sarah and Liam jogged across the pavement. Book Mark It. It sat in the middle of the block. The front windows were filled with a variety of titles—both newly released bestsellers and well-known classics. Liam reached around Sarah to grab the handle and pull the door open. His chest pressed into her back. His breath washed over her shoulder. A little shiver of excitement danced down her spine.

In the bookstore, the scent of paper and ink mixed with the aroma of coffee. Sarah inhaled deeply, and her shoulders began to relax. Her jaw loosened. At least for a few minutes, she could let her tension slip away.

"Are you okay for a few minutes?" Liam asked. "I want to find a quiet corner and text my boss. They're waiting for an update in DC."

"Go ahead," she said. "At least you have good news to share."

"Thanks a million." He pressed his lips onto her cheek. Her heart skipped a beat. Then again, it didn't matter what she felt. Any affection was part of the act.

The shop was filled with neat rows of books. The genre fiction section filled three of four walls. Mystery. Romance. Sci-fi and Fantasy. Nonfiction shelves were toward the back. Tables, heavy with discounted reads, were scattered throughout.

Running her fingers over a shelf, she scanned the titles.

"Excuse me," a woman called out. "Can I help you find anything?"

Sarah turned to the sound of the voice. Her heart ceased to beat.

Standing in the middle of the store was her sister Frannie Colton.

Hands on hips, she stared at her sister. "Sarah," she said, the single word ringing out like a thunderclap. "What are you doing here?"

Pulse racing, she stared at Frannie. Her sister wore her golden hair loose around her shoulders. For the day, she'd donned a pair of jeans, a cardigan and a T-shirt emblazoned with Read Banned Books. It was nearly identical to the shirt Sarah owned and loved to wear.

"I, uh, well, I..." Her mind froze up, spluttering, like a car that wouldn't start. She glanced over her shoulder, looking for Liam and some support. He'd disappeared into the racks. Great. She had to face her sister alone. "I didn't know you owned this store. I mean, I knew you owned a bookstore, but I never heard which one." She realized her mistake, but only once it was too late. "I should've looked you up or asked Jessie just now."

Frannie narrowed her eyes. "Your mom was here?"

After Robert's death, Jessie had tried to sue for his estate. Her mom's plan didn't work but it had certainly made Sarah and Nate's attempt at any relationship with Robert's other children more awkward. Still, Sarah couldn't deny the truth or ignore the question.

"Yeah, I met her here for brunch." She wondered if roadkill felt as beat up and flattened as she did right now. "I better go."

"No, wait." Her sister reached for Sarah's arm. "I don't want you to leave. I mean, you can, if you don't want to stay. I'm not kidnapping you or anything. It's just, well, we've never had a chance to chat." Frannie inhaled. She let out a long exhale. "Sorry. I was rambling. Can I get you a coffee? I mean, you just had brunch, so maybe you aren't really thirsty or anything…"

Was Frannie nervous, too? "Do you have tea?"

"I have so many different types of tea. What kind do you like?"

"I'll try your favorite."

"Aw, that's so sweet of you." Frannie walked toward the café. It was just a few tables on the far side of the bookstore with a pastry case and espresso machine. "Do you like hibiscus green tea?"

"As long as you have honey."

"How could I call myself a bookstore café if I didn't have honey?" Frannie slipped behind the counter and filled a mug with hot water from an electric kettle. She dropped in a tea bag and placed the mug on the counter. As the tea steeped, she said, "I heard you're a librarian in Boise."

Sarah nodded. "I started my job after finishing up grad school."

"Must be exciting to run a big library—all those books." Frannie sighed and leaned her forearms on the counter.

"I love my job. My favorite thing is to put a reader together with the perfect book. But administration is a lot of unglamorous work."

"Obviously, running a small business is hard. Owl Creek is supportive of the store, so we do okay," said Frannie. "But I'm with you. The best part of my day is when a book shows up at the store and I know which customers will love it." She paused. "It's nice to meet a fellow Colton who's also a bibliophile. I never fit in. Everyone else is so active and physically fit."

Honestly, she didn't know much beyond the basic details about her other siblings. "In Boise, it was just me and Nate." Then again, Nate was a police officer. He went for a run every morning and visited the gym several times a week. If there was ever a fight, he was in the middle, trying to break people apart. So yeah, he was definitely one of those active Coltons. "When we were kids, he was the athlete. I was just happy to sit in a corner and read."

"It sounds like I finally have someone who understands me. What a relief." Frannie slumped comically. For a moment, neither woman spoke. Frannie pushed the mug of tea across the counter. "Looks like this is ready. The honey's over there," she said, pointing. A ceramic sugar dish, cream pitcher and matching honey pot all sat on a table at the end of the counter.

Sarah picked up her tea and walked to the table. As she put a drizzle of honey into her tea, she said, "I love your shirt, by the way. I have the same one. Mine is blue."

"Oh my gosh, really?" Her sister approached with her own mug of tea in hand. "We'll have to wear them at the same time and get a picture. I'll hang it up behind the cash register in a frame and call it 'The Colton sisters against censorship.'"

"I'd like that," she said. She'd love to have a picture with Frannie. She took a sip of tea. It was warm and sweet. "This is really good."

"Glad you like it," said Frannie with a smile.

When she smiled, her sister looked just like their dad. For a moment, grief filled her chest. Sarah couldn't breathe.

"How long are you in town?" her sister asked.

"My friend Liam has some work in Owl Creek. We're here over night, for sure. After that?" She shrugged.

"Can I be honest?" Frannie asked. She didn't wait for an answer and continued, "I'm so happy you stopped in today. It's kinda like fate. I've been thinking about you a lot." She nodded toward a table. "Do you have a minute?"

"Sure." Sarah carried her cup to the closest table and slid into a chair. Frannie took a seat across from her and set down her own mug. "What's up?"

"Well, it's about what happened after my dad—correction, our dad—died. Everything was so chaotic. Jessie came looking for money, and then we all found out about you and Nate." She paused, blew on her tea and took a sip. "Well, none of us Coltons behaved the way we should have. You're part of our family. You lost your dad, just the same as me, and Fletcher and Lizzy and everyone else." She took another sip of tea. "I know you came to the wedding, but I wanted to call over the past few months. I wasn't sure if you wanted to hear from me. Sorry for not reaching out."

Sarah's throat tightened, filling with emotions. "I appreciate your apology and I accept."

"Are you sure you forgive me? I don't want you to just to be polite."

"I absolutely forgive you."

Frannie reached across the table and gripped Sarah's wrist. "I couldn't bring a baby into the world knowing that I had a sister out there and we weren't speaking."

She looked at Frannie again, taking her in from the top of her head to her feet. How had she not noticed the baby bump before? "A baby? That's so exciting!"

"I'm sure he or she will love their aunt Sarah very much."

"Aunt Sarah?" she echoed. "That's not something I expected to hear today. Or tomorrow. Or for a long time."

"Well, we'll all have to wait for this little one to start talking first." Frannie placed a hand on her middle.

"And, of course, we will get the little one reading," she joked.

Frannie said, "Dante loves books, so it'll be in our baby's DNA."

"There you are," said Liam, approaching from the bookstore side. "My one text turned into a long exchange. When I looked up, you were gone." She imagined that his superiors with the FBI would have questions about his progress.

"Liam, I want you to meet Frannie Colton, my sister. She's one of Robert's daughters."

"Sarah said you were here for your job," said Frannie. "What kind of work do you do?"

Liam repeated his cover story. He worked for a bank and was looking for property for a client. There was extra money for a local charity, maybe one in Owl Creek. Blah, blah, blah. "We just had brunch with Jessie and Markus."

"Oh, him." Frannie rolled her eyes.

"Sounds like Markus isn't your favorite person," said Liam.

Sarah wasn't going to let her sister get dragged into the

investigation. Rising from her seat, she reached for Liam's arm. "We should probably get going. You have work to do, I'm sure."

Her sister stood, too. "Maybe we can get together before you leave. What're you doing for dinner tonight?"

There was a lot she didn't know about an undercover investigation—like what was she supposed to do until they visited Jessie and Markus in the morning. "I'm not sure what we have planned."

"Our night is pretty open," said Liam. "Getting together for dinner would be great."

She hated to be suspicious. But she had learned the hard way that Liam was always focused on his investigation. So why was he so keen to have dinner with Frannie and Dante? In the end, it didn't matter. Pulling the phone from her pocket, she opened the contact app. "Give me your number," she said, handing the phone to her sister. "I'll send you a text."

Frannie typed in her contact information, then held out the phone to Sarah. "Here you go."

After saving the contact, she typed a long line of hearts and hit Send. "Now you have my number, too."

Frannie's phone pinged. Pulling it from the back pocket of her jeans, she checked the screen. "We'll keep in touch. There's a lot of missed years to make up for."

She opened her arms and her sister stepped in for a hug. "I'm so glad that I wandered into the store today. It feels like a new chapter for me."

Her sister squeezed her tighter. "It's a new chapter for everyone."

She wanted to believe that everyone would get a happy ending, even her.

There was more to the story. How would all the Coltons feel once they understood the plot twist? Would Frannie still want to make up for lost time when she learned that everything Sarah just told her was a lie?

Chapter Ten

Sarah and Liam stood on the sidewalk that ran between the bookstore and Main Street. A cold wind blew from the mountains. Tucking her nose into her collar of her coat, she trudged down the sidewalk.

"Anything you want to do right now?" Liam asked. "We still have time before check-in."

"After sitting in the car all morning, I'd like to walk. We can explore Owl Creek a little bit."

"Works for me," he said.

They walked without speaking. With each step, it was easy to let her mind wander. How different would her life have been if she'd grown up in a place like this, surrounded by family?

"You seem happy," said Liam, nudging her side with his elbow.

"I guess I am," she confessed. "I was worried about coming to Owl Creek. My mom. Running into one of my half siblings. The fact that we're pretending to be dating for the sake of your case." She glanced over her shoulder to make sure they were alone on the street. They were. "So far, this trip has gone better than I hoped."

"You think your mom will be okay once she knows the truth?" Liam asked.

Staring at the concrete as they walked, she stepped over a break between the slabs. Even now—as an adult—the childish rhyme filled her head.

Don't step on a crack or you'll break your mother's back.

As a kid, Sarah was terrified of hurting her mother in any way. Because of her father's frequent absences, Sarah always felt responsible for her mother's happiness. Time had changed a lot of things. Like now, she was working with the federal government to send Markus to jail. Her mother's life would be upended when that happened.

"There's no getting around it. My mom's going to be furious when she knows that I helped the FBI. But she needs to be saved, too. Otherwise, she'll end up in jail with Markus." She stepped over another crack in the sidewalk. "Running into Frannie has made this trip special. Not only is she my sister, but we have a lot in common."

"I noticed," said Liam with a wide smile. "You'll get to know her better at dinner."

His smile left her heart racing. She dropped her gaze back to the sidewalk. "Maybe we should cancel." She kicked a stone, and it skittered over the curb.

"Cancel? I thought you liked Frannie. Don't you want to see her husband?"

"I like her, and I'd love to see Dante again. But getting together means continuing the lie." She added quickly. "You and I aren't a couple. It's all pretend. I might get to know more about her, but she won't know anything about me."

"Go without me," he said, shoving his hands deep into his pockets. "That way, I'm not part of the equation."

Sarah glanced up, but she forgot whatever she planned to say. A black SUV sat at the end of the block. Her hands went icy, and she started to tremble. Looping her arm through the crook of Liam's elbow, she pulled him closer. "Look at the next block. Do you see it?"

The muscles in his arm went taut. "You mean the vehicle?"

The shadows of two people were visible in both the driver's and passenger seat. "What're the chances it's the same one that brought my mom and Markus into town?"

"That's definitely the same SUV." He paused. "It means that they took your mom and Markus home. Then, turned around and came back to Owl Creek."

"Why'd they do that?" she asked, although she already knew the answer.

"They're spying on us," he said. "On me."

It was just like Markus to be suspicious. "Then we have to give them something to report," she said. "We should kiss."

"Are you sure?"

She stroked the side of his face and smiled. "Remember, this isn't for me or you. But for them." She tilted her head toward the SUV.

He wound his arm around her waist and pulled her to him. Her breasts pressed against his chest. He placed his lips on hers. She was keenly aware of the security guards at the end of the block. Were they watching with binoculars? From a distance, would they be able to tell that the kiss was a fake?

She wrapped her arms around Liam's neck, pulling him closer. He moaned, his breath mingling with hers. Sarah couldn't help herself and she parted her lips. Liam understood the invitation. He slipped his tongue inside her mouth and kissed her hard. It was a kiss meant to conquer and claim. With a sigh, she surrendered.

He moved his hand from her waist to the small of her back. He pulled her closer, until there was no room between them. The muscles in his shoulders and pecs were tight. His abs were hard. His legs were long and lean. In short, he was everything a man should be.

Then again, the kiss was only for show. By now, the guards had seen enough.

She placed her hands on his chest and pushed back. Running her teeth over her lower lip, she peered down the street. It was empty. "They're gone."

Liam pressed his forehead into hers. "Should we talk about what just happened?"

"I think that this kiss was better than the last time," she said, teasing even though he'd sent the butterflies in her belly into a frenzy. "I'm sure we fooled the guards."

After drawing in a deep breath, he blew it out. "Very convincing for anyone watching."

"Good." The ghost of his kiss lingered on her lips. Hot blood ran through her veins. How was she supposed to work with him now?

"The thing is…" Liam began. His cell phone began to ring. Pulling it from his pocket, he glanced at the screen. "It's the hotel." He swiped the call open. "Hello?"

The speaker function wasn't turned on, but it didn't matter. Sarah could clearly hear the caller on the other end of the line. "Mr. Hill, this is Rakai Paku, the manager of The Inn on the Lake. I wanted to let you know that your room is ready. You can check in anytime you like."

THE INN ON THE LAKE overlooked Blackbird Lake. The front porch was surrounded by white railing. Tables and chairs were clustered in groups. If the weather was nice, it would be a perfect place to sit and enjoy the view. The lake was to the left and the mountains rose beyond the water. At one time, it had been the home of Owl Creek's founder. Made of golden bricks, the luxurious estate had been renovated to a resort. An outdoor pool, closed for the winter, sat behind a wrought iron fence. A tennis court was on the other side of the pool.

Liam sat in the passenger seat of Sarah's car. She maneuvered the station wagon into a parking place marked with a sign: Reserved for Guests.

His pulse pounded, echoing in his ears. The memory of Sarah's body pressed against his own still warmed his flesh. The scent of her soap and floral shampoo clung to him, as well. He inhaled deeply.

"This place is nice," she said, misreading his intake of breath.

It was better if she didn't know that the kiss left him drunk with lust. Because Sarah was like a fine wine—sweet, light and intoxicating. He'd only gotten a taste of her, and now he wanted more. Spending the night in the same room would be a special kind of torture. Then again, he had recruited her, so he was wholly to blame for his own mess.

She continued, "I wonder how much a place like this costs for a night."

"It's expensive," he said, happy to keep the conversation neutral. "I live in DC, where everything is pricey. But booking the room brought a tear to my eye and I was paying with an expense account."

"I guess this is one of the perks of working undercover."

She pressed a button on her steering wheel and the trunk opened with a pop. "Let's go."

Liam exited the car and then grabbed his duffel bag from the back seat. Sarah rounded to the rear and got her small suitcase from the trunk. After setting the luggage on the ground, she extended the handle and slammed the trunk closed.

A set of glass doors opened automatically as they approached the front of the hotel. The check-in desk was at the far side of the room. A grouping of chairs, upholstered in buttery-yellow fabric, surrounded a low table. A TV hung on a wall that separated the lobby from a restaurant. The television was set to a local news station. A meteorologist stood in front of an Idaho map. "A storm system is moving down from Canada. Expect more snow over the next few days. Seems like Old Man Winter isn't done with us yet..."

A dark-haired man stood behind the registration counter. He wore a name tag that read Mr. Paku, General Manager. He smiled as they approached. "May I help you?"

"We have a reservation under the name Hill."

"Nice to see you, Mr. Hill," said the manager. He slid a small envelope over the counter. "You're in room 317. The keys are inside here—" he tapped the envelope with a pen "—along with the password for the Wi-Fi. If you need anything, just press zero on the room phone. It rings to the front desk. The elevator is at the end of that hallway." He pointed to the corridor that ran to the left.

Liam scooped up the keycards. "Thank you so much," he said, giving Mr. Paku a small wave.

With Sarah at his side, they walked to the elevator. He waited as she pushed the call button. The doors opened automatically, and they stepped into the car. She pressed the button for the third floor and the doors slid closed. She stood a few feet in front of him. It gave him the perfect view of her from the back. Her round ass. Her hips. The way her jeans hugged her thighs. The light from overhead shone down, bringing out the fiery highlights in her hair. His fingers itched with curiosity. If he touched her hair, would he get burned?

In the small elevator, Liam was trapped with the truth. Sarah was more than pretty, smart and funny. She was even more than someone with whom he had a shared history. She was the kind of woman he'd choose to date if he ever made time for a relationship.

It was too bad that she and he were separated by an entire continent. If they were together, things might be different. But he hated the idea of a long-distance relationship. To him, loving someone from afar was worse than being alone.

The door opened. Sarah stepped out of the elevator, her rolling suitcase trailing behind her. Liam followed. A plastic sign hung on the wall. Rooms one through twenty were to the right. Twenty-one through forty were on the left.

"Looks like our room is that way," she said, before turning. He followed her, his feet suddenly too heavy for his legs. She glanced over his shoulder. "Are you okay?"

"Just tired, I guess," he lied. Because there was one other truth he had to finally admit. He wanted to take Sarah as his lover. It didn't matter that the relationship was a sham. His desire for her was real.

But there was something else he knew. If he slept with Sarah, he'd lose more than his chance at the promotion. He'd lose his job, as well. It meant he couldn't let anything happen between the two of them. Remaining professional was going to be the hardest part of an already complicated investigation.

SARAH STOOD IN front of the door to room 317. Liam tapped the keycard on the lock before pushing down on the handle. As the door swung open, she had a clear memory of sitting in Allison's childhood bedroom.

The two girls sat on the bed, crisscross-applesauce. Each girl held a pillow.

"Now, you have to hold it like this." Using the pillow as a fake torso, Allison continued, *"One hand behind the head. The other behind the back."*

Sarah copied the hold.

"Now, you lean in and kiss." Allison smooched her pillow. She set the pillow down, an unmistakable slobber mark on the case.

"I'll try." With an inhale, she puckered her lips and brought the pillow to her face. Like a million bubbles came out of her middle, she started to giggle. Burying her face in the pillow, she squealed, *"I can't."*

"Yes, you can. And you have to. How else are you supposed to know how to kiss when it comes time?"

At twelve years old, it was a reasonable question.

"I guess I'll just figure it out," she said, already thinking of the love scenes she'd read in the romance novels that had been purloined from her mother.

"It's not something you can read in a book. It's something you have to experience."

In seventh grade, Allison was already the star of the middle school lacrosse team. There were rumors she would be moved up to JV in the spring. Sarah usually stood on the sidelines, only playing when it was a blowout, and she couldn't do much damage. Even then, her feet always got tangled and the ball never stayed in the pocket of her crosse.

"Try again," Allison urged.

More giggles.

"Honestly," Allison huffed. *"Concentrate."*

"How is this even practice? I know the difference between a pillow and a person."

"You gotta use your imagination. Close your eyes."

Sarah did as she was told.

"Now, think of a guy you really like. And not my brother. That'd be so gross if you practice kissed Liam with my pillow. It has to be someone from our grade."

How was Sarah supposed to find any of the guys in her class attractive? All of them were defined by the three S's. Skinny. Spotty. Smelly.

With her eyes still closed, Sarah's mind filled with an image of Liam standing next to the pool in the Hills' backyard. Wearing nothing but swim trunks, his abs and pecs were defined. A thin line of hair ran from his navel down the front of his shorts. He smiled. His teeth were brilliantly white against his tanned skin.

"Do you have someone in mind?" Allison asked.

"Yes."

"Is it Liam?"

"I'm not thinking of your brother," Sarah lied.

Allison continued, *"Keep your eyes closed and imagine what it's like to kiss him. Then, kiss the pillow."*

Sarah brought the pillow to her face and puckered her lips. In her mind, Liam's hand rested on her cheek. Her fingers were wrapped in his hair. *"Oh, Sarah,"* he'd whisper. *"You are so beautiful."* And then, he'd place his lips on hers.

She set the pillow on her lap.

"How was that?" Allison asked.

"Not as bad as I thought." Her pulse raced, as the pretend kiss still buzzed through her mind.

Flopping onto her back, Allison asked, *"What'd you think your first time with a guy will be like?"*

Sarah lay on her side. *"I dunno. Awkward. Messy."*

"You're too literal. Don't you want romance?"

"Okay, what's your first time going to be like?"

"Prom night with Topher."

"No way. He's the same age as your brother. When we're eighteen, he'll be—" she paused and mentally did the math *"—in law school. No way will he take you to prom."*

"See, there you go, being all literal." Allison swatted Sarah with her pillow. *"Come on, what do you think your first time will be like?"*

Again, she thought of Liam. *"We'll check into a fancy hotel, where it's just the two of us. He'll be gentle and loving."*

"See, that's romantic. Who with?"

"Billy Frierson," said Sarah. Billy was an interesting combination of cute and smart.

As it turned out, her first time had been with Billy on prom night. It had been awkward and messy and sweet. But now, standing in the hallway of a fancy hotel, it was like her preteen fantasy was about to come true. But there was one huge difference.

Now, Sarah knew what adults did behind closed doors.

As she crossed the threshold, her luggage rolling behind

her, the phone in her pocket began to vibrate. She pulled out her cell and glanced at the screen.

Caller ID read: Frannie Colton.

She swiped the call open.

"Hey, Frannie," she said. "What's up?"

"I hope I'm not interrupting but I was wondering if Malcolm could join us for dinner. He stopped by the store today and I told him about meeting you and how we had plans for dinner. He asked if he could tag along. I didn't know what to say, but figured I should call you and ask." She paused. "No pressure, though."

"Of course," she said. It was funny that she'd been worried before about being rejected by her Colton siblings. Now, it seemed like they wanted to get to know her. "I'd love to see Malcolm."

"Great. I'll tell him. He'll be so stoked. Let's meet at Tap Out Brewery at seven."

"See you then," she said before the call ended.

With the phone pressed to her chest, she pivoted.

Liam stood right behind her, hanging his coat in a small closet. She stumbled back. Her thighs hit her bag and she started to fall. He reached for her, catching her wrist before she went down.

"You okay?"

"Yeah, thanks. It's the second time you've kept me from going ass over tea kettle."

He smiled and let go of her arm. "Glad to help."

"I'm a bit of a klutz. I guess that's why I've always been such a book nerd."

Gripping her suitcase, she rolled the bag toward the room. Liam moved at the same moment. She placed her palm on his chest to keep from colliding. His heartbeat raced beneath her touch. Dropping her hand, she said, "Sorry for touching you."

"I don't mind." His voice was deep and smoky and sounded like sin.

She swallowed. "What's that supposed to mean?"

"I… Well, I mean, it's no problem, I guess." He worked his jaw back and forth. "I feel like I'm covered in road grit. Unless you need anything, I'm going to grab a quick shower."

"I'll just get settled, then."

"Pick whichever bed you want." He set his duffel bag on the chest of drawers. Rummaging through the contents, he pulled out a pile of clothes. "I'll be done shortly."

She moved to the bed at the far side of the room and hefted her suitcase onto the mattress. The sound of the water's spray coming from the bathroom was unmistakable. An image of the two of them, naked and covered with water, came to her. Liam's mouth was on hers.

Without thinking, she crossed the room and placed her hand on the door. It would be so easy to go inside. If she did, would he send her away?

Chapter Eleven

Liam wanted to kiss Sarah again. But that would be wrong on so many levels. Standing under the shower's spray, he set the temperature to scalding. He really didn't need to get clean—what he needed was time away from Sarah. It wasn't like he hated her or her company. That was part of the problem. But there was a bigger issue. He knew how she tasted. He knew how her lips felt, how her body fitted perfectly with his, and how she sighed when he put his tongue in her mouth.

He could still feel the imprint of her palm on his chest. He scrubbed his breastbone with a cloth, but the echo of her touch remained. Over the past several days, she'd seeped into his pores until her scent was part of his own.

Ironic how he'd worried she'd redevelop feelings for him. After all, she'd had an epic crush on him when they were younger.

Who knew that he'd be the one who wanted her?

A vision struck him with a startling clarity. In it, he wore nothing other than a towel. Sarah's shirt lay on the floor of their current hotel room. The cup of her bra, lacy and pink, was lowered. He ran his thumb over one nipple as he licked the other one.

Without thought, his hand drifted to his groin. He stopped before gripping his length. He wanted Sarah, not just time alone in the shower. Maybe he was just horny, and he'd feel the same intense draw to any attractive woman. The last time he had sex was six—no, make that eight—months ago. He'd dated an analyst from the violent crimes division. Turns out, the only thing they had in common was their job with the FBI.

With a curse, he turned off the spigot. The shower stopped and a trickle of water leaked down his face. "Get it together, Hill." He emptied his lungs in one breath. "You cannot screw up now—not with everyone in DC watching the case."

He ran a towel through his hair before buffing his body dry. His strokes were hard and fast—a punishment for wanting Sarah so damn bad. His clothes sat on top of the vanity. Stepping from the tub, he reached for his skivvies. There was a single pair of jeans and a button-up shirt and nothing else.

Damn it. How could he have forgotten underwear?

Well, he wasn't going to walk through the room in just a towel, his fantasy aside. He'd have to go commando, at least for a minute. After stepping into his pants, he opened the door. A cloud of steam rolled into the room.

The first thing he saw was Sarah. She lay on her side, her head in her hand. A curtain of chestnut hair fell, hiding half her face. A book lay on the bed in front of her.

His fantasy from the shower was fresh in his mind. He couldn't help it, his arousal growing. Perhaps he should've taken care of things in the shower. At least it would've taken the edge off his sex drive.

She glanced up, her gaze meeting his. "That was fast."

He moved his duffel bag from the dresser to the unoccupied bed. "I forgot some things is all..." He found a pair of boxers tucked into a side pocket. "How are you, by the way?"

She drew her brows together. "What?"

"You tripped over the suitcase just a minute ago. I was making sure that you didn't get hurt."

She waved away his concern. "I'm fine. I've just never been graceful on my feet is all. You probably remember from when we were younger. Like the time Allison and I lost Bruno."

Oh, yeah. The two girls had walked the family dog. Sarah got tangled in the leash and Bruno had run as soon as he was free. "Who knew an arthritic Labradoodle would be so fast?"

She laughed while setting her book on the small table that separated the beds. "On the lead, he could barely walk. Off the lead, it was like he'd been launched out of a cannon or something."

"I haven't thought about him in years. He was a good dog. I still miss that old guy."

"He had a good family who loved him a lot," she said.

For a moment, he was surrounded by the ghosts of everything he lost when he left Boise. Friends. Family. Pets. A home. "I guess the only real guarantee we get is that time changes everything."

"Funny." She swung her legs around to sit on the side of the bed. "I still feel like the same old dorky kid."

"Trust me, you're fully grown up."

"I can't tell. Is that a compliment?" she asked, "Or are you saying that I'm old?"

"You've become a beautiful woman. Smart. Funny. Perfect." Sure, everything he'd said was true. But he hadn't meant to share so much. He ground his teeth together to keep from saying anything else.

"Wow," she said, rising to her feet. "That's one of the best compliments I've gotten from a guy."

"Sounds like you need to hang out with better men." He moved toward her.

"If you know any good men, let me know."

She was flirting. Inviting him to do more. To say more. To be more. The question was, did he want to cross that line? "I lied to you once," he admitted, "but I promise to be honest from now on. And honestly, if anything happens between us physically, there would be consequences."

She closed the distance between them. "Because if your superiors knew, things would be bad?" she asked, her voice sultry as a starless night in the summer. His cock grew to its full length.

The heat from her body warmed his bare chest. He took a step toward her. "It would be very bad if they knew."

"There's only one way to solve that problem," she said. "Just don't tell them."

"What do you want from me?" he asked.

"I want you to kiss me."

Liam turned off the part of his brain that knew he was making a huge mistake. Pulling her in close, he placed his lips on hers. He ran his hand over the fabric of her sweater and gripped her breast. She mewed with desire.

He didn't think it was possible, but his dick got harder.

"I want you," he said, breathing the words into her mouth.

"I want you, too," she said. "Make love to me, Liam."

He didn't need any other invitation. Lifting her from the floor, he set her on the mattress.

Sarah lay back, her hair spread out like a halo. "Come here," she purred, opening her arms.

Kneeling on the edge of the bed, Liam stretched out next

to Sarah. Starting at her collarbone, he traced her body from shoulder to thigh.

"You are so unbelievably soft." Kissing her again, he explored her mouth with his tongue. He knew that if anyone ever found out, he'd be in a hell of a lot of trouble. The thing was, to be with Sarah he was willing to sacrifice it all.

SARAH PRESSED HER hips into Liam's pelvis. He was hard. She was already wet. He kissed her slowly, seemingly prepared to take his time. Usually, she was fine with a leisurely round of sex, but with him it was different. She'd always had a fiery passion burning for Liam. For years, that flame only smoldered. But with him, here and now, that tiny spark had burst into an inferno.

She wanted him inside her.

She unfastened the top button of his pants before pulling the zipper down. She reached into the open fly. "Oh," she said, surprised to find his hard length and nothing else. "Do you always go without underwear?"

"Just today," he said, placing his lips behind her ear. "Just now."

The sensation sent a shiver of desire down her neck. "Is this a special surprise for me?"

"I wish I was that creative." He slipped his hand inside her sweater. His touch skimmed over her skin as he moved to her breast. His hand slipped into the cup of her bra. Brushing a finger over her nipple, he said, "Let's see if there's anything else I can do to astonish you."

He gently bit her other nipple through the fabric of her sweater.

She sucked in a breath, pleasure mixing with pain.

"You like that?" he asked.

She nodded. "Yes."

"Take off your sweater." He stretched out on the bed.

She lifted the garment over her head. After tossing it to the floor, she lay down at his side.

He gently pulled down on the cup of her bra, kissing her nipple before scraping her with his teeth. The pain was almost too much.

"You like that, too?"

"Yes," she said, arching her back and pulling him closer. She needed to feel Liam, skin to skin. He kissed her, harder this time. She reached for him again and ran her hand up and down his body.

"I want to be inside of you."

She wanted him inside her, too. Sitting up, she pulled the bra straps over her shoulders and unhooked the latch. "Do you have a condom?"

"In my wallet." He pointed to his duffel bag on the other bed. "Give me a second."

He rose from the bed and kicked off his pants. Naked, he crossed the room. His shoulders were wide, tapering down his back to the tight muscles of his ass. The sight of him left her mouth dry.

Standing quickly, she stripped out of her own pants. When she looked up, he was watching her. A slow smile spread across his face.

"What?" she asked.

"You are so damn sexy."

Sarah never thought of herself in that way. "You can't be serious."

"Look at you. Your long hair, tumbling over your shoulders. Your breasts are perfect." He came toward her, a condom packet in one hand. "Seeing you in just your panties is too much."

Maybe she did feel a little sexy. After removing her underwear, she stood in front of Liam. "What do you think of me now?"

"I think I'm going to enjoy being inside of you."

She sat down on the bed and opened her thighs. "I think I'm going to like that, too."

Liam opened the foil wrapper before rolling the condom down his length. She scooted back and he knelt between her open legs. He pressed his thumb onto the top of her sex. She was already swollen with want. A wave of pleasure rolled through her.

"You know what else I'm going to do?" He didn't wait for her to answer. "I'm going to like finding out what else it is you like."

"You're doing a good job so far." She placed her lips on his, kissing him softly.

"Do you like this?" he asked, slipping a finger inside her. "Or this?" He added a second finger to the first.

Her muscles tightened around his fingers. The wave of pleasure grew. "Oh, yes."

"What about this?" Still rubbing her, he slid his length inside her.

"Oh, God, yes." Sarah felt like she was being carried away onto an ocean of longing.

"This," he asked, sliding in deeper.

He was in deep, but not deep enough. "Harder, Liam. Harder."

He slid inside her all the way, and she moaned. Closing

her eyes, she let the sensations wash over her. His mouth on hers. His hand on her breasts. The heat of his body and feeling of him inside her. Every part of her was alive.

But for her, it was more than just the merely physical.

This was the exact moment that had occupied her daytime fantasies and filled her nights with erotic dreams. Yet, nothing she imagined over the years compared to this moment. Wrapping her legs around his waist, she pulled him in deeper. "Oh, Liam."

"You like it like this." He drove in hard.

"Yes," she said. Her orgasm was starting to build. She still felt as if she were riding a wave on the ocean. The swell rose higher, moving faster.

He lifted her leg, setting one calf on his shoulder.

God, she couldn't stop herself from having an orgasm. "Harder," she panted. "Deeper. Faster." Like a wave crashing on the shore, Sarah cried out with her climax. Her pulse thundered in her ears, making her deaf to every sound save Liam's ragged breath.

He drove into her faster. Throwing back his head, he let out a low growl. He came. Then, he slumped on top of her, his body melding with hers. Liam propped onto one elbow and kissed her slowly. "That was fantastic," he said, gazing at her. "You are fantastic."

"I feel pretty fabulous right now," she said. Funny, Sarah thought she had memorized every part of Liam's face long ago. But with him so close, she saw that his dark eyes were more than brown. Streaks of gold, like rays of the sun, radiated out from his pupil. "You should probably take care of the condom."

"I probably should." He rose from the bed and padded

across the room. Then, he disappeared into the bathroom, before closing the door.

Sarah sat up. Her panties lay on the floor. Her bra was on the bed, next to her sweater. As she redressed, the fog of lust started to clear. Without all the tingles and throbbing parts, it gave her space to think.

She and Liam were supposed to be working together. What's more, he didn't have some regular job. He was an FBI agent. Sure, she had reasons for wanting to have sex with him. But she should have ignored her yearning.

JESSIE SAT ON the sofa and looked out over the mountains. The internet was working, *thank goodness*. With her tablet computer propped up on her knees, she scrolled through one of her favorite clothing websites. They had just launched their fall/winter mother-of-the-bride collection. Honestly, Sarah was the kind of person who'd want a simple wedding with a few dozen friends and a plain satin dress.

But that wouldn't do for Jessie. She wanted to be mother of the bride at an event. She'd given birth too many times not to plan a fancy wedding. Since she was estranged from her other kids, Sarah was her only chance.

It looked like the popular colors for the season were wine and blush rose. Wine was too dark for her complexion, but the blush rose might work…

She heard Markus before she saw him.

"Keep digging." He entered the room, a delivery box tucked under his arm. He set the box on the table. "I know that he used to be a fed and is now a banker, but I want to make sure there's nothing we've missed before bringing him in deeper."

Obviously, he was talking about Sarah's new beau, Liam Hill. She understood that he had to be careful, but what would Sarah think if she knew that Markus was meddling in her love life? He nodded, listening to what the caller on the other end of the line said.

The computer froze, and a colorful wheel popped onto the screen. Markus had stolen all the internet in the room and the beach ball of death meant that her connection was lost. She still needed to send Sarah directions for tomorrow but had gotten sidetracked with shopping. Closing out the site, Jessie tossed the tablet onto the coffee table and sighed.

Markus ended the call and sat next to her on the sofa. He pulled her feet onto his lap. "What're you up to?"

She flicked her fingers toward the tablet computer. "I was shopping, but your call kicked me off the internet." She didn't care that her tone was filled with annoyance.

"I'm off the phone now," he said, rubbing the arch of one foot. "You can get back on."

She sighed and leaned into the pillow at her back. "There wasn't anything interesting to buy." She paused, knowing that there was more to her mood than no time on the internet. "Why are you so interested in Liam Hill?"

"I'm always careful about anyone who visits our compound, you know that."

She knew. "But he's with Sarah now. If she trusts him, so can you. Besides, I like him. I was just looking at mother-of-the-bride dresses. What do you think about me wearing blush rose?"

Ignoring her question, Markus said, "Your daughter might've spent time with his family a decade ago, but they haven't seen each other in years. I don't like the fact that he used to be with the FBI. I want to make sure he doesn't still have good friends in the Bureau. The kind of friends who could make my life difficult."

"What's that supposed to mean?" It felt like someone had just poured ice water down her back. Sitting up straight, she shivered. "Everything you do is legal, right?"

"Of course it's all legal." Markus dug his thumb into the arch of her foot.

"Ouch." Jessie pulled her leg away. "That hurts."

"You know I'd never hurt you and that I'd never break the law." His tone was petulant. "All this attitude from you and I just bought you a gift." He nodded toward the box.

"A present? It's not my birthday."

"It doesn't have to be a special day for me to get you something. Or maybe I should say, every day with you is special."

Like the sun coming through the clouds, Jessie's mood improved. She pressed her lips to his cheek. "You are good to me."

"Go on," he urged. "Open it."

She picked up the box. It was sealed shut with tape. "Just a minute. I'll grab scissors."

"I've got you covered." Markus stood and emptied his pocket onto the table. There was his money clip, filled with twenty-dollar bills. A phone charger. A utility knife. He opened the knife and sliced through the tape. After folding the blade into the metal scale, he handed her the box. "I hope you like it."

Inside the shipping box was another box. This one was from a designer she loved. Excited energy left her giddy. She was a kid at Christmas, if her parents could've afforded the best. She opened the store box. Tucked inside tissue paper was a beautiful cashmere sweater. She lifted it up, holding it against her shoulders. The fabric was long enough that it skimmed the top of her shoes. It was the exact sweater she'd seen online dozens of times. But it was so expensive that she knew enough not to ask. "I love it," she said, breathless. "I've wanted this coatigan for so long. How did you know?"

"Well, I noticed that you kept going to the same site and looking at this sweater. I figured you must like it a lot."

"How's that?" she asked, confused.

Markus frowned. "How's what?"

"How do you know what I look at on the internet?"

"Oh, that? I check your search history," he said.

"You what?" Now she was mad. No, not mad. Jessie was filled with venomous fury. "That's an invasion of my privacy. You have no right."

Markus was on his feet. "I have every right," he said, his voice booming. "This church belongs to me. Everything here is mine. You are mine." He pulled the sweater from her hands. "Remember what you were when I found you."

Of course she remembered. Sarah had just gone to college. Sure, it was only to Boise State, twenty minutes from their home. Yet her daughter had chosen to live on campus. She wanted the whole college experience, or so she said. But Jessie knew better. What Sarah wanted was to get away.

At the time, Nate was already working. His busy schedule didn't leave much room for his mother. It meant that Jessie was all alone. In those days, the guilt was too much. She was a woman who'd abandoned one set of children to give birth to another. Robert had left her, going back to Saint Jenny.

In a lot of ways, it seemed easier to end it all.

That's when she met Markus.

He offered her hope. A purpose. Love and a life of luxury.

"Do you remember how broken you were?" Markus asked, his voice softer.

Jessie nodded.

"Why give me grief if I'm interested in what you look at on the internet?" He chuckled. "Not that it's much. All you do is scroll through one designer's website after another. I don't even mind that you still conduct a search for the kids you had with your first husband." He paused. Markus wanted her to fill the silence with an explanation. She didn't. She wouldn't. He'd uncovered her secret. She still kept tabs on all her children, even though she hadn't been a mother to them in years. What he wanted was her motivation. Even if she knew why she always looked up her kids, she wouldn't tell him. Some things she would keep to herself.

After a moment, he held out the sweater. "Try it on. Let's see how it looks."

She took the garment. It was soft and warm, flowing over her hands like bathwater instead of wool. She slipped into the floor-length cardigan. Rubbing the fabric between her fingers, she sighed.

"You like it, then?"

"Like it? I love it," she said. "I think I'll wear it tomorrow."

"You know how much I like to spoil you." He picked up her computer from the table. "Let's take a picture. Then, you can send it to Sarah."

She knew that he was trying to make up for their earlier quarrel. Fluffing her hair, she moved to the front of the fire-place. "How do I look?"

"Cozy and chic," he said, before hitting the home button on the tablet. "Damn it. It looks like the battery died." He tsked. "I wish you would keep your devices charged."

"It had enough juice just a minute ago," she said, her teeth clenched. Jessie picked up the charger from the table and shoved it into her pocket. Once her computer was charged, she'd text directions to Sarah. But right now, it would do no good to point out that Markus had stolen more than the internet connection. He'd taken all the power, as well.

Chapter Twelve

Every table at the Tap Out Brewery was filled. The tangy scent of wing sauce mixed with the salty smell of deep-fried food and the crisp aroma of hops, barley and beer. The din of conversations mixed with a college hockey game that was on TV. Boise State versus Idaho State. Everyone at the restaurant had a favorite team—even Sarah.

Of course, she was rooting for Boise State. What's more, she was thrilled that they were ahead by 3 to 1 after the first period.

Thankfully, her group had been sat at a booth in the back corner, where they could hear each other talk. And Sarah could see a TV.

Sarah and Liam sat on one side of the booth. Frannie and Dante sat opposite. Malcolm pulled up a chair at the end of the table.

Picking up a menu, she scanned the entrée list. For months she'd wondered about her siblings. Now that she was with two of them, she couldn't find anything to say.

A female server with a long black ponytail approached the table. "Hi, I'm going to be taking care of you guys tonight. What can I get started for you?"

"Um," she said, not able to focus on anything listed. "What do you recommend?"

"Do you like pepperoni pizza?" Malcolm asked.

"Who doesn't?"

"Why don't we all get pizza and wings to share?" She could already tell that he had the same take-charge personality as her brother, Nate. But Malcolm's eyes were the exact green as her own. "And add in two pitchers of beer."

"Hey," Frannie protested, resting her hand on her baby bump. "The pregnant momma can't drink."

"Okay, make that one pitcher of beer and one pitcher of water," he corrected.

"I'll get that order in and be back with your drinks," said the server.

"So," he turned to her. "Frannie shared a little bit about you, Sarah. But it's not enough. Tell me about yourself."

She laughed nervously. "What do you want to know?"

"Favorite flavor of ice cream. Favorite holiday. Favorite Halloween costume." He lifted a finger as he counted off the questions.

She exhaled. "Favorite ice cream has to be cookie dough. Favorite holiday is Thanksgiving, because it's just about food, friends and family. Favorite Halloween costume as a kid." She paused, thinking. "In tenth grade, I dressed up like Jane Austen." She pointed to Liam. "And his sister was Amelia Earhart."

Liam shook his head and laughed. "I'd forgotten about those costumes. It's no wonder you and Allison were best friends."

"What's your sister do now?" Malcolm asked Liam.

"Actually, she's a fighter pilot in the air force."

"That's impressive," said Malcolm. "Sounds like you both knew what you wanted from life at an early age."

"I never thought about it that way," she said. "But I guess you're right."

Frannie asked, "Is she single? We need to find someone nice for Malcolm."

"I can find my own partner, thank you very much."

The server returned with two pitchers and a stack of plastic cups. Malcolm poured a glass of water and handed it to Frannie. "What would you like, Sarah?"

"Since I'm driving, I'll stick with water."

He filled the cup with water before passing it over. "I know Dante will have a beer with me. What about you, Liam?"

"You can't have wings and pizza without beer," he said.

Malcolm filled three glasses with beer. He handed one to Liam. "So, Frannie said that you're a banker from Washington, DC."

Liam took a sip of his beer and nodded. "I am."

"How's a DC banker end up in Owl Creek?" he asked. "I know I'm prying, but Sarah's my sister. Grilling her dates is part of my job."

Funny, to think that she shared a parent with both her brother and sister. It didn't take long to get a sense of her siblings. They were good people. Dependable. Hardworking. Honest.

True, Jessie and Robert hadn't been any of those things. But somehow, between them, they'd raised children who became decent adults.

"I'm looking for real estate in Boise," he said, using his lie. "I stopped by the library, ran into Sarah, and the rest is history. Now, here we are."

"If you're looking for real estate in Boise," Malcolm asked, "why are you in Owl Creek?"

"It's a chance for me to meet Sarah's mom. We met for brunch this morning at Hutch's Diner." He paused. While Frannie was the child of Sarah's dad, Malcolm was the son of her mother—Jessie. "I guess she's your mom, too."

"Yeah, I guess she is." He rolled a glass of beer between his palms. "So, Jessie was in town today."

"I'm sorry that she didn't stop by to see you," Sarah said. Still, her words weren't enough.

"Not a problem." Malcolm lifted the beer to his lips and took a long swallow. "I'm used to it by now."

Sarah doubted that was true. "You know," she said, "after my dad died and I found you all, I was furious with my mom. I really thought that we were the ones who were wronged." She paused. Maybe she shouldn't be so candid at a get-to-know-you dinner. But Malcolm looked so much like Nate. They had the same build and same unruly brown hair. She felt as if she were talking to the brother whom she'd known her whole life. "But Nate and I were the lucky ones. Mom—as imperfect as she is—stayed with us. She left you all behind." She paused a beat. "I am so sorry."

Her brother nodded slowly. "It's not your fault. You never asked for any of this."

"Well, neither did you…"

"Sometimes I wonder, even now, if I did something and that's why she left."

It seemed like she wasn't the only person willing to be painfully honest.

She blinked hard. "It wasn't you. I haven't known you for long, but I can tell that you're great."

He smiled. "You're pretty great, yourself."

"Must run in the family," Frannie added. "Nate's a good guy, too."

Sarah was always proud of her brother. "Nate's the best."

"How's he doing?" Frannie asked.

Honestly, she'd been avoiding Nate. Not that she was upset with him, or anything. It's just that she'd have a hard time sticking to Liam's cover story. After all, Jessie was his mom, too. He had a right to know what was going on. Then again, Jessie was also Malcolm's mother. Did that mean she should confide in him? Sarah took a sip of water and answered Frannie's question. "Nate's good—like always."

Malcolm pulled his phone from his pocket and glanced at the device. The screen was illuminated with an incoming call. "I have to take this," he said, rising from the table. "Be back in a minute." He swiped the call open and spoke into the phone. "Give me a second to get out the door. I'm at Tap Out."

He wove his way through the crowd, toward the door. Once he was gone, she turned back to Frannie. "Did I scare him off?"

"I doubt it," said Dante. "He's made of pretty tough stuff."

"True," Frannie agreed. "He lives on the Colton family ranch, and there's always something happening there. Plus, he volunteers with a K-9 rescue unit. It could be anything and he definitely didn't make up an emergency to get away from you." She squeezed Sarah's arm and smiled. "Trust me."

Did she trust Frannie? As it turned out, everything she knew about her life and her family had been a lie. Even she'd gone down the rabbit hole of deceit. Now, she didn't know what to believe. "Tell me how you two met," she asked, changing the subject.

"Dante was my best customer," said Frannie, reaching for his hand. "Every time he'd walk into the store, I'd get butterflies. He always loved to talk books, so I knew he must be a good guy."

"I'm a lawyer by trade." Dante Santoro wore his dark brown hair and beard cut short. A bit of gray was starting to show on his cheeks and chin. Lacing his fingers through Frannie's, he continued, "You can't become an attorney without liking to read a lot. But usually, what I'd read was legal briefs and other boring stuff. My family has some unsavory connections, and I was trying to stay off the radar."

"By unsavory do you mean organized crime?" Liam asked.

"Unfortunately, I do," said Dante with a shrug. "I've always stayed out of the family business, though."

Dante picked up the thread of the story. "Once I saw how much Frannie loved books, I started reading everything, just to have something to talk about with her."

"That's the sweetest story I've ever heard," said Sarah.

"It's almost as sweet as you and Liam. Who'd have thought that you'd grow up together and then later, fall in love?" said Frannie.

"Agreed," said Dante. "That's a top-notch love story."

Sarah's cheeks got hot. What would they both say once they knew that her whole story had been bogus? Frannie obviously had no love for Jessie. Maybe she could trust her sister with the truth. Before she could say anything, Malcolm strode up to the table.

"The call I got is for a missing person from the Ever After Church." His jacket was draped over the back of his chair. After pulling the garment free, he shrugged into the coat. "The K-9 unit has been called in to search. It's going to get frigid tonight. Anyone who's out in those temperatures risks severe frostbite or worse."

"If they're from that church, they might not have gotten lost. Maybe they tried to escape. Best to just let them get away," said Dante before taking a swig of beer.

"I don't care who's in the woods or why. It's my job to try and find them," said Malcolm.

"Take care of yourself." Frannie rose from her seat and pulled him in for a quick hug. "We don't want anything to happen to you."

"I'm always careful," he said, before turning to Sarah. He opened his arms. "Mind if I get a hug, too?"

"Listen to Frannie," she said, scooting to the edge of the booth. Standing, she pulled him into an embrace. "Be careful."

"It's good to know you. I'd like to stay in touch."

"Absolutely," she said. "I'll get your number from Frannie."

Frannie said, "I'll start a group chat and call it the Colton Crew."

"You call it that, then everyone will want to be a part of the text thread," said Malcolm.

"I don't mind." Sarah couldn't believe that things had changed so much for her over the course of a single day. This morning, she'd been terrified by the prospect of getting together with one of her siblings. Now, she had new affection for her brother and sister and the possibility of so much more. She gave Malcolm another tight squeeze before letting him go.

She slid back into the booth as he walked away.

"I don't mean to pry," said Liam. "But I have to ask about

the Ever After Church. You said that the missing person didn't just wander off but perhaps tried to escape."

Dante lifted his glass of beer and took a sip. "I was just being glib. I shouldn't have said anything about someone who's missing."

"Anything you know about the Ever After Church would be helpful. I met Markus today. He's trying to get me to invest in a project." Since Liam knew all about the church leader, Sarah assumed that he was just trying to get more information.

"You want some expensive legal advice for free?" Dante asked.

Liam said, "I never turn down a bargain."

"Stay away from the Ever After Church."

This was the exact kind of information Liam needed. She asked, "Why's that?"

"I don't know anything for certain," Dante said. "It's just a vibe I get."

"That doesn't sound very lawyerly of you." Sarah smiled wide to show that she was teasing. Still, she wanted to know everything Dante knew or suspected. "Besides, if there are issues, I need to know. My mother's engaged to Markus." Sure, Sarah thought Markus was a pompous jerk from the first time they met. But her mother might be in real trouble.

"The reason nobody knows much of anything is because there's a lot of security around the church compound." Frannie glanced over her shoulder, looking at the door. "Too bad Malcolm left already. He's been in the area on other searches and turned away by security."

"That sounds expensive." She'd seen the images of the church members already and she knew how they lived. Still, she was interested in what Frannie and Dante would say. "The church must be really nice."

"With all the nice cars Jessie and Markus are driven around in, you'd think that the compound was like the Taj Mahal," said Frannie, an edge to her tone. "But a few members have come into town. They're all filthy and cold and hungry. I can't understand why they don't just leave. I mean, they aren't prisoners."

Dante gave her a side-eye. Letting go of his hand, she grabbed her glass. With her back ramrod straight, Frannie looked toward the TV. The air between them became muddy with irritation.

"What aren't you saying?" Sarah asked the couple.

Dante exhaled. "Let's just say that we have different ideas about what's happening at the Ever After Church."

"What do you think is going on?" Liam asked.

"I grew up with connections to the mob. I've seen how people can get sucked into an organization and brainwashed. That's not a church in those mountains. It's a cult. As far as people coming into town and being a nuisance." He sighed. "I think those people are desperate."

The photos from the compound were tattooed onto Sarah's brain and into her soul. "It sounds like they're trapped without any hope."

"I guess if you think about it that way, they are." Frannie gave Dante a wan smile. He lifted her hand and grazed her knuckles with his lips.

The server approached the table, a large tray balanced on her shoulder. "I got pizzas and wings." She set two baskets of saucy wings on the table and then two large pizzas.

Sarah hadn't eaten anything since brunch. As the mellow

scent of melted cheese surrounded her, her stomach contracted with a grumble. Pressing a hand to her belly, she said, "That all looks delicious."

Finally, the server placed four plates and four sets of silverware on the table. "Enjoy."

"I'm definitely going to get heartburn from all this, but it'll be worth it," said Frannie, reaching for a slice.

Sarah took her first bite of pizza. The sauce was the perfect blend of tangy and sweet. The pepperoni had the right amount of spice. The cheese was melty and mild. She chewed and swallowed. "This is great pizza. Too bad Malcolm had to leave before getting anything to eat."

"If there are leftovers, we can drop them off at the ranch on our way home." Dante plunged a buffalo wing into a dish filled with ranch dressing and took a bite.

Frannie had already finished one slice of pizza and reached for a second. "The first three months of my pregnancy, I had horrible morning sickness."

"She couldn't even look at food without feeling ill," said Dante. "Crackers and ginger ale were all she could keep down."

"Now, I'm making up for all the meals I missed," Frannie said before taking another bite.

"Tell me about the baby," said Sarah. "Is it a boy or girl? When are you due?"

"The due date's not for a while." Frannie placed a hand on her belly. "We don't know the gender yet but have an ultrasound appointment in a few weeks. If the baby cooperates, we'll find out then."

"Any guesses?" Liam asked.

"It's a girl," said Dante. "She'll be beautiful and brilliant, just like her mother."

"You are a keeper," said Frannie. She cupped Dante's cheek with her hand. Pulling him to her, she kissed him softly.

Sarah hadn't known Frannie for long. Yet, she was happy to see her sister so happy and in love. It was the kind of relationship that other people envied and Sarah had been wanting for years. Would she ever find someone? She glanced at Liam. He was watching her. He gave her a slow smile. For a moment, she could feel his lips on hers again. His mouth on her breasts. His hands on her thighs. Her cheeks warmed with the memories.

Soon, there were only three slices of pizza and five wings left. "That looks like enough for Malcolm. I'll get a to-go container." Dante lifted his hand, waving to the server.

"Looks like you all enjoyed your meal," she said, while approaching the table. "Can I get you anything else?"

"Just a to-go box and the check," said Dante.

The server was prepared. She set a black check presenter on the table. "I'll leave this with you and be back in a second with your box."

Dante looked at Liam. "Do you want to split the amount down the middle?"

Liam picked up the bill. "Better yet, I'll pay."

"You don't have to," Dante protested.

"Trust me, I'm on an expense account," he said, setting enough money onto the table to cover the tab and a tip. "Besides, you gave me some good insights on the Ever After Church. That's helped me out more than you know."

Sarah scooted out of the booth and glanced at the TV.

There were only five minutes left in the third period of the hockey game. Boise State was still winning. The score was 4 to 1. She imagined the team could hold on to the lead until the end. *Go, Broncos!*

"Let's keep in touch," said Frannie, pulling Sarah into a hug. The one thing she was learning about her sister was that she liked to give hugs. She whispered, "You and Liam are a cute couple. I love the way he looks at you."

"I was thinking the same thing about you and Dante," said Sarah, giving her sister a final squeeze.

"Remember, we have to get a picture in our banned books shirts."

"It's a deal," she said, hoping there would be a next time.

Chapter Thirteen

Snowflakes danced in the headlight beams as Sarah drove back to the hotel. She parked in the same spot, the ground already covered in white.

"I guess it won't be snowing in DC tonight," she said, joking about the weather.

He leaned forward and gazed out the windshield. "Probably no snow in Washington, but even a few inches will send everyone into a panic." He laughed. "Remember that weekend it snowed so much we were all stuck in the house and my mom had to stay at the hospital?"

"Of course I remember the blizzard of oh-eight." She put the gearshift into Park and turned off the ignition. "Your dad turned it into a party. We camped out in the living room and watched movies. He made pancakes for dinner. Those were good times."

He sat back in the seat but stared out the window. "I miss living in Idaho. I miss the weather. The people. Finger steaks." He gave a weak chuckle. "I just didn't realize how much I missed everything until coming back."

Sarah had friends. A job she loved. A family that might be growing, thanks to her trip to Owl Creek. From what she'd picked up, Liam didn't have any of those in Washington. "Sounds like you're pretty lonely in DC."

"It's hard to connect with anyone in a city that big. I work twelve, sometimes fourteen hours a day. Then the commute." He rolled his eyes. "Horrendous. It takes me an hour to drive fifteen miles. By the time I get home, I want to eat something—anything—drink a beer and maybe watch a little TV. Then, I call it a night. I get up the next morning and start over."

It sounded like his whole life was horrible, not just his commute. "What do you want?"

"I don't know," he said, with a shake of his head. "The irony is, if this case goes well, I'll be a shoo-in for the promotion. That will only mean longer hours, less time at home, less time to make a life."

"It's the modern paradox," she said.

"You're right, it is. I've been thinking that I'm the only one who works too much. But I'm not."

"The question is still the same," she asked, "what do you want to do?"

He turned to her. In the car's dim interior, everything was shades of gray. As if the world had been sketched with charcoal on paper. "Wise and beautiful," he said. "That might be the perfect combo."

"What about a burger and fries?" she teased. "Or peanut butter and jelly?"

"You are much better than a burger and fries." He smiled, his teeth bright in the darkness. Leaning onto the console between the seats, he said, "I guess we should talk about what happened in the room before we left."

They'd made love but Liam's rebuff from years earlier was

a wound that had never completely healed. What's more, she wasn't ready to be rejected again. "It doesn't matter," she lied. "We're both adults."

"Oh." He was silent for a minute. "Well, if that's how you feel about it, then I guess we really don't have anything to discuss."

"For the record, I don't usually tumble into bed with any random guy after a few dates."

"I'd like to think I'm more than just some dude who took you out for finger steaks."

She smiled at the memory. At the time, she'd believed that Liam coming into her life was just luck. She didn't have an inkling that her world was about to change. Or maybe it was Sarah who was growing. "That date seems like it happened a million years ago."

He rubbed the back of his neck. "It's been a long week."

"It's going to be a long day tomorrow."

"I need to reach out to my boss and brief her on what happened today," he said.

"We should probably go, then." She opened the car's door and stepped outside. Cold bit through her jacket. Snow had already filled in the tracks left by her tires.

"Be careful." He reached for her to keep her from falling. "It's slick."

Truth was, she liked the feeling of his hand on her arm. She liked that he was worried about her safety. She liked having someone who cared. Could be that she liked it all a little too much.

Walking slowly, they made their way to the hotel's front entrance. Compared with the outside, the lobby was stifling. She unzipped her coat and followed Liam. He pushed the call button and the elevator doors slid open. She stepped into the car. Liam followed. Without speaking, they rode to the third floor and exited the car. After walking to their room, Liam swiped the keycard over the lock. It unlatched with a click. He opened the door. "After you."

Slipping inside, she flipped the light switch. The room was just as they'd left it. Sarah's suitcase sat on a luggage rack. One bed was made, the other was mussed. The musky scent of their lovemaking still hung in the air.

It was almost as if they'd never left.

Sarah hung her coat in the small closet. "Thank you for bringing me to Owl Creek. Without this investigation, I never would've run into Frannie."

Liam sat on the edge of the bed. Kicking off his shoes, he said, "You two would've found each other eventually."

Sarah imagined a golden thread tethering her to all her Colton siblings. Then again, the fact that she'd been lying to them all along would eventually come out. Would the truth cut that tie?

She sighed. "They're going to find out why we came to Owl Creek in the first place. They're going to know it's all a scam." She bit her bottom lip understanding what scared her the most. "They're going to know I'm a liar and no better than Jessie."

"First, it's a federal investigation, not some swindle. Second, you're doing this to save your mother from ending up in jail. Or worse." He stepped closer and placed his hand on her arm. His touch sent her pulse racing. "Trust me, your brother and sister will understand. And they'll know that you're a good person."

Her whole life she'd tried to do the right thing. Get good

grades. Be a loyal friend. Be honest and helpful. What if she was nothing but a fake?

He opened his arms. "You look like you need a hug."

Honestly, she didn't know what she needed. And yet, "A hug would help," she said, stepping into his embrace. He wrapped his arms around her, and she leaned into his chest. His scent, sweat and healthy male, surrounded her. She inhaled deeply. It did nothing to slow her racing heart. She took a step backward, slipping out of his arms. "I feel better," she said, already digging through her suitcase. She found her toiletry bag and pajamas. "I'm going to get ready for bed. Do you need the bathroom?"

"I'm going to send my boss a text and fill her in about dinner. Take your time."

Once inside the bathroom, she turned on the light and closed the door. After setting everything on the vanity, she studied her refection. Sarah would never be a classic beauty, like her mom. But she had bright eyes, an easy smile and, yes—she was happy to be sweet. The world needed more sweetness.

So, what was a sweet girl like her doing in a hotel pretending to be an undercover FBI agent's girlfriend?

She cleansed her face, applied moisturizer and stripped out of her clothes. Standing in her underwear, she looked at herself again. She ran a finger over her curves. Her breasts were full, her hips were round and her butt was muscular. Her beauty was completely opposite her mother's. But that didn't make Sarah any less attractive.

Her childhood memories were filled with moments of her mom's disapproval. Most nights after dinner, Jessie would give the kids a treat. Sarah would reach for a second cookie or the larger slice of pie. Jessie never said anything, but it was impossible to miss the scowl that passed across her mother's face. A cloud blotting out the sun.

It's one of the reasons why Sarah constantly read. She could live a new life and learn about different worlds. In short, she'd go places that her mother couldn't follow.

It's also why she stayed with the Hill family so much.

But Sarah was no longer a child.

If she wanted to be an adult, she had to step away from her mother's shadow. For the first time, she'd walk in her own sun.

Her thoughts moved on to Liam. He was another enigma.

Sure, they were in a fake relationship. But she could still lose herself in his arms. Without another thought, she opened the bathroom door and stepped into the room. Liam had changed into his own version of pajamas—a white T-shirt and pair of gray sweatpants.

He looked up. For a moment, he just stared. Then, he stood straighter. "This is a nice surprise."

"I was thinking about what you said. I've been thinking about a lot of things, really. My mom. My siblings. You…" No, she wasn't doing it right. Sarah should think of something sexy and seductive to say. Instead, she was starting to ramble. Drawing in a deep breath, she tried again. "I'm not sure what will happen tomorrow—or the day after that. But right now, I want you."

He pulled her to him. She sighed as he slipped his tongue into her mouth. The future would bring its own troubles and joys. But for tonight she would just let go.

She ran her hands over Liam's chest. Even under the fabric, she could feel the hard muscles and planes of his body.

She lifted the hem of his shirt. He had to duck down so she could pull it over his head.

Once his shirt was off, she traced his chest. Collarbone. Pectorals. Nipples. He hissed with ecstasy. She ran her tongue over his other nipple, her hand traveling lower. She slid her hand inside the waistband of his sweatpants and underwear. He was already hard. She ran her finger down his length.

"Jesus, Sarah," he moaned. "What're you trying to do? Drive me wild?"

"Basically," she said, feeling both playful and sexy.

Liam gripped her face in both his hands and kissed her hard. She didn't mind the pain. "I want you," he said, breathing into the kiss, "so bad."

"Not just yet."

"Not yet?" he echoed.

Before he could say anything else, she'd dropped to her knees. Liam let his pants fall to his knees. Honestly, Sarah had never done anything like this before. Oh sure, she'd occasionally taken a guy in her mouth. But never clad in only her bra and panties and in a hotel, no less.

Then again, today had been a day for firsts.

She ran her tongue around the tip, watching Liam through her lashes. Eyes closed, he let his head hang back. She took him in her mouth, and he moaned with pleasure. "Oh, Sarah."

She swirled her tongue over his length.

He massaged her shoulder as his breathing turned ragged. Liam pulled himself out. "You gotta stop doing that, or else I'm going to explode. Literally."

"That's kinda the idea," she said.

"I have a better idea. Get on the bed," he said while stepping out of his pants. Completely naked, he lay down on the bed.

Bending forward at the waist, she stretched out on top of him. She took him with her hand as he moved aside the strip of her panties. He slipped two fingers inside her before placing his mouth on her. Every part of her body was alive with sensations. The climax claimed her with a speed that was both exhilarating and frightening. She bit the inside of Liam's thigh as wave after wave of pleasure washed over her and through her and pushed her under until she couldn't breathe.

She panted. "Oh my God, I don't know where that came from."

"Roll onto your back," said Liam. "I want you."

"But you haven't come yet."

"I will," he said as she shifted to the mattress. "Besides, I don't think my leg can handle another one of your bites."

There, on his thigh, was a red ring of teeth marks. "Jeez, I'm sorry."

"Don't apologize," He rose from the bed. His wallet sat on the nightstand. Holding up a foil packet, he said, "This is my last one." After opening the condom, he rolled the rubber down his length. "If we need any more, we'll have to stop at a drugstore or something."

Would there be another time? Lying back, she opened her arms. "Come here."

Liam moved between her thighs. She watched as he slid inside her. The erotic vision was burned into her brain. He began to move inside her. She met him thrust for thrust. Neither spoke. The shifting of the bed and their heavy breaths were the only sounds in the room. Sarah could feel a new orgasm building. Reaching for the top of her sex, she rubbed the spot. Every part of her body began to tingle. Her feet. Her hands. Even her hair felt as if it was pulsing with an electric current.

Wrapping her legs around Liam's waist, she pulled him closer, driving him in deeper. Her hand was trapped between their bodies. It didn't matter, her climax was close. Liam reached for the headboard, using his arms to pump deeper inside her. It was all she needed.

She cried out as she came.

Liam was near, too. Funny how she'd learned to read his body after such a short time. Eyes closed, his brow was drawn together. A thin sheen of sweat glistened on his forehead and chest. A rumble of thunder began in his middle, and he groaned as he came. For a moment, they lay in silence as their heartbeats shared a rhythm. He kissed her slowly.

"The condom," she said. Sure, Sarah was willing to take a few risks and live dangerously. But she wasn't stupid. She wasn't ready to be a parent just yet.

"I'll be right back," he said, getting out of the bed.

She rose as he entered the bathroom and found her discarded panties on the floor. She removed her bra before slipping back under the blankets. Since her pajamas were still in the bathroom, she'd have to wait to get dressed.

Coming out of the bathroom, Liam stepped into his underwear. "It seems silly to sleep in the other bed," he said. "But I will, if that's what you want."

In a way, sharing a bed felt more intimate than having sex. If she wanted to create distance between them, now would be the time. But he was right—making him sleep in the adjoining bed bordered on ridiculous. Pulling back the cover, she joked, "I'll try not to snore too much."

He turned off the light before snuggling next to her. Her back was pressed against his chest. His breath washed over her shoulder. Bits of ice tapped against the window. She was warm and dry and sated from sex. But there were people living on the Ever After Church's compound who went to bed hungry and were sleeping in tents tonight. She was tired of wondering what her mother knew. Or wondering if Jessie even cared.

By helping Liam, she was doing the right thing. Would it be enough?

"What's going to happen tomorrow?" she asked, her words a whisper.

"Just getting onto the compound will be step one." Liam wrapped his arm around her middle and pulled her closer. "Next, I need to get into Markus's office. He has a computer that's never online. All his financial records are stored on the hard drive."

Rolling over, she faced him. "How're you supposed to do all that?"

"I'm not sure," he said. "I'll improvise."

"We," she corrected. "We'll have to improvise."

"I like having you on my team." She could sense more than see his smile.

"Once we get you into the office, how are you supposed to access the files you need?" she asked.

"I was given the password to the computer," he said. Before she could ask how he'd come across such sensitive information, he added, "A receptionist who worked for my mom's medical practice got sucked into the Ever After Church after a divorce. Because of her administrative background, she worked as Markus's secretary. When she realized what was

happening, she contacted me. But she knew his password."
His words disappeared into the darkness. "Cases like this
can take years to develop, but you've helped me get close to
Markus in just a few hours. If you ever want a change of career, you should consider the FBI."

Of course, he was teasing. "I'll leave all the clandestine
operations up to you."

"You've sacrificed a lot for this case. I'd say 'thank you,'
but it doesn't seem like enough."

"No need to thank me," she said. "Just get that evidence
and put Markus Acker in jail."

Chapter Fourteen

Sometime in the middle of the night, Jessie had texted Sarah directions to the church's compound. She had them on her phone first thing in the morning. For the day, she decided to wear a green cashmere sweater and tan slacks. Sure, she also had to wear snow boots, but the sweater was the nicest thing she owned.

Liam wore a flannel shirt, jeans and boots. When he'd shown up at the library he'd been in a pressed white shirt and loafers. Now he was much more casual. Was he getting comfortable being back in Idaho?

Since they were going to her mother's house for breakfast, neither bothered eating before they left the hotel. By 8:15 a.m., she was driving on a four-lane highway that led out of Owl Creek. Several miles outside town, they traded the interstate for a sparsely populated county route. That led to a two-lane road, which hugged the side of a mountain peak.

Liam sat in the passenger seat. Looking out the window, he said, "You never get views like this in DC. It's breathtaking."

She glanced out the window. Last night's storm had blanketed the mountains with six inches of new snow. Powder clung to branches, and it looked like the trees were covered in sparkling diamonds. In the distance, another mountain peak rose from the valley's cloud cover. Turning her attention back to the road, she said, "It is beautiful." But it was also secluded. She hadn't seen a house for miles. This far from civilization, would they be able to call for help if they needed it? "Do you have any cell coverage?"

Liam pulled his phone from his pocket and glanced at the screen. "Nope."

"Check and see if I have any bars." She nodded toward the cupholder where she'd tucked her device.

He picked up the cell and pressed the home button. "Nothing."

"My mom's internet is always spotty. But hopefully, there's a little coverage once we get closer to the church."

Liam glanced in her direction. "I hope you're right."

She didn't know what they were about to find, but without cell service, they were on their own. Sarah was so wrapped up in her own thoughts that she almost missed a wooden sign that was tucked into a copse of trees.

Property of Ever After Church had been stenciled in large, block letters.

Another note had been painted on by hand: Trespassers Will Be Shot.

Easing her foot onto the brake, she let the car idle next to the sign. "That doesn't seem very welcoming."

"Not like any church I've ever attended," Liam agreed.

She gripped the steering wheel tighter. "I guess there's nothing for us to do but see where this road leads." Pressing down on the gas, she turned onto the narrow track. Piles of snow lined the road. "At least they plowed this morning."

In the gully, a guard shack, made of plywood and painted

tan, sat at the roadside. The road was blocked with a large iron gate, attached at both sides to a metal post. From each post, a metal fence stretched out as far as she could see in either direction. Loops of razor wire, the barbs glinting in the morning light, topped the fencing.

A dark-haired man, dressed all in black, stepped out of the guard shack. Standing in the middle of the road, he held up a hand for her to halt. She dropped her foot on the brake, stopping several feet from the man. The guard stepped up to the car and wound his hand in the universal sign to lower the window.

She pressed a button set into the armrest. The window lowered with a whirr. All the warm air in the car was sucked out into the cold morning.

"This is private property." The guard wore a gun at his hip. It was a fact she hadn't noticed until now. "You can't be here."

Dragging her gaze from the firearm to the man's face, she said, "I'm, uh, Jessie Colton's daughter. I'm here to see my mom."

"You got some kind of ID?"

"Yeah." Her purse was on the floorboard of the passenger side, next to Liam's feet. He handed her the bag. She dug through her pocketbook until she found her wallet. Her driver's license was stored in a pocket with a clear plastic window. "Here you go," she said, holding up her ID.

The guard took her wallet and examined the license. He shoved it through the window, giving it back. He pointed to Liam. "What about him?"

"My mom and Markus are expecting us," she said, projecting more courage than she felt.

Liam leaned past Sarah with his own license. "It's okay," he said. "I'm sure this guy is just doing his job."

The guard examined the ID for several seconds. With a grunt, he held it out to her. As she reached for the license, he said, "Go ahead."

"Is it easy to find my mom's house?" she asked.

The man nodded his head once. "Just follow this road."

"How am I supposed to know which house belongs to my mom and Markus?"

"Oh, you'll know," said the guard. "Trust me."

Without another word, he opened the gate and stepped aside. Sarah raised her window before easing her foot from the brake. She stepped onto the accelerator and the car slowly climbed farther into the woods. She glanced in her rearview mirror. The gate was once again closed. "My God, they are serious about security here. Did you see that fence?"

"Honestly, I've seen friendlier prisons," he said.

She understood that he was trying to be funny. In a different situation, she might've laughed. Now, she couldn't even manage a smile.

The tree line broke, opening to a muddy field. Like she'd seen in the photos, tents and shacks made of boards were haphazardly set up around the compound. There was a large metal building. With a single door and no windows, it almost looked like a warehouse. A sign hung above the door.

Cafeteria/Sanctuary.

Next to the cafeteria/sanctuary was a residential trailer.

Administrative Building.

A guard, another fit-looking man in dark clothes, stood outside the office door.

She kept her eyes on the road. "You see that building and the guard, right?"

"I see them both."

For a moment, neither spoke. Then, he said, "For what it's worth, you're doing a good job as an undercover agent. But we need to assume that we're always under surveillance while we're here. Just because we're alone doesn't mean Markus isn't listening."

"That's an unsettling thought, but I won't say anything that'll blow your cover." She corrected herself, "Our cover."

She glanced out the window. The Ever After compound was large. Several miles of forest had been cleared away on the hillside.

A dirt track wound through a slushy field. Either side of the single lane was lined with more tents and shacks. Several children, elementary school-aged by the looks of them, surrounded a muddy puddle. Using a stick, they slapped the water. Droplets flew into the air. The game stopped and thin faces with red-rimmed eyes regarded the car as they drove past. Despite the cold, none of them wore coats.

At the top of a rise stood the wooden frame of a large, rectangular building. The sound of hammer strikes rang out into the cold morning. Sitting next to the construction site was a beautiful A-frame house with a timber exterior and roof of green tin. She'd seen enough pictures to recognize her mother's home at once.

Even before Liam showed up in her life, her mom had sent several texts with photos of the property. But now that she was here, Sarah knew the truth. All the pictures had been carefully selected to only show what Jessie wanted her to see. It wasn't a mistake; her mother had seen the ugliness and chosen to look the other way.

A circular driveway, covered in gravel, looped in front of the house. After pulling up next to a set of steps, she placed the gearshift into Park and exhaled loudly.

"Are you ready for this?" he asked. "Because if you aren't..." He let his words unravel.

"There's no way we can go back now," she said, turning off the ignition. "Let's just get this over with."

The front door of the house opened. Jessie stepped onto the wide porch. She was clad in an ivory silk blouse and wool slacks. Atop it all was a long cashmere cardigan that almost swept the ground. Smiling brightly, she waved.

Sarah stepped from the car. Liam came up beside her and held out his hand. She took his palm in her own. How was she supposed to prepare for a moment like this? Yet she smiled at Liam, hoping the expression looked loving. "Showtime," she said quietly, before walking toward the house. Speaking to Jessie, she said, "Wow, Mom. You really do live in the mountains."

Her mother leaned on the railing. "Isn't the view breathtaking?"

She glanced over her shoulder. All Sarah could see was the tent city and children who needed coats and a hot meal. "There's a lot of people who live around here."

"Well, Markus is such an inspirational pastor, people just flock to his congregation," she said. "I hope you're hungry. I made your favorite."

"Apple cinnamon pancakes?" she asked.

"Apple cinnamon pancakes," her mother echoed.

A set of steps made to look like tree trunks led to a wide

porch, complete with a set of Adirondack chairs. She climbed the stairs. Liam was right behind, his hand resting on the small of her back.

"Give me a hug," said Jessie, pulling Sarah in for a quick embrace. "Now, get inside. It's freezing out here."

Jessie held the front door as Sarah and Liam crossed the threshold. The walls at the front and back of the house were made up of floor-to-ceiling windows. A large stone fireplace bisected the room, separating the living room from the dining room.

The decor inside the house matched the rugged log cabin look, while also being tasteful and expensive. In the living room, a fur rug was spread out on the floor. A large green leather sofa filled the middle of the room. The table and the frame of a coordinating chair were made out of roughhewn logs. The adjacent dining room table was already set for four. There was a carafe of coffee, a pitcher of orange juice. Platters were filled with savory bacon, spicy sausage and sweet apple cinnamon pancakes.

"So?" her mom asked, "what do you think? It's a lot nicer than our old place in Boise."

"This place is lovely, Mom." She tried to smile.

"I'm glad you like it. Markus lets me do whatever I want with our house."

Markus came from a hallway to the right of the door. He wore jeans and a blue sweater with a collared shirt underneath. "I always let your mother do whatever she wants," he said. "She's such a persuasive minx."

Persuasive minx? Was this guy for real?

Jessie giggled.

Sarah thought she might barf.

Markus stepped forward and placed a dry kiss on Sarah's cheek. Reaching out his hand for Liam to shake, he said, "I'm glad we could finally get Sarah up here to visit."

Funny, she hadn't recalled ever being invited before.

Markus continued, "We should eat. I'm starved."

The choice of phrasing hit her like a punch to the face. For a moment, she saw stars. "*You're* starving?" she echoed.

"Yeah," said Markus, walking to the dining room table. "I skipped my early breakfast so I could eat with you all."

"What about all those people?" She pointed to the windows at the front of the house. "Who's supposed to feed them?"

"There's hunger all over the world," said Jessie, being willfully obtuse. "Our church sends money to ministries that feed the hungry."

"I'm not talking about anywhere else," she said, "there's hunger right here."

"Why don't you have a seat," said Markus as he sat. "The food's going to get cold, and we won't help anyone else by being miserable ourselves."

What did Markus know about misery?

Jessie slid into a seat next to Markus. He reached for her hand and pressed his lips to her knuckles. "This all looks delicious."

Liam caught Sarah's eye and shrugged. Obviously, he wasn't here to fight with her mom and Markus. What's more, her persistence could cause a rift that would jeopardize the investigation.

Still, an argument pressed against her chest until her ribs ached. She exhaled loudly before dropping into a chair. "Thanks for making the apple cinnamon pancakes, Mom. They really do look good."

Liam took a seat, as well.

Markus picked up a platter filled with bacon and stabbed four thick slices with a fork. Grease dripped from the ends as he transferred the food to his plate. "Here you go." He handed the platter to Liam. Aside from the meat and pancakes, Jessie had also set out dishes filled with berries, yogurt and granola.

There was little talking as everyone got their own food. Sarah took one pancake, one slice of bacon and a small dish of yogurt with granola on top.

"That's not a lot of food," said Jessie. "How are you feeling? Usually, you eat so much more."

It was just like her mom to wrap a criticism inside concern.

There was no way she was going to be able to eat while hungry children were playing in a mud puddle.

Markus took a large bite of pancake. Speaking as he chewed, he used his fork to point. "Everyone, eat something. I feel like a pig at the trough right now."

Sarah used the side of her fork to cut a wedge of pancake. She took a bite. The sweet apples and spicy cinnamon mixed perfectly with the fluffy batter. The food was more than delicious—it tasted like her childhood. All the best memories were of Sarah, Nate and their parents eating breakfast. "Thanks for making this for me."

"Of course," said her mother. "You know I'd do anything for you."

Was that true? Could she ask her mother to leave Markus? Even if there was nothing criminal happening with the church, he was still a bad man.

"Hey, what's this talk about doing anything for Sarah?" Markus asked, his tone jovial. "I'm going to get jealous."

Liam had eaten half of his pancake and two slices of bacon already. "Thanks for making us breakfast. You're a very good cook." The distant sound of hammers could be heard at the back of the house. "Looks like you have a lot of construction going on around here. What're you building?"

"I'm glad that you asked, Liam. Because this is the project that I want to discuss with you. Our community is always growing. What we need is a house of worship that's large enough for everyone. We have the labor on-site but what we need is materials."

Sarah tried to swallow another bite. It stuck in her throat. She washed it down with swig of orange juice. "House of worship?" she echoed. "What about plain old housing?"

"What do you mean?" her mom asked, her eyes wide.

Oh, she couldn't take the act anymore. "Don't play dumb with me, Mom. You must notice how poorly all these people live. It's freezing outside and you have people sleeping in tents. Why waste time and money building a church? People have to have their basic needs met."

Her mother said, "Everyone has come here because of Markus. They want to hear him preach. We need a church for all of us to gather."

"Then why spend all this time and money on *your home* when there are children living in shacks?" Sarah asked.

"I can see where you're confused." Markus chuckled as he wiped his mouth with a cloth napkin. "The congregation named me as the pastor. Since I'm their leader, I need a home befitting my position. It's kind of like the US president living in the White House." Shaking his head, he chuckled again. "Could you imagine me in a shack? How would anyone respect me? Or your mother?"

Honestly, she hated his smug tone. She hated Markus's too-perfect appearance. She hated his views of the world. But mostly, she hated that her mother had fallen for his crap. "In Valley Forge, George Washington lived in a tent until quarters had been built for all of his men."

"What?" Markus asked, a slice of bacon halfway to his mouth.

"You said that because you were a leader that you needed the best house. During the winter of 1777, which was brutal by all accounts, Washington lived in a tent like a common soldier until the Continental Army built housing." She paused and took a bite of pancake. "I think George Washington is a pretty respected leader."

Markus's face turned scarlet. "You listen here, Missy..."

"You know," said Liam, interrupting whatever else was going to be said, "I'd like to hear more about the church. Since I'm here for my client, maybe they could give an endowment to help with costs." He paused. "That way, we can all go back to being a happy family."

Sarah bit her bottom lip. The pain eased away her anger. After a moment, she reached for Liam's hand. "Now you see why I love him."

"You were always a good kid, Liam." Her mother held up a platter. "More sausage?"

The conversation about the living conditions and the extreme poverty was forgotten. Markus spent the rest of the meal discussing his plans for the church and the grounds. Aside from a large sanctuary, which would welcome visitors, there would be a retreat center. Those who lived on the church property would each be given a home. He was careful to point out that families with children were a priority. The congregants would all have jobs—cooking, maintenance, teaching at a school that would be built. They planned to raise their own food and sell artisan goods at a store that needed to be constructed, as well.

"What my people want is an oasis of peace in the desert of chaos that is the modern world. They want to create a community where everyone is equal, useful and appreciated," said Markus. "I'm the leader because I was blessed with the vision for our own little slice of paradise."

If Sarah were being honest, all the plans sounded lovely. Too bad she knew that Markus was full of crap.

Chapter Fifteen

"Eventually, we'll need a library." Breakfast had been eaten. A thin woman with gray eyes had cleared away the dishes and taken them to the kitchen to clean. Liam was with Markus in his home office. The pastor was eager to share all the plans the church had—assuming they could raise the capital. Sarah and her mother sat on a plush sofa in the living room. The view from the tall windows was a study in contrast. A mountain vista in the distance, with a collection of shacks and tents that looked like nothing more than a refugee camp. "That's something you could do, right, Sarah? We could work on that together. The library could be a mother-daughter project."

She held a mug of tea and squeezed the handle tighter. The porcelain bit into her flesh. "Yeah, Mom, it'd be great to start a new library."

"Like Markus said," her mother continued, "there are a lot of other things to address before we go worrying about books. But once everyone has a house, we can expand to schools and parks. I'll need your help. You'll be there for me, right?"

She hated lying to her mother. Taking a sip of tea, she swallowed all the facts she wanted to share. Then, she said, "I'm always here for you, Mom."

Inaudible voices came from the hallway a moment before Liam and Markus stepped into the room. "You two look as pretty as a picture," said Markus. "But I need to scoot for a few minutes. It's almost lunchtime and I say a few words before each meal. If you'd like, you can come with me, Liam. Then, you can see all the good we do."

Liam said, "That'd be great."

Then, like a light bulb moment from one of her favorite books, she knew how to get Liam into the office. Rising from the sofa, she said, "I'll go with you."

"I was hoping to keep chatting," said her mother. "I haven't even showed you around the house yet."

"You can show me once we get back. Right now, I want to see what you and Markus have done."

"Well." Markus inhaled, expanding his chest. "I'm happy that both Liam and Sarah have taken an interest in the church. Once you see how truly happy everyone is in this congregation, you'll feel better."

"That's what I'm hoping, too," she lied.

"Let me call my driver," Markus said.

"No!" *Damn.* She'd been a little too forceful. "I'd rather walk."

"You want to walk to the cafeteria? Are you kidding?" asked her mother. "That's almost a mile from here."

"A mile isn't that far," she said, setting her mug on a table. "Besides, Liam and I were looking at wedding dresses online last night. The ones I like are slinky. So, let's just say I could use a walk."

"Wedding dresses. Did you hear that, Markus?" Her mom's eyes glistened with unshed tears. "Oh, my baby's getting married."

"Well, it's not officially official." Sarah had lied to her mother so many times over the past few days, she shouldn't care about one more untruth. But for some reason, this fib mattered. "We're just talking."

"Doesn't this seem sudden?" asked Markus. "After all, you've only known each other for a few days."

Who'd have thought he'd be the reasonable one?

"Actually, we've known each other most of our lives. The time wasn't right when we were kids." Liam reached for her hand. "But the minute we saw each other at the library, I knew."

"I think it's romantic," said Jessie. "Sarah used to have a horrible crush on Liam when she was younger. Remember that?"

Anything her mom said was always honey mixed with vinegar. "I remember." Leaning into Liam, she rested her head on his chest. "Looks like I had good taste, even as a kid."

"Well, if we're going to walk, we ought to get going," said Markus.

He strode to the front door and pulled it open. Cold seeped into the room. Damn. Picking up her coat from the back of the sofa, she made eye contact with Liam. She narrowed her gaze, while slipping her arms into the sleeves.

He regarded her for a moment and grabbed his own jacket. Was the look enough for him to know that something was up? Hopefully, he'd take advantage of the situation.

The group stepped onto the porch. Jessie hadn't bothered with another coat. Folding her arms across her chest, she pulled the long sweater tight around her body. "It's too cold out here," she grumbled.

"Get another jacket or something," she suggested.

"Everything I have is too short. It won't look right with my outfit." Jessie was only a few steps behind. Arms still folded, she mumbled, "And what about the hem of my pants? Nobody seems to notice that they'll get stained or ruined. Definitely, nobody cares." She sighed dramatically. "The things we mothers do for our children."

She slowed until her mom was next to her. Linking her arm through the crook of her mother's elbow, she said, "We'll walk together, and I'll keep you warm."

"Thanks, hon. It'd be better if we could drive."

"Getting out of the house is good, too."

"One day soon, this will be a lovely community. Right now…" Jessie let her words trail off. Liam and Markus had pulled ahead and were talking in hushed tones. Leaning close, her mother whispered, "Are you mad at me?"

"Why would I be mad?"

Her mom said, "What I said yesterday about my bag being worth more than your car. I guess it was rude."

"I don't care about your bag," she said, her jaw tight.

"To be honest, you sound pretty pissed right now."

Now, Sarah remembered why she never visited her mother—aside from Markus not allowing her to come to their house. She and her mom were oil and water. They never mixed, even when they were together. "Can we drop it, Mom?"

"If you were mad, I wanted to tell you that I'm sorry. I also wanted to tell you that I have a bag from the same designer. It's from last season. But if you want it, it's yours."

What was she supposed to do with a designer bag? If it was worth something, she could hold a raffle to raise money for the library. Then again, her mother was trying. The least she could do is accept the kindness. "Thanks, Mom. I'd love it."

"Oh, good." Jessie squeezed her arm tighter. She leaned in closer. "Now tell me all about those wedding dresses you saw."

"Markus might be right. This is a little too early to be talking about forever."

"Miracle of miracles—you agree with Markus," said Jessie with a giggle. "But he's wrong, you know. I've seen the way Liam looks at you. He's in love."

With a shake of her head, she chuckled. "I heard that before."

"From who? Margaret?"

The library in Boise seemed like it was a million miles away. "Actually, it was Frannie." Sarah cleared her throat. "Frannie Colton."

Jessie stiffened. "When did you see her?"

At least she didn't have to lie about seeing a few of her half siblings. "I ran into her yesterday."

"Oh?" Jessie let go of her arm. "Where was this?"

"At her store right after I had brunch with you and Markus."

"Imagine that," her mother snorted. "You ran into Frannie in her own store."

"You don't have to be sarcastic. I didn't know who owned the store when I walked through the doors."

"How could you not have known? Book Mark It is the only bookstore in all of Owl Creek." Her mother's voice was shrill.

"How was I supposed to know about anything in Owl Creek? You never talked to me about that place. Or the fact that Nate and I have ten half siblings." So much for not arguing with her mother.

Markus glanced over his shoulder. "You girls okay back there?"

"We're fine," her mother called out. "We are fine, aren't we?"

She exhaled. Her breath caught in a frozen cloud. "Sure, Mom. We're fine."

Sarah shoved her hands deeper into her pockets and trudged over the uneven ground. The tents and shacks they'd passed before were now empty. There was no longer the sound of construction ringing over the field. Even the children had abandoned their game at the puddle, leaving it eerily quiet. It was like they'd all disappeared. The only thing that remained was the scent of refuse that hung in the air.

"Where is everyone?" she asked. A gust of wind caught her question and whipped it away.

"They're in the cafeteria, which doubles as a sanctuary—at least for now," Markus called over his shoulder. He gave Liam an oily smile. "I give a sermon right before the meal. Everyone is waiting to be fed both spiritually and physically."

"What's your topic for today?" Honestly, Sarah didn't care. But she wanted everyone to be busy and talking.

"I'm not sure yet," said Markus. "I usually just let inspiration take over."

"Wait till you see him," her mom cooed. "He's so impressive."

The office was close. A guard still stood outside the door. Sarah inhaled. Icy air burned her lungs. Holding her breath, she counted. One. Two. Three. Then, she stumbled and hit the ground.

A white burst of pain exploded behind her eyes. Her fall had simply been meant as a diversion. Instead, she'd landed on a rock. Damn. She could already feel the bruise, blossoming like a flower, on her foot.

"Are you okay?" Her mom knelt at her side. Liam was right behind Jessie. Markus stood, looming behind them all.

Her ankle throbbed with each beat of her heart. "I was stupid and not paying attention."

"Here, let me help you." Liam gripped her elbow and pulled her to standing. "How's that feel?"

The man who'd been guarding the office jogged up the road. He called out, "Everything okay?"

"Looks like Sarah twisted her ankle," Markus sighed. Turning to her, he asked, "Can you make it to the cafeteria? You can sit in there and get some ice on your foot."

She placed her left foot on the ground. Okay, so maybe it wasn't that bad. But this was the exact distraction that she needed. "I don't think I can," she said, hoping to sound anxious and distraught. "I'd rather go to the house than have to limp through a bunch of strangers."

"Honey, Markus has to speak to the congregation," said her mom. "They're waiting for him."

"I don't want to hold him up. You can stay with me, right Mom?"

"How're you supposed to make it all the way back up the hill on a busted ankle? The cafeteria is right over there." Markus pointed to the large metal building. A few people stood near the door watching and waiting for the pastor.

The thing was, Markus had a point.

"I can run back to the house and get the SUV," the guard offered. "It won't take me a minute."

Markus waved the guard away. "Go, Roger. Hurry back."

The guard turned and sprinted up the hill.

"I'm already late," Markus huffed.

"You should go," her mother said. "Sarah has been clumsy her whole life. This isn't the first time I've taken care of a twisted ankle."

After placing a kiss on Jessie's cheek, he jogged down the hill.

"Start the music," he called out to the men waiting near the entrance. "I'm coming."

Markus entered the makeshift sanctuary. The doors closed, and the morning was filled with silence. Sarah wanted to smile, but she couldn't. She limped forward. "Maybe I should walk a little. That way my ankle won't get stiff."

Liam held on to her arm. "I've got a hold of you," he said. "You can lean on me."

Squeezing his wrist, she mouthed the word *Go*. It was all he needed.

Liam gave a slight nod and let his hand slip away.

"Hey, Mom," she said, turning to Jessie. "Remember when I slid down the driveway on my Rollerblades in middle school? I had road burn on my knee for a week."

"I remember you wanted those Rollerblades so bad for your birthday. Because of your fall, you used them once and never again."

Her mother kept talking about the incident. How her father, Robert, had been angry to waste money. How the Rollerblades had ended up going to Allison, a much more athletic kid, who could stay upright. Sarah listened but kept walking slowly toward the house. She didn't know how long Liam needed to be in the office, but she'd done all she could. The rest was up to him.

LIAM SCANNED THE hillside to make sure that he was alone. Sarah and her mother were already more than a dozen yards away. She was close enough that he could see the piping at the edge of Sarah's coat, tan on dark blue, but so far away that he couldn't hear what they said.

Other than the women, he was alone.

Slipping a hand into his pocket, he wrapped his fingers around the flash drive. It was cold and solid, a reminder of his determination to get the job done. He walked slowly to the office.

That was another rule from undercover training.

Those who look like they belong go unnoticed.

His footfalls clanged on the metal stairs, the sound ricocheting like a gunshot. He paused, waiting for someone to stop him. The hillside was empty. He gripped the handle and turned the knob. The door opened, swinging inside.

Since a guard had been posted outside, he wasn't surprised the building was left unlocked. Hopefully, everything else was just as easy. Stepping inside, he looked around the space. Light from a window filled a converted mobile home. What would have been a living room had been turned into workspace, complete with a sofa beneath the window and two metal desks. A row of filing cabinets filled the back wall. There was also a kitchen, complete with a round dining table and refrigerator and stove.

Two rooms, one at either end of the trailer, were closed. His intel didn't include which one Markus used as an office. For a moment, the indecision rooted him to the floor. There was no way to know which was the right one. But guessing wrong would waste time he didn't have.

The room to the right was closer. He strode through the outer office. The room was unlocked. Inside was another office. Desk. Chair. Filing cabinet in the corner. An open laptop sat in the middle of the desk. He knew one thing for certain: Markus wouldn't use a utilitarian and impersonal office.

Quickly, he walked to the other side of the trailer. He turned the handle of the second door. It didn't budge.

Kneeling, he examined the lock. It was typical of interior doors, meant to deter polite people from entering without warning. In fact, Liam could force his way inside with quick kick to the jamb or a shoulder to the flimsy fake wood. But that wouldn't do. He needed to be able to sneak out of the trailer, too.

This required a bit of finesse.

In the FBI Academy, agents were taught how to pick locks, especially simple ones like this. Sure, he hadn't had the need to use this particular skill but at least he knew how.

After rising to his feet, he hustled to the kitchen area. He opened several drawers before finding what he needed. A plastic caddy was filled with flatware. Spoons. Forks. Knives—both smooth luncheon knives and sharp steak knives. He grabbed a steak knife and returned to the room. He slipped the narrow end between lock and jamb. For a moment, metal grated against metal. Then, the lock released, with a soft click.

Standing, Liam set the knife on a nearby desk. He'd put it back once he was done. He turned the handle and opened the door. The floor was covered with an expensive-looking rug with a floral pattern in reds and golds. The single window was covered with velvet drapes, blocking out the sun. Yet, there was enough light for Liam to see.

A leather sofa sat at an angle in the corner. A matching chair was next to the sofa. A bar on wheels was tucked in the crook behind them both. In the middle of the room stood a large desk. The polished wood reflected the scant light. Sitting on the desk was a computer monitor and keyboard. The device was so old that the tower for the hard drive stood next to the desk.

Bingo.

It was the computer that Helena had seen Markus use.

Liam entered the room. The door closed behind him with a thud. Without the open door, there was no light. He didn't care, he'd seen enough to know the layout.

At the desk, he touched a key on the keyboard. The screen began to glow. A password field appeared. Helena had told him the password. It was Markus's birth date in reverse order. He had long ago memorized the numbers and didn't think while typing.

The password screen disappeared, and he held his breath.

It took a moment for the computer's menu to appear. He didn't have time to analyze all the data. Once he was back in DC, he'd have the luxury of time. Then, he could look at all the files. Placing the flash drive into the front of the tower, he entered a set of keystrokes.

A new message appeared. Copying hard drive. 10% complete.

25% complete.
45% complete.

Sweat snaked down his back. He didn't know how long it would take to copy the hard drive. But he only had a few minutes before someone noticed that he was missing.

Chapter Sixteen

Jessie held tight to Sarah's arm as they walked up the hill. True, it was still cold outside, but she was now warmed by the fact that her daughter needed her. Truth be told, she hadn't been a good mother—not even to Sarah and Nate. But here Sarah was, still wanting her help.

"How're you feeling?" she asked.

"It hurts, but I think I'll be okay." Sarah hobbled forward, dragging her right foot. Funny, Jessie could've sworn she twisted her left ankle. A chill ran down her spine and it had nothing to do with the temperature.

"Do you remember the Christmas when you were eight years old?" she asked. "Your dad and I gave you and Nate sleds."

"We had gotten a foot of snow on Christmas Eve, so we both spent the morning sledding down the hill in the backyard." Sarah smiled before adding, "You made a homemade pumpkin pie and mashed potatoes. Dad roasted a turkey. When we came in—cold, wet and tired—the food was ready."

She recalled sitting around the table, as savory and sweet scents filled the small kitchen. Sarah and Nate were rosy cheeked with exertion and the cold. It was a nice memory. "I hope we can all be a family again. I know that you're making your own life, but I want us to always be close."

Sarah gave her arm a squeeze. "I know we don't always agree, Mom. But I do love you."

"And what about Markus?" Her fiancé didn't like to be discussed. More than once, a member of the church had questioned his authority. The punishment was always swift and severe. But outside, with nobody around, Jessie could ask.

Sarah snorted. "He does seem to love you. That counts for something."

"I know he's not your real father..." Jessie began.

Sarah stopped walking. "Mom, I'm a grown woman. I don't need a replacement dad. Besides, I'm not even sure that I knew my own father."

"You shouldn't say that," she chastised.

"Why not? It's true. You and Dad had a whole other life that we never knew about. You both had children from other marriages. What's worse, you never said a word to me or my brother. Or should I say, 'Nate,' because I have so many other brothers."

Sure, she deserved some of her daughter's wrath. It's just that Jessie didn't want to take it. "Can we please change the subject and talk about something pleasant?"

"Yeah, sure." There was a weariness to her tone that made Sarah sound older than her years.

"I have a confession to make." She held on to her daughter's arm tighter.

"A confession?" Sarah echoed. "That sounds serious."

"It's nothing too bad. It's just that I was looking at mother-of-the-bride dresses. I think I'd look good in dusty rose. If you're thinking about colors for the wedding, that is."

"I'm not sure that Liam and I are there yet."

Jessie looked over her shoulder. The camp was empty and quiet. "Where is Liam anyway?"

"He went with Markus."

"I don't think so..." Jessie brought back the moment that Sarah fell. The congregation was already assembled. Her daughter said she couldn't walk to the cafeteria. A guard had left his post at the office as Liam had helped Sarah to her feet. At the same time, Markus ran down the hill. She recalled him telling a man to start the music as he entered the building. What's more, he'd been alone. "Liam wasn't with Markus, I'm positive."

Keeping her eyes on the ground, she said, "Remember, he kissed me on the cheek and told me to be careful."

Jessie slowly shook her head. "That's not what happened."

"Yes, it is." Sarah's jaw flinched. The gesture was gone as quick as it came. But it was same tell she'd had all her life. Her daughter had just lied. But why?

Her heart started to race. The metallic taste of panic coated her tongue. She didn't know how Markus would react when he found out that Liam had wandered off. But she did know it wouldn't be good. He told her that all the security around the church compound was to keep nefarious characters out. But deep in her heart, she knew better. They were here to keep people in. She had to get Sarah and Liam off the mountain and back to Owl Creek. Or better yet, back to Boise. She gripped her daughter's arm tight. "Now, you listen to me."

"Ow," Sarah protested, trying to pull her arm away. Jessie only tightened her grip. A little pain now was better than what might happen later. "You're hurting me."

She leaned in close and whispered, "Markus is not a man

to be trifled with. Here, he's not just God's representative on earth. For this community, he is God. His word is absolute."

She drew in a shaking breath. Her galloping pulse slowed. "You've got to come clean with me. What in the hell is going on here? Where's Liam?"

"Nothing's going on, Mom." But her daughter glanced at the office as she spoke.

"Is that where he went?" she asked. "The office? What does he want?"

With a defiant glint in her eyes, Sarah met her gaze but said nothing.

"We don't have much time. Be honest with me." She paused, waiting for her daughter to say something. Anything. Sarah remained mute. She tried again, "Keeping you safe is the only thing that matters to me. I know something's going on. But I can't help if you don't tell me the truth."

FUNNY THING, SARAH had wanted to be honest with her mother from the beginning. Now that her mom was begging for the truth, she hesitated.

She heard the revving of a motor a moment before she saw the black SUV. The vehicle was coming toward them fast, like a bird of prey. They didn't have much time now. Once the guard showed up, the conversation would be over.

It didn't matter what her mother had said, Sarah wasn't sure if she was to be trusted. Then again, what other choice did she have?

"Markus is a crook," she said, starting with the obvious. "He's been stealing money from his congregation. Using his money to buy nice things." She didn't add that many of those nice things had gone to Jessie. She didn't need to.

They both knew the truth. "He's embezzled millions of dollars. The FBI is investigating him. You have to leave him before it's too late."

"Liam's still with the FBI, isn't he?" her mom asked.

"He is."

"And he's the one investigating Markus. Is he in the office looking for evidence?"

There was no reason to lie to her mother anymore. "He is."

Her mother asked, "You two aren't really a couple, are you?"

"Let's just say that it's complicated."

A tear ran down her mother's cheek. She wiped it away with the heel of her hand. "Why didn't you come to me from the beginning? Or is that complicated, as well?"

"Mom, there's a lot for us to discuss," she began.

Her mother waved a hand, as if wiping away Sarah's words from a whit board. It was almost like she'd never spoken. "There's only one thing to worry about right now. Liam has to get out of that office. If Markus ever finds out that he's been fooled, there'll be hell to pay."

She turned and looked at the trailer. From where she stood on the hill, the building looked smaller, like a child's toy. They'd walked too far to get Liam out now. Had Sarah been wrong to have kept her mother in the dark? Questions jumbled together in a big pile until she couldn't parse one from the next. But there was only one question that really mattered. "What kind of hell is happening here, Mom?"

Before her mother could answer, the black SUV stopped in the middle of the road. The guard, she remembered his name was Roger, put the vehicle into Park. He opened the driver's side door. "Where's the other guy?"

Her mom looked Sarah in the eye. "I sent him to the office." Slipping her hand into her pocket, she turned to Roger and smiled. "Markus brought my phone's charger with him to the office yesterday and forgot to bring it back. When I remembered, I sent Liam to grab it for me."

"Nobody's supposed to be inside that building without permission," said Roger. "That's why I'm posted outside all day."

"Then we won't tell Markus that you left your post."

The man opened his mouth, ready to argue with Jessie. He seemed to think better of it and gave a single nod. "Let's find your charging cable and get you all back to the house. Like you said, I've been away from my post for too long." He opened the back passenger door—a sure sign that they were supposed to get into the SUV.

Jessie slid into the back seat. Sarah limped toward the open door and got into the back seat, as well. The SUV had three rows of seats. In the front, there were two captain's chairs. The middle row was also made up of two captain's chairs. TV monitors were set in the back of the front headrests. The back seat was a long bench.

She ran her hand over the buttery-soft seat. "This is like a very fancy spaceship," she said, making a bad joke.

Nobody laughed.

The guard slid behind the steering wheel. He put the gearshift into Drive, and they rolled down the hill. He slowed in front of the office. "You both relax. I'll get the other guy and your phone's cord."

Jessie opened the door before Roger put the vehicle into Park. "I can do it myself. It'll just take me a second."

Obviously, everything her mom told the guard had been a lie. And honestly, she didn't know what was going to happen next. But she wasn't about to let her mother go alone. Opening her own door, Sarah dropped down to the ground.

"Hey," Roger called out. "I thought you twisted your ankle. Doesn't look like it hurts you now."

"It doesn't," she agreed. "Must be a miracle."

THE OFFICE WAS DARK, save for the light coming from the monitor. In the middle of the screen, a line marked off the percentage of files that had been copied and transferred to Liam's flash drive. The machine was a relic, as far as computers were concerned. The slow download had worn even his patience thin. But he'd come too far to leave without his evidence.

"C'mon," he said, as if his urging could get the computer to process faster. "What's the freaking holdup?"

The line filled in another inch.

Download 79% complete.
84% complete.
99% complete.
100% complete.

"Thank you," he said, entering the keystrokes that erased any trace that he'd been on the computer at all. Once the computer was shut down, he removed the flash drive. He stuck the stick into his sock. It wasn't an ideal hiding place, but it was better than his pocket.

Then, he heard it. The crunch of wheels on gravel and the idling of an engine. At the window, he pulled back the curtain an inch. One of the black SUVs sat next to the building, a cloud of exhaust surrounding the vehicle in a haze. Jessie

Colton exited the vehicle and hustled toward the office. He hoped to get into and out of the building without any witnesses. Obviously, that wasn't going to happen now.

He needed to think. Yet, he couldn't hear his own thoughts over his pulse slamming into his skull.

The door to the trailer opened, hitting the wall with a crack.

"Where is he?" He recognized Jessie's voice.

"He's in Markus's office," said Sarah.

Had he been double-crossed by mother and daughter?

The door handle jiggled. Then, someone knocked. "Liam, we have to go," said Jessie, before adding, "Now."

He didn't know what to believe or whom to trust. But staying in the office wasn't an option. He opened the door and stepped into the reception area. The door closed behind him. Jessie stood on the threshold. Sarah was behind her mother. Without saying a word, Jessie pulled a thin white cord from the pocket of her sweater and shoved it into his hands.

The outer door opened again. One of black-clad guards followed—to him, they all looked the same. He pointed a finger at Jessie. "I told you to wait in the SUV."

"And I told you that I could handle this myself," said Jessie. "And see, he has my phone cord."

There were too many moving pieces in this game for his liking. But his training kicked in. Another rule from undercover agent's training. *Always stay in character.* He held up the plastic cord, letting it dangle from his fingers like a dead snake. "Found it."

"Thank you." Smiling, Jessie took the cord and shoved it back into her pocket. She patted the guard's arm as she passed him at the door. "Lock the door behind you and take us up to the house."

Sarah reached for his hand and pulled him into her mother's wake. The flash drive in his sock snagged on his pants. He stepped outside. The air had the icy bite that promised more snow. The back door of the SUV was still open. Jessie slid into the back seat. Sarah squeezed his hand once and followed her mother. Liam got into the front seat of the passenger side. The driver rounded in front of the bumper and slid behind the steering wheel.

Roger slammed the door and shoved the gearshift into Drive. The air in the SUV was rank with anxious energy, like the moment before a bomb was set to explode. He watched Roger from his periphery. The other man gripped the steering wheel. His knuckles were white. The ride to Jessie's house took only minutes. Yet in the silence of the SUV, it felt like hours.

The guard slowed next to the steps that led to the porch.

Jessie leaned between the two front seats, "Roger, I think it best if we don't mention that Liam was in the admin building. You know that Markus won't be happy that you neglected to lock the door."

"Yes, ma'am," he said. "Thank you."

Liam opened the door. He drew in a deep breath and exhaled. Sarah and Jessie stood beside him. They waited as the SUV drove away. He turned to the women. "What in the hell is going on?"

"I should be the one asking you that," snapped Jessie. "How dare you put my daughter in danger."

He wasn't about to break cover. Looking at Sarah's mom, he said, "I don't know what you're talking about."

"Yes, you do," said Sarah. "I told her."

The three words hit him like a fist to the face. For a moment, he saw stars. "You what?"

"I had no choice. Roger had just shown up with SUV. If you tried to sneak out, he would've seen you. My mom helped, face it." The steel in Sarah's words surprised him.

True, he knew that she much was more than the kid with a bad case of hero worship. The wind caught her hair, blowing it around her face. She gripped her locks and held them in her fist. Snowflakes danced, swirling and swooping, in another gust. She reminded him of a Nordic warrior, and he admired her even more.

"Let's go inside," she suggested. "There's a lot we all need to discuss."

"No," said Jessie. "We don't have time for a tête-à-tête. You both need to leave."

"What're you talking about, Mom?" Sarah asked.

"You know how I said that Markus rules this community?" She exhaled. "There's no telling what he'll do to either of you. Please, just go."

Liam had never seen the serious and intense side of Jessie before. To him, she'd always been flighty and dramatic. For the first time, he wondered if he'd underestimated her.

"If it's so dangerous that I have to leave, then you're coming with me," said Sarah.

"I can't leave," said Jessie. "He'll come looking for me."

"The FBI has ways to keep you hidden," he said. "You'll be safe."

"What about Sarah? Or Nate? Or Malcolm? Or any of my other kids? Can you shelter them all?"

He knew the FBI wouldn't bring all the Coltons into protective custody. "I'll do what I can."

"That's not enough," she said with a mirthless laugh. "Now, you both need to go."

For Liam, leaving now would be perfect. He had the evidence he needed. But he didn't like leaving Jessie behind. Markus sounded like more than just a crook, but a sociopath, as well.

"Won't that seem suspicious?" Sarah asked. "What will you say to Markus?"

Jessie gave a small shrug. "I'll tell him that you and I got into a fight or something. And that's what you have to say at the guard shack. They won't worry about letting you leave."

"Mom, listen to what you're saying," The pain in Sarah's voice cut deep into his chest. "You cannot stay. Who cares about your nice house and your fancy purses. They aren't what make you the person I love. They don't make you who you are—my mother."

Jessie said, "To keep you safe, I need to stay, at least for now."

"I'm not leaving without you," said Sarah.

The sound of music, faint but unmistakable, rolled up the hill. The congregation had been released. Liam's time was up.

Chapter Seventeen

Roger stood in front of the crappy converted mobile home that was being used as the church's administrative building. The cold seeped in through the soles of his shoes. Shoving his hands into the pockets of his coat, he watched as the people, skinny and sad, shuffled by. They all sang, like they were happy. He'd heard all their stories. Lost souls, who finally found a place in the world. People who couldn't find a direction now had a leader to follow.

He he'd been let go from the Bingham County Sheriff's Office six months earlier. One late night, another deputy had swiped a baggie of weed from the evidence locker. They'd all toked up. In the morning, the sheriff figured it out. Everyone was questioned. Roger was the only one who confessed. By noon, he'd been fired.

In the small eastern Idaho county where he lived, his misconduct was a scandal. Roger became a pariah in his family. With no other options, he'd answered the online ad for security personnel. Markus hired him after a single interview.

When he thought about it that way, he was like all the hollow-eyed people who shuffled past.

But in a lot of other ways, he was different. After six

months on the job, he hated the Ever After Church. He hated standing around sweating in the summer and freezing his balls off in the winter. To him, everyone on this compound was a bleating sheep. Except for Markus, that is.

He was a wolf.

And speak of the devil—literally.

Striding up the road, Markus watched Roger.

Shifting from one foot to the other, he lifted his chin in greeting. "The sermon go well today, sir?"

"My sermons always go well."

"Glad to hear it," he said.

Roger had never been the churchy type. He didn't believe all the mumbo-jumbo about heaven or hell. You lived your life. Good happened when you worked hard. Bad happened when you screwed up. In fact, he was a prime example of that belief system.

"Did you get Jessie and the others back to the house?" Markus asked.

He didn't want to find out what would happen if he lied to the pastor. So thankfully, his answer was the truth. "I did, sir."

"How did Jessie's daughter seem? Will she need a doctor?"

"Actually, I think the injury wasn't as bad as we first thought."

"Good. Good." Markus walked up the set of stairs to the office building. He reached for the handle and pulled on the door. Neither budged. "Why's the door locked?"

"Since I wasn't on guard, I figured…" He reached into his pants pocket and removed a heavy ring of keys. He climbed the steps and stood next to Markus. Now would be the time to confess that Liam had been in the office unattended. He didn't believe Jessie's story about needing her phone charger. Then again, he'd learned a tough lesson about telling the truth. Sliding the key into the lock, he opened the door and stepped aside. "There you go, sir."

"You can come inside," the pastor said. "We can chat while I collect some of my things."

That's how it started last time. An invitation for a friendly conversation. Roger wasn't a brainiac or anything. But he was smart enough to not piss in the same well twice. "I really should be outside."

"Nonsense," said Markus with a laugh. "You're here to protect me. Besides, the office is better than standing out in the cold."

"Well," he chuckled. "I can't argue with that thinking, sir."

Markus touched his temple. "I'm the smart one. That's why I'm in charge."

The pastor entered the trailer. Roger followed. The room was warm and smelled of coffee. He'd grown up in a mobile home like this one. He hadn't talked to his mother in months. If he called now, would his mom invite him to come home?

"I won't be a minute," said Markus, pulling him from his thoughts. He pointed to a sofa. "Have a seat."

Roger dropped onto the soft cushion. The ache in his back was eased. His feet warmed up a little. That's when he saw it. A knife sat on the edge of a desk, the blade glinting in the light. His chest tightened, making it impossible to breathe. It was proof that Liam, that son of a bitch, hadn't just been in the office for Jessie's phone cord. But worse than that, it was evidence that Roger had failed at his job. What's more, he'd lied to the pastor.

Now, all he could do was hope the cutlery was overlooked.

Markus walked to his office door. From his pocket, he produced a key that worked into the lock. After turning the handle, he pushed the door open.

His pulse slowed as he made a plan. Once the pastor closed his office door, he could put the knife away.

Markus turned. "I forgot to ask…" His question unraveled as his gaze dropped to the desk. And the knife. He looked up at Roger, his eyes narrowed. "What the hell is going on?"

Roger's mouth was dry. He swallowed. "Um."

"Um?" Markus echoed. "Is that all you have to say?" He picked up the blade and pointed it at Roger. "I think there's a lot you know and you better start talking."

SARAH WASN'T GOING to leave without her mother. But what was she supposed to do if Jessie refused to go?

She tried a new argument. "If you want to keep me safe, get in the car. Because I'm not leaving without you. So, if you're staying, then I'm staying, as well."

Liam said, "Listen to your daughter. If you don't, I'll forcibly move you to the car."

"You are the most stubborn people I know," her mother said, pointing. "Both of you."

Sarah's purse was still in the house, but her car keys were in the pocket of her coat. Using the fob, she started the engine and unlocked the doors. "Let's get out of here."

Her mom opened the rear passenger door. Sarah reached for the handle on the driver's side. Liam held out his hand. "Let me drive."

She placed the keys in his palm. He wrapped his fingers around her hand. Their gazes met and held. There was so much she wanted to say. But every second was precious. "Let's get out of here."

Her hand slipped from his grasp, and she opened the passenger side door. Sliding into the seat, she put on her seat belt. From the driver's seat, he held out the flash drive. "Tuck this under the floor mat," he said. "Or someplace nobody will see."

Did he really think that the car would be searched? Well, until they'd left the compound, Sarah didn't know what to expect. She took the stick and pulled back the carpeted mat. There was a groove in the flooring. She tucked the flash drive into the recess and replaced the mat. "It's hidden for now."

He started the ignition and put the car into Drive. Snow had collected on the windshield, leaving them in a cocoon of white. Liam turned on the wipers and eased around the circular drive. He slammed his foot on the break. Sarah rocked forward, bracing herself on the dashboard. When she looked up, she saw it.

A black SUV was right in front of them.

Liam eased the car to the right, trying to pass the vehicle. The SUV nosed forward, taking up the whole road and blocking their path. Both front doors opened. Markus exited the vehicle first. Roger followed.

Liam rolled down the window as the two men stepped up to the car.

"Where are you going?" Markus asked, leaning an elbow on the car's cowl.

Liam said, "Sarah and her mom started talking. Well, Jessie wants to reach out to Malcolm. None of us have cell service, so we figured we'd drive to the road."

Honestly, she was impressed. Liam was a convincing liar. No wonder she'd bought his story about being a banker.

Markus turned his gaze to the back seat. "That true, Jessie?"

"I'm not sure that I'll reconcile with all of my kids." Her mother's voice was thin and reedy. She cleared her throat. "But Sarah convinced me to give it a try."

"You know what I think?" Markus asked. "I think you all are lying to me."

"Don't be ridiculous," said Jessie. "Why would anyone lie to you?"

"You're right, I am being silly." He shoved a hand into his pocket and pulled out a knife. "Except for this." Holding up the blade, he asked, "You recognize this?"

Liam gunned the engine, swerving around the rear bumper of the car. The force shoved Sarah back. Her station wagon jostled over the side of berm. There was a crack. The back windshield exploded as a bullet punched a hole into the dashboard. Smoke snaked out of the vents. Sarah looked over her shoulder. Roger stood in the middle of the road with a gun in his hand.

"Get down." Liam shoved the back of her head toward the floor.

Another gunshot rang out. The car bucked to the side.

Holding the steering wheel with both hands, Liam cursed. "He got the tire."

Then, time splintered into a thousand different shards.

Another bullet was fired. Another tire was struck. The car skidded across the road before hitting a snowbank. The world turned upside down as the vehicle flipped onto its roof. Her stomach lurched as the car tumbled end over end.

Hanging upside down, she was pinned in place by the seat belt.

There was the drip, drip, drip of blood landing on the roof of the car.

Everything was stark. Bright white snow. Blood so dark, it looked black. The sides of her vision were hazy, like a photograph that had started to fade.

In the distance, she heard her mother's cries.

Liam's voice came from everywhere, echoing in her head. "Sarah. Are you okay? Can you hear me?"

She wanted to answer but didn't know how to speak. And then, there was nothing.

LIAM STOOD ON the uneven ground. Cold bit into a cut on his face. The back of his head throbbed. Running his fingers over his hairline, he found a knot already forming. Markus and the guard with the gun had dragged him from the wreckage. They'd pulled Sarah and Jessie out of the car, as well.

Jessie sobbed. "What just happened, Markus? You shot at us. You shot at me. And for no reason!"

"Shut up," Markus snapped. "I'll deal with you later."

Jessie's makeup was smeared, but she seemed uninjured. Sarah was a different story. The accident left her unconscious. A cut ran along her forehead. Red ran down her cheeks, making it look like she was crying blood.

"Let's go," said Markus. He'd traded the knife for a gun. Using the barrel, he pointed toward the house.

Roger carried Sarah. Liam's fingers itched with the need to hold her. He wanted to kiss her and whisper that everything would be okay. But if he told her that now, it would be a lie. They were trapped.

His training as an undercover agent had covered a lot of topics. They'd discussed how to behave if captured, but they never discussed what to do if hostages were taken. Had he been on his own, Liam might've tried to run—the evidence in the car be damned. But there was no way he was going to leave the compound without Sarah.

The walk to the house took only a minute. Markus opened the front door and stepped aside. "Both of you," he ordered to Jessie and Liam, "get inside."

He hated to obey but there was no sense in getting shot for bravado. Without a word, he crossed the threshold. The faint scent of cinnamon and apples still lingered in the air.

Pointing to the sofa, Markus said to Roger, "Put her down there. Then call everyone else on your team. I want all the congregants gathered in the cafeteria. After that, get all the security personnel up here."

"I'm on it, sir," said Roger, before setting Sarah on the couch and leaving through the front door.

Jessie stroked her daughter's hair. "Can you hear me, hon?"

Sarah moaned and her eyelids fluttered. That had to be a good sign.

Markus lifted the gun. "I'm only going to ask you this once. How'd the knife end up on the desk in the admin building?"

A million answers came to him in a downpour of ideas. But he wasn't about to break cover. "What knife?"

"You think I'm stupid?" He pulled a chair out from the dining room table. "Have a seat."

He wasn't going to let the other guy get the upper hand. "Thanks, I'm fine standing."

"You need to get in that chair, or else I'm going to put you there." He leveled his gun at Liam, aiming for the chest.

"You know what I think? I think you're not going to shoot me. Assault with a deadly weapon is quite a crime." Especially when the victim is a federal agent. "I don't think you're stupid. In fact, I think you're smart enough not to get your hands too dirty."

He smirked. "I like you, Liam. I really do. But you see, I can't have people here that I don't trust. I know you were in the admin building. What's more, you used the knife to pick the lock on my office door. But I need to know why." He paused. "Tell me now. Are you still with the FBI?"

Truth be told, Jessie's story about the phone charger wasn't the best. But it was all he had. Besides, there was no reason to deny that he'd been in the office. Obviously, the security guy had ratted them all out. Then there was the problem of the knife on the desk. "Jessie asked me to get something for her, which I did. I might've poked around a little. But if you don't trust me, why should I trust you? Just remember, it's you who wants a lot of money from my client."

Markus rocked back on his heels at the mention of cash. "Why'd you drive away?"

"You used an SUV to block the road. You threatened us with a knife. What kind of man would I be if I didn't get Sarah and her mom somewhere safe?"

"Your story is convincing," Markus agreed. "But it's a little *too* convincing for me to think it's true."

"Stop it," Jessie yelled. "Leave Liam alone. He's answered all your questions. And why is nobody worried that my baby girl is hurt?"

"I told you," Markus said through gritted teeth, "that I would deal with you later."

The front door opened. Four guards, all dressed in black, entered the house. The large room became smaller. Markus smiled and handed the gun back to Roger. The other man slipped the firearm into a holster he wore at his side. Looking at Liam, he said, "I'm only going to tell you once more. Sit in the damn chair. Because if you don't take a seat now, you'll be begging for it later."

Sure, Markus wasn't asking for much. But he wasn't about to give in. "I'll pass."

"Take care of him, Roger."

Roger stepped forward. His gaze locked with Liam's, the security guard drove his hand into Liam's gut. The pain was instantaneous and drove the air from his lung. The first punch was followed by another. This one connected with his chin. For a moment, Liam saw stars.

It didn't matter that he was supposed to be a banker. He wasn't about to get beaten up and not fight back. He swung out wide, catching Roger in the side of the head. That's when the other guards started fighting dirty. All three came at him at once. One guy grabbed his arm, while another landed a blow to his side.

Breakfast threatened to come up. But he'd be damned before he puked in front of these bastards.

Jessie started pleading with Markus. "Tell them to stop."

"See what you've made me do? Did you really send him into the office for your phone charger? What were you thinking?"

"I'm so sorry. He's family."

"That's enough, boys," said Markus. The beating stopped, but the pain remained. "Sit him in the chair."

He was dragged across the floor and propped up in the

seat. He was exhausted and would've preferred they'd left him on the ground to pass out.

Hands on his knees, Markus looked him in the eye. "Now that I've got your attention, I need to know why you were in my office. Are you still with the FBI?"

"Just trying to find out about you for my client," he said, shocked by the conviction in his voice. "But I gotta be honest. I won't be recommending your project."

"You keep saying that, but the thing is, I don't believe you." He paused. "Roger, go to the kitchen and get me a glass of water."

"Yes, sir," he said, before disappearing into the kitchen. A moment later Roger returned with a glass filled with water. He held it out to Markus. "Here you go."

Markus rose to his feet and took the glass. He walked to the sofa and let the liquid trickle onto Sarah.

She coughed as the water ran over her face. Rubbing her eyes, she sat up. "What the hell?"

"It's time for you to wake up," said Markus. "Because your boyfriend won't tell me the truth. But you are all the motivation I need."

"Leave her out of this," said Liam. His lips were thick, and it hurt to speak. Holding on to his ribs, he tried to stand. A guard pushed him back into the chair, knocking the wind out of him.

"Give me your gun," said Markus, holding out his hand to Roger.

The guard placed his hand on his holster but didn't hand the firearm over. "You don't want to do this."

"Oh, don't I?" Markus turned to another guard. "Gun?"

The man removed a pistol from his holster and handed it

to Markus. For a moment, the pastor held the firearm in his palm. Then, he pointed it in Liam's direction. "Now, tell me the truth. Who are you and what do you want?"

It was a risky move to call Markus's bluff. After all, he'd ordered a group of thugs to beat the crap out of Liam. But roughing someone up and shooting them were two different things. "You know who I am and what I do. Don't believe me, look on the internet."

"Wrong answer."

Pivoting, he aimed at Sarah and pulled the trigger.

Chapter Eighteen

Sarah didn't have time to think, only react. She tensed, bracing for the bullet's impact.

"No!" her mother screamed, shoving her to the floor.

A flash of fire erupted from the gun's muzzle. There was a blast that left her ears buzzing. The acrid scent of gunpowder filled the room.

But the pain never came.

Jessie was slumped over on the sofa. Her long blond hair fell over her face. Her breaths came in a wet wheeze.

She looked at her mother and fear gripped her throat. "Mom?" Sarah rose to her knees, kneeling next to her mother. "Are you okay?" She pushed back her hair, and saw bloody foam clinging to Jessie's lips. "Mom?"

Jessie slumped to the side. Her ivory outfit was dark red with blood and gore. That's when she understood it all. In pushing Sarah to the floor, Jessie had caught the bullet.

"Mom!" Rising to her feet, she lifted her mother's sweater. The bullet had torn a hole between her breasts. The wound wept blood. Sarah struggled out of her own coat. Wadding the fabric, she pressed it to the gash. "Mom, can you hear me?"

Jessie opened her eyes. "Are you okay, Sarah?"

"I'm fine, Mom." Her eyes burned. "The important thing is that you'll be fine, too." She looked over her shoulder. The room was filled with men—Markus, Liam and four guards—staring at her. "Damn you all. Help."

"I shot her? I shot Jessie?" Markus was pale. The gun slipped from his hand, clattering to the floor.

Liam rose from the chair. "There has to be a first aid kit around here somewhere."

Roger said, "There's one in the admin building."

"Go get it," said Liam. "And use the phone to call 9-1-1. Tell them to send an ambulance." He stood and scooped up the gun. While slipping the firearm into the waistband of his jeans, he pointed to the remaining security guards. "You gather up all the towels you can find. We have to stop the bleeding."

They all rushed from the room.

One guard emerged from the kitchen with a stack of clean dishrags. He handed them to Liam.

Holding the towels, Liam knelt next to Sarah. "You need to pull your coat away when I tell you. Got it?"

She nodded.

"Now."

Sarah lifted her jacket, now soaked with blood, as Liam pressed the towels onto Jessie's wound. Blood pooled on the leather sofa and leaked to the floor. Her mother's lips were blue. She reached for Sarah's hand; her skin was cool.

Scooting next to her mother, she stroked the hair from her forehead. "Roger went to call an ambulance and get a first aid kit. We'll get you fixed up in no time." The towels Liam pressed to the wound were stained crimson. Her mom had

lost a lot of blood. How much more could she lose before…?
No. She wouldn't think that way.

Looking back at her mother, she tried to smile. "You just
hang in there."

"You were always an easy child, Sarah. I'm sorry I wasn't
a better mother."

"Don't say that. You were a great mom. The best."

"I tried." Her mom swallowed and grimaced with the pain.
"I need you to do something for me."

A guard helped Liam switch the gore-stained kitchen towels for a large bath towel. To Sarah, it seemed like the blood
wasn't soaking the fabric as quickly as before. It meant something important. But was it good or bad?

"Anything," said Sarah.

"I want you to talk to your brothers and sisters—not just
Nate—but everyone. Let them know that I made bad choices
and they suffered. Tell them that I'm sorry. But make sure
they know, I'm proud to be their mom. And Jenny's kids, too.
I'm proud that I was their aunt."

The burning in her eyes was too much. Tears leaked down
her cheeks. She wiped them away with her shoulder. "I'm
going to let you tell them yourself, Mom. Once we get you
to the hospital, I'll call them all. They'll come and see you,
I'm sure of that."

"Oh, Sarah," said her mom. "I hate to leave you. But I
won't make it to the hospital."

"Don't say that, Mom. Please."

"I'm sorry that I won't see you get married. Or have children of your own. But I know that you'll be a beautiful bride
and great mother."

"You're going to be okay," she said. But her mother's lips had turned gray, and her hand was like a block of ice.

"He's here," said her mother, into the distance. "Your father's come for me."

"Mom. Mom. Mom. Don't go. I need you."

Jessie smiled and closed her eyes. She exhaled, and then she was no more.

MARKUS STOOD IN the corner, his hands trembling. A keening wail echoed off the walls. For a moment, he couldn't find the source. Then he realized, he was the one crying. "Ohmigod. Ohmigod. She's dead. I can't believe it. She's dead." There was empty space in his soul now, one that only Jessie could fill.

"She's dead because of you, sick bastard." Sarah stood. Her sweater and hands were covered in Jessie's blood.

"I didn't," he began. But, of course, he had. "I didn't mean to." He'd aimed at Sarah. "If she hadn't shoved you out of the way, she wouldn't be dead."

Even after everything he'd given to her, Jessie still loved her kids more than she loved him. Someone had to pay for his pain. He might've pulled the trigger, but it was all Sarah's fault. Balling his hands into fists, he lunged forward.

"I wouldn't do that if I were you." Liam aimed the gun at Markus.

He froze, arm lifted and ready to strike. Three of his guards stood to the side. They all had guns. "One of you," Markus barked. "Do something."

Two of the men backed away. They opened the door and sprinted from the house.

That left a single guard. "You," he ordered. "Shoot him."

"I can't do that," the young man said. "You need to leave. Roger went to call an ambulance. Because it's a shooting, the cops are going to show up, too. You don't want to be here when they arrive."

"Like I said." Liam lifted the gun. "Don't move."

A sour taste filled his mouth, but he wasn't about to submit. Turning, he ran around the fireplace and toward the kitchen.

"Stop or I'll shoot," Liam warned.

Markus ran faster.

Pop. The air sizzled as a bullet whizzed by his ear.

Pop. Pop. Pop. Pop. Liam fired at him as he ran. The bullets slammed into the wall, sending splinters flying through the air.

He skidded to the back door and turned the handle. Before he could pull the door open, Liam ran into the kitchen. "Step away from the door."

Markus pulled the door open.

Leveling the gun, Liam pulled the trigger.

Click.

Markus didn't have time to gloat. He ran outside. Cold air bit his hands and face. He glanced over his shoulder. Liam came up from behind but was slowed by a limp.

Running down the back stairs two at a time, Markus skidded on the fresh snow. Somehow, he kept on his feet. Heart pumping and legs burning with exertion, he sprinted toward the tree line.

He didn't know how far he'd gone when he realized that the only sound in the woods was his own breathing. He slowed, then stopped. Fat snowflakes fell from sky, lazily twirling in and around the bare branches. Leaning on a tree trunk, he looked back the way he'd come. His shoeprints were filling with snow, and soon they'd be gone. It'd be like he vanished.

No, that wasn't true.

His old computer was still in the administrative building. On it was his entire financial life. If anyone ever saw his bookkeeping, he'd be a wanted man. It wouldn't just be the authorities who would hunt him down.

Hidden in the forest, he trudged through the trees, always keeping the compound to his left. The hammer strikes that usually filled the day were silent. Good, he was glad that all the members of his church were waiting in the cafeteria. Honestly, he didn't care what they thought. He didn't need them anymore.

It took only a few minutes to circle around to the administrative building. There was no guard outside. The door was unlocked. He still had the key to his office, and he opened that door, too. He didn't bother to download the files or destroy the hard drive. Markus picked up the tower and left the same way he'd come.

As he trudged back to the woods, a pang of grief stabbed him in the chest. Jessie's loss would haunt him for the rest of his life, he knew. But he had a new reason for living—to avenge the death of his beloved and make every one of her children pay dearly.

SARAH SAT ON the floor and held her mother's cold hand. Liam had found a sheet somewhere in the house and draped it over Jessie's body.

He knelt at her side and held out a steaming mug. "Green tea with honey," he said. "Sorry, I couldn't find a lemon."

How could she even think about something as simple as

tea? Her mother was gone—dead because of Sarah—and her world was shattered. "I'm not thirsty."

"Drink," he said. "It'll help you feel better."

Right now, her emotions were a blank canvas and she felt nothing. Her whole life, she'd been Jessie Colton's daughter. Sure, her mom could be exasperating. But without her mother, Sarah didn't know who she was.

"Drink," he insisted.

She reached for the mug because she didn't have the energy to argue. She took a sip. The tea warmed her from the inside out. Yet, now she could feel the grief. It was a black shadow that closed in on her from all sides. The dark so complete that she might never see the light again. "My dad is dead. My mom is dead." Her voice cracked on the last word. "At twenty-six, I'm an orphan. Too young to lose both my parents. Too old to have anyone care for me. It means that I'm all alone."

"You aren't alone," Liam began.

She wasn't in the mood to be pacified. "Don't," she said. "Just don't." And then, "What's going to happen now with Markus?"

"He ran into the woods. Because of the snow, I lost his trail. A warrant will be issued for his arrest. Once everyone gets organized, a search party will start to look for him."

"Will they find him?" she asked, taking another sip of tea. "Will that bastard ever be made to pay?"

"They'll find him," said Liam.

"Soon?"

"I can't really say for sure. But a lot of resources will go into bringing Markus Acker to justice."

It wasn't exactly what she wanted to hear, but she knew it was the truth.

"She really loved me," she said, as the first tears started to fall. She drew in a shaking breath, trying to control her crying. It was no use.

"She really did love you," Liam agreed. He took the mug from her hand and set it on the floor. Then, he reached for her shoulders and pulled her into his chest. He was solid and warm and comforting. The black shadow of grief swallowed her whole. Leaning into the embrace, she let the tears come. In the distance was the lonesome wail of a siren. The ambulance, meant to save her mother, was on the way. Yet, it was too late for them all.

THERE WAS NO reason for Liam to maintain his cover any longer. Official vehicles—ambulances and police cruisers—lined the rutted lane that ran through the Ever After Church compound. Lights atop cars strobed, turning the constantly falling snow red and blue. Standing in front of the house, he briefed a contingent of local law enforcement.

Fletcher Colton was a detective for the Owl Creek PD and one of Sarah's half siblings. At first glance, it was obvious that Fletcher and Sarah were related. They had the same brown hair and green eyes. There was also Archer Mackenzie, a forensic analyst, and Ajay Wright, part of the search and rescue team with the Idaho State Police. Pumpkin, a yellow Lab, sat next to Ajay's feet. She regarded Liam with her head cocked, as if she, too, were listening to what he had to say. Both Archer and Ajay were romantically involved with two members of the Colton crew—Hannah and Lizzy.

He'd begun by telling them about the undercover operation, meant to retrieve the data from Markus's computer. He ended with the events of the past few hours. "After the car wreck, Markus took us all to the house to be questioned. He knew something was off because I screwed up. I used a knife to pick the lock to his personal office but didn't put the blade back. Once he saw it, he ordered his goons to rough me up."

"Looks like you got more than a little roughed up," said Ajay. Ajay kept his brown hair short. He wore a heavy coat. The words *Idaho State Police Search and Rescue K-9 Officer* were emblazoned across the back.

Liam hadn't taken the time to look in a mirror. But he could tell that he'd been beaten badly. Pain seared through his chest with each breath. His lips were swollen, and one tooth was loose. He shrugged. Pain stabbed him in the side. "I'll survive."

"And then what happened?" Archer coaxed. Where Ajay was clean cut, Archer was scruffy. His dark brown hair fell past the collar of his coat. His cheeks and chin were covered in stubble, like he hadn't bothered to shave in days.

"Markus turned the gun on Sarah, but Jessie pushed her out of the way. She caught the bullet instead." Liam pointed to his own breastbone. "She bled out in minutes. I chased Markus but he got into the trees before I caught him. I'm not prepared for this weather." He held out a hand. Several snowflakes landed on his palm, melting instantly. "I figured that it'd be better to let the professionals find him."

Fletcher sighed. "We all know my mom didn't approve of how Jessie took off, leaving her kids behind. Then, there was the whole episode of Jessie trying to get a portion of my dad's life insurance. Still, it's a tragic way to die." He paused. "Where's Sarah?"

Liam pointed to one of the ambulances. "She's getting checked out by the EMTs."

"We need to search this entire area. Aside from the financial crimes, there are some murders linked to this church. Who knows what evidence we're going to find," said Fletcher. "Before we get started, I'd like to speak to Sarah."

"I think she'd like that," he said, walking toward the vehicle.

Ajay, Archer and Pumpkin hung back.

The ambulance's rear doors were closed. Using the side of his fist, Liam banged on an inset window. The impact sent a bolt of pain rocketing from his hand to his teeth.

A female EMT opened the back door. A lanyard with an ID card hung around her neck. Her name was Zoey. "Can I help you?"

"Yeah," said Liam. "Detective Colton would like to talk to his sister. Is Sarah up for visitors?"

From inside the ambulance, Sarah called out, "I'm up for a visit."

Zoey jumped to the ground. "You fellas have a few minutes before we head back to town." She pointed at Liam. "And you should come with us."

"I'm fine." He wasn't going to let a few scratches and bruises take him away from the investigation.

"Everyone is always fine until they aren't," said Zoey. "But my recommendation is that you get checked out, too."

Eventually, he'd see a doctor. Right now, he wanted to see Sarah. Holding on to the handles on either side of the doors, he hefted himself into the back of the ambulance. Sarah lay on a stretcher. Her bloody clothes had been traded for an Owl Creek EMT sweatshirt and pair of dark gray sweatpants. A bag of fluids hung on a hook. Clear tubing led from the bag to a needle that was taped to the back of her hand.

"They put you on meds?" Panic raced like a raging river through his bones. "Is anything seriously wrong?"

"This?" She touched the gauze pad that covered the needle. "It's just a saline drip. The EMT wants to make sure I stay hydrated."

A jump seat was pulled down next to the stretcher. He dropped into the seat, suddenly weary. "That's good news."

Fletcher pulled himself into the back of the ambulance, as well. "Hey, Sarah," he said.

She smiled weakly. "What're you doing here?"

"Well, I'm a detective in Owl Creek," he said before adding, "I'm sorry about Jessie."

"Thanks," said Sarah. "I still can't believe she's gone. I keep hoping this is the worst dream of my life and I'll wake up at home." She paused. "What happens now?"

She'd asked Liam the same question. He didn't blame her for being concerned and wanting answers.

"Right now, there are several teams getting ready to get to work. One team will search the compound. The other team will start searching the woods for signs of Markus. There are also officers on hand to question members of the church."

Liam was looking for evidence of financial crimes. "I'll process the admin building. I'm looking for records associated with fraud. Whatever I find will have to go back to the Hoover Building with me."

"I'm going to help you," said Sarah, swinging her legs to the side of the bed. "I can't sit here, alone. Besides, I'm a librarian. It makes me an expert at organizing lots of information."

"If you're up to it," said Fletcher, "you can join the team.

You and Liam can take the admin building. I'm going to bring everyone together for a final briefing. Then, we can get started. See you in a minute." Fletcher climbed out the ambulance, leaving them alone.

"Do you mind if we chat for a minute?" he began. But he didn't look like he knew exactly know where to begin. "I'm sorry about your mom."

"Like Fletcher said, it's tragic."

"No, it's more than that. I was the one who got you involved in this case. If it weren't for me…"

"We aren't going to play what-if," she said, interrupting. "Neither of us will win that game. I'm devastated that my mom is gone. But the only person I blame for what happened is Markus."

Liam reached for her hand. Having his palm next to hers felt like coming home. "Markus won't get away. I promise," he said. But there were other things that he wouldn't say. He was the one who let Markus Acker escape, which meant that it was Liam's job to find him.

Chapter Nineteen

Zoey, the EMT, returned to the ambulance. "Ready to take a trip back to Owl Creek?" she asked Sarah. "There's only a medical clinic in town. If any of your injuries are serious, you'll get sent to Conners." Conners was a town located more than thirty miles away. "But I think you'll be released as soon as the nurse practitioner gives you an exam."

"Change of plans," said Sarah. "I'm staying. Can you get the IV out of my hand?"

"I'd advise against it," Zoey warned.

Sarah appreciated the advice, but her mind was made up. "I'm staying."

The EMT removed the needle and placed a bandage over the puncture mark.

"Are you sure that you're up to this?" Liam asked.

The bruise at the back of her head throbbed. Her eyes were gritty from crying. What's worse, she felt like a rag that had been wrung out and then thrown in a corner to rot. But she couldn't rest while Markus Acker was at large. "I'm fine," she said. "Lead the way."

Liam didn't bother with the short ladder attached to the

back of the ambulance. He dropped down and landed with a curse. "Damn it."

Sarah backed out, climbing the rungs to the ground. "Are *you* sure that *you're* up to this?" she asked, copying his question.

"I'm fine."

To her, he didn't look fine. Both of his eyes were blackened. There was a bruise on his cheek. A cut to his chin. And his lips were swollen. But she knew that he wasn't about to leave without completing his job. So, Sarah didn't argue.

Liam said, "Looks like the briefing is over there." A group of people were gathered on the driveway in front of Jessie's house.

"The Statie is with Lizzy, right? The other guy dates your sister Hannah." He paused as they both walked slowly toward the group. "Ajay. Archer," said Liam.

"Hi, Sarah," Ajay said.

"Hey," said Archer. "I'm sorry about your mom."

Ajay added, "We'll find the bastard who shot her. Don't worry."

"Thanks," she said. A yellow Lab nudged her hand. She scratched the dog's scruff. "Both of you. Or should I say, all three of you."

"This is Pumpkin," said Ajay. "She works with Search and Rescue."

Before she could add anything else, Fletcher whistled. "I need you all to gather around."

A group formed around her brother. Some of the people wore Owl Creek PD uniforms. Others were clad in street clothes. Sarah and Liam approached. The wall of bodies separated, making room for them in the circle.

"Now that we're all here," said Fletcher, "let me introduce everyone. Archer Mackenzie will process the house, collecting evidence associated with the shooting. Ajay will take a team from Search and Rescue into the woods to look for Markus. Hopefully, he hasn't gotten too far, and we can wrap this up tonight. Liam Hill is with the FBI. He's going to go through the records in the admin building. Sarah's going to help organize everything for transport back to Washington, D.C. The uniformed officers, Muriel and Kate, will lead a team from the PD to talk to all the church members. Hopefully, someone knows where Markus might go or who might help him." He paused. "Any questions? Comments?"

There were none and the group dispersed.

Sarah paused, looking at the house. Her mother had been so proud to own a nice home. But it had come at the ultimate price. Turning her back, she walked through the snow. The drifts were over her ankles and there was no sign that the storm was done.

Her car, a twisted hunk of metal now, lay on its roof. The SUV that blocked their escape was in the middle of the road.

"Hold up a minute," Liam said.

She stopped.

He crawled through one of the broken windows of her car. The vehicle teetered. Without question, today had been the worst day of her life. It would only be fitting for some other horrible thing to happen—like Liam getting crushed by the wrecked station wagon. She couldn't take a second loss today. "Be careful," she said, bending at the waist to be heard through the open window. It didn't seem like enough. "What's so important that you can't wait for the car to be taken to impound?"

Liam backed out the same way he entered the car. Rising to his feet, he dusted snow from his knees. "I needed this." He held up a slim piece of black plastic.

"The flash drive." Her mother had lost her life for that information. "I hope it's worth it."

"Me, too." He shoved the device into his pocket.

They walked in silence to the admin trailer. Liam held the door open and Sarah crossed the threshold. Her eyes were drawn to one of the desks and the landline phone. "Do you think that phone works?"

"Roger called 9-1-1 from here, so yeah. It works."

Roger. She hadn't had time to think about the burly guard—or any of the other security personnel Markus employed. They had all seemed to disappear along with their boss.

"If you need to make some calls, I can give you a minute," Liam offered.

"You can stay…"

He waved away her offer. "I'll just be outside." He opened the door and stepped onto the landing. "If you need me, just yell."

"Thanks." She dropped into a seat. As the door closed, she lifted the receiver from the cradle. Holding the phone to her ear, she entered a set of numbers that had been memorized long ago.

Her brother answered after the third ring. "This is Nate."

Sarah's chest constricted. She tried to find the right words. But how was she supposed to tell him that their mother was gone?

"Hello?" he said again, annoyance evident in his tone. "Is someone there?"

"Hey, Nate," she croaked. Tears gathered in her lashes. She wiped them away with the back of her hand.

"Sarah, is that you?"

She cleared her throat. "Yeah, it's me. Listen, I've got bad news. We need to talk."

"Hold on a minute. Let me close my office door." On the other end of the line, she heard the soft click of a latch engaging. "What's up?"

"It's Mom," she began.

Nate groaned. "What'd she do this time?"

"You don't understand," said Sarah. "She was shot."

"Shot?" he echoed. "By whom? Although I bet that I can guess. It was that piece of crap. Markus." He cursed. "Hopefully, now she'll kick him to the curb with the rest of the garbage."

"Nate," she said. "She can't do that."

The line went silent. Had the connection been lost?

After a moment, he asked, "How is she?"

The question stretched out, filling the miles between the two siblings. But more than that, it filled the years. Memories—both good and bad—washed over Sarah in a tidal wave. And then came the knowledge that death was another word for *never again*. Never again would Sarah receive a text from her mother, excited with a new purchase. Never again would she eat her mother's apple cinnamon pancakes. Never again would she tell her mother about her day. Never again would she hear her mother say, *I love you*.

Nate's question had gone too long unanswered. "She's not good. In fact, she didn't make it."

"What happened?"

She spent a few minutes giving him the barest details about

the past week. Sometime soon, she'd tell him everything. Finishing her story, she said, "She lost her life saving mine."

"First of all, I don't want you to feel any guilt," said Nate. "None of this is your fault. The bastard who shot Mom is the one to blame."

"If it weren't for me, she would still be here."

"You can't carry that baggage. You were a good daughter. I cut Mom out of my life years ago. You always tried to maintain a relationship." His voice was hoarse, thick with emotion. "I guess I always figured there'd be time for us to reconcile. But now, it's too late." He paused. "What do you want to do for a funeral?"

"Honestly, I haven't had time to think about anything."

"I'm going to take a few days off. I'll come to Owl Creek. Not sure if I'll leave later today or first thing tomorrow. A lot will depend on Vivian's schedule." Vivian Maylor was Nate's new girlfriend. Always classy and kind, she was the one person who made Nate happy.

"It'd be great to see you both. I'm staying at the Inn on the Lake," she said.

"Once I have plans, I'll check in with you," he said before ending the call.

Nate was lucky to have found Vivian. At least he wouldn't be alone while dealing with the loss of another parent. Her mind wandered to Liam. Like a switch being flipped, their charade was over. Too bad her feelings for him couldn't be turned off in the same way.

There was a light rapping on the door before it opened. Liam stepped inside. "It sounded like your call ended, so I figured I'd check on you."

She tried to smile. Her cheeks were tight. "I reached out

to Nate. He needed to know what happened." She paused. "He asked about a funeral. I don't know where to begin."

"I hate to tell you this, but it might be several days before the authorities release your mom. They need time to collect evidence from the body."

Was she supposed to stay in Owl Creek until her mom could be buried? Sarah had a job. A cat. Not to mention that a room at the Inn on the Lake was more than she could afford. There was too much to think about and she was suddenly exhausted.

"Hey." Liam patted her shoulder. "You've been through a lot. I can get you a ride back to the hotel so you can rest."

The word *ride* brought up a whole new set of problems. "My car's totaled. That's another thing to worry about."

"I'm sure the FBI will work something out with you." He paused. "But what about now? Do you want to go back to town?"

Sarah didn't want to sit in a hotel room, alone, without any company. "I'll stay," she said, thankful for at least one decision made. She stood. "Having something to do will help—especially if it puts Markus in jail." Drawing in a deep breath, she asked, "Where do we start?"

AFTER SEVERAL HOURS of searching the admin building, Liam had to admit that the paperwork kept by the Ever After Church was surprisingly organized. A forensic audit would have to wait, but everything he found looked legit. Soon, he'd box up the documents and have them shipped to the Hoover Building. There, a team of financial analysts would comb through every sheet of paper.

Then again, he knew that there wasn't anything incriminating to find in the filing cabinets. That's why he'd come to Owl Creek, to see what Markus kept on his personal computer. And sure, someone had taken the actual processor. But it didn't matter. Liam had the memory stick with a copy of the hard drive. Or so he hoped.

Taking the flash drive out of his pocket, he held it in the palm of his hand.

Sarah stood next to him. She'd been right when she claimed to be good at organizing documents. If it wasn't for her help, Liam wouldn't have made as much progress.

He held up the memory stick. "I hope I got enough evidence."

His ribs and side ached with each breath. The pain made it hard to concentrate. In fact, all he wanted to do was rest. Yet too much had been sacrificed for him to leave before the job was done.

"We should find out." Sarah sat behind one of the two workstations in the reception area. An open laptop was on the desk. The password was written on a sticky note, taped to the base panel. She entered the keystrokes and held out her hand.

Liam hesitated for a moment, before handing her the flash drive.

She inserted the drive into the port on the side of the computer. A menu appeared and she opened a document. Liam stood behind Sarah and watched over her shoulder as she opened a spreadsheet.

Suddenly awake, he scanned the lines and columns. As it turns out, Markus was an exacting bookkeeper all the time. "I'll be damned."

"What'd we find?" Sarah's cheeks turned rosy.

Liam leaned forward, pointing at the screen. His arm

brushed her shoulder. He remembered the moments after they made love. He held her in his arms, placing a kiss on the same spot he now touched. But he couldn't get sucked into the memories. Now, more than ever, he needed to focus. "See that? It looks like Markus has been receiving large amounts of money from an account in Colombia. Then, they get listed as a donation to the church. He doesn't spend any of the money, just sends the funds to an account in Delaware."

"That's illegal?"

"It depends on who sent the money in the first place. Colombia makes me wonder if he wasn't working with one of the drug cartels." Had Liam just gotten the evidence that Dubois needed? He continued, "Delaware is a banking-friendly state. But like with everything, criminals can take advantage. Now, we have account numbers. Once I get a subpoena, we can unravel this accounting mess."

"Is this what you needed?" she asked. "Will it be worth all the sacrifices in the end?"

"Nothing will ever be worth the loss of your mom. But what we have here will help to put Markus in jail for a long time to come."

"Good," she said. "That'll be a start."

She was so near that her breath washed over him and mingled with his own. The look in her eyes was so sad. Liam was the one who'd caused all her heartache. He wanted to ease the sorrow. He also wanted to feel her lips on his, despite the fact that his mouth still throbbed.

Even though the relationship had been phony, he knew that his feelings for Sarah went beyond friendship or even their shared history. But their weeklong affair was about to end.

In an instant, he saw their future. And he knew it was bleak.

With the evidence needed to build a case against Markus Acker in hand, Liam would be called back to DC. He'd be given the promotion, but then all his time would be spent at work. Sure, he could suggest a long-distance relationship. Sarah could come to Washington for a visit. But with her, it wouldn't be enough. They'd get frustrated with the separation until finally one of them called it quits.

Better to avoid the heartache before it started.

"Thanks for all your help." The need to touch her again was like a hunger. "There's nothing else for us to do here." He checked his phone. He didn't have any coverage, but the cell still gave him the time. It was 3:26 p.m. "Let's get back to Owl Creek. I need to call my office and we should get something to eat."

"I'm not hungry." Sarah closed the computer and removed the flash drive. She held it out to him. His fingers grazed hers. He ignored the electric current that ran up his arm and shoved the memory stick into his pants pocket. "But I agree we should get out of here."

Sarah stood and walked across the room. She opened the door. Thick gray clouds hung low in the sky. Fat white flakes drifted slowly to the ground. Snow covered the bottom two stairs of the steps.

His coat sat on the sofa. He picked it up and held it out to Sarah. "You want this?"

"I can't," she began.

"I'm not going to let you go out with just a sweatshirt," he said.

"Let me?" she echoed.

"Okay, that came out wrong. You've been through a lot and the last thing you need is to get sick or something."

She reached for the jacket. Standing on the stoop, she shrugged into the coat. She pushed the sleeves up to her wrists, but the coat hung down to her knees. "Not very stylish," she joked. "But at least it's warm."

He was glad that she still had a sense of humor. It'd help her get through the next few months. Finding Markus, assuming that the pastor was found, would only be the beginning. After he was taken into custody, there'd be a trial. Appeals would follow. Through it all, there would be media attention.

He'd do what he could to shield Sarah, but he could never give her back her quiet life.

Fletcher Colton strode through the snow toward the admin building. "I was just coming to check on you. What'd you find?"

"We've got everything we need," he said, patting his pants pocket. The flash drive was still there. "Once Markus has been captured, there's enough damning evidence to put him away for years. Any chance we can get a ride back to Owl Creek?"

"I'll get you a ride with one of the uniformed officers," he said.

A female officer, Juliette, gave them a ride back to the Inn on the Lake. By the time they arrived, it was after 4:00 p.m. Liam hadn't eaten since breakfast. Despite Sarah saying she wasn't hungry, he was ready for a meal.

Housekeeping had visited the room while they were gone. The beds were made, and the towels had been refreshed. Everything was the same and, yet, different. "Want to grab something to eat? Or there's a restaurant downstairs. I can get room service to deliver," he asked.

Sarah took off his coat and laid it on a bed. "I need a

shower, and then I'll do whatever you want. Just don't ask me to make a choice. I'm done with decisions for the day."

A menu for the hotel's restaurant was tucked into the drawer of the bedside table. He scanned the pub fare. Burgers. Soups. Chicken wraps. Finger steaks.

He should get his fill of finger steaks now. In a few days, Idaho would be a memory.

Before ordering food, he had to get in touch with his office. Enabling the encryption app on his phone, he placed a call to Constance at the Hoover Building.

"I was wondering when I'd hear from you," she said. "How'd it go?"

"I was able to download the hard drive. There's a lot of information we need to go through. But I'm confident we have what we need for an arrest, indictment and conviction. But it came at a high price."

"How high?" she asked.

"Jessie Colton was shot and killed by Markus. He ran into the woods. The local and state police are looking for him. It's been snowing all day, so I don't know what kind of trail they'll find."

"Hey, don't be so down," she said. "In the eyes of the federal government, your operation was a success."

Funny. With the loss of life, he didn't feel successful. "I'm going to send you all the data taken from the computer."

"I'm sure Dubois will need a debrief, but that can wait until you get home."

Home was something Washington, DC, would never be for Liam. "I'll see you when I get back."

"You know, the promotion will be yours. Honestly, you deserve it," Constance said before ending the call.

How was it that Liam ended up with everything he wanted, and nothing that he wanted at all? He picked up the coat Sarah had left on the bed. He brought the collar to his nose and inhaled deeply. It smelled like her, like flowers and sunshine. He couldn't help but wonder how long the fabric would hold her scent.

Chapter Twenty

Five days later
Washington, DC
Hoover Building

Liam was in the same conference room where it all started. This time, every seat around the long table was filled. Beyond A-DIC Dubois and her entourage, Nadia Starkey, assistant director, was also in attendance.

Much of the information copied from the computer's hard drive had been analyzed. It looked like Markus Acker was laundering money from some very bad people. He had cleaned money for a drug cartel from South America as well as a group in North Carolina that bombed a day care center. For funneling the money through his church, Markus was given a commission. Over the last five years, he'd made over six million dollars.

He and Constance were giving the briefing. This time, they'd compared notes and even practiced what they were going to say. So far, everything had gone well. Liam clicked a remote he held in his palm. The final image for the briefing filled the screen. In it, Markus and Jessie embraced as they admired their new home. In the foreground, a thin and dirty child cried. It was the same picture he'd shown Sarah—back when he needed her to help him get onto the compound. He and Sarah had spoken on the phone several times since he left. She'd returned to Boise when he left for Washington, DC. The Bureau had provided her with a rental car until her station wagon could be replaced. She'd been planning Jessie's funeral. It would be held in Owl Creek the next day.

Obviously, Liam wouldn't be attending.

Refocusing his attention on the meeting, he said, "The facts prove that Markus Acker was a rich man. A man who claimed to also serve humanity. Why did he steal money from those who couldn't afford it? Markus is still at large, presumably in the woods near Owl Creek, Idaho. If he's found—when he's found—that's the question I will ask. After I arrest him for his other crimes, of course." His joke earned him a few chuckles. "Any questions?"

"I have one," said Assistant Director Starkey. "What's being done to find Acker?"

Constance answered the question. "The Idaho State Police has taken the lead on the search. So far, there hasn't been any hard evidence for his location. There are three theories. First, is that he's found an abandoned cabin and is holed up there. The second is that he's gotten help from one of the criminal groups he's worked with in the past."

"And what's the final theory?" asked Dubois.

"Well," said Liam, "Markus could've died in the woods. Hypothermia. Animal attack. A minor injury in that climate could be deadly. If that happened, we may never find him."

"That's not good enough for me," said Starkey. "I want to set up a task force in Owl Creek. The FBI needs a full-time presence to work with state and local authorities until this Acker character is caught." She turned to Dubois. "Make that happen."

"Yes, ma'am," said the A-DIC as she scribbled a note on a pad of paper.

Starkey turned her attention back to Liam and Constance. "I heard that a supervisor position has opened in your unit and both of you are the top candidates. The career board met and made a decision. Both of you are well-qualified, but Special Agent Hill will be given the job."

"Congratulations, Liam," said Constance with a smile. "You'll be a great supervisor."

Liam's gut twisted into knots. Yet, he smiled and tried to look proud. "Thank you, all, for your confidence. But Constance did an amazing job organizing things here. All I did was get beat up."

"Talk about taking one for the team," Starkey joked. When he'd gotten back to DC, he'd been seen by a doctor. Thankfully, none of his injuries required treatment. "You really did go above and beyond for the investigation and the Bureau. I like that you recognize everyone on your team. The FBI is lucky to have you in management." She rose from her seat and stepped forward. Her palm was outstretched. "Congratulations again," she said, shaking his hand. She also shook hands with Constance. "Don't worry about your career. Good things are coming your way."

"Yes, ma'am," said Constance.

The room emptied.

A-DIC Dubois was the last person to leave. "Good job, both of you," she said on her way out the door.

"So, what's first on the agenda, boss?" Constance asked.

Liam knew what he wanted to do. But the question remained, was he willing to abandon his life plan? Then again, a life is exactly what he wanted. "Hold on a minute," he said to his colleague. "I need to grab Dubois."

He jogged down the corridor, catching up with the A-DIC. "I have a suggestion for who could run the federal task force out of Owl Creek."

Dubois raised her eyebrows. "You do? I'd love a recommendation."

He laid out his plan, much of it coming to him as he spoke. As it turned out, he had a knack for improvising.

When he finished, she asked, "You're sure? You know how this will affect the decisions that have already been made."

"I know," he said. In the end, it would all be worthwhile.

"Alright," she sighed. "I'll make it happen."

He turned, walking slowly back to the conference room. For the first time in years, Liam knew exactly what he wanted.

The following day
Owl Creek, Idaho
Abel's Funeral Parlor

THE FUNERAL DIRECTOR, a Black woman named Letitia Abel with her braids coiled into a bun, had deposited Sarah in a sitting room to wait for the funeral to start. The room was filled with a sofa and two wingback chairs, all upholstered in blue velvet. A wooden table stood in the middle of the seating arrangement. The top was polished until it gleamed with the glow of the overhead lights.

As Letitia had explained, the room was meant for the family to wait before the services began. But aside from Nate, she didn't expect any other family to attend. He was already here, along with Vivian. They were both seated in the small chapel, which meant that Sarah was alone. Again.

The thing was, she didn't know who else might show up. It was no secret that her mother had burned many bridges. She hated the idea that nobody would come to the funeral. But she was prepared to deliver her eulogy to only Nate, Vivian and Letitia.

She glanced at the wall clock: 9:58 a.m. It was almost time. Leaning forward, Sarah reached for a cup of water. The papers on her lap scattered to the floor.

"Damn it," she cursed, before pressing her lips tightly together. Was cussing in a funeral home as taboo as swearing in church? She didn't know. Placing the cup back onto the table, she dropped to her knees. She sorted the pages, placing them in order.

"I think those who plan to attend the services have gathered." Letitia stood on the threshold. She was dressed in a pantsuit of silver and white that coordinated perfectly with the room.

"I didn't hear you come in," said Sarah while standing. For her mother's funeral, she'd had borrowed a black sheath dress from Margaret. On her friend, the dress came to the knees. On her, the hem stopped at midcalf. She dusted off the front of her outfit. Was anyone ever prepared to say a final goodbye to a person they loved? Yet, she couldn't put off the inevitable. "I'm ready," she said.

She followed the woman into the chapel, where the funeral was to be held. At the front of the room was Jessie's casket, closed now, with a spray of roses draped across the top. There was also a photograph of her mother on a stand.

Next to the casket stood a lectern with a microphone. Pews filled the room. None of the seats were empty.

As expected, Nate and Vivian were in the front row. Next to them were Frannie and Dante. Malcolm was there. Fletcher Colton was also in attendance, along with his girlfriend. She thought her name might be Kiki. Archer Mackenzie was with Lizzy. Ajay and Hannah were there, as well.

In the middle of them all sat Jenny Colton.

Sure, Sarah knew that Jenny and Jessie were identical twins. But looking into the crowd and seeing her mother's double stole her breath. She inhaled and searched for the one face she knew she wouldn't see. It was ridiculous to think that Liam might come. Yet she had secretly hoped that he'd find a way to make the trip.

Rolling back her shoulders, she stepped up to the lectern. Setting her notes on the upper tray, she leaned toward the microphone. "My mother wasn't a perfect person," she said, beginning with the truth. "Then again, none of us are perfect, either. I know that I'm not. My mom was fiercely proud. She loved to laugh and loved to love. She was passionate and never did anything halfway. And when it came down to it, she laid down her own life so that mine would be spared."

The door at the back of the chapel opened. She paused and looked up. Light shone from behind, cloaking the new arrival in shadow. But the shoulders were familiar. She recognized the tilt of the head, the way he moved. Her heart skipped a beat as the door closed softly.

So, Liam had come after all.

The bruise under his eye had faded from violet to gray. Stubble covered his cheeks and chin. His hair was mussed, and he wore a sweater and jeans. She imagined that he'd taken an overnight flight to Boise and driven directly to Owl Creek. And he was still the most handsome man in the world.

She looked down at her written eulogy. The words she worked hard to perfect were no longer sufficient. Holding tightly to the sides of the lectern, she let out a long breath. "I knew my mother better than anyone else. Sure, she could be maddening. But I was with her when she died. Those last few moments as I held my mother's hand will always be the most precious and painful of my life." She paused, swallowed and wished that she'd thought to bring her glass of water. "But at the end, when she knew that she wasn't going to make it, my mom had one thought. And it was of all of you. She asked me to deliver a message to everyone. She knew she had been in the wrong. She was sorry for all the hurt she caused. Because of that pain, she didn't know how to start over. But do not doubt how she felt. Jessie Colton loved you all." She drew in a deep breath. "Thank you for coming today. It would've meant the world to my mom, and it means the world to me."

Soft music began to play. As instructed by the funeral director, Sarah walked down the middle aisle. She was followed by Nate and Vivian. There was a reception area at the back of the chapel, where the siblings could greet their guests.

The first person in line was Jenny Colton. From a distance, the sisters had looked identical. But now that her aunt was closer, she could see differences between the two women. Jenny's profile was softer. Her hair was shorter. There was a light in her eyes that Jessie never had. "Hi, Sarah," she said, opening her arms for a hug. "You gave a lovely eulogy. Your mom would've been proud."

She let her aunt embrace her. It was almost like being

hugged by her mother. "Thank you for coming. I know you two were estranged," she began.

"But she was my sister, and I never would've stayed away. I only wish that things had worked out different between the two of us." A dark-haired man stood next to Jenny. She reached for his arm. "This is your uncle Buck."

Buck Colton was taller than her father had been. But the brothers shared the same green eyes—the same ones that Sarah had inherited herself. "If you ever need anything," said Buck, giving her a quick hug, "don't hesitate to call."

"Thank you," she said. "It's nice to finally meet you."

"I know all of this—losing your dad, finding this whole family you never knew about and then losing your mom, too—is overwhelming. But as far as I'm concerned, you're a Colton." He included Nate in his words. "Both of you are family."

"We're both leaving in the morning," said Nate.

"Well, stop by tonight. Heck, I'll invite everyone. We can raise a glass to the memory of Jessie."

She looked at her brother. Nate shrugged. "Obviously, we don't have any other plans."

Sarah said, "We'd love to stop by. What can we bring?"

"Just yourselves," said Buck, patting her shoulder. "I'll be happy to get to know you better."

Jenny gave her another hug. It seemed like Frannie had picked up her affinity for hugs from her mother. "I know I can't replace your mom. But I'm here for anything. Good news. Bad news. I'm only a phone call away."

Sarah's chest ached from the kindness shown by her aunt and uncle. She gripped Jenny's hands. "Thank you both, so much."

The next people in line were Frannie and Dante. Frannie pulled Sarah into a tight hug. "I'm so sorry for what happened. I'd love to chat with you more. Do you have time to grab a cup of coffee—or should I say, tea?"

"Buck wants to have everyone over for dinner tonight," said Nate as he shook hands with Dante.

"Great." Frannie gave her another hug. "I'll talk to you then."

The line of Coltons seemed endless. Malcolm gave her a hug. There was Ruby and her boyfriend, Sebastian. Wade and his girlfriend, Harlow. Chase and Sloane. Greg and Briony. They were all kind with their condolences and warm with their welcomes into the family. Jenny had been right, nothing and nobody could make up for the loss of her mother. But maybe time with her newfound family would help ease the ache from her loss.

Then, the receiving line was down to only one person. Liam.

Nate shook hands with him. "Vivian, his younger sister was Sarah's best friend when we were all kids. He's with the FBI."

"Nice to meet you," said Vivian.

Nate said, "I guess we should go outside and get some air."

Then, it was just Sarah and Liam. Her chest was tight with grief and loss. But in seeing him, there was also happiness and hope.

"You came," she said.

"There's no place else I'd rather be." He reached for her hand, lacing his fingers through hers. She liked the way they knitted together, fitting perfectly.

She hadn't spoken to Liam in two days. True, they'd both

been busy. Yet, she hoped it wasn't a sign of things to come when they neglected to call the other. "How was your presentation?" No, the FBI didn't call it a presentation. "Brief," she corrected. "How was your briefing?"

"It was good. The career board met. I was offered the supervisor's position."

She wanted to be happy for him. But once Liam got sucked back into working long hours, they'd never have time to speak to each other. "Congratulations," she said. "I know that's what you wanted."

"I *did* want the job. That is, until I realized what's important. I want a home and a family. I want someone in my life that I love and like and respect. I want more than a spouse. I want someone who can be a true partner. My job's important, but I want more." He paused. "I turned down the promotion."

"Why did you do that?"

"Because I finally know what I want in my life. It's you." He pulled her close and wrapped her in his embrace. Her cheek was pressed to his chest. She felt as well as heard everything he said. "I love you, Sarah."

"I love you, too." Still, she wasn't sure what came next. "Don't tell me you left the FBI. I won't believe that story again."

He laughed quietly. "I'm still with the Bureau. But my job's changed a little. I'm going to oversee a federal task force, coordinating with other law enforcement agencies, to find Markus Acker. I'll be in Owl Creek most of the time. But it's a hell of a lot closer to Boise than Washington, DC."

Sarah wasn't sure of the rules about kissing in a funeral home. Yet, she rose to her tiptoes and brushed her lips over his. "Welcome home, Liam."

Hand in hand, they walked out of the funeral home and onto Main Street. The sun, a white ball, hung in a sky of robin's egg blue. A breeze blew past Sarah, ruffling her hair. It held the first kiss of spring and the promise of something new.

Chapter Twenty-One

The Colton Ranch was located outside Owl Creek and surrounded by acres of farmland. Nate had driven, and Vivian sat in the passenger seat. Sarah and Liam were in the back seat. Cars, trucks and SUVs already lined the long driveway that led to the Colton family home. The focal point of the structure was the red barn, but rooms spread out from the main building and looked to be more functional than for aesthetics.

Sarah leaned forward, poking her head between the two front seats. "I think it's kinda charming," she said. "But Mom would've hated living in a place like this." She bit her lip. How long would it be before she stopped worrying about her mother's opinions?

"Agreed," said Nate. He blew out a long breath. "Let's go."

He turned off the ignition and opened the driver's side door. Vivian followed. Sarah remained, rooted in the back seat. Sure, the Coltons had been nothing but kind. But by now they all knew that Sarah had been working with the FBI from the beginning.

Liam reached for her fingertips. "It'll be okay," he said. "I'm with you."

She squeezed his hand. His touch was all the assurance she needed.

She opened her door and stepped out of the car. Liam followed. Nate and Vivian stood only a few feet away. As a group, they all walked toward the front door. The sun was dropping below the hills, but there was a lingering warmth in the air. "Looks like spring finally decided to make an appearance," she said, not really speaking to anyone but not able to stay silent, either. "How are the cherry blossoms? They must be at their peak now."

"They started to bloom, then we got a horrible storm. The wind and rain stripped the trees bare." Liam huffed out a breath.

Nate stepped up to the front door and knocked.

The door was opened by Hannah's daughter, Lucy. If she remembered correctly, the little girl who stood before them was five years old.

"Hello." Lucy's diction was clear. "Aunt Sarah. Uncle Nate. I haven't seen you since the wedding."

Well, she might look like a five-year-old with her pigtails, but she sounded more like she was fifty. Sarah crouched in front of the child. "I'm happy to see you again."

"It's nice to see you, too. Come in," Lucy opened the door wider. Sarah and the rest stepped into the large room. It was filled with lights, voices, laughter—and people. Every one of them was related to Sarah. Could they also become her family? Lucy continued, "How have you been?"

Nate nudged Sarah in the ribs. "Look, another brilliant Colton. I bet Lucy likes books, too."

"I love books. I'll go and get some of my favorites. They're in the back bedroom." Lucy ran toward what must've been the back bedroom, her pigtails bouncing with each step.

From across the room, Frannie waved. She was wearing another T-shirt with a quote. *I'm with the banned.* Images of famously banned books were also on the shirt. *A Wrinkle in Time. Of Mice and Men. To Kill a Mockingbird.* Among others. The fabric was tighter across her stomach, making it obvious that Frannie was pregnant.

Arms opened for a hug, Frannie pulled her into an embrace. "I've been looking for you. There's something I want to talk about with you in private."

Sarah's heart sank. So, it was going to happen now. Frannie was going to yell at her for being a bad daughter. At least she was classy enough to want some discretion. Fletcher was talking to Nate and Liam. Lucy had returned with her books and was showing them to Vivian. But there were still too many people around to chat in private. "Let's step outside."

Back on the stoop with the door closed, Frannie asked, "How are you feeling?"

"Sad," said Sarah. "Guilty."

Her sister shook her head. "I can't imagine what you've been through. But for what it's worth, don't feel guilty. You were a good daughter. If Jessie hadn't gotten involved with Markus, then none of this would've happened. I won't speak ill of the dead, but don't give up because of your mom's choices."

"That should become my mantra," she joked. "Don't give up."

"Never give up. And you have all of us here to support you."

Sarah inhaled. She could breathe a little easier. "Thanks for the pep talk. It helped. We should get back inside."

"Can I get another minute?" Frannie didn't wait for an answer, and said, "I know you've dealt with a lot recently, but I have a favor to ask."

This wasn't how Sarah expected the conversation to go. "Sure," she said. "If I can help at all, I will."

"You know how I told you that we had an ultrasound appointment coming up? Well, there are some complications. Nothing too serious now, but the doctor wants to keep it that way and suggests bed rest."

Sarah reached for Frannie's arm, suddenly protective of her sister and the child she hadn't met. "Should you be standing here? Let's get you back inside."

"I'll put my feet up in a minute. But I wanted to talk to you first." She paused. "Would you consider running Book Mark It? I know you have a job, but I wouldn't trust my store to anybody else."

For a moment, Sarah said nothing. And then, "You aren't mad at me for lying to you? After all, Liam and I were faking our relationship."

Frannie shook her head. "Neither of you were faking anything. And besides, you ended up together. So, the only person you lied to was yourself."

"I never thought about it that way."

"Well, think about my offer. Besides, it'd be nice to have you here, with family."

"Let's get you back inside," said Sarah, opening the door. "And I promise to let you know my decision soon."

Inside, Liam approached. "There you are," he said. "I was wondering where you'd gone."

"Think about it," said Frannie before wandering to the sofa.

"What's all that about?" he asked.

She said, "Frannie wants me to run Book Mark It. She's having issues with her pregnancy and needs some time off."

"What are your thoughts?"

Honestly, Sarah hadn't had time to consider the offer. There was a lot she'd be leaving behind in Boise. Her friends. Her job.

But something about moving to Owl Creek felt right. She said, "If I came here, I'd get to know all my siblings better."

She scanned the room. Was this her place? Honestly, she would love to share her favorite children's books with Lucy. Talk about popular fiction with Dante. Visit Frannie for tea and a chat. Go to Tap Out Brewery with Malcolm for wing night and a hockey game. Plus, Liam was going to be in town.

Well, when she thought about it that way, there wasn't really a decision to make.

"If I moved here," she asked, "what would you think?"

Liam answered her by placing his lips on hers.

Were all of Sarah's dreams finally coming true? Then again, her mother wasn't around to share in her joy.

"There you are." She recognized the voice but knew it wasn't Jessie who'd spoken. She broke away from the embrace to see Jenny approaching. She pulled Sarah into a hug. "I'm so happy to see you."

"I hope you like the looks of me," said Sarah. "You'll be seeing me a whole lot more."

"Oh?"

"I've decided to help Frannie out by running Book Mark It."

"Oh good." Jenny hugged her again. "Frannie needs help, and we all want you here."

Buck approached with a bottle of beer in his hand. "Good to see you both," he said, shaking hands with Liam.

"Did you hear the news?" Jenny asked. "Sarah just decided to move to Owl Creek."

"Well, how could I know if she just decided?" Buck reasoned.

Jenny swatted his arm playfully.

"But it's the best news I've heard in a long while. We'll be happy to have you around more." Buck kissed Sarah's cheek. "And I heard that you were coming to town, Liam. I suppose you are going to be needing a place. We've got lots of nice places listed with Colton Properties."

"We haven't really talked about where we'd live," said Sarah. Moving in together after only a few weeks seemed sudden. Then again, if she'd learned anything this month, it was to take risks. "We can stop by in the morning and see what's available."

"You want to talk to Chase." Buck pointed to another brother with brown hair and green eyes. And then, he pointed to a long table that ran through the center of the adjacent kitchen. It was covered with platters and bowls that were filled with food. There were several kinds of salads, steaks, grilled chicken, steaming baked potatoes and green beans. "Go grab a plate. The steaks are from our own cattle and the rest of the produce is from our own farms. I can't have you leave here hungry."

Jenny squeezed her shoulder once more, before walking away with Buck.

"They're nice people," said Liam. And then, "What do you think? Should we move in together?"

Sarah was definitely thinking *yes*. But she still needed

some time. She slipped her hand into his. She loved the way they fit together. Would they always be perfect for each other? "Let's see what's available tomorrow, and then we can decide."

Hand in hand, they walked toward the buffet. Sarah felt like she was walking into a dream. But really, it was the life she'd always wanted.

Ten days later
Owl Creek, Idaho

THE GRAY LIGHT of a new day filtered around the drawn curtains. Liam eased onto the corner of the bed, careful not to make too much noise. He worked his foot into a sock as Tolstoy slinked across the comforter. The cat butted his head against his forearm. One sock on, he scratched the cat under the chin.

From the other side of the bed, Sarah rubbed her eyes. "What time is it?"

"It's too early for you to be awake," he said, leaning over to kiss her cheek. It was 5:32 a.m. A call had come into the task force hotline. A man who owned a cabin ten miles outside town had stopped by his property before dawn. One of the windows had been broken and the glass was covered with a piece of wood. The man was worried that Acker had been—or was—on the premises. That's when the cottage owner called. Liam was on the way to check out the lead. "Go back to sleep."

"I'll get up and make you breakfast," she said, her voice hoarse.

"I don't have time to eat anything right now," he said. "Besides, you have a big day."

Tolstoy sauntered over to where Sarah lay and curled up behind the bend in her knees. By the time Liam put on his other sock, they were asleep once again. For now, he and Sarah had rented a house three blocks off Main Street. The two-bedroom house was owned by Colton Properties, and while it was small, it was perfect for them.

In his sock feet, he walked quickly and quietly down the hall, through the living room and to the front door. A pair of work boots sat on a mat next to a table in the entryway. Liam picked up a set of keys and his cell phone from the table and shoved them into his pocket. Next, he worked his feet into his boots. He opened the closet door and removed a blue windbreaker. FBI was stenciled in large yellow letters on the back and smaller white ones on the left front. Also in the closet was a gun safe. Liam pressed his thumb onto a sensor and the latch opened with a *click*. He removed his Sig Sauer and the magazine. After loading his firearm, he placed it into a holster at his hip.

Opening the door, he stepped into a new day.

His official Bureau car was parked in the driveway. He unlocked the door and slipped behind the wheel. As he started the engine, his phone rang, connecting to the in-car audio. Caller ID flashed on the dashboard.

Fletcher Colton.

Using controls on the steering wheel, Liam answered. "I'm shocked to hear from you so early," he said, not surprised at all. If Liam had gotten a call for the task force, then so had Fletcher. "You on your way to the cabin?"

"I am," he said with a yawn. "What're the odds that this is another goose chase?"

He understood Fletcher's skepticism. Over the past week,

the task force had received more than thirty calls. Residents had heard something or seen something or had a feeling that Markus was close. It wasn't up to the task force to decide if the lead was credible or not—they investigated them all.

In fact, the night before, they'd been called by a hysterical woman who heard someone trying to break into her garage. As it turned out, nobody was trying to get in. But a raccoon had gotten stuck and was trying to get out.

"I'll tell you this. Even if a raccoon broke that window, he didn't repair it with a piece of wood."

"I guess you're right," Fletcher grunted. And then, "Is it weird that last night I dreamt that I had rabies?"

"I'll see you up there," said Liam before ending the call.

It seemed like the search for Markus was driving everyone a little bit bonkers. Although he didn't blame Fletcher for his odd dream. The raccoon in the garage had been mad. And who knew that the chubby trash pandas had such sharp-looking teeth.

Soon, he pulled onto a lawn that surrounded the cabin. Driving a police cruiser, Fletcher parked next to him a moment later.

Liam exited the car. The sky was a clear, soft blue. The ground was frozen, the brittle grass crunching under his feet. Fletcher exited his car, as well. He held a printout from the task force's call center. "Looks like this property belongs to Gus and Amanda Ferguson. It was Gus who came up early this morning to turn on the water and to start getting the house ready for summer. He noticed the broken window that had been covered with a board. With all the media coverage about Markus, he got spooked. That's when he left and called us."

There were two windows on the front of the house. Curtains were drawn, but both were intact. "Let's check it out," said Liam. They walked around the side of the house. One window was covered with a piece of plywood. "Bingo," said Liam.

"What're the chances that Gus broke the window last winter and patched it up, but forgot?" Fletcher asked.

"That seems unlikely. But you never know." They walked the perimeter, checking to see if anything else looked suspicious. Nothing was amiss. Standing next to the front door, Liam asked, "Did Gus give us permission to search his property?"

Fletcher held up the printout. He pointed to the page. "He did. Says so, right here."

That's all he needed to enter the building. Still, Liam knocked on the door. "This is the FBI. We're coming in. Put your hands up." It was standard procedure to knock before entering. He turned the handle. To his shock, the door was unlocked.

Wide-eyed, he looked at Fletcher. The detective reached for a gun he carried on his hip. Liam removed his firearm, as well. He nudged the door open with his toe. From the entryway, he could see the whole cabin.

There was a living room/kitchen combo. To the left was a fireplace. Along the back wall, two bedrooms straddled a bathroom. At one time the furniture had been covered in cloth. But now, the sheets were piled in a corner. Empty cans and boxes of food sat on the kitchen table. The remnants of a fire filled the grate.

"Someone's been here," said Liam. "And I don't think it's a raccoon."

"We need to get someone here to collect evidence. And then, get the K-9 units out and looking for a trail." Fletcher reholstered his gun and then pulled a phone from his pocket. He placed a call. "Hey, Archer. Sorry to bother you so early but we found something…"

SARAH STOOD AT the counter of Book Mark It. It was her first day on the job and she hadn't been sure what to expect. The store had only been open for thirty minutes and already half a dozen customers had come through. Of course, one of them had been Aunt Jenny, who stopped in to say hello.

As the last customer paid for their purchase, the door opened. Liam entered the store. She couldn't help it, just looking at him made her heart race.

"Hey," she said. "You were up and out early."

"I was. But first, how's your day so far?"

"Well, I was able to walk to work, which was nice. Aunt Jenny stopped by already and Frannie will come in after lunch." She opened the front of her loose cardigan to show Liam her T-shirt underneath.

"Read banned books," he said. "Nice."

"Dante's going to take a picture." She pointed to a spot on the wall behind the cash register. "Then, we'll put the photo right there."

"Sounds like you're having a good day."

She was. "You know what would make it better?" She came around from behind the cash register. Reaching for Liam, she answered her own question. "If you kissed me."

He placed his lips on hers. Sarah was exactly where she needed to be.

"So," she began, "what happened with your early-morning call?"

"It was him," said Liam. "Or at least, I think it was Markus. Archer collected fingerprints. We'll run those later today. If it's a match with him, we'll know. Ajay and Malcolm have taken out a team of K-9s. If there's a trail to follow, they'll find it."

Sarah started to shiver, even though she wasn't cold. If Markus was still in the area, then none of them were safe. Especially her. "What happens now?"

"I will continue to love and protect you," said Liam. "Not just until Markus is arrested, but always."

Sarah sank into his embrace. It wasn't like all the books that she'd read over the years. This wasn't The End.

It was the beginning of a whole new life with the man she loved.

* * * * *

COMING SOON!

We really hope you enjoyed reading this book.
If you're looking for more romance
be sure to head to the shops when
new books are available on

Thursday 19th December

MILLS & BOON

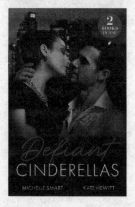